ALSO BY JANET PEERY

Alligator Dance
The River Beyond the World

8/07

What the Thunder Said

What the Thunder Said

Janet Peery

St. Martin's Press
New York

This is a work of fiction.
All of the characters, organizations, and events portrayed in this novel
are either products of the author's imagination
or are used fictitiously.

www.stmartins.com

Parts of this work appear in different form in *Black Warrior Review, Best American Short Stories 1993, 64 Magazine, Kenyon Review, Blackbird, Shenandoah,* and *Southern Review.*

Design by Kathryn Parise

LIBRARY OF CONGRESS CATALOGING-IN-PUBLICATION DATA

Peery, Janet.
    What the thunder said / Janet Peery.—1st ed.
        p.   cm.
    ISBN-13: 978-0-312-25263-2
    ISBN-10: 0-312-25263-3
        1. Sisters—Fiction.   2. Oklahoma—Fiction.   3. Dust Bowl Era,
1931–1939—Fiction.   4. Farm life—Oklahoma—Fiction.   I. Title.

    PS3566.E284W46 2007
    813'.54—dc22

                                                                2006050744

First Edition: March 2007

10   9   8   7   6   5   4   3   2   1

For Natalia and Sophia,
new people, new stories

Acknowledgments

～

I am indebted to George Witte, Leigh Feldman, Mary Flinn, Sheri Reynolds, Lee Abbott, David Lynn, Daniela Rapp, and Sara and Bob Schwager for their patience, insight, and counsel, and to the Virginia Commission for the Arts and the John Simon Guggenheim Memorial Foundation for generous support.

Contents

We thought it was our judgment,
we thought it was our doom.

—Woody Guthrie,

"The Great Dust Storm"

And our name shall be forgotten in time, and
no man shall have our works in remembrance,
and our life shall pass away as the trace of a
cloud. . . .

—Wisdom of Solomon 2:4

By some chance, here they are, all on this
earth; and who shall ever tell the sorrow of
being on this earth. . . . May god bless my
people . . . oh, remember them kindly in their
time of trouble; and in the hour of their taking
away.

—James Agee, *A Death in the Family*

Prologue

***

Set Me as a Seal upon Thine Heart

After waking from a dream so real it shook him——on Judgment Day not only was he missing from the glory roll, his mind had taken leave of him to wander in the past——the old man sat up and took stock.

He was certain who he was. McHenry Spoon at ninety, give or take. And where. His solitary room for over half a century, its window giving onto what amounted to a grassland outpost where he'd landed in the dust storms, never meant to stay. The question of when was easy. All his life he'd tracked the seasons, his land man's memory an almanac. A Sunday in the month of June, the last year of the seventh decade, the early-morning moon a waxing crescent. He was dying faster than he could live, that much was clear. His frame, he calculated, was rusted past repair. But his faculties were fine. In the dream he'd heard no voices, he could tell the living from the dead. So far the dead—his brother John Hardy, his wife Billie Ann, maybe his daughter Etta—had kept their distance. It was unsettled business with the living that gnawed at him.

At noon he expected the arrival of the woman who had been, in what had come to seem another life, his eldest child. After several long estrangements—he blamed hard times, his faulty fathering, her pride—she had begun to travel every Sunday along the northern Oklahoma line the hundred miles that separated them. She brought groceries, bread and cheese, tinned milk, a bag of gingersnaps he rationed to make it last the week. In fair return he stood by while she assayed his decline, suffered her devotion while she daughtered past the silence on his part that kept from her the fact that she was not his daughter but his niece.

Her name was Maxine but she was called Mackie, as if a shared nickname indemnified her from his brother's violence in her begetting. From his own. Home to the Missouri Ozarks from the horrors of the Meuse-Argonne in that year of 1918, hearing a woman's screams in the woods where he was tracking a buck, Mack had mistaken John Hardy, in the brutal act, for a stranger. Into the moonlit darkness he shouted, "Whoa up!" Aimed the barrel high, meaning to fire a warning, but when he clambered up the ridge he learned he'd shot his brother in the back, a mortal wound. Later, when he sought out the girl to make amends—it was his given curse to want to make right out of wrong—the end of it was that he married her to give the coming child a name. When he found a spread of ranch land at a tolerable price, he moved them out to Oklahoma.

His desire had been to leave his sin behind and never have to tell it. Whether his act had been an accident or not, he had committed it, and though there was atonement, there was no forgiveness. His single shot rang in his ears as a reminder of John Hardy's long resentment of him for the way he'd held himself above his brother, how he had tried to father him with goodness to the point John Hardy called him

"Jesus Mack." Hundreds of miles away at Salt Camp he hoped to found the orphan's vision of the paradise of kin, a plot of well-loved ground, a crowded, ample table and a happy life for generations, love abundant, room enough for all. He had failed at this so grandly that it stunned him still, but at last he understood his sin of sins. Because he wanted to be good, he asked the same of others, held them to a light too bright to bear, and when they let him down he trained on them the full force of his disappointment with himself.

This June morning, shaken by his dream, he made up his mind to talk Mackie into driving him to see the place he'd stayed away from for forty years. He had no plan, at this late date, to tell her the degree of their relation. What purpose would the truth serve if his was the only mind it eased? But he had sensed in her a kindred affliction. She moved from town to town, roaming the desert of the Southern Plains like the Israelites, failing to take root, as if trying to outrun judgment. He wanted to warn her away from dwelling in the wasteland of remorse, whether she burned up the road to do so or stayed put.

Times before, when he suggested the trip, she came up with excuses. The drive would eat up the day and she had work to do. There was nothing left to see but go-back land and anyway his eyesight was so bad he couldn't tell what he was looking at. His boots were an embarrassment. Said she.

He wondered if her shilly-shally rose from qualms that going back to see the place might rattle loose a failing of her own. Hers too was one of clouding the truth. Just before the end of the Second War, after their first estrangement, she came home for a visit with a boy of four or five, saying she'd taken him to raise. The practice was common in Depression years, when stray people and loose-ended children roamed the blistered plains, but still he wondered. Schooled in keeping his own counsel, in the exacting counterweights of shame and pride, he had let her story stand, no matter that the boy looked like John Hardy, spit and image.

Whatever were her reasons for not wanting to go back to the old place, it galled him that her counts against him weren't far wrong. He could no longer see to drive—his pickup rusted in the shed—and his toes, for want of tending, had crabbed over on themselves, the nails grown antler yellow, hard as horn. He'd tried every tool—the ordinary mill bastard file, the polling shears, the pig-tooth nippers—but he couldn't get the angle right, couldn't bend right, couldn't see. His hands were stiff as plankwood, all drawing tendons and swelling joints. His feet were worse. No boot or shoe would fit. For months he'd shuffled around in carpet slippers, but in honor of the day's errand he worked to rig a pair of Sunday wingtips bought in higher times by cutting out the toe box. If he looked like a funny-papers bum for his trouble, at least he'd be able to walk the land, get her up onto the rise, and feel that old lost living ground still swelling under him.

By the time her El Camino pulled into the yard, he had passed muster in the kitchen mirror. His thready hair was water-spruced, furrowed with comb tracks, the stubbled crosshatch of his chin free of tobacco juice, and he waited on the lean-to porch, busying himself with inspecting a tenpenny nail worked out of the baluster.

A small, spare woman nearing sixty, she appeared, in the week since he'd seen her, to have made herself over. Revamped herself into some kind of youthful cowgirl. Instead of the shapeless housedress he expected, she wore a pair of Levi's, a crisp snap-buttoned shirt with a Western yoke, a Spanish belt. The hammered conchos glinted in the morning light. New earrings, some kind of crystal that reminded him of the salt crust at the Rock Saline, glittered at her earlobes. Her hair, once worn in a knot, was loosely gathered with a leather ornament. He'd never known her to be vain; she hadn't been a beauty, but she had a pretty, bright-eyed face with color quick to rise. The changes were becoming, and from her blush he saw that she was pleased with them herself. He decided she had either met some man or given up on men entirely, but then it struck him that maybe her retooling meant he wasn't the only one who had a mission.

From the seat she pulled out grocery bags, her pocketbook, a box of Oxydol. "Morning, Dad."

He cleared his throat, thick with the quid habit he'd taken up to hurry sundown on the long, solitary days, and made a show of looking at the sky. "Seems to be, yes. Sure enough."

She squinted against the sun's glare off the porch's tin roof, already ticking with the heat. "How are you doing?"

He grinned; he'd made the joke before. "Mildewing."

Dutifully—at least *that* was unchanged—she laughed, shading her eyes to take him in.

He put on a little shuffle, a creaky, bone-jarring step to take her attention from the cuspidor he'd forgotten to hide, a sludge-filled Mason jar beside his bench. Her quick eye spied it. He tapped again to shift her notice to his shoes, but he stepped down wrong, flinched when pain knifed up his ankle. He wondered, not for the first time, why he took to clowning when he felt the possibility of blame.

She shook her head at his spit jar, then lengthened her gaze to survey the place. The mounting pile of tin cans beside the porch— Luck's, Dinty Moore, Hormel—the wracked timbers of the far barn, the nearer barn collapsed into a creature haven overgrown with trumpet vine and brambles, the windmill, spavined as a burden-broken horse, folding inward on itself.

He readied for reproof. Truth told, for all he'd yearned for family life, the decades she'd stayed away had come as relief. Alone, he had to bear no judgment but his own for his boar's nest or the habits he refused to break. Tobacco, cold canned chili, guilt.

"I brought you something. Look"—she held a stewpot—"field peas. Your favorite."

They weren't. At some point he must have made over them, given her a false impression.

Her efforts to please him often pained him. If he was guilty of believing he could mend the worn-out world with God and spit and baling wire, she behaved as though it could be nursed to health with false cheer and hot food.

When she thrust the pot into his hands, he was relieved of the awkward chance of an embrace. Touch was not their way.

In a fit of dithering she took back the pot. "Oh, never mind. I'll set these on."

He followed her across the porch, propping the screen door for her with his cut-down shoe and showing it to advantage. "Maybe you hadn't ought to settle in so fast."

A barn cat with her ears laid back was what she called to mind. Not spooked enough to run, but watchful. She thought he was either telling her to go away or passing judgment on her rootless ways. She was as thin-skinned as her mother.

"In case we go somewhere, I mean," he said.

If her fault-finding grated, it was her fear of him that nerved him up. Maybe she was wary by nature and maybe he was to blame. He had favored her sister Etta, born two years later, the child of his contentment, his reward, flesh of his flesh. He'd been bewitched by her quicksilver ways, although he tried to hide his partiality. He didn't know if it was the eldest's history or her affliction—her foot curled slightly inward, causing her to limp—that caused his wife to watch for slights, but Billie Ann's vigilance set further hindrance to his dealings with his brother's child. Even now they couldn't talk straight, couldn't find a way to meet each other in the middle.

He sheaved the papers on the table, his budget, advertising flyers for things he didn't want or need. "Not too big a mess to clean up in here this week."

"Not bad at all." Her voice was bright, agreeable, a signal of her willingness to try again. She set the pot on the burner, lighted the flame, then went to the pantry. She came out carrying a torn sack of cornmeal.

He didn't like it when she took it on herself to tidy up, especially when it meant a wasted nickel. "I might have use for that."

She dropped the sack into the trash bin. "Weevils got it, Dad."

He started to protest, but then he decided to pick his battles. "Say," he began, thinking that a little saddle soap about her new wardrobe might ease the way for her to notice his improvements, set them on their way, "is that the latest style?"

She fiddled with her shirt cuffs, rolled up her sleeves. The dungarees were spanking-new, still stiff. "Oh, I just threw it on."

Irked that he was shambling around his topic when he ought to state it outright, he pulled out a kitchen chair, but before he could sit down and lay out his plan, he was seized by the urge to get away.

In his prime he could have stumped out to the fields, stayed gone all day, and come back empty-minded, but his range had narrowed to the mailbox on the road. "Going to the box. Might be the check's here."

"Nothing's come. I looked. Besides, it's Sunday."

To leaven their standoff, he gave her a wily, mock-suspicious look. "It's the government. You can't tell what kind of fast one they'll pull next."

Her earrings jittered, seemed to throw off sparks. "You can't take someone else's word?"

Pretending he hadn't heard, he headed down the steps and across the yard, his spine held straight, the posture Etta used to call his "riding back." When he believed she was no longer watching, he slowed to save his feet. Even the softest leather rubbed, and the split toe box threw off his gait. The ground was hard, the going slow, giving him time to mull again the question that had vexed him all his life: How could it be that things he meant to do so right could end up so wrong?

In his dogged hunt for the first wrong turning, starting with his boyhood in the Baptist Home for Boys, his mind took him past his youth, past early manhood, past French forest and Missouri woods to fix on an April day in 1935, his middle years at Salt Camp.

. . .

That morning too, Palm Sunday, he had awakened at first light, just as the Dominecker rooster muttered and hens grudged awake. He went to stand on the back steps in long-handled drawers, sock feet. A faint warm breeze, stars pot-iron gray, the moon an aging quarter in the west. East, a spill of crimson at the cloud line. Red sky at morning. He had let his spirits rise.

For several years the droughty earth had blown, fine farms and ranches gone to ruin. Somehow his escaped the damage. He credited his faith—he'd trusted heaven to provide, and heaven had repaid him. If the promise of sunrise meant anything, the coming thunderstorm would be a drencher, the pastures soaked to pan, the creek high and rising, froth boiling in the eddies. The hay was nearing bloom. With rain, his field would be a sea of blue, the winter wheat a billow. Let Noah's flood come, yes, he thought, for once not caring that he borrowed God's own voice: *Let there be rain.*

Upstairs, his family slept in bedsteads of his own carpentry, under the gabled roof of his own shoring. Billie Ann with her face unpinched, too early in the season for hay fever to clot her breathing, in rest as not in waking satisfied. Mackie at fourteen a nerve-strung sleeper, legs atwitch. Contrary Etta, at twelve in her last year to be a child, curled for once into a compact stillness, his spitfire. He counted his blessings, sending up a grateful word.

He went inside to take his bib-alls from the peg, stepped in, and hoisted up. Stretching, he felt his neck pop, his backbone righting itself like a signal deep within. He eased on his boots and started for the barn.

This is the church and this is the steeple—always the Sunday school rhyme as he heaved open the great doors. He loved the deep-bayed cow barn, the place cathedral-like as dawn broke through, the smells of neats'-foot oil and polished tack, feather dander, livestock, hay dust from the winter-cure. He loved the stamp and shuffle of his shorthorn milchers, the beasts ungainly, yawing on their hooves, the chuff of hide against the hand-hewn rails, the heft of swollen udders. He forked ensilage into the manger, and the cows moved in, heads lowered, as if coming forward at an altar call. He set the stanchion bars and settled in to milk.

In church, he couldn't pray. The sanctuary was too close with must and sizing, scalp, the sour whiff of snuff, the woman's monthly smell. Too human and too carnal, reminding him of flesh. A shaft of sunlight streaming through the Gethsemane window might cast a patch of fire across the stuff of his thin black trousers, turn them redder than Mercurochrome, and the heat might cause him to look up into the choir loft for a certain pigeon-y soprano.

His musing would inflame him, and he'd have to rest the hymnal on his lap. To clear his mind, he sent it to the fields, slew panic grass and shattercane, thwacking at the seed heads with a scythe until more righteous thoughts returned.

In the barn, alone but for the cows, hot daydreams didn't plague him. Instead, something calm and holy seemed called out of him, and he felt clean as a boy, light in his bones. Here, he was moved to pray his constant prayer, *Thank you, I am sorry.* To sing hymns in his cracked morning voice, starting low, more murmur than music. By the time the milk pail filled, his dark thoughts would be washed away.

"Though like the wanderer, the sun gone down," he sang against the red whorls of a shorthorn's flank, hearing the reach of his warming tenor to the rafters. "Darkness be o'er me, my rest a stone." Outside the half door, low clouds scudded whitely by, lamblike and fleet.

After church, beside the stand of stunted creek willows in what was called the pasturage, the congregation lingered, speculating. A passable crop if it didn't blow to China. If jackrabbits didn't get it. If it would rain. The little children chased around the circle of parked automobiles while the BYF youth played a kissing game forbidden from the pulpit. Off behind the privy he had found them, his lame girl and the preacher's son, locked in an embrace. Mackie's look was rapturous and stupid, spellbound. Before he knew what he was doing, he snatched up a willow switch.

The boy fled, but she stood, head bowed, taking his blows. She wouldn't cry, refused to, stood there with a saintly look on her small features, and so it wasn't the noise she made that drew the others but his own, a stream of bellowed hellfire that he hadn't known was in him. All he knew was that the blood had risen to his throat, and he was shouting, bringing down the switch against her legs.

A group of deacons stopped him. "Mack, let go. She's just a little girl. She meant no harm."

Back home in the lull of afternoon he stretched out on the front room rug to nap. The dinner hour had passed in stony silence. Troubled by what he'd done at the pasturage, he'd had a hard time dozing, but when he finally did, he slept too hard, too long. He awakened to a hot and airless house, to the heart-sunk understanding that he'd lit into the child in penance for his own unruly lusts.

Bleared with sleep, he went to the window. Outside, a long low cloud glowed red. Strange light seemed to overtake his wife as she stood in the chicken yard. Out near the currant bushes Mackie sat among the flock of Dutch Everydays, playing quietly. He looked for Etta, taking in the barn, the silo, her rope swing, but the child was nowhere to be seen. Sand gusted at the window glass, but even then he let himself believe the cloud portended rain.

He exulted at the first huge drops, the shudder of unstable air, heat-charged, then frigid, but then the rain ceased and grit needled at his face. Forearm shielding his eyes, he waited for the spate to pass, but the front came on, a blistering wind, a seethe of sand and hay straw glinting in the sifting dirt, tattered paper scraps white as the cattle egrets that flew before a great black roller cloud.

He called for Etta, but the wind, cold as winter now, tore the breath from his mouth. At last in the blowing dust he caught a glimpse of her on the roof of the washing shed, saw Mackie standing there beneath the eaves.

Instantly he knew what Etta had done, her trick forbidden as the kissing game; she'd sewn her feet together in a spectacle she called the Hindu Needle. She sprawled facedown, half-on, half-off the roof, her sister tugging at her bound feet. He broke into a run and closed the distance, and his heart cracked when she whimpered, "Please don't hit me!"

Mackie yanked and Etta dropped, her weight pitching the two girls backward. He ran to pick them up, carried Etta through dust already drifting, the other coming on behind.

When he set the child inside the door, she buckled, crumpled to the floor. "It's all right," he told her, "I won't hit you."

Billie Ann lit the lamp, took in the scene, went for the rope-webbed rug beater. Mack had threatened that if he caught Etta at her trick again, there'd be a reckoning.

"I'll take her in the front room," he said. There, away from the others, he could lighten his hand.

His wife hardened her eyes.

A renegade idea coursed through his mind, *Refuse.* But Billie Ann had snipped the thread, pulled Etta up, and turned her around to ready her for punishment.

The lamp flickered, dimmed, the globe already filmed with dust.

He loved her then more than he ever had, his stormy Etta-girl, her face defiant, streaked with mud and tears, and he knew, even as he raised the rug beater, that he would lose her, if not this day, then soon. He wanted to say something about a father's love, about Abraham and Isaac, about sacrifice, to liken her wrong to her sister's in the pasturage. He wanted to teach a lesson that just then he couldn't put words to, except to wonder if the lesson would be his.

His first blow was a glancing one, but Etta wailed.

Billie Ann and Mackie watched him, eyes like judges. Wind

lashed at the weatherboard as again and again he brought down the beater, brought it down until he was spent with loathing, sick with the knowledge that he was bringing down his hand on all of them except the one he struck.

Now he reached the lane end to open the mailbox he knew was empty. Walking, he had willed a letter to appear, a check, a flyer or a handbill, anything to justify his errand, but there was nothing.

On the way back to the house he took the measure of his gumption, discovered that he still wanted to see Salt Camp, now more than before. He would tell Mackie he was sorry for the way he treated her. He would get her to remember better days, show her how he tried. Remind her of the kiddie wagon he'd pulled her around in. A lamb they'd bottle-fed. A wooden hutch he'd built beneath the cedars where she played café, serving lettuce leaves to rabbits on her dollhouse plates.

Somewhere in a bureau drawer there was a tintype of her at two, her hair still baby-fluff. In the front yard of the Salt Camp house beside a trellis of Cherokee roses, he'd stood for the photographer while she perched on his shoulders, her legs around his neck, her dimpled hands pressed into his eyes, wild delight in hers. He would find the picture, tuck it in his shirt pocket, show it to her once they got there, proof. And then he would tell her that he loved her, letting the words he found himself unable to say—not to her or to her sister, not to anyone—stand for every other lesson he would like to leave behind. If they left soon, they could be back before the sun went down.

In the kitchen, tin cans had been stowed in grocery bags and set by the back door. Sudsy water steamed in the sink. The smell of vinegar and Bon Ami stung his eyes. On the stove the field peas simmered.

"Smells good in here." He rubbed his hands in a show of heartiness, hoping to right the day, and suddenly he meant what he said. The earthy, fragrant steam had chased away the staleness. With the window open the room felt light, the day seemed new.

"Why, it's just peas."

He took a chair at the table, easing gently off his feet and trying not to groan. "But what's that you put in the pot for seasoning?"

"Salt and pepper. Ham hock. A little blackstrap if I'm feeling venturesome."

"Venturesome," he repeated. An inroad. But before he could follow through, she clamped the pot lid on the peas.

"I've got something to say." She hooked a strand of hair behind her ear, then grabbed the broom to sweep under the table, her strokes brisk and determined.

His own preoccupation with confession bracing him for hers, he asked, "You planning to tell me what the something is?" His voice sounded gruffer than he wanted it to, and so he winked to ease things up. If she had a bone to pick, he'd pick it with her.

"I'm going by a different name."

He tried to remember the last time he'd called her by the name they shared. How *had* he addressed her?

Whisk went the straw broom. "Maxine is what I go by over there."

A phrase came to him from eighth-grade Latin: *Nomen est omen,* but he couldn't puzzle out its meaning. To show her that he would take her decision at face value, he said, "Well, that's near enough I won't forget it, and it's your given name, besides."

"It's what they know me by. In case you ever had to call, or needed to find me . . ." Her voice trailed off, and in the silence the shadow of her sister hovered. There was bad blood between the girls, and he knew his favoring played a part. Long ago he'd tried to track Etta, but he found no trace of her. The hired boy he thought of as a son had taken off to fetch her, came back empty-handed, and after that the boy had no heart to go on. Mack never heard from him again. He blamed himself for that as well.

He suspected that the news about her name was just her first run at the wall. She was a blurter like her mother, saving up a storm of words to blast him when he least expected it. The waiting could be maddening as dry thunder. If she finally came out with the truth about her son, he would do her the honor of not asking questions. Her wrongs would dovetail into his, and he could speak his piece.

She swept dirt into the dustpan, then propped the broom beside the door, looking around for the next chore. She picked up a sponge and stooped to scrub at a sticky spot on the linoleum.

Winding sideways toward his ends—Salt Camp was on the way to the panhandle town she'd moved to a few weeks before—he asked, "Aiming to settle down out there in No-Man's-Land?"

She had taken his question as rebuke. He could tell this by the cant of her head, her hooded gaze, trying to meet his but failing.

"I might just." She appeared to want to say more, but her sponge just then needed wringing.

He got to his feet, steadying himself with a hand on the table. If he waited for her to come out with her confession, he'd have to wait all day. If she planned to tell him, she could do that just as well once they were in the car. He thought of Salt Camp in the spring, the pastures green with timothy, and he saw the two of them flying down the highway, his 3X Stetson squared, the warm wind against his sleeve.

"Maxine," he said, using her name to show he was a model of give-and-take, "I want us to go over home."

"To Salt Camp?" She opened the oven door to peer inside. "Dad, what have you been roasting in here? Ox?"

"If it's my shoes . . ."

She faced him, no downward glance, no hem-haw. "It's your feet. You had to creep out to the mailbox. Hobble was more like it. I'll drive you over there to Salt Camp, but first you'll have to fix your feet."

"They're fine. They reach the ground."

No smile for his old joke, she turned back to regard the blackened oven. "How about next Sunday? That way we can plan it."

He wanted to walk back down the lane, take himself away to collect his thoughts and work himself back up, but he'd done that already. Why did it have to be so hard to get something across?

"Now, today."

"All right." She shut the oven door. "But first let's have a look."

"No horse-trading. My feet are fine. Let's just get going. Daylight's wasting."

She angled out a kitchen chair for him. "Dad, sit down."

"I said they're fine."

She shrugged, picked up the broom again, suddenly intent on knocking cobwebs from the corners.

He sat, began to work at the knots he'd labored to tie. By the time his socks were shucked, she'd filled the enamel roaster pan with warm water and Epsom salts. She lowered the pan to the floor, pushed it nearer his chair. The water wavered, sloshed.

"Soak them a good long while. Then you can doctor up your toes and your boots will fit. And then we'll see about going."

"We'll see about?"

She pursed her lips, the picture of her mother. "We'll go."

Where it wasn't jaundiced, his skin was milky blue and scaling, the overgrown nails yellow-gray as polled horn stubs, his toes clawed, crippled things. Exposed in the patch of sunlight that stole across the linoleum, the wreckage of his feet shocked him. He eased them into the water, not to do her bidding but to hide them, and as he did so something in him turned against her. Who was she to call him on his ways? On his broken windmill or his spit jar or his feet?

While she busied herself in the back room, he looked at a *Reader's Digest*. Even the large-print version blurred. Mack Spoon, who'd once maneuvered wiry and surefooted on the frets above the stockyards at Baxter Springs, who'd driven cattle up the Chisholm Trail, who'd taken fire near the Hindenburg Line, that man's worth was spilled out on the ground or dumped into the trash bin, swept away, and what was left was useless as a pail of water in a drought. He was no more than a memory, a side trip in somebody else's life.

She returned from the back room where she'd been changing the bedsheets. She ladled some field peas onto a plate. She set this on the table with a glass of milk, beside which she laid out three gingersnaps, a child's meal. "Eat a little something."

He spooned up some peas and tasted them. Too hot. He tried a gingersnap, and before he knew it he had eaten all three, and she had caught him in the act. "Dad, you'll spoil your appetite."

"It's a hard life if you don't weaken." He didn't know why he'd said the phrase, a Depression saying. What he meant was that old age was bad enough, the narrowing of vision, the hobbling of his senses. She didn't have to point it out.

"Keep at it. I'll go find the clippers, and we'll get you doctored up." She was gone before he could tell her he'd already tried them.

He spooned up some more field peas, tried again to eat them, but he'd lost his appetite. Somehow that too was her fault. He started to call after her, but he felt a quaver rising in his throat. He never swore, but he was moved to add a word to tamp the tremor. "Dadgummed things won't work. They're rusted shut." They weren't.

She returned with a towel, the La Cross clippers, rust-spotted but in working order, a pair of snips, forged steel but black with tarnish, and the hoof rasp. "Daddy, if you'd soaked them before, they'd have clipped easier."

She never called him Daddy, and it set him off. "I'm not a child."

"Then don't act like one."

When she was a girl she lived to please him. Anything he did was fine. "You never would have talked to me like that in the old days."

Sitting cross-legged on the floor in front of his chair, she lifted his foot from the water, dried it with a towel. His skin was waterlogged and soft, his toes were puckered. He drew back. "That hurts."

"I haven't even started."

A breeze wafted through the open screen door and with it a rise of ticklishness he willed away. The hoof rasp muttered across the softened nail, setting his teeth on edge. He said again, he didn't know why, "It's a hard life if you don't weaken."

She smiled gently. "Dad, nobody's perfect."

"Isn't *that* the truth." He was proud of his comeback, one lick closer to the topic. If the way he said *that* didn't lead into the next part of her news, he didn't know what would.

She went on filing until it was clear the hoof rasp wouldn't do the job, its gauge too wide. She picked up the clippers. "Just keep imagining how good you'll feel when this is done." Her eyes were light brown, John Hardy's eyes now aged and deep-set in a web of wrinkles. "Just think, 'How beautiful thy feet with shoes . . .' "

For reasons he couldn't name, the verse from Solomon hit him crossways. *He* was the one who knew the scripture inside out. "But not without?"

"Oh, Dad."

If she didn't hurry up and get what she came to tell him over with—he wasn't born yesterday, it was coming, he'd bet a dollar on it—he was going to kick away the roaster pan, splash water on the floor, and stomp out to the porch, bite off a big fat plug. She was trying to help, but the fact was that her forced patience only made him want to hurt her.

Her breath on his feet was warm, too close. The foot-washing service at the Salt Camp church at Easter had always made him cringe. The ritual was embarrassing, too private—his feet in a stranger's hands—and he wanted to wrest them away.

One of her earrings cast a rainbow on the water in the roaster. A deep *clip* sent a shard pinging against the cupboard.

He asked, "How's the boy?" She'd shown him a picture of the great-grandson—his great-grandnephew, he guessed—he'd never met, a toddler on a plastic tricycle. For all her own wrong turns, she'd ended up with what he'd always wanted. Family. How was that fair?

"Buddy's fine. Jesse and Kay live west of Albuquerque." She clipped, then clipped again.

He was goading her, but he was too far in to stop. "Did Jesse ever straighten out?"

Her son was her sore spot, the boy—the man, he guessed— headstrong and lazy. Aimless, no direction whatsoever, and so he fired in any one that came to mind. She said he'd had a bout with po-lio and it left him jittery and nervous, but Mack was skeptical. Jesse came to him a few times in the 1960s, a rangy long-hair with a blue bandanna tied around his forehead, a cheap guitar, a smell of burning stinkweed. Wanted Mack to show him how to cowboy, but like his true grandfather he was wound too tight, was jumpy as John Hardy, couldn't stand still long enough to learn a pastern from a fetlock, a curb bit from a hackamore, and by then Mack had strung a five-strand fence around his heart.

"He's trying." She kept clipping. "He and Kay are on-again and off-again. Hard-headed, both of them. Mr. and Mrs. Kiss and Scratch." She went on, making idle conversation that he didn't care to hear.

Driven to work from sun to no-sun, he had put his own restless energy to purpose. The force that pushed him then to tong and whang at things under his hand until they came to something or else shattered drove him now, made him want to harry the truth out of her. He felt in his pocket for his quid pouch, but it was out on the porch under his bench. He longed for a cheekload of bitter juice. "Did Jesse never," he asked, fixing on the question guaranteed to trip her spring, "want to know his real mother?"

He wasn't sure what she would do. Burst into tears and make a scene the way her sister might have, standing up to him until the last dog died? Give him the long-suffering look she gave him at the pas-turage those many years before that fueled his wrath? In truth he'd whaled at her so hard because in her he saw his own do-gooding no-tions. Turn the other cheek. Go the second mile. Give up your cloak, lay down your life. The desire to break her shook him now as fiercely as it had seized him in the pasturage. "Did he ever ask to know the truth?"

She looked up at him, dry-eyed and sorrowful, and he understood she saw him the way in his worst private judgment he saw himself—feeble, mean, embittered. She had written off his cruelty to age.

One foot was finished, and she set to work on the other, the nail shards falling like so many nutshells. As if she'd worked it all out in her mind a long time back, she said levelly, collapsing every stave and board he'd used to build his grudge against her, "I had him, Dad. He was my own. He always knew. I've done plenty to him, I suppose, but that one thing I couldn't."

"Well," he said. "Well, hell."

For once she didn't lower her eyes but met his straight. "I'm glad you know. I didn't know how to tell you. I didn't want to disappoint you, then it got to be too late. The lie got too big to take back. I thought you'd . . ."

"Judge? I'd never." He looked at the Mason jar upended in the drainer, immaculate and shining. "I'd never."

It wasn't lost on him that she saw his claim for the untruth it was but didn't trouble to dispute it.

Radiant—with relief, he guessed—she scooped the nail parings into the dustpan, then pushed up from the floor. "It's done. Shoe up, and we'll go out there. I'd half like to see the place again."

She wiped her hands on her Levi's, looking around to see if anything else needed doing before they left. Her gaze came to rest on the ruined wingtips beside the chair where he'd abandoned them, as if he'd stepped out of them to be taken in the Rapture. "Try them now, why don't you?"

The silence drew out long. Into it he could confess his wrongs, not just his failings but his sins, the truth he'd kept from her. He could come clean. She had to have wondered, given Etta's outbursts.

But how did anyone begin to tell a tale like that? And how go on after such knowledge, after so long a time? What did such silence
make him?

She smiled encouragingly, and it occurred to him she was the one
person who still walked the earth who would forgive him anything.
But something had shifted outside his power to reckon or foresee,
outside the guiding of his hand. "Maybe another time," he said. "It'd
be dark by the time we got there."

She seemed to be waiting for him to change his mind, but he
would not, no matter how long she stood there smiling. At last she
said, "Well, I should be going anyway. Your bed's changed if you
want a nap."

She stowed the cleaning supplies and dumped the water, rooted
in her pocketbook for keys.

He wanted to mark what had taken place between them, but he
wasn't certain what it was. "Well," he said, "those peas sure tasted
good."

She clasped her pocketbook. "Did they?"

This was what he meant about the pattern of their dealings, the
skittish back-and-forth. She was either doubting him or fishing for a
compliment, but he couldn't tell which. Both made him want to spit.
What he wanted—what was needed—was clean, straight, simple
talk, gloves off. "Why can't you take me at my word?"

Her eyes teared up. She blinked. "I'll bring you something else
next time. What do you think you'd like? How about some . . ."

"Look," he raised his voice to make it stick, "the peas were good.
The peas were fine and dandy and I'll eat them till they're gone. One
at a time if that'll prove to you I like them."

She didn't even pretend to be bewildered by his outburst.

He wanted to back up and try again. Say what he meant to say.
That he was grateful she had come so far to tend him. That he was
sorry he was acting like a jack mule.

She gave the table a last swipe, straightened the shoes, and tucked his socks inside. Sometimes at the end of a visit, she would say, "I love you, Dad," and he'd have to look away, or pretend he hadn't heard. Or if she put him on the spot, he'd have to mumble "You too," or some such. He wanted her to say "I love you" now, so he could hear it right, so he could say it back and mean it. Give her that at least, get it off his chest.

"Well," he dropped the word into the silence to give her time, but when nothing came of it, he finished with, "you'll have a long drive home."

"I don't mind. It gives me time to think."

Her answer went contrariwise to his intention, but he decided she was trying to be gracious, and so he let it ride. He walked her to the porch and down the steps, stood by while she loaded up.

When she swung into the driver's seat and shut the door, he wondered why, although the day had gone crosswise to his plan, he felt so oddly gleeful. It wasn't just his shriven feet or that they'd dealt with one another to the metes and bounds of their imperfect powers, or that the fire he'd felt to say his piece had come to smoke. Something else had left him.

His faith stood fast—from the porch steps he'd looked into the cloudless sky to test it and found God as ever in His heaven—but it came to him there was no need to square himself and no undoing in a lesson what was laid down in a lifetime. There was no coming clean, not now or ever. If this meant that when the roll was called on Judgment Day his name would not be heard, that would have to be— it *was*—all right, but if there was a place apart, a holding pen, for those who wanted to be better than they knew themselves to be, who couldn't get their acts to match their faith, he'd have to hope for that. Or maybe he should aim for hell. In either place, he reckoned, there'd be kin to spare.

Although the urge to boyish foolery made him wonder if his wits had left him, he felt like acting up, and a reckless feeling in his bones moved him to try a tent-show buck-and-wing. He jutted his elbows, essayed a step that came off as a jerky, sideways hop. He tried to catch her eye to see if she would smile.

She started the engine, her near arm elbowed out the open window. "You're feeling all right, Dad?"

He made a show of patting himself down—chest to belly to hip pockets—and mugging his amazement. "Last time I checked."

One laugh, not given out of duty but sincerely, would be sign enough for him to hear the unsaid words he least deserved to hear but now most needed. When it came it was more a puff pressed through her lips that made a little air-leak sound, but it rang truer than a silver dollar.

When he reached out to pat her arm, sunlight glinted off the side view mirror—an unkind glare that if it were in his sway to do so he would soften—to cast a square of light across her eyes, her brow raised in unguarded startle at his touch.

"Well, then," she said. She shifted into gear. "Well, then," she said again, as if she could think of nothing else to say. She headed down the lane.

At the lane end she always made a point of looking back as she turned the car onto the road, and just before her last view of the old man he knew she saw as he stood barefoot in the front yard of a makeshift place on stopgap land, a word he should have said came to him, a word so sentimental that his vision clouded and he knew and didn't care that he wasn't long for this or maybe any world, a blessing that he prayed would dwell with him, would follow her like mercy, like his better ghost, and he willed it to her understanding, *Godspeed.*

Book One

What the Thunder Said

1

Fits and Starts

Downstairs in the café a few days back two half brothers went to blows. Cap and Wheeler, fools as old as I am and so far past fighting age you had to shake your head to see them roostered up and feathers flared. The younger boxed the elder, blacked his eye. Gus Wharton, know-it-all and self-appointed hero, by his own account the oldest living black-faced cook in white-faced Oklahoma, took it on himself to fetch our thickest Angus beefsteak to put on the rising bruise.

The brothers' set-to, feeble as it was, had been a lifetime coming. Everybody said so. What would you expect, two men as unlike as Cap and Wheeler, Cap a born-again-and-loud-about-it stockman and Wheeler a state-your-business judge, the way they shouldered up against each other all their lives, brothers as different and the same as, well, as sisters? Their argument concerned the afterlife, as near as anyone could tell, and didn't last a minute. Before you blinked, the two made up, and by and by they left, each to his peculiar progress.

After they were gone Gus groused about the bunch that meets on Thursdays here in the café, the Old Bulls. A pack of long-eared cof- fee hounds, neck backs gullied down as sand draws? Have to occupy their sacred window table? They're your boys.

"Hot air the lot," Gus grumped, "blowhards and gasbags to a man."

I told him, "Gus, what scares you most about yourself is what you pick to fuss about in anybody else." I told him that the truth was, as far as Old Bulls went, Augustus Adam Wharton looked a little beefy and long in the tooth himself.

His royal self banged down a pot lid, hoisted up his old sag- bottom pants, gummed around his everlasting toothpick, "Maxine, you'd better palsy out and water your petunias. Things out there are looking wizened-up as you."

"Well," I said—or wanted to—"and after all we've been through, Gus, and me the café's boss and ranking you in age and wisdom both." Bit my tongue for knowing he'd come back with, "All right, Max Factor, let's sit down and have a head-to-head about the wisdom part," and remind me for the umpty-hundredth time about a stupid thing I'd almost done to wreck my life a final time a dozen years be- fore.

No matter what the brothers' trouble was or what the hornet was that buzzed around in Gus's Denver Broncos ball cap bonnet, the fight unhinged me. In the middle of it all I had to take myself upstairs to cry. Cried hard. Even muffled in a pillow, the noise I gave out sounded like a seized-up dowser or a gate squeaked open on a rusted hinge.

See, their squabble opened up a well of want too deep for flower- tending or smart comebacks to fill up. Brought to daylit fact the sneaky way the past can loop around your feet—you just walking on and tending to your beeswax, blind enough to think you know the progress of your days, what will happen where and how and when, and journeying along—this same old past can loop like rope around your feet and snatch you up and string you upside down, shake you loose till what falls out of you is sadness at there being no one left to love enough to fight with.

Out of my own mouth came four words I didn't know I had in me to say. *I miss my sister.* It had been half a life since the girl I was had turned my back on her as if there wasn't blood between us and I wasn't wrong as she was, another half a life since it had hit me what I'd done. *Who on earth,* I asked Maxine Jane Spoon after yet another half a life had passed, *were you to judge?*

Anybody reading, did you ever feel like jumping out a window while nobody watched? That day while down below those two clowns had their fistfight, upstairs on my own, the want of Etta fallen sudden on me, I lurched and floundered like a creature with the staggers. Carried on a wrestling match against myself, the way I cried. Flung myself from bed to davenport to chair, clutched the curtains like a let-go lover in a drugstore romance, which I once upon a time had been. Lonesome was one word for what I felt. Abandoned, left behind, for others. Not word-one of them a stretch.

If what I've just put down makes the crying I'm describing sound embroidered, puffed up with feeling to the point you have to squint, I am here to tell you, young or old, it *hurt,* which counts for something.

Everything I've learned in life—the hill of beans it pleases Gus to tell our regulars this knowledge won't amount to—I've learned in fits and starts. Do a thing and let the reasons catch up later. See the road bump that will crack an axle only miles beyond it. Repent a good half century too late. What happened was that after all this time I came awake again to what I'd lost, and worse than that, I saw again the mark on it of my own telltale hand. Fact was plain as day too many years to count, then dawned sudden as a change of wind.

Maybe it was world times. Across the country far away, on the
clearest blue September day, an awful thing had happened to us all,
and no one knew just yet what was to come. Maybe it was Cap and
Wheeler's fight. Maybe it was just the way regrets roll quietly along
behind you where they ought to stay until you get to going good
along a downhill patch, and of a sudden they start rolling of their
own accord, dragging you behind them.

Once, the man I thought of as a husband fixed an eye screw to a
bowling ball and tied it to his old dog's collar. John figured ball and
chain would fix the creature's rambling. Days that hound dog
dragged the weight around the yard until he found a squeeze hole in
the fence and made his break for freedom. Tail-wagging proud old
Rover was until he got to zipping down a slope and then the ball
rolled past him, jerked his neck so hard he scrabbled hindparts-over-
hell-to-come the whole way down, which is the long way round to
say the yanksome way that dog looked was the way I felt, and so I flat
wanted to jump out of the window.

Even if I jumped, the landing wouldn't kill me. Luck would land
me right side up, for I'd lived eighty-something years with not one
broken bone, no accident except the one at birth that left me with a
slewed right foot, as if the Joker Up on High decreed that one short-
changement to a customer would do. And so I didn't jump but only
wanted to with every never-broken bone. Wanted to land in that dirt
parking lot and hoist what's left of my behind, take off like Jesse
Owens, hotfoot off as far away from Hatcher, Oklahoma, as the one
good leg would take me. Do the thing I'd done before, which was to
put safe distance between myself and me. All this went through my
mind while I was deciding not to pry the window.

I wouldn't really. Jump. But I thought about it to the point-of.
Then I got hold of myself and splashed some water on my face and
went back to the café and the fighting men, the plan in mind to give
all three of them what for.

Disrupting the peace, I planned to tell them. Tell them I had been bequeathed this café, run-down as it was, for my old age and my security. They'd blighted one and wrecked the other. Tell them I was staying put come hell, high water, or the wrath to come, and no amount of anything could chase me off. Which of course I didn't, for this last part was beside the point, and, anyway, the two were finished with their fight, then the lunch rush came and set me onto other things.

But I started wondering again about my sister. If after all this time she'd know me and would I know her? If she wandered off the road to Tucumcari and found this little diner, sat down to order breakfast, would I recognize her by the birthmark catty-corner to her eye that sometimes looked a little like a coffee drib and others like a pale brown tear, or by the way she walked—light-footed, as if she meant to sneak around the earth and play a trick on it, nodding slowly side to side as if she had all day to figure how to do it? Would she look beyond my bone white hair, my loose-skinned sack of body, would she see older, smaller, sorry me, say, "Sweet bejeezus, didn't I know you a long time back? Weren't you once upon a time my sister?"

Who knows what we would come to after that, what we might have had? A blood companion to live out our days beside. To laugh about old times. Or cry about the same. Or fight ourselves to kingdom come the way those brothers did. The point is that I wanted her so much just then—all good, all bad—my chest felt torn apart. The cross-grained selves we were and likely would remain meant nothing, and I wanted to lay eyes on Mary Etta Spoon. Hands, too. Wanted to kiss that jut-jawed face and squeeze the stuffings out of her. Barring that, to know what happened to her. Where she went and how she lived. Had she gone to California like she swore she would, or had she wound up closer by than anybody'd guess? She had a little daughter named Georgette. I saw the child one time, yearn, now, to see the grown-up woman she turned into.

Oh, I've played the story out a dozen ways, and all ways featured Etta trying to find me. All ways wound up with us taking up where we left off before the dust storms winnowed us to our worst selves and scattered us like chaff, the two of us old women at the turning of an age, our last days rendered peaceful as the latter end of Job's. But more often than not I wonder if she might well have been one of the wayfarers who make their way out here, could well have sat down in the corner booth for me to pour her coffee, looked up at me through stranger's eyes, then moved on.

History's past changing, and the answer as to whether it will travel past redeeming is beyond me, but I've kept my memories to myself for so long that there's hardly anybody left to tell them to, so I've made up my mind to write them down. Here I sit this pretty September evening while the shadows gather in the way they always have to make me think there's something other than the sun behind them, a way those shadows can persuade a person past her own intelligence that not one season is forgotten in the long memory of earth.

In the bad years you had to wait until the dust storms cleared to see the damage they had done. I expect it is the same with inside weather. Strike or miss, for good or ill, the dust storms scarred a person, deep. Our kind can't throw away a penny pocket handkerchief for fearing future want, can't be stopped from pasting rows of odd-sized stamps along an envelope to make the postage come out right. Jars and butter tubs, don't even ask. The fear is, see, that even if the item had cost next to nothing, somehow even that price was too dear.

In those old days what separated us was hope. Either Etta lost hers early, or it grew so large it couldn't be contained. Whichever was the case, it made her cut her losses and get out. I held on, but which of us was better served by hope is up for grabs.

In hard times, if we needed light, we used kerosene if we had it, candles if we didn't, the wax stubs melting down to puddles smelling high of paraffin and pig. Now, this solitary night, the electric lamp over my shoulder is just bright enough to see the pens and pencils laid out straight, an almost-empty notebook with a sheaf of pages. Here under my writing hand, some thousand ruled blue lines to hold a crooked tale that maybe won't amount to much beyond some long-gone years when people carried on like anybody else and made the same mistakes until they got them right or didn't, and at least one person had the luck to live beyond them. Anybody reading, if I forget to burn them when I'm finished, take these pages how you want, a testament, a tale, a caution. I mean them as atonement.

~

Before she left for anywhere-but-here, my sister Mary Etta was the kind of girl you called a pistol. High-tempered, quick-tongued as a garter snake, more wayward even than a place like Land-Grab Oklahoma in the 1930s had the room for. She didn't want to be a girl, forget about a good one. She would have rather wandered all day on the creek, building huts and lean-tos, hunting arrowheads and lizards. She would have rather struck fat matches on the run-board of Dad's sky-blue Model A and set a fallowing field on fire. She'd get an idea in her head and couldn't get it out until she did the thing, whatever.

Anything that came to her to do, that was the thing she did. Slide down the barn roof on a gunnysack and skin her bottom raw. Race around on coal black Sultan all tricked out in paper streamers, catch the corral's lintel beam and drop down to the ground. Walk around the silo rim in patent-leather Sunday shoes, her wiry arms akimbo, gingham blowing in the wind and fifty feet between her daredevil self and earth.

She threw fits, she pouted, and she lied. When she got mad she was a hornet. When she was glad there was no limit to her gladness. If her mads were madder than a mortal person could abide, her glads were gladder, and so they carried you along. When she was small, she laughed a lot, she played like there was no tomorrow. Before she tossed them down the silo in a fit of pique, she had two Kewpie dolls she called the Kids, a snub-nosed boy and a pigtailed girl, and the Kewpies had adventures Etta put on like a show. The boy would get himself into tight spots—caught up a tree during a lightning storm or drowning in the stock tank, stuck inside the grain chute of the combine—and the girl would have to rescue him. Etta would get so caught up in her play you wished tomorrow *wouldn't* come. She had one bright idea after the next, but all the Kids' adventures seemed to end in fights, doors slammed, the ruin of the game my fault and me not knowing what had hit me. Notional, Dad called her, but he would grin as though she were a miracle on feet. My secret grief was that he favored her.

I was dutiful, domestic. Looked it. Lank, straw-colored hair, pale skin, and light brown eyes that had a sorry way of looking down if anyone looked in them straight. Freckled as a sparrow. Blushy. If in flesh I was the house wren to her harry-hawk, in spirit I was Martha to her Mary, making sacred duty out of keeping house while she went dreaming on her way. But you had best discount the Jesus part of that comparison, as Etta had no use for church. "Judas Priest," she'd say outside Dad's earshot, "don't we have enough to scare us half to death?"

Most of our girlhood I spent waiting to see which rule the whirl-wind known as Etta would break next, then deciding if I ought to tell. Mostly told. But did or didn't, mostly I decided wrong. Tell she broke a pickle jar, get in Dutch for failing to sweep up the shards. Don't about those lucifers, take the blame for burning stubble and a blackened hedgerow, Etta's darkish curly hair singed crisp. I'd get so tangled up in what to tell, what not to, when was witness false and when could it be true, so bollixed-up in sorting out which wrong was righter than which right, which right was wronger than which wrong, I tied myself in knots. The point is that I was so busy count-ing motes, I couldn't see the beam, which was my pride.

If I loved Mam for all the reasons children love their mothers, not

the least of which was that she took my part when Etta teased, I idol-
ized our father. Thought he was the be-all-end-all, went about my
business trying to please him. Nearabout hung out a shingle lettered
with the word *Perfection,* opened shop for business. Tried to make
myself so right-thing-doing I would have to be anointed or at least
had a badge of honor pinned to my lapel.

Tale-bearing was the dark blot on my record, and so every now
and then I would reform. Pledge to let my sister go her wayward
way alone, let nature take its course. I was holding a revival for myself the day the big storm hit.

Even in these latter days I don't know how to talk about the dust
storms. Worse than any single windstorm ever hoped to be. Twisters
touched down once or twice then moved away. Dust storms lasted,
one after another, day on day and week on week until years passed.
You had to see them to believe them, and even then you couldn't. No
single picture ever tells the story of their devastation. Wind and dirt
a hundred miles across and two miles high, the noonday sky gone
black as night, the sun, when you could see it, paler than a blister,
the moon a glowing ember. Biblical, no stretch in that word either,
lifted of a piece out of the crazy Book of Joel, terrible wonders in
the heavens and on the earth. The southern plains had been in drouth
for years—no rain, no rain, no rain—so when the winds came up,
which was always, the soil peeled off and blew away with nowhere
firm to settle. Some people prayed, saying it was a punishment. They
held tent meetings, hired rainmakers, plowed, and listed. Some
killed snakes and draped them belly up on fences, hoping to draw
rain. Out west they dynamited clouds. Many died and many left, but
most people stuck it out, banking on tomorrow, on an uncloudy day.

Some years back, when I was driving out to visit Dad near War
Drum, a sandstorm hit and swallowed up the car. I had to stop.
Couldn't see the windshield, couldn't breathe. Felt kicked deep in
the ribs, kicked hard and backward into that old helpless, awful fear
of being buried. Feeling dwells in you for life and haunts your sleep.

Ask anybody who lived through those drouthy times; I'm not the only one who says this. Scratch Okies of a certain age—whether they're gone-aways or stuck-it-outs—and it'll be as though you struck a match, that fear will flare.

It wasn't the first storm that sealed our downfall—by the middle thirties the dirt had blown around for years, and we had been all right—but the biggest, the April storm of 1935 that turned day into night. In history books it's called Black Sunday. To us it was the beginning of the end.

All that warm spring day we felt some *something* gathering in the west. A blue-sky day, and yet the sun went darker by the hour. At the silent Sunday table there fell over us a sense of time awry, a feeling of the clock hands and the light gone off in separate wrong directions. By two, the air was charged and still. Gusts of hot wind needled us with blowing sand. Across a swale of go-back land dust devils whirled like dervishes. But until we saw the cloud—a dark, wide anvil taller than a thunderhead and blacker than dried blood, we'd not known what was coming.

On her way across the yard, a clutch of guinea hen eggs bundled in her apron, Mam thought it was the Rapture come that far across the land to seize her. She'd hoped to leave the threat of End Times back in Joplin, but here it came to catch her out, she later said, just standing there unready but so oddly, oddly willing. She dropped the eggs. They shattered hard against the ground. For a time she only stared, waiting to recall her wits, and then she cried "McHenry!" to our father, who was by then walking from the hay barn to the windmill, looking west. Even then, he would allow, he hadn't known the cloud for what it was.

Beside the currant thicket I plinked dent corn into Ball lid plates with the plan in mind to serve the hens their supper. In my mind's eye I could fairly see their scrappy, peckish flurry as I set their orders on their dining table, an enamel basin overturned and covered with a hankie. Playing restaurant was my game, early on and even at four-teen. Chickens as the patrons, chicken on the menu, didn't matter.

When Mam called, "Girls!" I glanced up, dazed between the play world and the real. I couldn't fix on where I was. "Mackie, Etta, come!" she yelled.

In those days and for too long beyond, I was called Mackie. Took up Maxine again when I was old, for the way a man I came to love could fit his mouth around it.

I looked across the yard toward the last place I'd seen Etta, on the tin roof of the washhouse where she'd been bent over her forbidden trick. This trick was to take a threaded needle to her callused skin and sew her heels together flat upon each other, then to sew her toe pads ditto. She used to call her act the Hindu Needle, Houdini being one of her heroes, but over time it turned into a little mocking sideshow known as the Praying Feet. She would pull the thread to make her toes come tight together, stretch the toes apart, then pull the string again, again. Made you grit your teeth, but still you had to snicker at the snake-oil-salesman speech she gave, making out the feet were praying of their own accord.

Of the lesser sins Dad couldn't cotton, mockery was first. Never mind the threat of spanking that she'd yet to have, Etta plied her trade behind his back until the pinprick holes along her toes and heels grew hard as kernel corn. Another look at the shed roof and the flash of yellow gingham told me she had failed to change out of her Sunday dress, a paddling crime as well.

For all my trying to be good, that day my spirits were as sore as the backs of my legs. At church that morning I'd had a working over, punishment all out of keeping with the crime. Playing kiss tag, I got snagged by Manfred Grover, dandy. Had to stand there while he planted one. Wet peck hadn't meant a thing, but still I got the switch. Skin still smarted. Ears did too, for Dad had called abomination on my head. I had yet to look Dad in the eye, planned never to again. If there was one thing I couldn't bear, it was to let him down. I had done that and then some, and I wasn't going to tell on Etta, love nor money.

The dust cloud rumbling toward us, Mam grabbed my hand to pull me up. "Where's Etta gone?"

I tripped over the pie plate. Hens and dent corn scattered, so I didn't have to answer. We shooed the biddies to the brooder house.

Once they were shut safely in, she asked again, "Where do you reckon she got off to?"

She was clutching at my shoulder, so I wasn't sure she felt my shrug.

Alongside her I gimped against the wind and wondered what to do. You could drown in dust, your mouth and nostrils stoppered up. I didn't want that on my head. I didn't want my sister dead. I was jealous, but not that so. But if I told, it would be tattling. I'd forsworn. Not only that, but Etta would repay in meanness. Midnight pinches, bed kicks, spite. No telling what.

Mam's work dress was plastered to her legs as we churned toward the house. "Mackie, do you know?"

Caught in dread and fear and waiting and no little gladness at the thought of scofflaw Etta punished and for once without my help, I shook my head.

After we got inside, we watched from the window as Dad ran helter-skelter, rounding up the horses, Sultan and the mares, brown Hetty and blind Stella, heaving doors and latching gates. In the gritty wind that whipped across us from the Panhandle, his voice gone staticky with swirling sand, he called Etta's name. No answer came.

Darkness fell around us. You could hardly see your hand in front of you. The front came on, the wind now wintry and cold. Beside me, Mam cried, "Oh, my land of Goshen, where can that child be?"

This is what I finally did. Etta was only twelve, but she was half-again as big. I was tiny, and I had that laggard foot. When I walked, a person hardly noticed, but if I hurried anywhere I bumbled like a bobbin on a crooked spindle, felt a fool. I didn't want to run, to call attention to myself, to her. Didn't want to make a scene, and so I decided I would brave the wind and walk out to save her. This doesn't make much sense as I recall it, but at the time it did. It was less like ratting, more like rescue, noble and unselfish. It would keep me on the right side of the strait gate and the narrow way.

I pushed open the door against the bitter wind and walked fast as I could into the dust, trying to reckon the familiar way in unfamiliar light, past blinded, calling Dad and to the lee side of the washhouse where I banged a fist against the slats and yelled, "Climb down quick, and they won't see you."

In that cold whirlwind, Etta's voice was small. "I can't. I lost the scissors . . ." She must have sucked in dust, then. She coughed and choked and cried.

I'd never seen her frightened. Wild hogs, rattlesnakes, and scorpions, she seemed to look them in the eye and stare them down. Just the day before, she'd shinnied up the windmill scaffold nimble as a monkey, skinned-the-cat the whole way down; but there was something fearsome in that storm, in the closed-in, suffocated way the dust could make you feel, like being buried in a box of dirt.

Break the thread, I told her, but she only whimpered.

I threw an arm over my eyes against the grit, began to climb one-handed up the three-rail fence. "Slide," I yelled, but had to shut my mouth against the dirt that blew inside it in breath's absence.

I made it to the overhang, reached out and touched a dirty foot, tugged hard. I gathered breath to tell her that if she slid down, I'd catch her, but I didn't have to for she scooted down to dangle. Her dress a tattered yellow flag, she let go her grip and tumbled onto me. Backward we went off the fence. We landed catabiased just in time for Dad to grab us up and see the tale told whole—she'd sewn her feet again.

Over his shoulder he threw her, Etta bawling loud about her arm. Her collarbone was broken, we would later learn, but at the time nobody knew. I don't remember running to the house behind them, only the vision of that silver needle in black dust, still attached by thread to Etta's feet as the wind snatched at it and it darted like a living thing.

We slammed the back porch door as though against an evil spirit. Outside, the wind howled louder than a belling hound.

Mam lit the lamp although it was high afternoon. Angrily, she hunted up some shears and angrily she snipped away the thread that bound the Praying Feet.

No matter that my sister earned the punishment Dad dealt, I felt as if my own flesh took it. Sick at heart. I don't know why. Maybe it was how her body felt when she tumped off the roof, its solidness, its trust, emptied out of everything but fear, of needing me, maybe how she cried as if her heart were broken, maybe that the way he beat her seemed the picture of the awfulness around us, seemed to strike again at me.

By morning the storm had passed. Dust eddied on new dunes. Hazed, weak sunlight, no stronger than light given by a quarter moon, struck the sifting dirt and made it glint like mica. Our ears had been so buffeted by wind and for so long our voices sounded far away, like voices on the radio—muffled, cottony, and hushed. It would be days before my hearing came back right. Etta claimed hers never did.

A few days later, after Etta moped around and lay in bed and otherwise went off her feed, the broken collarbone came to light. Mam set it. We weren't big on doctoring; in those times and in that place, nobody was. She bound Etta's shoulder with a torn bedsheet. Dad couldn't look at her, he felt so rotten. "I didn't know," he said, "I didn't know."

After this, Etta carried on like Mrs. Puny, Mrs. Sickling Child. Go get me this and pass me that. Poor, poor me, and look what Dad had done. If I had to mark the moment when she set herself against him, this was it.

⟶

At first we thought the great black storm had been a one-time thing, but more and more came on. Not so violent but more relentless, steadier. As time went by, we learned to tell the wind's direction from the color of the blowing dirt—black from the Dakotas, brown from Colorado, red from Texas. One by one we sold the stock. Mules to start, then horses one by one. Stella, Hetty, Sultan, off they went. We grieved each one, but Etta took their loss the hardest. She was growing fast, shooting up to leave me even further behind, but even so she seemed to narrow down each time an animal was sold away.

We traded the spinet piano for two tires and a new battery. Bartered the silver service for a sack of flour. When we got down to a tractor and a truck, one cow, six pigs, a dozen chickens and no rooster, it didn't matter if the storms were natural, divine, or human-made, we understood that something large and slow had overtaken us, and there wasn't much between us and the end.

Out on open ground the dust lay fine as flour. Walk down a road, dirt hovered ankle high, and if you traveled at a faster pace than ambling, the cloud of it rose higher than your head. Not even weeds took root.

We lived west of the Rock Saline, which is an otherworldly seabed plain of crusted salt where nothing grows, on three hundred twenty acres of good ranch and farmland Dad called Salt Camp. He had great hopes for it. The place was Kiowa hunting land, he said, in times before, and it had once been beautiful and wide as any open heart.

At first we tried to keep the house clean, to stay ahead in work, but the windows clouded up with windblown dust and salt and oil silt from the southern fields, sometimes ash and cinders from a burn. Dirt was everywhere. Open any door to find a ridge along the threshold. Take a dampened cloth to it and all you did was make the reddest mud. Shake a sheet or blanket, out it billowed, dust, so that even with your mouth and nose bound tight in huckabuck you couldn't draw a satisfying breath. Minutes after any bath we were begrubbed again. Dirt settled in our eyes, our ears, our nostrils, and our lungs. Our necks were ringed with grime, our faces smudged and gray as miners.

Just when we thought a storm had passed and no loose earth could possibly remain, on another came. One afternoon a flock of blinded blue-winged teal fell from the sky, a knobby line of buried birds, necks broken, feathers weighted. We could still make out the V of their formation. "They went quick, at least," said Mam. "That's mercy working somewhere."

Static charge killed off the melon crop, the pretty little fingerlings electrocuted, wasted black. Jackrabbits got the rest. The dirt was sifty as face powder, piling up in mounds around the house. We used the wheat scoop to carry it away, making a path up to the door like a tunnel shoveled in black snow. Sometimes with the dust there came ball lightning or dry thunder cracks to stop your heart, but hardly any rain except for sprinkles only fit to make the bare dirt look like a spotted pelt and crueler than none at all.

To save the dying land, Dad mortgaged up to buy a lister. Lots tried the same. The theory was that this machine would hold the soil by plowing furrows deep enough to trap the blowing dust. But you had to know which way the wind would come out of in order to plow them right and so the lister only scarred things worse. All around, the countryside was stark and barren as the sands of Egypt, and after just a year the Salt Camp ranch was lost for want of seven hundred dollars and a dime. It wasn't the seven hundred, Dad said. He could live with that. It was that dime. You'd think they could forgive that sorry dime if ten cents was the going rate for pride.

He talked of heading down south for the oil fields. We could rig up a chuck wagon and sell box lunches to the roughnecks and roustabouts. Mam would cook, Etta and I could serve. I liked this idea, had visions of a starched blue uniform, a perky hat, a name tag with *Maxine* in fancy script. But when the governor, Alfalfa Bill, shut down three thousand oil wells to drive up the barrel price, Dad changed his mind. There were food riots in Oke City. Tulsa the same story. You heard of families camped in boxes, huddling in dug-out holes with pasteboard roofs. Mam said she'd rather tenant farm than that, or go back to Missouri or out to California like the rest. "Just once," she said, "I'd like to pick my shame before somebody beats me to it."

"Most who leave have family out in California," Dad told her. "We don't."

She picked at grit under her thumbnail with the sliver of a kitchen match. "We don't have family anywhere."

She was given to dark sayings, had a way of looking back as if to see some old haunt trailing close behind her. She came from down near Joplin, from some Ozark Spruills, pale-eyed folk who ran to temper, the women to root medicine, the men to stern religion. Her father was the leader of a splinter church of Two Seeders. Thought he was a prophet. Once, he stretched himself across a trestle bridge to prove the Rapture would arrive before the Katy made its milk run. When the locomotive set the struts aquake he held on fast, but just as the cowcatcher loomed, he bailed, shattered his backbone on ravine rock. He lived another year, wasting into gravel-throated growl and nasty spirit, whacking his hickory prod against the floorboards when he wanted tending.

"Never," Mam said, "get your heart so set on something that there's no way to live on after you don't get it."

In the harder times that were coming, neither I nor Etta heeded her advice. No amount of warning scared us off the hell-bents that we were, and both of us would be undone by our set hearts. But here I'm jumping over time when I mean to tell the story straight.

About the shames remaining to us, Mam couldn't fix on one. She left the choice to Dad. By then I'd watched them long enough to know that any choice he made would be in her eyes wrong, and blame would come his way no matter. I imagine that he knew this, too. But before you take it that she stood against him any way he turned, before you take it that she was sour or bitter-hearted, put the word *beleaguered* to her. Let it go at that. I've come to think some unkind, gloomy spirit troubled her, dark as the woods she came from, the darker of the two seeds her people put their faith in, and that this spirit rode her to the ground. Also, everybody has their hidden reasons, and she would have been no different. Unless before she went she passed those reasons down to Etta, who, time would show, had reasons of her own, she took them with her.

Down deep, for all the sad-sacking he put on, Dad was more hopeful in his nature. He believed we could wait out the storms and drouth, and he believed in prayer. "We've asked for help," he told the Lord one suppertime, "but now we pray for guidance. Teach us Thy will, O Lord."

When we raised our heads, Etta said she had already had a word with God, and He told her we should head for California, fast. Mam said we should think about Saint Louis, she'd dreamed of all that river water flowing by. A few days later when I lied—no word at all had come no matter how I tried—and told him God said that whatever Dad decided would be fine, Etta rolled her eyes and whispered, "Goodie Two-shoes."

Against every westward push bred in his bones, he moved us east around the barren Rock Saline to middle ground and backward to a place below the Arkansas River for what little water this could give, out of the heart of the Dust Bowl and to its edge, but only just. We would take up living on a tenant parcel near the one-horse town of War Drum on a shallow clay bed stream that rose with every little rain but parched into a gully with the drouth.

"There's no shame in a backup step," he said. "It can help you set your stance." Lots of people then had shifted a few counties east, hoping to outride the storms.

Mam said, "You've prayed us out of Hades into limbo. McHenry, don't you think this same wind reaches over there?"

"Don't blaspheme, Billie Ann," he told her, but then he made hearty, as if to take her crabbing as a joke, which was his way. "It's a setback, but we'll weather it. This way we can keep an eye on things. We'll head west the minute things look better. Besides, we're fine. Nobody's dead."

She gave a dark harrumph, went back to packing plates. We were hurrying against the sheriff's sale. In the yard the truck was groaning on its axles, our last cow, Big Babe, tethered on behind.

In oil and cattle land below the Cherokee Strip, the new place was set into a rolling countryside of pinkish sandstone, cutbank hills, and upland pastures rising out of sand draws. Pretty enough, and green, just as he promised, but nothing like the grassy glory Salt Camp used to be. On the banks of Tebo Creek grew cottonwood and willow, redbud, dogwood, coffee trees. You had to go more easterly for blackjack oak and cedar, but still the timber looked like woods, and ran with fox and deer and coyotes, pheasants, songbirds, quail. More rare were bobcats and red wolves, and once a cat so tawny and enormous that we had to think it was a cougar.

The tenant house was no more than a shotgun bungalow sided with boxcar sections, their red paint weathered ruddy. Front room, kitchen, a bedroom off the back, a dormered attic room where I and Etta slept. Set sideways on the grid, the house faced east. The front porch boards had gone to carpenter ants and dry rot and had fallen off, and the roof overhang was stobbed with timbers so the front door gave out onto nothing and you had to use the back. Still the place, by tenant standards, was more an actual house than most.

"Not so bad," Dad said. He kicked at a tractor tire planter some other tenant left behind, some dry-hay-colored sweet-flag strag-glings. "Before long we'll go back."

Except for the fact that it wasn't ours, after the desert we had left behind, the War Drum place seemed paradise to everyone but Etta, who grudged it from the start.

Some girls when they grow to women will slough off their spunk, will quiet down and nicen up in hopes of catching boys. Not Etta. At fourteen, she liked boys well enough. As we lay in bed at night she whispered about one or another of the few left at school, and of the men who sometimes worked around. But she vowed that any catching would be done by Mary Etta Spoon. She had not outgrown her willfulness, and she waxed even stronger in her nature. The broken collarbone had changed her, though. There was a grieved and bitter edge to her there'd been only a glimmer of before.

By her lights the new place was a piddling dirt farm, not a ranch at all. She missed the horses, Sultan in particular. She drew horses in the margins of Dad's *Capper's Monthly,* named them Ink or Midnight, Raven. The War Drum school was sorry, just a bunch of lowland ragtags. She was hungry all the time. There wasn't anything to eat.

"There's plenty here," Dad said. "The greatest of it. Think of this as a new start. 'Ye were hungry and I fed ye.' That's the promise."

Etta sulked.

He tried again. "Just think, before long you'll have more horses than you can count."

Etta said she hoped they tasted good.

She wanted a gun, as well. A six-shooter. Said she needed it to plug herself if things got any worse.

"Don't talk like that," Dad said, "not even as a joke." He cast an eye at Mam, who pursed her lips and looked away.

"We'll make the best of it. It's a hard life if you don't weaken," he'd tell Etta. This was a saying of the time. It meant, buck up and tough it out. Everybody knew this, but Etta said, "What in the samhill's *that* supposed to mean?"

A different father would have slapped the daylights out of her.

On the day we left Salt Camp, he cranked the truck with us inside it, straightened the chain we dragged to ground the vehicle from static charge, and climbed in. "We're off," he said, fixing the choke. "First one who doesn't fuss along the way will get a big surprise."

Slumped between a dish barrel and a roll of quilts, Etta crossed her arms. "Is this a trick?"

"No trick."

He wouldn't give a hint. I guessed a fried hamburger sandwich at a roadside stand. I'd tasted one before, so good it figured in my dreams.

"A coal black Morgan horse," said Etta.

Mam said, "A flat tire."

"Billie Ann, you're out," he said, but he was in high spirits, and even Mam had to ease up.

We hadn't gone five jouncing miles along the road before I needed a necessary stop. Another mile of wheedling got me the empty lard pail in a dry creek bed, so I was out. That left only Etta. Judging by the surprise, he'd had her in mind all along.

On one of his land-scouting trips he'd bought a buffalo, a motherless bull calf, stick-thin, all head and ribs. When he saw the creature in the roadside pen a mile from War Drum he took it for a sign and bought him, never mind the dollar. We would name him Titan, fatten him on mash, charge passers-through a dime to look, another dime to ride, and that way keep us in food money. "You can start your own Wild West show," he told Etta. In higher times, he'd taken us to see the Miller Brothers 101, where once the great Geronimo, brought low, had skinned a buffalo before a watching crowd.

Though Etta should have been too old for the idea, she took to it. She loved any kind of feat, saw herself bareback on the beast, one hand gripping the rope around his neck, the other hand hat-waving. Titan was no horse, but he would do.

It took a calf a while to grow big enough to bear a load, so in the meantime she got Mam to sew her a costume—a cowgirl skirt out of a saddle blanket, a checkered shirt cut down and darted. She got Dad to make a lariat of henequen and teach her how to rope. She practiced until she could whirl the loop around her feet as smooth as whipped meringue. Dad painted a wooden sign that read *See the Titan of the Plains.* Etta made him add *Roped Every Day by Mary Etta Spoon.* She planned an act in which she lassoed Titan and pulled him around a ring, then jumped astride.

We fed the calf on sorghum fodder, oats and grass and milk, but day by day he sickened. Mam said, "You should have named him Herbert Hoover. He's that worthless."

"He'll perk up." Dad scratched his neck back, wandered off.

Etta spent her days in Titan's stall. She slept beside him on a pallet. Brought him grass and hay and tried to feed him cow's milk from a bottle. But finally the little creature foundered, his belly fast with bloat. We'd been at War Drum but a month when he gave up the ghost. No one with extra dimes had passed through anyway, and so when the sign blew over in a bad turn-wind, Dad let it be.

He mended tools for trade and change, got by with farming on the halves for Emil Holloway, a suitcase-farmer whose family lived in a big rock-chimneyed mansion house in War Drum. He brought in meager dry farm crops of kaffir corn, Sudan grass, wheat, alfalfa hay. When Etta asked what farming on the halves meant, Mam shushed her. Later, when Dad had gone out to the barn, she said, "It means sharecropping. Hush about it, hear?"

He took day work with the road crews when he could, or went out west to shovel dirt for a dollar a day. He hatched another plan to sell the extra eggs and milk, but this plan didn't either come to pass. Except for clabber, which I had to swallow for having had the rickets to the point my bones were weak, we had no extra anything.

When the weather followed us and found us in our hiding place, Mam didn't say a word, but everybody felt her prophecy come true. Storm on storm on storm and banshee winds that blew you down. Static charge that made it so you couldn't touch each other without jumping back. Blue sparks raced along the barbed-wire fences and fireball lightning traveled up the windmill, lit it like a derrick. Snow and dust and wind and dust and dust and dust. By March of 1937 the place looked almost as bad as what we left. But for the coming of Audie Kipp, which allowed Dad to hold out hope, we might have given up and headed west to have ourselves five different lives.

―⌐

Lots were on the road then, not just Okies. Hoboes, bandits, bindle stiffs. Some of them rough customers. The Barrow Gang had come through more than once, and there were Alvin Karpis and the local-boy-made-bad Choc Floyd, their like. Etta followed Pretty Boy's adventures especially, but she took an interest in all their doings. She listened fierce-eyed to news reports when she could get Dad to hook the Philco to the Ford truck's battery. She scissored out newspaper articles. On the raw boards of our attic bedroom wall she tacked up grainy pictures of her heroes. She found an old felt hat and wore it pulled awry like Bonnie Parker's. The hard-times tales of crooks and robbers shook the outlaw bone in Etta, but most people ran scared of them. Rumors flew like feathers, got the county all jumped up.

One March sundown when we were at the supper table we heard out on the lane the sound of someone riding in on horseback, the slow clop of a walking gait. Dad went for his .45 and Mam seized the belaying pin we kept beside the door. I crept behind the stove, heart hammering. Etta, with her robber hat jammed low, raced to the door as if behind it there was someone come to save her. Against Dad's warning, she threw it open wide.

A gust of cold spring wind blew in. When she saw what stood outside, scuffing his down-heel boots along the dirt, she shrugged and said, "Oh, pitiful," went back inside to finish up her butterbeans and mine.

Our stranger was a big dark boy. He wore an army dreadnought, bullhide boots of prison issue, the kind they gave out at the Indian school. Behind him in the dooryard was a blood bay mare so close to foaling she was barrel-square. The stranger worked his face as if to compose a speech, and when he spoke, his voice was deep and sure, past the froggy affliction of cracking back into his boyhood voice. "First off," he said, "I come out of Chilocco. So you'll know."

Up east near the Kansas line stood Chilocco, the Indian boarding school. Some called it Prairie Light and others called it hell on earth. The place stands to this day, a ring of gloomy castle-looking buildings made of cut gray limestone. We'd heard of children stripped from families, sold into bondage, runaways brought back and whipped, boys and girls strung up by their thumbs for speaking in their olden language, or worse, their tongues slit longways like a flock of talking crows.

"I'd be pleased to work for board-and-found if anybody had a job that needed doing. You wouldn't have to pay."

Dad crossed his arms, narrowed his eyes. "How old are you? Don't fib."

The boy looked at his sorry-looking boots. "Almost eighteen."

"How short of almost?"

"Seventeen. Next month."

Dad took this in. "What name you traveling under?" He meant this as a sideways kind of joke. If you were quick enough, you could see his face had shifted just a hair off stern. You could tell that he was liking what he saw.

Three times the stranger had to give his name before we understood it to be Audubon Jay Kipp.

"Audie's good enough," he said, and here he seemed to grin without a muscle moving. Some inner light, as faint-but-there as Dad's, went *flicker* in his eyes. "Or even Hey, if that's a supper I smell fixed."

Dad wouldn't bow to his good humor or his hint for food. He drew back and eyed the mare hitched to our post. "You ride that creature in or did she follow you?"

"No, sir. I led her."

This was a good sign. The mare was nigh, the boy too big. "She stolen?"

Audie Kipp looked down the lane, then sideways to the timber of the Tebo, where the sun was sinking behind a fringe of trees and lining them with glow. Then he looked back at the mare, and from the softening around his eyes it was plain he loved the creature. "Well, she's borrowed, yes. Adopted, more like."

"Her brand is BIA." Dad stepped off the back porch stair into the yard, patted the mare's neck. "Go on and turn her loose. She'll find her way."

This was a test. If the visitor let go the horse, it might mean Dad would hire him. I drew a breath and held it, waiting, for with Audie's no-muscle grin something had happened in me. A pleasant shock that traveled foot to hairline, made my knees go all to water and my arm hair stand on end. If I'd been born a bug, my feelers would have quivered.

Behind me, Etta muttered, "Keep the horse and let *him* go."

When Audie Kipp unhitched the blood bay, slapped her on the rump, and sent her in a heavy, pregnant walk back up the lane, I breathed.

A silence stretched between the two men as they seemed to size each other up, then Dad ran a hand up across his forehead and over his frowse of sandy hair, a sign he meant to deal.

Lately, grim had been the word put to him as he worked against the weather. He bit off words as though they cost him money. Before, at Salt Camp, he had been a talker. Loved to tell a story on himself. How he came back from the war on fire for land like every other fool and hied himself back home to Joplin with the plan in mind to buy a team of horses and at least one good cow pony, how he wound up with two blue mules, a staggered jennet, and a wife. When McHenry Spoon made plans, he liked to say, all heaven noted them and took the necessary steps to gum the works. In his stories he cast himself a rube bamboozled by Almighty God, short-ended in the trade by a Jehovah who was combination faro dealer, gypsy horse thief, and hanging judge. But the truth was he believed in prayer, and because he was a hopeful man, his back broke slowly, bone by bone, so steadily you couldn't mark the moment it was broken past repair. But in that long-gone year of Audie Kipp's arrival and for a few beyond, he was still able to believe in second chances.

"This is how it is," he said. "I've no sons here to speak of." He cut his eyes as if an afterthought had struck him. "Or anywhere, I reckon." He waited to see if Audie would laugh. Audie—watchful, smart—obliged.

This pleased Dad, who came on stronger. He held out a hand to take in me and Etta, who had returned to the door and was peering out, her hat pulled low across her eyes, one hand on a jut-out hip. "And these two girls are busy with their mother in the house. The neither much for outside help. Spoiled, you see."

This wasn't true. We worked hard, had chores inside and out. But it was the way men talked to each other in those times, as though the household females were a burden. It was a measure of pride for a man to be able to say he had a sickly wife. It meant he was well-off enough to keep her, and it called attention to his own hard work. Then, we didn't pay it any mind, but time would come they had to be broken of it and the breaking would be hard.

Dad stuck out his hand. "Mack Spoon. We'll give you a fair try. Room and board. Two bits, if I can spare it, for a day of work. If you work out, nobody at Chilocco has to know. My word on that."

Audie took his hand. They shook.

Later, when they knew each other better, Dad told Audie that the turning point was that his shake was strong, had met his own grip notch to notch, and that he'd looked him in the eye. At Chilocco, Audie said, they taught the boys to shake like that. It was not the Indian way to squeeze and pump, but if learning to had got him out of there, it served its purpose.

On that March night, to seal the deal, Dad spoke his creed. "Man's work is his solemn business, and no bank, no bureau, and no government had ought to meddle otherwise."

Audie made the sign of praying hands, and gave out a loud "Amen!"

This stopped the show. Dad drew back. For him, this was a holy word, not something you said just to agree. You didn't amen-this and amen-that, throwing its weight around. Said the way Audie said it, by Dad's reckoning it was blasphemy.

Mam pretended interest in a fleck of white paint on the doorjamb. Again I held my breath. Even Etta scuffed her foot against the threshold, looked at our visitor as though remeasuring. Something about the stranger had lifted us already and we didn't want to see the lifting end, we all of us had been so long so grim.

Dad said, "If you mean to second the motion, say, 'Hear, hear.' Save the dynamite for when you need it." He clapped Audie on the shoulder.

By Dad's lights, Audie was honorary kin. An orphan like himself. Dad and the brother who died in a hunting accident—the gun misfired as John Hardy climbed a split-rail fence—had grown up in a home they never called their own. Audie was more than welcome with us as long as things worked out. He could bunk out in the hayloft of the near barn, board with us at the table. If he wanted to come to church with us, so be it.

"Hear, hear," said Audie.

"Fix our guest some supper," Dad called over his shoulder. To Audie, he said, "There's not much, but you're welcome to it."

Etta stood at the doorway, her eyes as narrow as a cat's. "The butterbeans are gone."

"Some corn bread, then."

"I ate that, too."

"Make biscuits."

Goodie Two-shoes hurried in and did.

—➤—

Audie Kipp was six feet tall, long-boned and barrel-chested. His shoulders slumped. He had a loping, splay-foot gait, and went about his business with his neck thrawn sideways, wry-necked as a jinx, as if he meant to listen for a message rising from the ground. Awkward as a grounded crow, he was that ill-made he knew it. "If I'd been born a horse," he liked to say, "somebody'd have to put me down." As for me, if my heart was called out by his body's awkwardness, it grew wings at hearing how he could make light of it.

Anyone could see that he had Indian blood. Choctaw, Dad guessed, as half of eastern Oklahoma bore the trace. They were known for industry, intelligence, and thrift. "Might as well be Scots, them," Mam said of the tribe. Sometimes she peered at Audie as though the just-right angle of regard would tell his bloodline. "He might be a dark Scot. People, chickens, horses. Tan and gray and brown and red. I never could see what the hubbub was."

For her, this was a speech. Somewhere buried in it was a notion she was mulling, but mostly things came out of her in sparseness. A few stark words you had to ponder. Since we moved to War Drum, she had grown even more inward, and as the days grew browner, something in her seemed to parch. When two of her front teeth fell out, she didn't say a thing. She put them in a jelly jar and set them on the shelf beside the dry sink where every morning when I went to look out the window there they were, two cracked, brown stubs gone rootless. Of the land, of moving from the Ozark hills to flat-land, she sometimes said, "It's not so pretty out here, but at least you can see far enough to tell what's coming at you." I had begun to won-der if she even saw the feet she put in front of her, but around Audie she perked up.

He was funny. He made faces. Not broad or clownish like an ac-tor in a show, but fleet and telling. His whole face changed. He would lift an eyebrow, sly, and try to snitch a biscuit. Tiptoeing around, the biscuit in plain sight, he pretended he was foxing her. He made over her cooking, saying she beat the pants off any hash house. Outcooked the boarding school hands down. Every now and then he threw a twenty-dollar word her way, putting on a high-toned accent to tickle her. He'd talk about her culinary skill, the gastronomic feast she laid out on the table, even though it was plain beans. With Audie around, she smiled more, covering her gapped teeth with her hand, so that she was almost pretty again. She saved him the sorghum mo-lasses she had once held back for Etta, who also had a sugar tooth, and one morning as she stirred the hominy for breakfast I heard her singing, a sound I hadn't heard . . . well, ever. "Wayfaring Stranger," its low notes minor, mournful, whisper-sung and quaky, but a song.

About his lineage, when we finally got up the nerve to ask, he said, "Almost full-blood and apt to turn incompetent." He meant this to be funny but there wasn't much to laugh about, it was too true. Anyone with blood enough and rights could be declared incompetent on white-man whim. Tribes lost their acres faster than the drilling companies found oil. Land-jobbing was just the start. Oilmen would find an elder with an allotment and a taste for whiskey, and that was the end of it. Their tactics ran to burnouts and murder. "Kaw," he said, shaking his head, "and nearabout the last one standing."

He worked alongside Dad. They talked or didn't, as it suited them. Dad called him Aud, and in the way he said the name there was no trace of poking fun or joking, just the word said short and whole and sounding like a wonder. Before the month was out, Dad loved him like a son and friend and brother, all in one. The way the two were like, they might have been related. One time I overheard Dad tell a story of his boyhood, about a sorrel mare he had saved up to buy. When he went to make the deal, the trader cozened him—a kid of twelve—into a skewbald hack. Outside the machine barn, my peeping eye to a crack in the boards, I spied on them. Not once in the telling did Dad look up at Audie. Only cranked the whetstone for the corn knife he was sharpening and shook his head as though to tell the story to himself, as though bewildered by the fact that as a grown man he was as far from that fine horse as the boy he had once been. Or so I thought, for after a silence into which I read the dashing of Dad's hopes from the birth bed on and felt his losses in my marrow, he put down the corn knife. "Fixed that old crook's wagon, you'll be glad to hear. Nag dropped dead before I got the nickel slug fished from my wallet." Dad and Audie laughed until they went to rubber, knee-slapping, raring back.

Our guest was big and kind and funny and imperfect. This made him perfect in my sight. I loved him and there was no brotherness about it.

⤙

Etta had grown beautiful. Anyone could see it, not just green-eyed me, who watched for evidence. Long-limbed, deep-bosomed, her skin coppery and smooth. She wasn't perfect in her features—her nose too pointy and her eyes too wide apart, that catty-corner-coffee birthmark, but she was startling in her aspect. She hardly looked the same way twice. Even her dark hair seemed to take on her temper— sometimes flyaway and bristly, others glossy, smooth. There was no telling which way the wind would blow against the weathervane she was, but she was beautiful.

A pinched place in my heart was glad she didn't take to Audie. She acted like he was a pest. At first I thought it was the extra food he ate. When Mam dolloped supper on his plate—a little less than Dad's but more than ours—a hard look came across my sister's face. She would make a show of hunger, ask for more potatoes even though she saw the bowl scraped empty. But that didn't seem reason enough. I considered it might be that he was Kaw, in those times and thereabouts the poorest of the poor, but she had never shown a prejudice before and we were schooled in red-and-yellow-black-and-white from Cradle Roll. Besides, her birthday wish when she was five had been to *be* an Indian. When it hit me she resented Audie because he took her place as favorite, this gave me, I'm ashamed to say, a bitter thrill. One day, wanting to see if she'd admit to it, I made up my mind to ask.

She was in the front room on the sewing chair, basting the kicked-out hem in her green school skirt. Etta at sewing was a strange sight for too many reasons. One, it brought to mind the Praying Feet and called me back to Salt Camp and our last days there. Two, she never sewed a lick if she could badger me to do it. Three, the sight seemed to contain the changes in her, all at once. I am saying that I saw her fresh and saw I didn't know her, which turned the baiting I intended into wanting, honestly, to know. "Why," I blurted, "don't you like him?"

She plied the needle through the skirt hem, drew up slack. "Who?"

"Well, Audie Kipp." It hurt to say his name out loud.

"Odd Bird? I don't."

I didn't like her name for him but knew that if I made fuss she'd call him Odd Bird all the more. "Don't what? Don't like him?"

"I don't *not* like him." She wound thread around a finger to make a knot, pilled it, then pulled taut the thread.

"Then why don't you talk to him? Why do you give him dirty looks?"

"Mostly I don't think of him at all. For all that he's a runaway, he's tamer than an old pet skunk." She bent to bite off the thread. "He reminds me of that old boy Kewpie. Dull and gatless."

Then and there I made up my mind to win him. Dull was good and gatless was just fine. Of course he wasn't either of those things, but if Etta thought so, that was all right by me. He was the first thing, save a foot repair, I'd wanted hard enough to pray for. My plan would be the one that always failed before, to be the opposite of Etta. If I outshone the sun, so be it.

Dad came in then, settled in his chair, picked up his *Capper's*, shook it out. For two years, since Etta's thrashing with the rug beater, he'd been trying to flatter her back into his ken. When he saw her sewing, saw the stitches fine and even, he said, "Why, I believe you could make a living as a seamstress." He meant to please her, but Etta only gave a baleful stare, and even I could see the April-Sunday ghost that flew into the room. Her grudge wore on.

As spring came on with thawing mud, a phantom greenness in the tops of trees, I put my plan in action. After what remained of school was out—there were only seven of us in the high school room, a part-time circuit teacher—I worked a full day at housework. Swept up my own dust storm, cleaned and cleaned and cleaned. Cooked, too. When the men came in for supper I do-gooded all around, lifting pot lids, going on about the savors I was fixing to dish up, sneaking looks at Audie's face. If it brightened, and he said, "Mm-mmm!" I smiled and pranced to beat the band. I left extras on my plate and said I couldn't eat another bite and would he like them? Etta beady-eyed me like a copperhead might watch a rat, but I was on a mission and I didn't care.

Out behind the far barn was a fallow field, and beside it ran an unused wagon trail. There, with a sharp stick, I scratched some love arithmetic into the dirt. MJS + AJK = True Love. To see the letters gave the feeling of a Ferris wheel I'd once been on, all risen hackle hair and goose bumps. One afternoon I etched out *Mrs. Audubon Jay Kipp*. Just as I finished with a curlicue, Mam called for supper help. I had to fancy-dance to scuff the name away. Grieved me to erase it. I wanted a marker that would last, and so a few days later, on the wormy lapboard of the toolhouse, so small it was no bigger than a dime and so far down only a passing mouse might see it, I carved our names and linked them with a plus, enclosed them in a heart as swollen up as mine.

Looking back, I see I featured Audie grander in my mind than any mortal boy could be. But I was sixteen, and I knew no other way to ponder love. My knowledge of romance I took from Lancelot and Guinevere, from love stories from the ten-cent store, but mostly from the Bible, and so it seemed only right to liken him to heroes. Moses leading us from Egypt, Gideon and his horn, Daniel in the den, and Shadrach in the furnace. Joshua before the walls and Samson and the pillars. I'd like to say that I stopped short of Christ, but of course there was no stopping me. Since he'd left Chilocco, where they made boys cut their hair, Audie had let his grow long. He wore it down his back, a braided stub tied with a piece of rawhide. He said it was a custom and that he'd cut it only out of grief. With his dark skin he looked like our *Sallman's Head of Christ* that hung over the horsehair sofa in the front room, the portrait with those haunted Jesus eyes that didn't only watch you but watched *over* you, so that in them you could imagine earthly and divine love, mixed. An old hymn went "I have decided to follow Jesus," and under my breath I sang it except I put Audie's name in Jesus' stead. No turning back, the hymn went on, no turning back. At night in bed beside my sleeping sister I sent my yearnings upward in his shape and form.

All hope aside, the coming spring would be the hardest yet, not only for the drouth and storms, but for the first true loss they brought.

~

Only one big snow had fallen the winter before, barely deep enough to ease Dad's worry for the wheat, some Turkey Red he planted on his own, a gamble. The cover hadn't lasted and the snow was blown to powder before it could soak the soil. The rain in March was sparse, two April rains just scarves of mist. The seedlings burned before the heads came on. Those that grew to milk stage cooked. The earth cracked into curling slabs as big as dinner plates, the Tebo narrowed to a thread between blanched sandbars and withered manna grass. The fisher-birds that used to stalk the backwater flew off. Each night coyotes slunk around the house, so close we heard their panting.

In middle May the hayfield dried too soon. There was no money to hire a reaper. "We'll cut by hand," Dad said, "ourselves."

Etta, Dad, Mam, Audie, me, all in a wide-spaced staggered line just in that order, armed with borrowed sickles, women forward, men behind, we cut. Snakes, jackrabbits, and fieldmice scuttered as we whacked against alfalfa stems that should have been knee high but only reached our ankles. We had tied kerchiefs around our heads against the dust and chaff, like cotton pickers. Though she bound her nose and mouth in skimming gauze because of her hay fever, Mam sneezed and sneezed, her poor eyes streaming, sneezed again, and more than once hung back. When he nearly nicked her on a swing, Dad called out, "Billie Ann, look sharp!"

At midmorning we rested. We had taken out the dasher from the butter churn and filled the crock with water. Into this we put the ice Audie had spent a nickel on. Acting like the Daddy Warbucks that he wasn't, he kidded Dad, "What do you bet we'll make double that in hay?" The night before, they augered out the ice block, chipped it with an awl, and now, at midmorning in the middle of the hayfield as we took our ease, white precious slivers floated in our water cups, and we felt rich. We drank until our teeth hurt and we saw small fleeting stars. "Butter water, hey?" said Audie, toasting. This struck us—even Etta—funny, and we laughed. We lay back on that cut green stubble, laughed. Alfalfa stems pricked through our shirts, grasshoppers spanged like bullets out of nowhere, and we itched like sixty, but no water since has tasted half so good. For noontime there were biscuits in the basket, plenty, and a quarter round of cheese.

The sun hazed over. Dad made a temple of his hands, looked out from under them toward the cloud-blown glare. "Rain, and after all this time." He shook his head and swore Job's oath, the words he used to keep himself from worse. "Curse God and die." If it rained, the hay would go to waste.

We cut faster, reaping silently and at a stoop with our short-handled scythes, swaths behind us broad, straight trails. With Audie working beside me, I thought of the Philistine army moving through the tares, their scimitars aflash. I remembered Samson and the foxes, how Samson tied torches to their tails to set the fields on fire. I thought of gleaners, Ruth, Naomi, Boaz at the threshing floor. Of what it might be like to sleep at someone's feet. A searing thought shot through me fleet as lightning and my hands went weak around the scythe—at Audie's, say, but next to him and head to head. I thought of kissing him, him kissing me. Then I remembered the long-ago switching at the Salt Camp pasturage, and so I gripped the sickle harder, whacked in rhythm with the others, put away the notion, hard. Planned to entertain the idea later, linger in it like a storybook and not the close-lipped Bible, which was big on entering-into-tents but deadly quiet on the subject of what people did together once the flaps were sealed.

We worked until my bones were burning and my hands crabbed up. Deep in my back an ache seemed to cut sideways through me, and my body was so tight and sore and burning that I couldn't think aught else, and so the afternoon turned into sweat and bug-song, slice and whick and slice and whick.

A wounded rabbit makes a certain sound, a high unearthly squeal that rives the air. This is what I thought had happened when we heard Mam scream.

We dropped our scythes and ran to her. She clutched forearm to her belly. Blood coursed between her fingers. Dad yanked off his shirt and tried to stanch the wound, a slice of flesh on the underside of her forearm, cloven to the bone.

Her face was ashen, empty, her gaze beyond us on the field's far end. It was a mercy when she fainted.

Dad knelt over her, working to tie off the arm above the elbow, looking from gash to sickle, gash to sickle, as though if he looked hard enough he could unmake the moment when his blade slashed upward on the swing.

When she came to, she tried to rise but fell back listless. Dad picked her up and carried her into the house. We followed. I couldn't look, but Etta, doctorly and quick, unfazed, sewed the wound with cotton thread. She dressed the arm in poultices, pinned a dish towel to Mam's dress to make a sling. Later, Dad told Etta that her work had been so fine she ought to study for a nurse. "Ish-ka-bibble," Etta said, "I'd rather rot."

The real doctor, Mam wouldn't have. "If there was nothing to pay field help, there's nothing left for this. Besides, a rest will do me good. I know what to do." She went to bed and closed her eyes and slept the soundest sleep, she said, she'd slept in years.

The men went out to gather the sickles we had left in the field. Working long past dark, they raked the hay into piles that mouldered worthless in the latter rain.

That night hailstones big as lady apples clattered on the roof. When they melted, on a rainstorm came, and after that a rage of blowing dust that settled into puddles the rain had left behind. By the time the puddles dried, the silt had turned to stone and Mam's right arm was proud and purple, and she couldn't touch it for the pain. A hot, red line snaked up her arm.

Dad came to stand before her where she sat resting her arm on the kitchen table. "Don't cross me, Billie Ann. I'm going for the doctor."

She smiled weakly, sweetly. "Don't, Mack. It's getting better."

Anyone could see he wanted to believe her. "You're sure?"

She looked up from the rag rug at her feet. Their gazes met, his skeptical and hers oddly serene. "I'm sure."

That night as I lay trying to sleep in heat that stuck me to the sheet, out of the deadest silence rose her voice, "Pray until you're ragged, Mack, but it won't change a thing."

She was beside herself with fever. Sometimes she raved. Said things that seemed to come from some quarter beyond her.

"You can't come over Pontio. Pontio is over Pilato."

"Dullix ix ux."

Numbers, spells and signs, singsong verses, nonsense. When Etta tended to her wound, she and Mam seemed to be speaking in some unknown language, for Etta said the strange words back. "Dullix ix ux. You can't come over Pontio."

I brought cool washcloths for her forehead, warm broth and sugar-water. With every sip she took I whispered in my mind, *Don't die.*

Although she tried to drain the wound of greenish ooze, it gave a stench to stop your breath, its foul smell trapped in the floorboards of the house.

One night I woke up from a supper table dream so real that I could smell the food. Potatoes, gravy, and roast beef set steaming on a platter. I got up to see if somebody was cooking, if there was something good to eat. Not everlasting biscuit, meat. The kitchen was hot, the firebox glowed. Mam stood beside it. The strange hot smell of burning punk and searing meat was from the flatiron pressed against her arm to shrive the poison.

She heard me, turned, her black eyes deep and dulled. "You'll be lost without me."

I made to go to her, but she lifted her good arm, the flatiron raised, and shook her head. "Dullix ix ux," she said, as though it made good sense.

I ran outside, meaning to hold the sound that rose in my throat until I reached my hiding place behind the toolhouse, where, in what seemed to have been another life, I had carved the low-down heart.

The wind was high, the air a haze and thick with dirt. A gust swept round the corner of the building. Grit sandpapered at my ankles, and the sting felt good.

Etta was there already, sitting on an upturned bucket, arms crossed over her chest. Her hair was loose and wild, her nightdress and her eyes so white her face looked like a shadow. She jerked her chin toward the toolhouse wall. "Dad's in there. Praying."

From inside came no voice, only an odd dry rasp, as from a wide-gauge file on wood rot, then a shuddered breath.

To the east a cloud bank scudded past a hatching moon that cast the slats in light as silvery as spinning flax. The cloud's tail drew a wisp across the moon.

"How can he dare when it's his fault!"

I whispered, "It was an accident."

She held a length of binder twine, winding it around her fingers, pulling tight, unwinding. "He might as well have aimed!"

"Etta," I said. "Etta." I tried reason. "You were on the end and she was in the middle. Etta, it was you, then Dad, then Mam and Audie and me. And we were up ahead of them, the men. You couldn't have seen."

She stood. The bucket, rattling in a hollow metal sound, clanked over, rolled. Her hair flew in the wind.

One time she accused a schoolmate of stealing her lunch pail. Set up a wail in the play yard that her bucket was missing, and she knew who had done it, a dirty boy named Bucky Madzey. Child's family was on the county and he begged food every day and so the teacher swatted Bucky with the paddle, sent him home. That day when we got back to our place, there was Etta's lunch pail in the ditch at the end of the lane just where she left it, fried bologna sandwich still inside. When I said she ought to tell the teacher about the mistake, Etta shook her head. "That little stinkpot must have left it there. Ran all the way out here and put it in the ditch to save his hide." This made no sense to anyone but Etta, but there was no arguing. Once something set her mind, the way she said it was, it was.

"If Mam dies," she said, "he'll be the one who killed her."

"She won't die. She'll be all right."

"He's done it before."

This was old news. "Etta, it was the war, and he was in the army."

"There are things you don't know. Things she told me. Awful things."

"Mamma doesn't know . . ." My breath caught and my gorge

rose, and suddenly it felt like dust had lodged inside my throat. I hadn't called her Mamma since I don't know when.

I swallowed, and then made up my mind to speak the truth. "She's delirious. She's sick. She can't tell what she's saying. Those words . . ."

"They're powwow magic from the Long-Lost Friend." She went on to say the strange words came from a book of Dutchy spells brought to the Ozarks from Pennsylvania by our Granny Spruill. In the book were remedies and potions, magic spells, but I had heard enough.

I ran from her, ran to the near barn to the cow stall where Big Babe lay, knob-knuckled legs folded beneath her, her big humped back a bony comfort I fell onto. I said her name, Big Babe, and this let me cry for how she smelled just like herself, of grassy breath and milk and hide, of mud, manure, and cowness. I cried until my belly ached. At sixteen, I felt three, a child in sweaty, snot-soaked misery. About that forsaken time, even now at eighty-whatsoever, I still do. I don't imagine that I ever won't.

Outside, the sand blew hard, then the wind stilled, and a spate of rain dashed against the boards, rain so fine it was the merest whiff of water and meant nothing. Then it ceased entirely, and whatever cloud had carried it moved on. I refused to let the cloud's passing mean the end. I worked it round and worked it round until I made it not mean Mam was dying.

A moon-cast shadow fell across me. Audie's. He came to hunker near Big Babe, reached out to stroke her ear. Out on the plain a coyote yipped, another answered him in kind.

"I heard what she said." He scratched behind the cow's ear the way you would a kitten's. "It was an accident. She'll come around. She has to think that way to draw the sting."

He moved his hand from the cow's head, brought it to mine and let it rest, its warmth a balm that failed to heal. I cried on past my strength, and he sat with me, quiet, but I felt no better, and I knew there had to be a harsher word than *accident* for what was happening.

In the morning Dad went for the doctor, promising payment in a cord of wood come fall. When the doctor saw her arm and said it was too late, she murmured something that I took to be "It never wasn't." In my hearing she didn't speak again.

That night Dad rousted us from sleep. "You girls get up and pray with me."

Etta balked. "There's nobody to hear it." But she got up.

I followed, skeptical as she was but too heartsick to admit it. I used to pray my foot would heal, pray with a want so hot and strong I fairly felt my bones abuzz, the holy shock and promise and the hush that surely came before a miracle, and I would fall asleep on the promise there would come reward for wanting something so, for having been so good. I would fall asleep in the hope that in the morning I'd no longer be a crooked little person. But always when I woke up I would see that ankle gone awry, the swollen knot of it, the patchy skin. I had prayed for Audie to be mine, to love me back, but out of longing, not belief. Now, with our mother twisting on the bed, it seemed too big a thing to pray for, too terrible, impossible, too lost. Still, I wanted to. Even though I knew a lukewarm prayer would be spewed out, I wanted to.

But I couldn't. Could only listen as Dad called on the God of Abraham who caused the seas to part, changed Moses' staff into a serpent, Aaron's rod to living wood. Watching his mouth and hearing that measured thunder, I saw it come upon him, that same holy shock and promise, and I knew it like my own blood beat and knew that it was doomed and had to turn away, for above his praying in that fevered room, above his sending up the name of His child Billie Ann Spoon for the Creator's blessing, I heard the rabbit cry she'd given in

the hayfield at the moment when her living spirit left her, departing in the chaffy, sunstruck air.

—

We set no stone, there being none. A few near neighbors came, the Holloways from town, some people from the War Drum church. We'd been to service only once or twice and hardly knew a face.

The funeral day was hot and still, the ground heat rising up to meet the sun's. It was no cooler in the house. Men gathered on the back steps where Dad sat, head in his hands. The women bustled in the kitchen. We ate and ate and ate. Ham, potato salad, greens, gooseberry pie and sponge cake, wooden vats of ice cream, food in such abundance that it gave lie to the wanting way we lived.

When Etta and I passed through, the women pressed our hands. They said, "It was God's will."

Toward evening, Etta came undone. She stood in the front room, third or fourth dish of strawberry ice cream in her hand, and when Dad came through from the porch, smelling of corn liquor and cheroot, she dashed the ice cream to the floor. "You did this. *You* did this. It was *your* will."

"Sister, don't." He tried to take her in his arms, but Etta wrenched away, stood crying. I went to stand beside her, tried to take her hand. She drew it back, cried on. From the back porch Audie came into the room. Walking slow but purposeful, he went to her and folded her into his arms. He held her tight and let her beat her forehead against his chest until she quieted. I led her upstairs to bed and tucked her in, smoothed her hair, and at last she slept.

When I came back down, the house was empty, neat and clean. The melted ice cream was mopped up. The women left the pans and platters with their names on the bottoms in adhesive tape. Their dishes sat on the icebox on the back porch until one morning they were gone. We never learned who fetched them.

.   .   .

Summer passed in heat and haze. Long, blank days so hot the sky was white. Nights, we slept with wet flour sacks across us. By midnight they were like hot skin. We went our ways apart, like creatures hiding out to nurse their wounds.

Etta said no more of blame. She hardly spoke at all.

Dad worked.

I left off writing in the dust, too tired. I couldn't get my mind to feature Audie's face or kisses or the threshing floor. He was just there, another mouth that chewed and swallowed what I cooked. I had taken over in the kitchen. Etta was to do the cleaning and the washing, but she didn't. Cobwebs grew and dust piled up and our clothes smelled sour, but no one cared. The clock moved slow as we moved.

Numbers, facts of math and science, rules of this and laws of that— I had no head for these. I never learned at school what I most craved to know, which was how people fit together in this life, how from the start we'd been put here and had lasted all this time and still knew next to nothing. I always got that best from watching how things worked or from books that told a story.

Etta didn't like facts any better. Worse, you'd have to say, given the evidence. But she was starved, she said, for company, and so when September came around, she talked me into going to school for one last term. Truth told, I ached to get off the place, to see faces other than our drawn ones.

School always commenced first Monday in September, and so on that morning just past dawn we dressed in our best clothes. I put on a yoked school dress of brown-and-yellow plaid with a sash that felt too young. Into my brown brogans Audie had tacked a piece of cedar as a shim to lift my foot. Etta wore a white blouse and that kicked-out-hem green skirt, let down and still too short, but all she had.

We had not yet cut up Mam's clothes, but in a box under Dad's bed we found her Sunday shoes, some bright green ankle-strap high heels that made Etta's legs look womanly and pretty. My breath caught when I saw her, this same girl who tossed in bed beside me in a hopsack gown. We went downstairs to the kitchen where Dad and Audie sat at the table, crumbling corn bread into milk.

Dad pushed back in his chair. "What's this?"

Etta flashed her skirt to show the shoes. "School starts today. Don't we look nice?"

Blankness came across Dad's face, as if he'd been going to tell us something but forgot.

Audie, sleepy-eyed and moving slow, spooned up some milky corn bread. "Don't go off and get too smart for us."

"Too late for that," said Etta, but she winked.

Audie looked gap-jawed and dumbstruck, and it hit me, *He likes sass.* Just that fast, my wanting him was kindled, stronger than before.

We set off across the section toward the schoolhouse. To save them from the dust, I carried our shoes in a gunnysack. Etta carried the lunch pails she had packed, cold biscuits and a jar of watermelon pickle brought up from the cellar.

We walked along the sand bed road, picking our way through sticker patches. Etta swung the pails, nodding, working up, it seemed to me, to one of her glads. "I wonder who'll be there."

Here I have to say that I was walking along dark-hearted, my nose out of joint about Audie's notice of her, for just as quickly as my feelings kindled, my old envy rared. I said, "Nobody, probably."

She quickened her pace and stalked ahead. "All I can say is that the farther away we get from that miserable place, the better I feel." She meant poking-along-on-purpose and dark-hearted me, and I could see I'd best not cross her.

The schoolhouse stood nearly hidden behind a stand of cemetery cedars, the kind of building people called a knowledge-box, a square, two-storied redbrick structure, flat-roofed and window-eyed. Etta waited at the front steps for me to catch up. We bent to brush off our feet and put on our shoes. Audie had sanded the shim so well, it fit so smooth that I could hardly feel it. This gave me a thrill and an idea. When school was done, I would hurry home and tell him how good it felt, thank him again. Then I'd think up something so prickly and smart to say his eyes would widen, and he'd give me that same gap-jawed look he'd given Etta.

"We must be the first," she said, her voice shrill, elated. "That means good desks."

I didn't care about good desks, but something about the solid brick, the orderly windows, quickened me. I remembered books, which I had missed, and of a sudden I was eager too.

We hurried up the steps, pulled open the green doors, and stepped inside, stood breathing in the smells of chalk dust, crayon wax, brown paper. Etta's eyes were brighter than if she'd had a fever. She whispered, "Doesn't it smell like town?"

We started up the inner staircase to the upper floor. When we reached the top, she sang out, "Katy-bar-the-door, the Spoon girls have arrived!"

In the classroom, desks sat empty, furzed with dust. From the stopped clock hung cobwebs thick as moss. In a corner some rac-coons had made a banquet. Gnawed bones and corncobs, leavings, lay about.

Etta went to the window, and I followed. Out in the play yard a board swing dangled from a cottonwood, the bark stripped bare by grasshoppers and deer. The backhouse door banged in the wind.

Her body seemed to take up all the window space. I felt myself a willow withe beside her, small and mean. I'd said "Nobody" to be cruel. I hadn't really meant it.

The sill was littered with moth husks, stirring at our breath.

Her eyes brimmed with a wet green light. "He knew the school closed down. He knew it, and he didn't tell us."

I blew on the sill. Husks whirried upward like a gust of chaff.

She gave a dark harrumph that sounded so like Mam's I nearly broke my neck to look at her. Dry-eyed now, she stared fiercely out the window across the fields toward War Drum. In the haze the town seemed shimmering and far away. "Everybody's gone. Just gone."

As though in contradiction, a host of blackbirds swarmed into the cottonwood. September marked the time of their migration, when braided rivers of them blacked the skies. They roosted thick along the barren branches, squawking, settling, but then, as if they heard her, they seemed to heave a shudder, then flew off into the bare blue sky.

She seized my arm and pinched it hard. "I have to leave. I'm going to run away."

I pretended not to hear her, yanked away, and turned to go.

She called after me, "Mackie, if you have the sense God gave a goose, you'll follow."

My threat of old sprang up. "I'm telling." I didn't know if I meant for pinching, blasphemy, or that she meant to run away. All three, I decided.

"Go ahead," she shouted. "You think you're fooling anybody? You think nobody doesn't see you think you're perfect? Goodie Two-shoes? Mrs. Nicey-nice?"

I didn't answer, didn't turn, kept walking down the stairs and out the door, onto the road. I was going home, and I knew what I wanted. I wanted what I left that morning in the kitchen, crumbling corn bread into milk. I'd hurry home to thank him for the shim, and then I'd sass him, bad. I had the whole way back to think up some, and if the road was dusty, it was just right for writing our names. Etta Spoon could hit the road for Jupiter for all I cared, and the world would turn just fine without her. Mrs. Nicey-nice knew what she wanted, and she wasn't stopping until she got him.

⤙

I didn't tell. What would have been the point? Dad was in no mood to care how anybody sinned. He wandered, plucked at grass blades and kicked at tires, sat for hours in the truck, the Philco set on the hood and hooked up to the battery, listening to tinny music or the news of coming war in Europe. And Etta didn't leave. No point there, either. There wasn't anywhere to go. Except for farming-out or housework, there was nothing for a girl her age to do.

She sank deeper into gloom. No one could coax her out. "Darken the corner where you are," Audie teased, putting some made-up words to the hymn to try to josh her out of brooding, but it didn't work. When she wasn't glaring at him, she ignored him. She spent most days in bed up in our room, a piece of soft barn wood on her lap. In loopy script with a lead pencil sharpened with a paring knife she etched *California, California, California.* The grooves went deeper, deeper.

So did my wanting Audie. I don't remember what I said to him that schoolless day when we got home. Something cockeyed that fell wrong. I wanted him too much, and this likely showed. Still, as the days of fall went by, and a chance arrived to tease him, I would try. If he said, "Mackie, will you pass the salt," I'd say, "Well, that's my name, don't wear it out."

"How long before supper?" he might ask.

"How Long is a Chinaman's name," I'd say. "Ha-ha."

Like that. So pitiful I'd get mad at my open mouth and vow to quit. It wouldn't have mattered anyway, as he stayed just the same, a brother-boy.

We went on as before. I took up my dust-writing again, marveled at the way our middle names started with the letter J. When we married and set up a place together, this could figure in our cattle brand.

That lonely fall even the dust storms stayed away, stayed south and west of us, and though the days were clear, with so much sun it should have warmed us, the cold seemed all the brittler for its brightness.

Winter set in early. Blades of ice sheared out of the west with naught between the mountains of New Mexico and us to catch it. We put on our nightgowns underneath the quilts, did likewise with our clothes each morning. We left off wearing skirts and went to poor-box flannel shirts and dungarees. From surplus cotton the Ladies Aid Society handed out, we sewed whatever else we needed, underdrawers and shifts, men's shirts, dish towels, and pillow slips. Almost every stitch we owned was limp and ghostly white. Our coats were made of cut-up quilts and blankets, lined with surplus batting. "California's always warm," Etta would say from time to time, but the rest of us were too cold to argue or to care.

To stop our walls, so full of cracks the wind sliced through, we brought newspapers from town and nailed the layers thick. Boarded up the windows with sheet iron. The house stayed dark and stale. Nothing bright or beautiful to look at except for once when I put a vase of cattail stalks on the kitchen table. They didn't last. In the dry stove heat the stalks sent seed puffs flying, and I had to toss them out. One night the lamp went out still full of oil and in the morning we woke listless, couldn't get the stove to catch. After that, we took turns opening the door to let the air in, took down one section of newspaper from the wall. Wind whistled through the cracks like someone's voice.

We wintered on what food was in the cellar, yard, or timber, what could be got for trade. Salt pork figured large. We couldn't kill a chicken, out of fear of wanting eggs. Up from the cellar came the last jars of put-up vegetables, and we ate pickle till our bellies burned from brine. Audie trapped for table meat. Rabbit, squirrel. Once he pistoled down a possum, but I couldn't cook it for the smell and so he threw it to the barn cats, who also turned away. All around us there were jackrabbit drives, when boys and men thrashed through the brush to round the creatures up and club them dead and send them east for food lines in the cities. The jackrabbits were called Hoover's hogs, but they smelled so bad to cook you didn't want to eat them.

We were hungry, all of us, began to gaunten down. At mealtimes I did as Mam had, loaded Dad's plate first, then Audie's except I matched theirs even, skimped on Etta's, shorted mine. At the table we were silent unless Audie saw a sight outside and told it. A little metal trailer house abandoned on the road—if no one claimed it he wanted to haul it in and fix it up to live in—a screech owl frozen to a tree limb, that cougar. He was not the kind of talker who needed nods or answers, but if he got one or the other, it was Dad or I who gave it. Etta wolfed her supper, looked for more. Broody, mad, she glared at Audie's plate. Every now and then Dad made to give a blessing for the food, but too often his words got choked inside his throat, and we gave up and ate.

Through all of this, in the interest of winning Audie, I tried to put a pleasant face on things, chippering around and trying to lift the sorrow. "Isn't the sunset pretty," I might say. Or, "Did you ever notice how warm it is here by the stove?" Kept it up and kept it up until it wore me out, and Etta said, "Judas Jones, Mackie, will you just give up!"

And so we went on in our ways, each to his own, until the days at last began to lengthen. It wasn't time or healing grief or anything I did or failed to do, but Etta's growing misery that led me closer to my goal. It helped that I'd made up my mind to make a move, stop dallying and get things going.

⟶

It happened on the night I stewed a cottontail Audie had trapped. I'd filled the plates and we sat down as usual, Dad at table's head, Audie at the foot, girls flanking. No prayer, and so Dad said, "Let's eat."

But he had no heart for the meal, and he laid down his fork. "Girls, I wonder could I trouble you to fix me up an egg instead? That one egg over on the safe. A nice fried egg. Aud and I broke up wood all day. You'd think I'd build an appetite, but I'm flat wearied out. No offense meant to the rabbit." He threw a look toward Audie, the ghost of his old teasing, then threw one to me. "Or the cook."

I pushed out my chair to get up to fix the egg, but Etta picked up her water cup and threw it. *Clang* it went against the sheet-ironed window. Audie shrank his neck into his shoulders like a terrapin, but he went back to eating. Dad sat, palms flat on the table.

I stood. "It isn't any trouble. I'll just fix it."

Color rose to Etta's ears. "You would!"

Dad said, "I only thought that if you didn't need it for something else . . ."

A rage was on her. "Mackie cooked this rabbit. You can eat this rabbit. This goddamned awful rabbit!"

Audie took his dreadnought from the hook and went outside. He had caught the rabbit, dressed it out, had fairly laid it at our feet.

I wanted to go after him, tell him Etta hadn't meant to hurt, but she jumped up, knocking over her chair. She stooped to pick it up, then seemed to change her mind and banged the chair against the floor. A leg slat cracked. She stamped across the kitchen to the safe.

"An egg? You want it? Here!" She snatched it up and smashed it to the floor.

Dad got up so fast I hardly saw him move until he was across the kitchen, his hand raised against her.

"Hit me," Etta screamed, "that's what you always do!"

His hand went down. "Sister, what's got into you? Where have you learned that kind of talk?"

"Don't call me sister! That's your trouble. You don't know who anybody is to you!" She went on, and it was as though she had opened her mouth and senseless things were flying out. I don't remember half of what she said, but in the middle of it all she stopped and looked at me as I stood, openmouthed as well, my hand on a chair back, and it seemed a storm had broken loose.

Her face went purple. Her birthmark took on color. "I'm telling her! She ought to know!" She grabbed me by the shoulders, shook me.

I wrenched away. "It was an accident. Everybody knows it. Et, you're wrong."

Dad came between us. "Mary Etta, let your sister go."

Etta glared, biting back the words that blamed him for our mother, words she must have been holding in, but in the middle of her fury something other came across her face, which seemed to crumple. "Why do I have to be the only one who knows? I don't even *want* to!" She sank into a chair, put head in hands to cry.

At the time, I couldn't fathom the mysterious grievance she'd built up against him, the dark hints she dropped about what she thought she knew and what I didn't know. I knew only that her anger with him had to be more than that long-ago punishment, more than losing a horse, and that whatever it was, she felt it strong enough to make a show. Back then you heard stories of farm women driven mad with want and isolation to the point they walked off in the dust and weren't heard from again, and so I decided it was madness that afflicted her, and that her mind had come unwound. I found the dishrag, bent to daubing at the egg mess.

Etta cried on. Dad's hands hung at his sides. A sad and ugly scene, our family.

I said again, "It was an accident."

He turned to face me, his gaze deep and searching. "What was?"

"Out in the hayfield," I began. I couldn't finish. I hoped my silence told him I meant everything that happened after that as well.

He went to Etta and stood over her. In his voice pain echoed. "Honey, can we stop this? Can we allow that done is done, and there's no help for it?"

I wanted her to say, "I'm sorry." Wanted him to say, "I'm sorry, too." For them to put hard feelings in the past, and we could go back to being ourselves, a father and two daughters coming out of grief. But it came to me I'd never heard those words come out of Etta's mouth. I'd never heard Dad say them either. Although my heart caught, waiting, you can't live with people all your life and fail to know what they can't do.

Etta stood her ground.

Dad's shoulders slumped. "All right, but if I hear that kind of talk again, I'll have to punish you. You're not too old for me to give you a good working over. Is that clear?"

From her place at the table, Etta said bitterly, "Clear as the bells in hell!"

Dad's look and his red face told me to go outside.

I put on my sweater and went outside across the frozen ground to the near barn. The air was crisp and clear. In the cow stall by lantern-light Audie ran a currycomb down Big Babe's flank. The old cow was asleep on her feet, her head held low, her snore a soft whuffle.

"She's an elderly old girl, but she still likes a little touch-up from old Audie-boy. She doesn't like all this consternation, and it riles her up."

Contrariness was on me; I'd forgotten all about making my move. "That cow is fast asleep."

He offered me his dreadnought. "You cold?"

I couldn't think whether I was or wasn't.

He took off the garment, draped it on my shoulders. Thing weighed one warm ton.

He asked, "They still going at it?"

"Worse."

He ran the currycomb down the cow's flank. "It's that they're like."

This irked. "They're not." I went on to tell him what any simpleton could see, that where Etta was mad-mouthed and fractious, Dad was even, steady to her changing moods, kind to her mean temper.

He pulled a hay straw from the currycomb. "Strong-minded,

both of them." He looked at me. "And you're a stubborn thing yourself, for all you try to hide it. Didn't fall that far from the family tree,
it looks to me like."

This made me angry, but there wasn't anyone to spend it on. I
gave a piffing sound that likely proved the truth. "Is that all you can
think up to say?"

I shucked off the dreadnought, climbed the stick ladder to the
haymow, stomped across the planks, and sat down loud.

Cobwebs hung in wisps above me, and I batted at them, daring
any spider to present himself for smashing. So swift and terrible
would be my hand the wretched thing would never know what hit
him but would curl his legs into his body and be dead.

When my eyes adjusted to the darkness of the mow, I glimpsed a
single thread drawn tight between rafter and joist. I watch the thread
for movement but no spider braved the filament, and this was somehow a proof of my good temper. Stubborn was the last thing in the
world I was. I was easy-natured, peaceable. I turned the other cheek.
All I wanted was for everyone to get along. In all the world there was
no match for my good temper. I felt misunderstood and sorry for
myself, which made me even madder, which felt better than I
thought it would and got me even madder. I saw the draw of being
angry, then, how big and righteous it could make you feel.

Later, when I worked the evening over in my mind and wondered
at the reason Audie followed me into the haymow when I was being
mean, it came to me he couldn't have done otherwise. A fractious,
spiteful person fit a groove already carved in him.

His dark head appeared in the ladder hatch. "So you'll know,
that's not all I can think up to say."

I picked at the pills on my anklets.

"Haven't thought of anything, of course. I just mean that's not
all." He knocked a knuckle against his head. "And there's plenty
more where that came from."

I held my peace, pill-picking. He was trying to silly me back to niceness and I did not appreciate it one iota. And then suddenly I did. Oh, I told him, come on up.

He had to hump along hunched over so as not to pick up splinters from the beams as he duckwalked to sit beside me. So close, he smelled of machine oil, supper, lye soap, cow. He rested his hands on his pant legs, his big, long-fingered hands, red-brown but ashy and plum-colored at the knuckles, his flat, half-moony nails.

I said, "So *you'll* know, I'm not stubborn."

"Are," he said.

"Am not."

We went on like this until he fixed me in a study. "I'll prove it." He held out his hand, palm up, and gave the count for Scissors, Paper, Rock. Across his palm he made the sign of scissors. I'd made scissors, too.

I gave the next count and we played again, smacking sign into our palms, again, again, each time showing up the same, paper to paper, rock to rock. Just as I made up my mind to do the opposite of what it came to me to do and this way end the sameness, he did likewise. I tried to trick myself, pretending not to know what sign I would make until I made it, but each time it was uncanny. At some point in the game I had remembered what I meant to do, and in my mind I said, *I'm going to kiss you.*

"That doesn't prove a thing," I said.

He chucked my chin. "You're a little Maude the Mule, like in the funny papers. I'm going to call you that. We'll be Maude and Aud, then. Cousins, would you say?"

He was teasing and I liked it. Liked it fine. I began to stare him down, to see which one of us flinched first, a schoolyard game I never won.

His face hove near until our foreheads touched, like billies in a standoff, his two eyes verged to one. His breath was crisp, fragrant as pepper. I blinked first.

And then, before I knew I'd do it, I had done it, kissed him.

Didn't know how to go about it right, but simply planted one, and it felt good. His lips were soft and smooth but for a little tag of chap.

He drew back, his wide, dark face a puzzle I couldn't begin to solve.

"Well, then," I said, which is what brilliance sprang to mind, and by and by this came to seem enough.

I stood up and made a show of brushing hay straws from my sweater. I left him—blank and staring—and climbed down from the mow, walked through the barn unseeing. If there had been a woolly mammoth in the manger I would not have seen it.

The kitchen was dark. The dishes had been washed and dried and put away. The big skillet was set ready on the stove for breakfast, the dishrag pinched into the oven door to dry. A first. If Etta had done it, there was something wrong.

Snoring came from Dad's room, a rattle that sounded as if his throat was pulling into itself. Upstairs in our bed, Etta lay still. When I crawled in beside her, she didn't move. Not even when I rubbed my feet together in the way she said would drive her to the bottle.

I nudged her side and whispered, "Et, guess what?" Yes, she'd had it out with Dad and probably was smarting over it, but that kiss burned in me to tell.

"Don't call me Et. Don't call me anything. Don't look at me."

I raised up on one arm and looked at her dark hair tumbled on the pillow, and suddenly I was weary of her moods, her food-begrudging and her high-hand notions, her accusations, of how nothing could be good and plain and simple. Had to be a spectacle. A show. I was as happy as I'd ever been, and her unhappiness would blight it. It was high time she was straightened out. I hoped Dad gave her a working over, whaled the road tar out of her.

Her back was to me, and as though to cast a spell, I willed her to roll over. I was going to tell her it was time she stopped acting like a stinkpot. For once, my stubbornness would be a match for hers.

"Dullix ix ux," I murmured, not knowing what it meant but hoping to get a rise.

"Don't," she said, her voice clotting with tears, "Mackie, don't."

She was crying, but it wasn't tears that turned my heart, it was the way she smelled of our shared bed, the must from the piece quilts we had slept under all our lives. "Etta, what happened? Did he hurt you?"

"He talked. He only talked." She reached a hand behind her, found mine and clasped her warm, moist fingers around it. "Remember when I was up on the washhouse roof on the day of the black duster? How you came to save me?"

In a small voice I said, "Yes." Though I wondered what he talked to her about, I couldn't ask. My mind was back in Salt Camp, remembering her weight, the fall we took together, how good it felt to know she needed me. A sister was a sister.

She was quiet for a time. "I wish we could go back."

"To Salt Camp?"

She drew a quavering breath. "Just back."

The sky outside was black; the moon was new. Frost flowers pinged the window glass. Her grip was tight.

"Did you ever know you shouldn't do a thing but you can't stop? That something in you won't let you *not* do it?"

Thinking of that kiss, I said, "Oh yes."

"Mackie, whatever happens, no matter what anybody tries to tell you, even me, *especially* me, you've been a good, good sister."

Although I couldn't feature what had spurred her flood of feeling, I felt bad for grudging her. Lying there, my hand in hers, heat from her body seeping toward me through the quilts, I made vows to be better. I would try to understand the workings of her mind, to have more sympathy. Whatever it was in her that caused her scenes, I'd try to understand. I'd be kinder in my heart.

"You didn't ask for this," she said. "You didn't do a thing to cause it. It's not your fault." Her tone was tender. She drew in a breath, and when she spoke again her voice was firm. "It isn't."

I wasn't sure what she was talking about, but I wanted to ease her mind. "Etta, it isn't anybody's. And don't feel bad for me. I'm happier than you think I am."

And I was. Happy, that is. I planned to wake up loving everyone. Dad and crazy, forlorn Etta and the world at large, the God who had brought Audie Kipp to me.

———

The month of May came around again, and things were looking better. Except for Etta, who rolled along at quarter speed, we began to lift a little, our sadness letting up. The weather seemed to break. The number of dust storms dwindled. We'd suffered only two sand blows since March, one red, the other brown, and both of them halfhearted. We thought the great black ones might be behind us. "Knock wood," said Audie, rapping his head. The love-struck girl who laughed as if this was the greatest wit was me. We hadn't spoken much since the night up in the mow, but it seemed to me our kiss had settled some unspoken something.

The café out on the highway opened up again, and it felt almost like before. The place smelled of boiled coffee and machine oil, the kind of weeklong working sweat you never in these cleaner days will smell. Men rolled cigarettes and smoked until the air was gray, talking of the local goings-on. Some were good—the WPA was planting shelter belts of bois d'arc trees and Russian olive. Some were bad—somebody robbed the hardware store and pistol-whipped the clerk, made off with a week's receipts. Some were up for grabs—an unwed mother left a newborn near a borrow pit, but people from the church had found the baby, and a childless couple took him for their own.

The New Deal had at last kicked in. Some spoke of Roosevelt as though he were a kindly uncle. Others made him out to be the devil camped down at the crossroads. Sometimes when the café's radio played one of his speeches, fights broke out, and so they kept the dial tuned to the stock report, the weather, which was holding, for a wonder, fine.

The days were warm and right. It rained. It rained again. Not torrents swallowed up by dusters, but gentle, soaking rain. Dad and Audie worked from dawn to nightfall. Every day they checked the wheat. It was knee high and green, with heads set on and safely past the milk stage. If you were a hopeful person, you could almost think we'd have the first good crop in years. Audie, feeling flush and manly, so he said, went into town and bought two 3X silverbelly Stetsons, one for himself and one for Dad. Dad would wear his till he died.

They tramped fields, poked at the earth. Sometimes I'd see them in the distance, two land men gazing into farther distance, as though if they held the contours long enough in sight, they could commit them to heart. Audie took on Dad's stance, hands behind his back, chin up. They looked like son and father, and the notion moved me. I began to feature weddings, me the given-away bride.

Nights around the table, they talked planting, what needed to be done. A neighbor had a rusted-out hammermill to sell and they could fit it with a new auger; wouldn't that shell corn like sixty? A good crop might see them getting up enough to buy a parcel if they went in together. Bonus Pay had finally come in for the soldiers of the Great War, and that little extra something just might do the trick. They figured and drew maps. In lampblack ink on the whited knees of his denims Audie drew a field map, a melon patch with dollar signs abloom across his knees. When they speculated, they didn't speak of *I* or *you* or *we,* but said *a man.* If a man had sixty acres, he could put in soya beans and make a profit. If a man had a four-bottom plow, he could work up a section in a morning. If he had a blooded

Brahma bull to stand at stud, a man could make a goodly piece of change. It was the way of talking then, and everybody did it, as if to put a buffer zone between themselves and disappointment. People still said it was a hard life if you didn't weaken, but there grew up an unsaid sense of what this meant. It seemed we'd weakened, bent to weather, had made do—had *had* to—but then we came back stronger, and life seemed for all the trouble we'd been through a little bit less hard. My gown would be a pretty eggshell white.

Lost inside their plans, the men paid little mind to what went on with me and Etta in the house. This was a disappointment, but I aimed to ride it out, bent as I was on showing what a catch I was. I aired the quilts and blankets, beat the front room rug, scoured the floorboards with lye water made from wood ash. I sewed the two of them new canvas shirts. In the root cellar—swept by me and spanking-clean—I came across some cans of paint. Hair tied back in a bandanna, I set to work. Bit by bit our winter-sooted rooms looked fresh, and it began to seem the clapped-out tenant house had come again, the way a burned pie covered with a dish towel will.

Etta's moodiness was the one blight, but even that was tolerable; she had begun to take herself away all day. Late afternoons she would amble down the lane, as though returning from another world. She had a walk like no one else, nodding side to side in a thoughtful-looking rhythm. She couldn't help it, she would say if someone called her gait to her attention. She just had to walk that way. Besides, she said, it was fun. Things looked different every time she turned her head. Mam had blamed her strange walk on tantrums—as a little child Etta had thrown fits, holding her breath until she turned blue and couldn't breathe. Mam thought the spectacle should be ignored, but Dad always ran to stop it, giving Etta attention enough for her to keep it up. I had wondered before if her tantrums had done damage to her head.

About her wanderings, she wouldn't tell me where she'd been.

"Around" would be the best I'd get. Where had the *Life* magazine, the vial of Ben Hur perfume, the bottle of Delaware Punch, the pink chiffon scarf she tied around her neck come from? "The getting place."

I checked, but no money was missing from the fruitcake tin where we kept the household change. Could be she was lifting from the ten-cent store in War Drum, but if I pressed her, saying maybe I'd like to come along on one of her trips, she laughed deep in her throat, as though she knew a secret. Which she did, I guess, but at the time I couldn't figure.

She began to look tired and blue-veined around the eyes. At night she smelled of salt and sweat, a worried, restless smell, like copper pennies held for too long in your hand. Once, when she crawled into bed after a day-long ramble, I caught a waft of another scent, strange and deep and flowery and animal, like creek mud and blown pear blossom, a smell I knew but couldn't place, a haunting smell that called me back to babyhood. Sometimes during the day as I was going about my work I'd get a phantom whiff and think I knew, but like a forgotten word on the tip of your tongue, the recollection wouldn't come.

Ignoring Etta as best I could, every evening when the men came in for supper I made them look at the improvements. Audie would nod, and say, "Looks nice," and Dad would say, "You girls have worked." Not-tattling so triumphantly that all could hear, I'd smile, and say, "Oh, we have. We *have*."

If the School of Silver Linings handed out degrees, I would have been a graduate for all the hope I held. But if I'd bothered to read down to that diploma's bottom, I would have seen the fine print, which spelled out the warning that just as trouble can beget a boon, the opposite will hold. The trick was knowing which was which and who the light shone on.

What happened next was up for grabs. Out of it, two people

died—one blameless and one guilty. Another found someone she thought would save her and another what he wanted. As for me, I saw the shadow that had rimmed my bright cloud all along.

———

On a rock-hard wedge of land across the Tebo lived a family named Birdsall, clannish folk from Broken Bow down in the Kiamichis. A first run of five rawboned boys, a latter run of five towheaded middling girls. The Birdsall brothers took odd jobs, but mostly they jalopied up and down the roads in a cut-down Essex green as bottle glass, and hooted through War Drum to scatter Indians and bulldog the colored family who did for the Holloways. They hung out at the Fish and Game, a juke joint down a dogleg road where there were punchboard games and knife fights. Becker Birdsall was the leader. He was beefy and brass-eyed, his eyebrows almost white. Word was he robbed a bank in Wellington. Did or didn't, Becker was the kind who wouldn't lay to rest a rumor. He put it out that he was Choc Floyd's running mate. Dad had no use for Birdsalls. He warned us to steer clear.

The little Birdsall girls kept house, such as it was, and peddled things around. Old jars and dishes, broken toys. They pulled around their kiddie wagon loaded full of scavenge. One June morning as I was hanging wash I met the one named Teeny. She might have been thirteen but she looked more like a knock-kneed nine-year-old. She wore a filthy flour sack shift torn out at the neck. Across the field she came to sell a clutch of pigeon eggs.

She was a smart thing, a natural seller, chattering about the eggs, their roundness and their speckledness, two cents apiece, a giveaway. I bought one, good for little but a batter-dab, and gave her a nickel. I told her, "Keep the change." This made me feel for the first time in a long time generous, and the feeling stayed with me all day. I would be going along and wondering why I felt so fine, and I would remember Teeny's rat's-nest braids, that flour sack dress, her speedy sales pitch, and the canny light in her blue eyes as she plunked the nickel in a Red Man pouch and went off looking for another sale.

The Birdsall father was in jail for making moonshine. He had the jake leg and could hardly walk, so everybody thought he sacrificed himself and served the time to spare his boys. They and their mother kept the business running. Beside the Santa Fe trestle over the Tebo, the tracks unused for years because of heat warp, they had set up a blind pig to sell homebrew. It was in this creekside shack a few days after Teeny had been out to sell her pigeon eggs that one of the brothers found her, her dress pulled up and tied like a potato sack around her head, her narrow body violated, warmth seeping from her even as the brother touched her. Her throat had been sliced open with a length of baling wire. In her hand she clutched a hank of hair.

Late that night we were awakened by voices in the dooryard, torchlight through the windows, licking up the walls. Outside, the Birdsall brothers and some others gathered, lofting oil-soaked rags tied onto two-by-fours. The air smelled of creosote and pine pitch. Dad went to the door. I and Etta stood behind to watch.

The brothers spoke in low tones, hats drawn down, torchlight making shadows of their eyes. Becker gave an account of how they'd found their sister.

Somebody spat.

Dad asked some questions, heard the answers.

The second brother—Bobby Jack—said, "Heard you had somebody on your place. Big fellow."

Another brother said, "Big Indian."

"That would be Aud," Dad said. "My hand."

"Where is he at?"

Dad looked off toward Audie's scavenged trailer house. Audie had been working on it, had it parked under a brush arbor on the rise just past the far barn. "What business do you have with him?"

Before any of the men could answer, Audie appeared, coming toward us. He stood off a ways, apart.

Bobby Jack walked over to thrust a torchlight closer to his face. The others ringed him, elbows out, the way fighting roosters jut their wings. A shotgun safety clicked.

In the orange light of the doorway while the night air swirled around my ankles, puffing at my gown hem, in the depth of that dark summer night, I thought of Teeny and her eggs, that nickel, thought that anything could happen here. There was no law at hand, the marshal miles away.

Audie said, "What's this about?" But he said it mildly, looking down. Any Indian—*anybody*—would beware of any Birdsall.

Becker nudged him with his rifle barrel. Again somebody spat.

Dad moved forward, cleared his throat, but before he could speak, Etta threw wide the door, rushed past me, out into the dooryard to stand by Audie. Later, Dad would praise her for quick thinking.

In a swooping, breathy voice, she said to Audie, "Oh, there you are!"

She slipped her arm through his. "Out in that barn again? Sugar, that old cow will be all right. You leave her be." She sounded cozy and come-hither. "I've been keeping your side of the bed warm." She threw a smile toward the men and shook her head in a show of exasperation. "My husband."

If the younger brothers glared, the eldest glowered. A lot of people didn't hold with mixing.

Audie had stiffened, but if he was ashamed at a woman speaking out for him, it was also clear her claim had thrilled him. His face went soft, and so in all the stiffness and the fear, he managed to look soft and curious, alert. I looked from him to Etta, him to Etta, sick a little, but not knowing why.

The torch went down. "Not him," said Becker, casting an appraising look toward Etta in her nightgown. "Hair was different."

Dad said, "You'll want some help. I won't do any shooting, but I'll help you bring him in."

"Geronimo comes too?"

"Man's name is Audie Kipp. It's up to him."

Audie nodded toward the men, and they left on foot, moving toward the creek, the torchlights growing smaller until they looked like fireflies in the distance. The group split into parties at the bank, one moving east, the other west along the Tebo. Then the westward bunch turned back, and all together they went eastward at a faster clip. We watched until the lights became too faint to see, then we watched some more.

Etta took two knives from the kitchen drawer, the butcher knife, the boner, put them on the table. We sat down to wait. "Blow out the lamp," she said. I did. Moonlight spread across the oilcloth and with it spread dark thoughts. If I pieced together her disappearances, the items that could have been gifts from Audie, her refusal to tell me where she'd been, the way he'd looked at her, the puzzle turned out easy.

Miserably, I said, "I thought you didn't like him."

She ran a thumb down the knife handle, then lay down the knife. "Audie wouldn't hurt a fly."

I wanted to know the truth, even if it hurt. "Etta, where have you been going?"

She shrugged. "To town to look at job ads. To look around. That's all."

Just then we heard a thump and clatter on the roof. We jumped. My heart beat fast against my breastbone.

Etta said, "It's just a trade rat." The place ran thick with them, their bargains mystifying. They traded one thing for another. Take a button, leave a blue jay feather, trade an eyebolt for a castor bean.

I said, "It sounded bigger."

We heard scrabbling under the eaves.

I waited for my heart to quiet down, then asked again. "Where do you go?"

She sat still, again fingering the knife handle, but she would not look up at me. "I told you. Don't you believe me?"

I got up to set coffee on to boil. I didn't want to be near Etta, so I went upstairs to look out the attic window, saw only blackness, the night sky, the evening star. But then I didn't want to be alone, and so I went back down.

Etta still sat at the table, the knives laid out in front of her.

"Etta," I began, but before I could repeat my question, two things happened, the kettle whistled, and a shot cracked in the distance. I took the kettle off the flame but before I could set it on the trivet, another shot rang out. Three more.

They shot him where they found him, sleeping in the shallow hole he'd scooped out in the creek bank and lined with newspaper. Near his campsite was a jackdaw pile of junk—blown tires, machine parts, cans. They found Aud's bullhide boots, Dad's auger. Nobody ever learned his name. Nobody called the law. He was a drifter, an old madman with child's blood on his trousers, wire marks not yet faded from his palms. From the dates on his newspaper nest, he'd been living not a mile away at least a year.

When the men came back, Dad's hands were shaking. His skin looked gray, his whiskers glinted in the lamplight. He went to the back room and shut the door.

"Who fired the shots?" Etta asked.

Audie looked at his hands. "The brothers did. One each. But the one called Becker took first aim."

She nodded, took a sip of coffee. "Did Dad shoot?"

He shook his head. "We neither of us did."

I watched the two of them, Etta with her hands clasped around her cup, Audie rubbing at a burn scar on the back of his hand. I watched them for a shared look, for a secret sign, but I saw nothing. Nothing.

.   .   .

The next morning Becker Birdsall came by in the green Essex. He brought two pullets and a quart jar of white mule. Help for help, he said. Said Birdsalls would be leaving before the month was out. Had family out in Colorado. He spat, then drove away.

Under a cottonwood the men set up camp to drink the liquor. Sprawled beneath the tree, they slept all day, woke up at suppertime. I had stewed the pullets, made some dumplings to keep my mind off the idea of Audie and Etta. In the daylight the possibility didn't seem so near at hand, and so I wrote off my suspicions to the horror of the night before, the closeness of true evil.

At suppertime we gathered at the table. Something off and wobbly about the day seemed to stop all four of us at once. It seemed that of one mind we took in all the changes in us, like travelers might look backward on a peril.

Once, Dad had been a broadish, bull-necked man, but he'd grown lean. He looked a decade older. Audie's thrawn neck had straightened. His hair had grown, the braid-stub well below his collar. Etta's eyes had hollowed out. Her cheekbones angled. I had to look hard to see her birthmark. When I reached out to take my water cup, my wrist looked bird-boned, breakable. It seemed a miracle that although we'd changed, we were still here.

We hadn't prayed over a meal for a long time but now Dad said, "I'd like us to return our thanks."

Audie bowed his head; I did likewise. Something caught in my chest, and I felt glad. My fears of the night before seemed far away and foolish, and I was as hungry for the words of his familiar blessing as I had been for food. Things would be all right.

Dad's voice cracked at first, and when he found it again it seemed to gutter like a candle. "For these thy gifts, O Lord, we ask to be made grateful, kept mindful of those less fortunate than we. We ask in Jesus' name this food be blessed to the nourishment of our bodies and us to thy continued service, Amen."

Etta hadn't bowed her head. She sat stiff-backed in her chair, cup raised as though to make a toast. "Lord," she said, "we further ask you to let us face the fact there's hardly anybody on this earth less fortunate, except for Teeny Birdsall. And that's up for debate."

She drank to her own toast, then set down the cup. "Amen."

Dad looked at her for a long time, as though composing in his mind what he should say. She held his look, the study of a dare.

Dad broke first, made busy with a dumpling.

I tried to catch Audie's eye, but it was on my sister. I felt a shimmer of the feeling of the night before, for in his gaze I didn't see what I expected, which was judgment. Instead, there was a searching, kindred look.

We ate then, each as though to swallow more than food.

<hr />

Instead of going off all day, Etta now began to wait until the sun went down to do her roaming. Where she had once been giddy and quicksilver about her trips, she grew reserved and even more secretive. Late in the night I'd feel her sliding in beside me, but if I asked her where she'd been, she'd say, "That's for me to know and you to find out."

Envy had worn a groove so deep into my heart I couldn't help suspecting she and Audie were sneaking off together. I kept watch. Sickened by the stealth I went about with trying to confirm my fears, and sickened by the knowledge even as I spied that things could be suspected into being, I knew his whereabouts at any given time. I tracked her progress up the lane to see which way she turned, traced her route over a field before she disappeared into the timber. Although I never saw a sign that they were meeting anywhere but at the table, my smarter heart told me I ought to school myself away from him. He was a lost cause, and it didn't take a genius to divine it. But in the crooked way of things, this only made me want him more. And so I held out hope.

About this time it struck me hard that if I left, nobody would miss me. In turnabout I took my own self off to wander, feeling peckish, put-upon, unnoticed. At the Tebo's bank I'd stop to peer into the shallow water where along the bed a crayfish bucked and scuttled, stirring up the silt, and feel a nameless want that there might some-day be someone I could say to, "Look at that," and have it heard in just the way I meant it. Someone to see the way a breeze flicked at a single leaf or hear a little spadefoot's calling to his mate, her answer. Meanwhile, I kept my ears pricked up, sharpened my eyes, and went on worrying and spying.

It turned out that I would win Audie's notice when I least wanted it.

It started on an afternoon when Etta and I were in the side yard, hanging out the wash. I had gone off to the backhouse for a minute, and when I got back she was unpinning all the clothes we'd hung. She pointed to the sky northwest of us. Stretching to the horizon was only wheat, a mild wind playing across the heads. The sky was azure. Not a cloud. "I don't see anything," I said.

"Look harder."

"Rain?"

She shook her head. "The other."

How she'd known the dust was coming, I couldn't have said. All that afternoon there was no sign that by evening the greater dark would come from dirt.

Dad and Audie battened down, shut doors and windows, wired the gates. Inside, we stuffed rags along the sills and plugged the chimney flue. Beyond this, there was little we could do.

The winds were straight-line, sixty miles an hour, Dad guessed, rattling the rafters. In the front room, I handed wetted handker-chiefs around. By lamplight, Dad looked at his *Capper's*. Licked his fingers, flipped the pages at a steady rate. Etta stretched out on the floor, eyes closed. Audie sat in the sewing chair, and I sat on the sofa. I tried to mend a shirt but couldn't for being too busy sneaking looks at him to see if he was watching her.

Dust sifted past the seals, so needlelike and steady you could almost daydream rain. Once, I caught Audie's eye, and daring rose. Across my palm I made the finger sign of scissors.

He smiled, and when he signed the same, my heart flipped faster than Dad's pages. Maybe things would be all right. Miracles could happen. You never knew.

Around true dark, the wind let up, and quiet fell so loud you heard it. We got up and went outside. The air was thick with dust.

"Not bad," Dad said. He started toward the wagon road beside the field.

We followed. Although the night was gauzed, we could see enough to tell the wheat was fine. Seed heads bowed a bit, but fine. Another wind would blow it off. "Not bad," repeated Audie.

Etta had turned back to the house, and Dad was moving through the wheat. A wild, doomed feeling of last-chance-for-gas was on me, now or never, and I moved closer to nudge Audie's arm. "All that wind for nothing, hey?"

He nudged back. "Looks like it passed on over."

If ever words were taken other than they were intended, his were. I took them secretly to mean my worries about Etta. Ahead of us on the ground, the rising moonlight cast our shadows long, his tall and broad, mine small, the image of a man and a woman.

Just as scars can show up on a wound you think has healed, dust can blow from ground to uncover furrows cut months before. When the moon broke through the clouds, the light threw shadows angled so that there before us, ridged with dust, lay some initials I'd forgotten to scuff out. MJS + AJK. A heart enclosed them, its arrow pointing toward the future, fletches aimed at me.

I could wait and hope he hadn't seen, or try to decoy him, get him back into the house and come out later to destroy the heart, or I could run over and quick-scuff it. When he pointed to the scratching in the dirt, and said, "What is that there?" that fast I did the latter. Bobbined over and kicked up a storm and scuffed it out, then ran away. Didn't care about the wampish way I wobbled, ran until I reached the tool-house, slammed the door, did not come out till morning.

At sunrise I sat on the cistern cover, watching a trail of ants go crooked-legging down the corrugated tin. Gritty-eyed, I hadn't slept. Up behind the hill where Audie parked his trailer house the sun was rising. I waited for the trailer door to open, for the glint of sunlight off the metal that would mean he was up and out, but even as I was watching, he appeared around the corner of the trailer. He saw me and gathered himself.

He came on toward the cistern. "I was looking for you," he said when he stood before me.

Sass at last arrived when I no longer needed it. "I wasn't lost."

I kicked my heel against the cistern as a punishment for shooting off my mouth, but then I shifted to make room, hooked my smarting laggard foot behind my good one.

He wiped his palms on his pants knees. The denim had gone white and smooth, one wash away from threadbare. His field map had faded. He smelled like the wood ash soap I'd made while lost in daydreams of future wifely offices.

Across the yard, a mockingbird swooped down to peck a passing barn cat on the head. At any other time I would have laughed.

"There's something I ought to have told you," he began, but I didn't give him a chance to finish.

"I already know."

"What do you know?"

There was no one word for what I knew. That only a fool would write initials in the dust when there was writing on the wall. That I could never look at him again. "Everything," I said.

"Then you know I think of you as a sister?"

"Don't think of me at all." This came out more peakèd than I meant it.

The mocker bombed the cat again. Audie pointed. Out of somewhere I coughed up a laugh.

Either because I had the need to make myself more miserable or because I had the need to make myself more miserable, I asked, "How long?" I meant, had he been in love with Etta.

When he nudged me with an elbow to remind me of my old pitiful sass about the Chinaman's name, my eyes stung.

"That first night when I got here, when she wore that hat. The way she looked when she told Mack the butterbeans were gone . . ."

"Good luck to you," I said, boosting myself off the cistern cover, heading for the house. "It's only going to get worse."

I left him there and went inside and took four quarters from the fruitcake tin and started off for War Drum.

I won't go on about how many times I wanted to plunk down on a curb, or duck into an alleyway and sink against a wall, how much my feet weighed when I put one in front of the other. Anyone who's felt the way I felt that morning after knows. An old verse from a schoolyard game played in my mind, singsong and sad. *The needle's eye that does supply the thread that runs so true. I stumped my toe and down I go because I wanted you.*

For lunch at the café I ordered a hamburger. It was so good it made me cry, and after that I couldn't taste it.

I read the job cards posted on the town hall board. One caught my eye.

> *Girl To Do. Christian young woman for cooking, housekeeping, care of invalid. Room and board in separate quarters. Sundays off. Pay negotiable. Must be 21. Inquire C. Lucas, R. R. #2, Belle Plaine, Kans.*

I took out the tack and slipped the card into my pocket.

I took the long way home, by the creek path rather than the road. When I passed the shack where they'd found Teeny, I found it burned to cinders.

Just before the path turned off to the tenant place was a deeper washout pool along the root-grown bank. It was called the Red Hole for the way the soil had washed away to show layers of the earth from pink to rust. I headed there and settled on a stump, meaning to sit until last light and think about the Girl To Do.

I had turned eighteen, but this was three years short of twenty-one. As for Christian, I teetered back and forth. I charged horns down at religion half the time, the other half I hid. I had been born again too many times to count.

I hadn't yet got my imagination on a bus to Kansas when I heard voices coming from a canebrake. From the dusky coolness, a man's urgent whisper and then Etta's high, wide, reckless laugh. A rustle, then a thump.

I crept along the bottom toward the voices. Crouched behind the stand of cane, I peered until I could make out two figures merging into one.

You can't grow up in the country and have failed to see the act. Horses down, I'd witnessed coupling, but now I watched as though caught in a light. There in the sand on a fallen log he sat, his long legs out, with her across him, her green skirt hiked high. My mouth went cottony as a cocoon. I couldn't draw a breath. Not because of what the two looked like entwined, but because even in the failing light it was plain that Etta's lover wasn't Audie.

⁓

Up in our attic room, in bed, I waited for her. She took her time. The moon moved from one corner of the window to the other. When she finally came in, she shucked her clothes, the green skirt shedding twigs and leaves to droop into a dark pool on the floor. I knew now what the creek-mud and pear-blossom smell had been. I propped up on an elbow. "Becker Birdsall?"

In the moonlight, her eyes went wide. "We're going to California. He has to do some business first but then . . ."

"What business? Robbing banks?"

"That's for me to know and you to find out." Her breath gave off another smell, sharp-sick and sweet, wood alcohol and fusel oil of white mule whiskey.

"What about Audie?"

She made an exasperated piffing sound. "He's got no claim. I only let him once. Just to see what it was like. Besides, it was a while ago, when . . ."

I stuck my fingers in my ears to plug them while she went on, but I heard more than I wanted to, vowed I'd never go again into the haymow where we'd played our baby scissors game.

Etta drew back. "Don't look at me like that. Audie wasn't yours. You didn't speak for him. How was I supposed to know?"

"Why," I asked, the truth of what had happened rolling over me, "if you don't love him?"

"He wanted it so bad. He asked so nice. He wants us to get married. He says he's going to ask Dad for my hand. Hell, I'd cut one off and give it to him if it would make him leave me be." Her laugh was ugly. "And if Becker knew, he'd kill him."

She raised her hands to her wild hair and tried to smooth it. "Mackie, you can have him if you want him."

I couldn't speak.

"Becker and I are leaving as soon as he takes care of things. Tomorrow or day after. The little girls . . . we're leaving them in Manitou with their aunt. Going on ourselves. He's got a plan."

"Etta, he's a no-account. A criminal."

"You don't know him."

"What's Dad going to say?"

"Who cares? You don't know *him,* either. You think he's Father, Son, and Holy Ghost."

All the years of her poor-mouthing Dad came to a head, and I burst out, "Why do you always talk like that about him? I've heard it and I've heard it and there's nothing at the bottom. You want me to hate him, and I don't know why. What's wrong with you? Are you just crazy? Do you just *want* to make trouble?"

Her tone grew ominous, her eyes glittery and bright. "You want to know? I'll tell you."

Out of her smeared-looking mouth came an ugly made-up tale that Dad had killed his brother in cold blood. It was no hunting accident at all. He'd simply gunned him down.

"Etta, that's a bald-faced lie."

"You don't believe me?"

"Not word-one."

"Mam told me."

"That's another."

It was ever Etta's way to worsen things, to up the ante, tell another lie to prove the first one, shake you off your point and put the blame on you.

"And Mackie, here's what you don't know. You're not Dad's girl at all."

What she said then was a bad bump in the road, but I ran over it. "I don't believe that for a minute. I don't believe she told you, and I don't believe it's true."

"She told me so I'd be nicer to you after she was gone. So I'd take pity on you."

Her spiteful lording look had stunned me quiet. So had the suspicion, but I shook it off. She was a liar. When she was in a corner, her cruelty knew no bounds, so I put her ugly talk behind me.

She shrugged. "Think what you want," she said. "I heard what I heard."

"And I," I said, the threat of telling what I'd witnessed in the canebrake not-so-buried in my words, "saw what I saw."

Dad called up the stairs. "You girls settle down!"

Etta pinched my arm. "You tell him anything I said, I'll kill you."

"Why don't you just let Becker do the honors?"

I got up and wandered half the night. Up on the rise, Audie's trailer house was dark, and inside he was sleeping, innocent, unknowing. If I felt pity for him, I felt also a big and righteous, wicked kind of justice.

———

Becker didn't come for my sister the next day or the day after that. A week went by, then two, but he didn't come for Etta then or ever.

Late one night Dad woke us to say the Birdsall place was burning. He and Aud were going over to help the bucket brigade volunteers. No one could find a Birdsall. They had packed up and left. "Let it burn," said Etta.

It strikes me only now as I remember this that Etta could have set the fire. Memory tells me she'd been punky and mean-tempered all that day, recalls a burn blister on her thumb and that I found up in our room where I went to fetch the suitcase her California board hacked with the paring knife to splinters. From then until I left for Kansas her hands and arms bore cuts, some fresh and some scabbed over. She had sunk for certain down into a mad.

By this time I had written to the Belle Plaine people, and they sent bus fare. In my letter I assured them that I filled the bill, only part of what I wrote a lie. If they caught on I wasn't twenty-one, I'd find work in a diner. I was to start the first Monday in August—a short week away—for a monthlong tryout period. But before I could break my news, Big Babe dried up and Etta's deeper problem came to light. Anybody could have seen both problems coming.

With Babe, at each milking there'd been less and less. The cow was too old for another calf to start the flow again. "She was a sweet thing, that's for certain. Saved us more than once. It's a wonder she held out so long," Dad said. He shook his head. "She kept us going all those years, but there's naught to do but butcher her. It grieves me, but there isn't any other way. We'll do it ourselves and sell the beef. Cut out the middleman. There'll be a piece of change for anybody helping."

At the sink I was scrubbing at the skillet, eased up scouring to hear. Audie took a seat at the table to listen. Those last days at home, knowing what I knew, I could hardly look at him except to see that he was as busy trying to charm Etta as I'd been busy trying to charm him, and that both of us might well have saved our breath.

They wouldn't be able to winch the cow high enough to bleed her into a barrel the way they did with pigs, Dad went on, so they would have to dig a pit in the far barn's earthen floor. The joists were strong enough to bear the load.

While Dad and Audie spoke of renderers and meat lockers, Etta paced and muttered, picking up things and slamming them down.

Dad looked up from figuring, explained patiently what anybody knew, that feeding Babe would cost too much. He numbered off the tons of fodder, dollars lost. He didn't say that there was nothing left of the bad hay from the year before, that this year's yield was so full of grasshoppers it was worthless, that the forage was played out. Etta knew these things.

She came to stand beside me at the sink. "That's what he does when something outlives its use."

I tossed my head as though to flick away a gnat. The Kansas letter crinkled in my pocket, my ticket to a better life.

"He slaughters it."

I scoured hard to drown her out. When I looked up, Dad had left the kitchen.

Audie looked hopefully at Etta. "Say, I could buy her from him, maybe. We could . . ."

"Audie, just shut up!" She slammed the door and went outside and took herself somewhere I didn't care to know.

By and by he got up and went outside, pretending some forgotten errand. Woe to him, I thought. Or if not woe, then some more of that other creek-mud thing he wanted bad enough to ask so nice for. I banged the skillet on the stove three times. Shock traveled up my arm, rang in my skull.

———

Saturday came and still I hadn't told Dad I was leaving. The task hung over me like dread. Any excuse to put it off, I took.

The butchering day dawned hot. When Etta came downstairs, she was already out of sorts. She wanted me to go to town with her. "Come on, Mackie."

I refused to look at her. "I need to cook for them," I said. "I've got too much to do." Truth was, I didn't want to be around her. Since the night I'd spied on her with Becker in the canebrake I had slept downstairs on the horsehair sofa, saying it was too hot in our room.

Her face was slick with sweat, her hair unwashed and clumped in hanks. "I don't want to hear the shot." She wore her nightgown, and when she puffed it up to air herself I caught a whiff of unclean body.

When the shot rang out, just one between the eyes, no more, efficient, merciful, I left the kitchen and went out behind the brooder house and lost my breakfast.

Etta was waiting for me at the door when I returned, her eyes narrowed. "We're next."

"Shut up," I said, and tried to put her from my mind. This was a day like any other. Two more and I'd be gone. Etta'd made her bed and now she had to lie in it alone.

She wore the limp nightgown all day, didn't wash or comb her hair. While the men were in the barn, she paced the kitchen, wandering from door to window, fretting about the heat.

Gone already in my mind, I threw myself into the housework. Swept the cobwebs off the porch and blacked the stove a final time.

Then I went to the garden to hoe weeds and pick some green tomatoes. The afternoon was windless, a din of locusts.

Around five o'clock I went inside to start supper. I'd saved a round of lunch meat and a loaf of store-bought bread. Thinking to fry tomatoes, I struck a match to light the stove.

Etta came out from the pantry to stay my hand. "Don't, Mackie."

I let the match burn down. "Aren't you hungry?"

"I'm burning up. It's hot."

"Why don't you take a bath?"

"I'd only drown myself."

Mam had once said things like this. The stark thought struck me like a slap that our mother welcomed her own death, that Etta, in her unsoundness, was courting hers.

She stood at the screen door. Light streamed through her stained cotton gown. Her body looked too thin. She'd scratched at bug bites on her ankles and the blood streaked down.

"Don't talk like that," I said. "Things aren't so bad."

"Anything would be better than this. Anything. Oh, Mackie, I'm so miserable."

Once again my heart turned toward her. Whether I approved of her or not, despite her meanness in trying to hurt me about not being Dad's girl, she was suffering. I went to stand beside her. "Etta, honey, is there something I can do?"

"Shoot me." She turned her gaze outside. "Look at all this nothing. All this nothing."

I looked outside the screen door down the long lay of the tenant farm, past the well and woodpile, cistern, sheds and barns, down to the tree line of the Tebo. Between the near barn and the far barn lay a field of dent corn, brown-tasseled, nearly ready for a harvest that I wouldn't see. The lowering light made the field look brilliant, each leaf, each sturdy prop root lined in gold. Outside the far barn door, I caught a glimpse of Audie. Walking weary as the day he'd come to us from Chilocco, he was headed toward the creek to wash. I didn't mark it then, but this would be the last time I would see him.

"Look at all those flies," Etta said.

I looked hard, but saw no flies.

In a hollow, stricken voice, she whispered, "Mackie, Becker didn't come."

"I know," I said. "I'm sorry." I wanted to say that it was for the best, but I knew not to. It would set her off and start a scene. If we could get through two more days, I'd leave her spectacles and scenes for good. I went to cut some lunch meat. Started making sandwiches for when the men came in.

"Sister," came her voice, faint, spoken from beside the door where she pressed her forehead into the screen, "I'm going to have a baby."

I kept on buttering the bread. I had to get the strokes just right. This statement I believed like my own breath; it wasn't said for any reason—spite or joke or meanness—other than it had to be.

"Did you hear me?"

From outside came the clank of the hand pump in the yard, the dowser's squeal, the rush of water. I looked past Etta, out the door into the yard. Dad was coming up the pathway, mopping his forehead with a balled bandanna, walking crabbed. When he looked up to see Etta waiting at the door, his expression seemed to lighten. He lifted his hand to wave, like Dad of old.

From out of one of those dead silences that come upon a house at summer dusk, she shouted at me, her voice now curdled, brutal, and the ringing sound of it was terrible. "Did you hear me? I'm going to have a baby!"

I ran into the front room, felt dizzy and light-headed, stars before my eyes, my vision narrowed to a tunnel, like looking through a stovepipe.

Out in the kitchen, the screen door clattered on its hinges. There came a muffled sound of struggle, then the screen door slapped.

I ran back to the kitchen door to watch. Dad pulled Etta down the path toward the barn, Etta scrabbling to keep from falling, trying to wrench away. At the barn bay door, he yanked her arm to turn her around. Shoved her inside.

I wiped the dust that settled on the table, the merest reddish powder. I tried to keep my mind on Kansas, tame and safe, a paradise of niceness and good manners, where people didn't scream and carry on and get themselves in trouble. Where people would be kind. Appreciate the work you threw yourself into. I tried to feature what the place might look like. Belle Plaine had a generous, rich-sounding name. Would the house have shutters on the windows, holly-hocks in bloom, a pot of red geraniums beside the door? What would separate quarters look like, would there be an iron bedstead with a feather tick, a crocheted coverlet?

Try as I might to summon pretty, peaceful visions, I could not, and so I smoothed the dishrag against a chair back and went outside, darting into the field of dent corn for cover, and made my way through the stalks until I came out behind the far barn. Through a crack between the barn boards I could see Etta and my father.

In the center of the earthen floor lay the pit where they'd bled Babe. Dad sat on a hay bale, Etta sprawled at his feet. He held her in a hammerlock, his free arm around her neck. The setting sun cast dusty rays across them. Flies, drawn by the blood in the pit, thickened the air.

"I don't know what to do with you."

She strained against his hold. "Shoot me in the back. Cut my arm off with a sickle. Butcher me."

He shifted his grip. "You have to stop this, Etta."

She tossed her hair, shook her head from side to side, tried again to break away.

He held her tight. "Look around here. This is killing. This is death. It's hard and terrible."

"Let me go!"

He held on. "I want to show you what you're saying. Do you understand it hurts me when you say those things?

"Daughter," he said after a time when Etta only glared, making his voice gentle, "I never would have . . ." Whatever else he meant to say was lost when she spat on the ground.

"Etta, you have to straighten up. This isn't good. It isn't good. And I don't care how mad you get at me, don't ever make light of an out-of-wedlock child. It's not a thing to joke about. Not a thing to use to make a scene. Not even to hurt me."

Doves cooed in the rafters. A lone white feather drifted down, catching the golden light.

He must have loosened his grip, for she broke from him and scrambled to her feet. Breathing hard, she threw back her head and gave an empty, anguished yell, the picture of a mad thing.

Something in her must have let him know she wasn't joking. His face seemed to collapse, and he looked old and haggard, broken. In a voice so low I barely heard, he asked, "Whose is it, Mary Etta?"

She faced him across the pit. "It's mine. And I don't want it."

He held her gaze. She broke first, looked up toward the haymow where sunlight streamed down, then cried out, "I didn't want to, but he forced me!"

"Who did?"

Sobs erupted, so overwrought and wild a fool could see that they were false. "Your favorite son, your prodigal, your golden boy."

Furious, confused, but knowing what I knew, which was that nobody forced anyone, and that Etta's lie would wreck Audie's life and ruin Dad's, I hurried to the house and slipped inside, grabbed up the broom, made busy sweeping dust I hadn't seen before. Crumbs on the floor. Hay straw and bug shells. Blood rang in my ears, my hands felt numb. On the table sat the plate of bologna sandwiches and I thought of Bucky Madzey and how he took a paddling for Etta's lie about the lunch pail. I'd felt sick then, I felt sick now. It seemed that almost all my life with Etta had been one long sickness, one long storm.

At last Dad came up the path alone. He stopped at the pump to wash again. He came through the door, let it close quietly, pulled out a chair and sat. He made a cradle of his arms, put down his head. Down his forearm ran a line of blood he'd missed. When I cleared my throat, he raised his head.

I pointed to the plate of sandwiches. "Dad, I'll bet you're hungry."

In a thickened voice, he mumbled something. I moved closer. "Come again?"

He cleared his throat. "Nothing. Coughed." He picked up a sandwich. "Where is he? Audie?"

In all my years of telling or not telling on my sister, this time what I had to do was clear. Truth was truth, no matter what. But when I opened my mouth to tell him about Etta and Becker Birdsall, what I said was, "Dad, I'm going away."

He took this in, considered me. "Things haven't been so good here for you, have they?"

I lied and told him they were fine. I told a bit about the job, the housework and nursing I'd be doing, how I wanted to make my own way, maybe to go to college. This last I hadn't thought of until I said it, but once I had, I began to think I could.

He scratched the back of his neck. "I know you'll make me proud. You've been a help. Don't think I haven't noticed. I don't know what I would have done without you."

To hear him say he noticed all the work I'd done would once have been my fondest wish, but somehow, now, it was too late. Even sixty years after the drouth and dust, I always water the barrel garden I've got going in the café's parking lot. Rain or shine I drag out the hose and give the flowers a good long soak. Gus will say, "Maxine, why mess with watering when rain is on the way?" but I learned a long time back that sometimes even rain is not enough. Still, it meant a lot, his compliment, and if compliments could serve for answers, I might have taken his to mean that all was well between us, all was just the same: He was my father and he would have told me if he wasn't.

He was looking at me deeply, his own eyes sunken, tired, mine watering from trying to hold his in my gaze, and I knew that if I ever planned to ask, this was the time. I'd mulled it in my mind, the way to ask. Just come out with it, plain. Speak up. But did I really want to know the answer, wasn't it enough to believe the story I'd been told? Didn't sometimes everything—religion, truth, the reasons people do the things they do—come down to that, to choosing what to think and sticking with it, come what may? Couldn't you belong to people other ways? For a long time we regarded each other, burdened both of us, it felt like, by the heavy silence in the moment. Then, as always, I broke first. "Thank you," I said.

He fell to eating, then, as if it were a task, ate until he finished all the sandwiches, then asked me, "Is there any milk?"

"We're out," I had to say.

When the reason for its absence dawned on him, he got up and started for his room, undoing his bib-alls as he went. Just as he reached the back room door, I called out to him to wait.

Hand on the doorknob, he turned.

I looked down at the floor, at my bare feet on the worn board floor, then back up at him. I gathered my breath. "Etta's telling you a story . . ."

Relief smoothed out his brow, and for a short minute I knew what it must feel like to have the power to unbreak a heart. "She's not . . . expecting?"

Many years later, a man I called my husband told me that some folks would rather tell lies for a lifetime than speak truth for a minute, and just then, as I looked into Dad's eyes, I would have gladly put myself among their number. If with a lie I could have undone all that had happened, the dust storms and his disappointment, my envy and Mam's dying, Etta's headlong dash at ruin, I would have fibbed like there was no tomorrow. But I shook my head. "He didn't force her."

He pinched his nose bridge, looked away, looked out the back door, his eyes hooded. "How would you know a thing like that?"

I thought quick and told part of the truth. "I saw."

Dad gave a shudder, and he seemed to settle something in his mind. "Aud's a good man. He'll do right by her."

Audie would try. They'd marry. A black-haired baby girl he named Georgette was born in April. My mean-hearted prophecy about its only getting worse would come to pass, as Etta floundered deeper into her unhappiness or madness, whichever one of those it was that plagued her. Maybe some of both that seesawed back and forth. But I didn't witness this. I didn't see the end of things for Dad and Etta, Dad and Audie, Audie and his wife and child. Later I would learn that Etta simply stole away, taking the child, that Audie tried to follow them across the country. For all his handiness at tracking, he must have lost the trail, or it went cold, and after that he went away. We didn't hear from him again.

Me, I was too busy hoping for the bright tomorrows everybody said were coming, and so I paid no mind to what went on back home. I was above it all, gone off to make my own mistakes, and wouldn't see my sister for another year, when she sought me in the bed I'd made and would insist on lying in.

2

~

Signs and Wonders

Before I go on delving back into the time that seems to run inside of time, it hits me that I ought to stop and make something of starting this fresh notebook. I don't know rightly what to say. What comes next in the story is the part I'd like to skip, jump over it and pick up in the present day, tell how things ended, maybe make some noise about how living on to tell or not to tell is all that matters, which might just be a dressed-up lie. It's funny that the longer I remember and the more words I put on these pages, the easier the words come but the harder comes the truth. *Seal up what the seven thunders uttered and write them not.* If I were still the girl I was, I'd likely take that crazy scripture for a sign and call it good. But up to now I've laid out Etta's wrongs and skimped on mine, and so I'll finish what I started.

.   .   .

The Belle Plaine place was not a rich farm, but it was nice enough the same. Wheat, alfalfa, flax, a herd of white-faced Herefords and a few stray shorthorns, a tidy green-roofed house on acres proved up by Call's grandfather in the Homestead Act. The place had been hurt by the drouth and dust, but not as much as some. The acreage was bottomland, sandy loam along the shallow Ninnescah, and willow brakes and sand plum thickets kept the damage down. Still, you could see the mark of weather in the harrowed look of things. A reddish ridge of dune where nothing grew, a crooked fence line turned into the backbone of a great sand snake, a dry stock pond in the middle of a pasture.

Lila Lucas was a tiny woman, her bones frail as a squab's, her hair fine blond as chick fluff. She wore dresses in a baby shade of blue. She was sickly, taking to her bed more often than not, but she wasn't yet what you would call an invalid. Rare times she would perten up and spunk around. I learned her ways and minded her in every word. Her husband called her Wife. She wanted me to call her Missus, so I did.

It was winter by the time I saw Call Lucas truly, though I'd seen him, sure, before. He met my bus in August when I stepped down in the middle of a sunny shower when the pavement steamed with the travel smell of rain on concrete and macadam. I had seen him every day thereafter. But at this winter meeting, ours was more a sudden notice, like a secret thought grown big, then bigger, till you blurt it out and nearly jump inside your skin to hear it said.

He was milking Boss, his flat man-rump on a T-bar stool, knees higher, spraddle-legged, shouldered into Boss's flank, arm hoist around her leg to hobble her, neck craned sideways, looking up at nothing, at the pigeons in the rafters, then at me, at Mackie Spoon, eighteen that past July, come in to gather eggs. Missus had an outlaw hen that roosted in the manger, and she'd sent me to spy out the nest.

What we did was wrong, but I wanted to believe there was a way of turning things, of seeing how what happened after might add up to make it right. It was milking time, five-thirty, warm inside from cattle, from the little things that live in hay to make it give its own green-breathing heat. The sun was tabby orange through the slats, dust and motes around me like I'd walked into a halo. Bars of orange slid across me smooth and light as water, and I smelled the warm grass smell of uncured hay, of cattle, linseed oil, and harness leather, swallows' nests of mud and straw and feathers, mice, the foam of milk from Call's pail when he set it down and milk lapped onto dirt as he came toward me, unwashed work when he came closer, myself in my red wool blanket coat with wet snow melting on the shoulders where it fell upon me from the eaves, myself under my dress, and we lay down in all of it, in a way that felt like all the world was gathered into one sweet skin, and though you knew that it was wrong, down deep, in bone and blood and muscle, you desired the one forbidden thing your head told you you weren't supposed to want, and in that wanting, in that knowing it was wrong, there was a stillness at the center, calm and full and sly, that came from knowing you would do it anyway, and you could tell your head to cease its thinking, to let the bone and blood and muscle have their way, glad, for what you were doing seemed the holiest of human acts, and in that time when everything was fighting in you you were whole as you would ever be, and how I knew the first went gladly out of Eden. I knew how Etta felt, and Audie, and even Becker Birdsall, how everyone since time began had felt, and why the world went round. Just that fast I backslid into Bible tales, turned into the Revelation woman clothed in sun, moon at her feet, head crowned in stars. I didn't travel in the verses far enough to recollect her end, but halted, stunned and come to life.

Call was quiet, after, gave out one shiver, gathered up his pail and eased back through the stanchion bars to turn Boss out, looked back at me as though he knew me to the center yet had never seen me in his life before, and in his eyes there was a blue-eyed look of staring too long toward the light, as if what we'd done had hurt him.

The ladies of the Hannah Circle doted on Missus, bringing covered dishes, cakes, and pies to tempt her. They were in the kitchen with her when I came back with the eggs, nine white, six brown, two banty. "Put them on the drainboard, Mackie," Missus told me. "You can wash them later."

One of the ladies handed her a plate. "Try some peach cobbler, Lila."

"Oh, thank you, no. Maybe after a while." She sighed. She pushed away the plate. "Right now I'm not too pert."

They clucked around her while I stood at the sink and scalded dishes I'd let to sit after our supper. I felt my neck go pink as the spots of rouge on Missus's cheeks.

One of the Hannahs asked after her health.

"Pretty punk," she said, "and tired. But I'll get on. There's Mackie, here. She watches after me."

"Call's so good to hire you help," another said.

"Yes. There's so much work. And we weren't blessed."

In a shaded plot north of the house were two small headstones, babies gone before they breathed.

The Hannahs started in on female trouble, and I tried to close my ears against the hollow, black-and-blue sound of the word *womb*. I dried the dishes in a hurry, wanting to get out because I knew Call would be bringing in the house milk to skim, and I didn't want the warm new smell of milk to rise into that kitchen where I stood, my head gone giddy and my insides sore, everybody watching.

Things just went along. I worked in the house, around the yard, and with the chickens. I took portions of what I cooked, and ate alone at my own place, so the three of us sitting together at the table didn't happen. It was all the bumping into one another. I'd be at the sink and he'd bring in the milk to separate and there we'd be, working, breathing, so close that we could fairly smell the time we both remembered, but neither one of us would speak. Neither acted like the other was alive, but in that ignoring, in that looking-off, that silence, there was more than if we'd tried to talk.

About this time I had two letters, the first from Dad, a few days later one from Etta. His spoke of weather—it was still getting better—and the farm. Holloways were going to Texas. He and Aud were getting up a plan to use the money from Aud's allotment and his bonus check. They were going in together to buy the tenant parcel. He thanked me for what I'd sent. I was paid ten dollars every week; I sent him half. Etta's child was due in April. She and Aud had married, which was good, he wrote. Etta carried on like world's end all the way to the courthouse but after that she went to bed. He wrote, *We pray she will adjust.*

Etta's started this way: *Maxine Jane,* no *Dear.* Just my full name stark. She went on to say she didn't appreciate it that I took things that belonged to her. A comb, some hairpins, and a handkerchief, that suitcase she had packed to go away with Becker into which I'd put my worldly goods—three dresses, underthings and whatnot, and that red wool blanket coat. There was no mention of the marriage, of the coming child. Her letter ended with the words, *How could you leave me here?*

I wrote to Dad that I was fine and working hard. I told a little of the place and of the work I did, the weather. Funny how the words arranged themselves around the big hole in the truth. Feeling past-it-all, I sent Audie my regards. Etta's letter I tried to put from my mind, for I had made up my own world, the one I knew could be, and what I'd left behind me held no part in it.

I went about pretending Call and I were married, that I was the wife and he the husband, that I ran the house and saw to things in such a way that didn't need reminding. When I saw something pretty or I had a pleasant thought, I featured telling him, though never did. When we met each other in the barn, I forgot all my pretending and just let be, then afterward fell back into the quiet way it was. That quiet way was fine with me, as ours was not a solitary love affair I carried on alone, but mutual, and this time there was proof.

I came to feel a power over Missus, that never mind my twisted foot and that our sizes matched, I was strong and she was weak and this was only right. I took to slamming things, not hard, but with an edge—her teacup at her place, a pair of scissors she asked me to fetch—pretending accident, my slamming, and she would take this with a narrowing of eyes, but say just, "Lightly, Mackie-honey, lightly." One time when I was brushing out her hair—she wore it coiled at her nape and it had grown too long for her to tend alone— I pulled too hard, and she cried out.

"Beg pardon, Missus," I said, though not meaning it until I saw that she was holding back her tears so as to hide her need and weakness. She was a banty hen, all scruff and feathers. She knew the power others held over her and tried to hide it with her ruffled ways. I understood how we were like, and love for her crept up on me. I stopped the slamming, cold.

I began to think I ought to leave. That I'd brought trouble to the house. Though we were quiet—secret—in our doings, how were they any different from what Etta'd gone and done? Nights, I sometimes dreamed that I was being stoned by white-robed figures ringed around me.

But, oh, I couldn't get enough of Call. He couldn't get enough of me. We were both of us that hungry for each other. So I stayed.

Dazed, invisible, lovesick, I made sly moves for him to notice me. I'd clang the triangle for supper, standing at the back door so he would have to pass me, close. I'd run a finger just above his belt to watch him shiver. Serving, I would cut my eyes to glance at him, and if he met my gaze, my knees went all to water. And so the days went by, the three of us moving around, bumping into one another, not talking much, but busy and working, like a box hive full of bees, until the idea of what was going on became an almost buzzing in my ears.

Then two things happened. Call took Missus to the doctor in Belle Plaine and when they came back home she went to bed for almost good. We put her in the spare room. She got up rarely, but would wander, touching things. To care for her, I moved into the farm-house. I slept on a cot in the small wake parlor off the front room, the kind old houses used to have. We put an old sheep bell beside her bed so she could ring for me. She took this fine, but with her small mouth tightened in a sweet, long-suffering knot, and it seemed her belly swelled as though her tumor fed itself on what it knew of me. But until the night in March when Boss had trouble calving and Call yelled out for me to come, I believe she only just suspected.

Boss bawled and bellowed like the earth was heaving while we worked by lanternlight to turn the calf, me kneading at her hardened belly, Call naked to the waist, his arm full up inside her, wrenching till I felt a give and shifting, slid his arm out red and warm and steaming and we saw the baby crown. Then, above our breath, we heard another sound, that sheep bell, but close outside, and when we looked around we saw her in her pale blue nightgown, coming through the doorway toward us in the cold, ringing, calling in a whisper. She cried that she'd forgotten something, cried because she couldn't think of what it was, and then we all three knew she knew, but none of us would say it, and so things went along, with Call and me inside the house like man and wife and Missus as our child.

"I got some broth down her," I'd tell him. "She fussed a little, but she took it."

"She never did eat much," he'd say. "Just picked."

This was how we talked about her, nothing deeper, and we never talked about ourselves or what we'd done or the names we'd have to bear, but my heart sang at the way things worked out, because the second thing that happened was that I was pregnant.

I knew the moment, marked it, felt it when the word begetting entered me the same time he did. It was a February night when I was bathing, the first time he came to seek me in my side house. I had heated water at the farmhouse, as I didn't have a cooking stove, and carried a steaming ewer out to my place. I lit the lamp and stood at the bureau, washing. I heard him outside, knew that he was looking in the window, but I didn't move to cover myself, only turned a bit because in all the weeks we carried on we hadn't seen each other without clothes. When he came in, I helped him to take off his things and washed him, washed him till the water cooled.

At first I just ignored the signs that even as Missus lay there I was incubating something of my own. My feet grew sore and swollen waiting on her, and I lost my breakfast soon as I could get it down, but I tried not to let this show. If it came to me to liken what was going on to Etta's trouble, I set my jaw against the thought. This—*I*—was different.

Since the night in March when we birthed the calf, Call had stopped coming for me. I understood, and if he had asked, I would have told him, "No, it isn't fitting." I didn't tell him about what I was carrying, but planned to wait until I grew big enough for him to notice on his own and when Missus died do the right thing and marry me and just go on, for in that quiet, grief-struck house, I was ecstatic, and the days could not be long enough.

I saw the rightness of the world in everything. When the brood sow farrowed eighteen piglets, I knew the number meant my age. If

I gathered thirty-seven eggs, it stood for Call's. In April, lightning hit the walnut tree and forked it to the roots, and I knew this meant Missus would go within the month. I vowed to make her comfortable, to ease her passing. I did this with divided heart, for I knew the reward.

The Hannahs were all over us, bringing their offerings of food. I was thickening by then. It had begun to hurt to hold my middle in.

"That Mackie Spoon's not missing any meals," I heard one say.

Another said, "She was so scrawny when she came she liked to blown away," but they said no more than this, as Call was known to be an upright man, a pillar.

One asked, "Where will you go when Lila passes on?"

"Don't know," I said. But, oh, I knew.

"You might find work down at Costin's. Zada's half-worn-out with all those children. Triplets, can you feature?"

Another suggested the café on the highway. "The Waco Wego's hiring. There's a big sign in the window."

I made myself busy folding bedsheets. "I'll worry about it when the time comes."

"Call's looking bad," one said.

"Feed him," they told me. "That's all you can do."

"I will," I said, "I will."

For all the signs I took out of the Bible, for all the signs I made of plain things, you'd think I would have watched for one that augured warning.

Late one night I sat at the kitchen table finishing Missus's cup of tea. She'd had a bad spell, and I'd tended her, reading to her from the Psalms, taking care to choose the peaceful rather than the warlike or lamenting ones. "I will lift up mine eyes unto the hills" and "The Lord is my shepherd, I shall not want." At last she dozed. Call was asleep in their old room, and the house had fallen quiet. I sat in moonlit darkness, thinking of what to do to make the place my own. Blue curtains, the color of Call's eyes. I had just started to think about the meals I might prepare for him once time enough had passed for us to take up living as a couple, when a movement drew my notice to the corner. A fleeting shape, a darting mouse.

As though touched by a phantom hand, from the high rail above the table where six Blue Willow plates were propped, a plate crashed to the floor and shattered. I'd dusted them, knew every chip and craze. I knew I'd set them firmly in the plate groove.

Another fell, the next in line.

Then or now, I didn't hold with ghosts or spirits, but the hackles prickled on my neck.

When a third plate crashed, I cried Call's name.

He pulled the light chain just as the fourth plate tottered, crashed.

He angled out a chair and stood on it, grabbed the last two plates and handed them down to me.

"Bull snake," he said.

Emerging from the shelf rim was a blunt dark snout, the flicking tongue, the spadelike head.

He snatched the snake behind the jaws, stepped down. The creature—thicker than a table leg—lashed and writhed. Call held tight, went out the door. A musky, dank smell seemed to slither in his absence.

When he came back in, he said, "After a rat, I guess."

He went back to bed while I stayed up to sweep the plate shards into the dustpan. I couldn't get out of my mind the picture of that serpent coiled round Call's ropy arm.

I was still standing in the middle of the kitchen when he came back to say, "It's best Wife doesn't know."

He didn't have to tell me what he meant.

⌐

By now I'd passed the early months of losing breakfast and was starting to show, but I loosened up my dresses and wore a tentish apron,
so nobody would suspect.

Missus held on. If anything, she rallied. One morning, when Call
was on the back porch lacing his boots, she shuffled into the kitchen
where I was redding up before the outside work. Gripping at the
doorjamb, she was frail and tottery, a wraith. I feared she would
look up toward the plate rail, whimper, "Oh, my pretty plates, what
happened?" and we would have to tell a story, but she said, more
strongly than she'd said another thing for days, "I want to see my
girlhood home. I want to have a picnic."

Call's voice turned in an instant to a tender thing that gave me
hope for how he'd someday speak to me. "Why, we could do that,
sure."

We planned the outing for the coming day. I killed and fried a
chicken, made potato salad and a lemon cake, some powder biscuits.
Then I remembered Missus wouldn't be able to get down a bite of it,
could only take the smallest tastes before she lost her appetite, and so
that night I stayed up late to make a marrow broth.

The next morning I washed her hair. It was white by then, though
she was only thirty-five, so thin that to get it to suds up it only took a
dab of glycerin shampoo. I bathed her, smoothed Pond's cold cream
on her flaking skin. She wanted out of her nightgown and into a
dress, so I put on her best, a blue jersey with a scalloped, eggshell-
colored collar. Her skin was creped, her flesh so gauntened that the
space between her neck and collarbones was hollow. To cover this
we put a pink scarf around her neck and pinned it with her lily of the
valley brooch.

I propped a mirror on the bureau and seated her before it so I
could comb out her hair. Thin, it spread across her shoulders like wet
string, but her eyes were gleaming. "Make me ready for the party,"
she said, her breathy voice a tiny girl's.

Pity for her welled up in my throat, and with it, love that moved me to kiss the top of her wet head. "You're already the fairest of ten thousand," I told her, and I meant it. She looked beautiful, looked heaven-eyed and holy.

She smiled. "Now that I'm scoured down to bone, I feel so light."

She went on, her voice a reed, but urgent. "You'll see it when your time to go comes round. How things come clear. You look back at your life, then you see it. Only at the far end. Sometimes you don't have to look back at all, you just see it. Every ragged scrap and tatter from the start on down. Right there looking at you with your own eyes."

Tucking her hair into a knot at her nape, I said, to humor her, "Oh, I know."

"Well, you don't."

I'd seen enough to think I did. I was coming on nineteen. I fixed the last hairpin into the knot. "There," I said. "All done."

She reached up to take my hand. She held it to my belly. Her grip was firm but gentle, and there was no malice in it. "Child," she said, "I know what's going on."

I stared at her reflection in the tilted mirror. The lily brooch had drawn the pink scarf crooked. I reached around to right it.

"Did you hear me?"

"Yes."

"Don't you tell him until I'm gone. Only then. Tell him I didn't know. It would kill him to think I knew. Pride's his downfall. It's his sin. You promise me."

I said, "I promise." I said, "I'm sorry . . ."

She laughed, a poor shred of what a laugh might be, but I hadn't heard a laugh for so long that it staggered me.

"I don't want you to be." She tilted her head to meet my gaze in the mirror. "Mackie-honey, look, I'm giving this to you." She fumbled to unclasp the lily of the valley brooch and tried to press it into my hand.

"I can't," I said. "I can't." When she wouldn't take it back, I dropped it in her lap.

"Come around," she told me. "Come here to me."

I went around and knelt at her knees.

"I want to tell you something so you'll see. Nobody's perfect. That's a simple thing, and you already know it, but you've just forgotten. Nobody's altogether perfect. The sooner you learn that for good, the better off you'll be. You might think I've never done wrong. Sugar-mouth around the way I do and act so sweet nobody'd guess. But I've done wrong."

I shook my head. I didn't see, would not believe.

She picked at the blue stuff of her bodice. "When I was a young woman, just married, there was a man. He kept the grocery store in Wellington. Every time I'd go in to look at this or that or do my weekly, we would talk.

"Now, you know Call, and you know how he is. Stormy, even with his mouth sewn shut the way it mostly is. I knew the way he was when I married him, but then I got it in my mind he didn't love me well enough to suit me. Didn't show me in the way I wanted, and I took it hard. But this grocery man . . . he made me feel a beauty. Even back then I was pale and small. Put me up against a clapboard house and all you'd see was eyes . . ."

She was tiring, her voice faltering. "After a long dry time when things weren't going well, and Call did something, I don't even remember what, maybe he just looked at me the wrong way or wouldn't answer when I asked a question. Something. Anyway, it made me mad and so I sought that grocer out. You know well what we did. Lord God. And more than once. Lasted about a year. I never told. I was ashamed, but I was also happy. Happy and ashamed all balled up into one big knot. But the funny thing was I was never sorry. Can you imagine? And the whole long time of our marriage, if I got angry with Call, I'd take out that time and what I did with that grocer, and I'd work it around my mind and think, Husband, you do not know me at all. Kept it all these years, took it out and polished it the way you do a grudge. Stored it in a little gilded altar in my heart."

She was breathless, but she went on. "I used to think those lost babies were the punishment, but they weren't. I didn't know enough back then to understand God's got no time to match the sinner with the sin or price out crimes and levy charges. It's easier than that. He just lets the world turn around and turn around until it hits a stopping place and jumbles everybody up and by and by you'll meet yourself in someone else's skin. Or else you'll do somebody else the wrong once done to you. Whichever way it goes, you'll get paid out in people. That's the true coin of this realm and don't forget it. And when that time comes round for you, you'll know it, and you'll say, 'Oh, my,' and be surprised. But way deep down you'll know."

She was quiet, picking at the brooch in her lap. "He gave me this. Call did. A present to make up for whatever it was he did. Or didn't do. Maybe it's for the best you didn't take it."

I started to get up, she tugged my hand to pull me back down.

"Wait," she said, the color of her face now yellow-gray, "this might well be my last say, and I aim to have it out."

She folded her hands around the brooch. The bedroom curtains billowed with a breeze. A fly bumped at the screen.

"Well," she finally said after a long silent time, "I reckon that's the size of it. Not much to speak of, was it?" She giggled, then held out her arms and I went into them. She stroked my head. Her hands were small and dry as leaves. Under her blue dress her heart beat like a bird's. "Honey, you cry if you want to," she told me, but my eyes were dry.

Call came in and found us so. I got up from my knees and made busy straightening. "Ready for the party," Missus said.

She'd grown up along the Medicine, in Barber County, a morning's drive. I expected her to doze after the morning, but she fairly perched on the front seat of the Chevrolet. The window was cranked down. Wind tossed her done-up hair to wisps as we drove westerly. She looked like an eager fledgling sparrow. "Oh," she sang out, "I can smell it." She turned to Call, and in the smile she gave him decades vanished. I saw her as she must have looked when younger, strong and hopeful, still a girl. "Oh, Husband, I can smell it!"

We passed out of the rolling pasture lands of the Ark Valley and moved into the Gypsum Hills, ranch land, a countryside of buttes and mesas, salt cedar and prickly pear, red outcrops shaped into spires and pillars, battlements, whatever forms you can imagine rock will shape itself to. When she pointed to a high butte rising from a scree, and said, "Look there, a horse hill," I took her meaning in an instant. Though no horse stood on its summit, what she meant was that a horse would look so perfect posed on such a hill, his mane a banner in the wind, his foreleg raised. Etta had pointed out horse hills on any trip that took us out of flatland. I had to ponder hard on scenery to put the sudden thought of Etta from my mind.

Call couldn't find the way to her family's homestead, and we turned down one wrong road, then another. We bottomed out in washouts, winding up once at a burned-out farm, and once at a dead-end road where a squatter family had made a house out of a wheelless boxcar and goats ranged in the red dirt yard.

Call bristled. He gripped the steering wheel as though to yank us down the right road through his force alone. He braked hard, backed up harder, gunned the engine, swore. Nasty oaths I'd never heard, animal and shocking. *Son of a she-goat. Son of a whore.* Beneath the hood the radiator boiled and steamed. Water gurgled in the hose.

"It's all right," she said. "Daddy, it's all right. It's fine enough you got us here." For one long minute I thought that maybe he would cry.

We made our picnic on a bluff over the wide red Medicine. To the south, the land seemed to fall off in stairsteps toward the plains of Oklahoma. Before I thought how it might be taken, what meanings lay within, I said, "Down there's the Dropping-Off Place." I gritted my teeth to think I had burst out with such a death-reminding thing, but Missus laughed.

"Why, yes," she said. "I haven't heard that name in years. We'd better watch our steps." She threw me a secret, confiding look, but I couldn't get my mouth to smile.

To the north lay a broad swale that caught the sunlight and the shadows of the racing clouds, as though the grassland were a moving picture screen laid out and green. Nearby, a wooden plaque nailed to a post marked a spot where the grass lodges of the Wichitas once stood. The plaque showed a wood-burned picture of a village of bound sheaves. The writing on it said that on this land a battle had been waged between two tribes. Whole, a phrase came to my mind unbidden but so sudden that I knew it was the truth: *Something terrible has happened here.* You could feel it in the rise of ground.

After our picnic, Missus napped beneath the canopy we made of sheets in the shade of a gnarled box elder. The sunlight filtered through the leaves, dappling her yellowed skin. A vein pulsed at her throat. A ways away, two blackbirds were at courting, flying at one another, one up, one down, then switching places and the other up, the other down, chittering all the while. If they mated, they did it beyond my sight.

Call went wandering in a wild plum thicket, the blossoms blown and new fruit setting on. From time to time I stirred myself to swat a gnat or to track his progress, but by and by I forgot to, forgot all else—her story and her knowledge, him as man, myself, the coming child—and just let be inside the day. I lay there on the great back of the grassy, rolling world, the sky so high and wide it ought to make you feel alone and small, but somehow made you rise up large, and thought of blessed nothing.

She heard Call's return before I did. I watched his presence come across her. Sickness fell away, and it was clear she loved him. She tried to rise on her elbows, but she couldn't. I plumped her pillows, helped her.

He had found a clutch of plums, still hard and green this early in the year, and he held them toward her. Her small, pale face was wistful, pleased, and somehow coy, and I understood the plums were a token of a time between them long before, some other place locked in her heart that she'd keep to herself. She clasped his hand, the plums folded inside it, to her breast.

Saying I needed to excuse myself, I went off. Crouched behind a stand of poke, I wept.

The sun set orange at our backs as we drove home, our headlamps on against the coming dark. She slept. Grasshoppers ticked and popped against the grille.

⟶

By now it was early May and the world had turned around by half. I wasn't the same person who had left War Drum, and the longer things went on, the more I understood I hadn't known exactly who that person was. I didn't now, so just went on.

One night I sat beside her bed in the spare room, sponging her with lemon water. It was that close to the end that she was wracked and failing for the final time, her body meager as an empty grain sack, her skin the color of wet ash, gray-blue and drowned. She lay still but for her hands, which fluttered at her flattened bosom, fingers plucking at her nightgown bodice as though to rid herself of something stored there. Suddenly, she spoke. "I want . . ."

I bent closer to hear. Her shallow breath gave off the smell of spoiled potatoes. "Mackie, will you put the pillow on my face?"

I stopped sponging.

"On my nose and mouth. I promise not to fight you. I'll hold still."

I told her that I couldn't.

"That brick." She pointed weakly toward the closet where we had to prop the door shut with a painted brick to stop it from swinging open. "If you did it fast, I wouldn't know."

I shook my head.

She was a long time getting out the words. "The pillow, then. A kindness. Mackie, please."

It was the only thing she wanted, the last thing left in her to want, but for everything I wanted that I took from her, I couldn't. I cried into my hands, "I can't," and she cried with me, tears rolling down her face and pooling on the pillow, saying, "Child, I know."

She lasted two more days, passing in and out of being while her body drew into itself. Call stayed out of her room all through this time, went on about his work, but I could hear him pounding in the anvil in the toolshed late at night, I saw the blisters on his palms, the ax marks gouged like splintered wounds out on the granary floor. Though I didn't love him any less, though I understood, I hated him a little.

The Hannahs performed last offices, dressing her, laying her out, and she was buried in the plot beside her stillborn babies. Dry-eyed, grim, Call took condolences. I helped with serving, spoke few words all that day. *Thank you. In the icebox. On the table. Yes,* and *Yes.*

I was in the kitchen after the service, after the last mourners had gone home, wrapping food in dish towels and covering bowls with dinner plates when I heard a howling sound like the one the wind would make before the dust began to blow, a fearsome, keening, human sound.

I went outside, my apron still around my middle, and looked about. The wail was coming from the barn. I crossed the yard and looked inside the bay. He knelt beside the hay. The sounds he made weren't words at all but wrath and anguish mixed. I turned and ran with my hands over my ears and the hard weight of the child a stone inside me. I went inside and slammed the door and cried. For her, for him, for me. For anyone who ever grieved for someone who was gone, for the world and everyone who rode its great broad back in bliss, forgetting what was coming. I cried for gratitude, for selfish love, for happiness and shame, for all things all at once.

In the morning when I got up, he was asleep in his own bed. I went around the kitchen quiet, boiling bedsheets, fixing his breakfast. I left a plate of eggs and scrapple in the warmer box and went outside to wring the sheets and hang them up to dry. The day was fine and beautiful. Swallows flew into the barn with wisps of straw to build their nests. From the high pasture came the bawling of a calf. Cottonwoods were sending off their seedling puffs to gather on the clothesline wires like batting. I went to turn the chickens out, feeling wifely and washed clean as the sickroom bedding hanging on the line.

In the air I felt a message that Lila was released, was happy, looking down at me with love and understanding, and I began to feel happy for myself. I believed I could make Call happy, too, and I began to hear the "Do Lord" song inside my head—*Oh, do remember me*—and then I whispered it and felt remembered—noticed—out of nowhere there in all the turning world, and when I came to the part about the home in gloryland that outshone the sun, the sun itself rose over the barn and glinted off the roof until it looked as red as flame. I took this as a sign the world had turned itself to right, all wrongs forgiven and all sorrow manumitted, and when the rooster crowed it was the trumpet blowing in the Year of Jubilee.

When I got back to the house my suitcase was on the step. On top of it and weighted with a rock rested a square white envelope, no writing on it or inside it, not my name, just five smooth twenty-dollar bills.

Vapor lay across the warming ground. Fog pooled softly in the low-lands, gray as the flannel wool the Hannahs had wound Lila in. I picked up the suitcase and started up the lane toward the road.

From the jimsonweed beside the road a locust gave out his electric warning. A kinglet swooped onto a barbed-wire fence to pull at a snag of cattle hair. In the shelter belt a mockingbird practiced his same song in a different tongue.

A warm, slow wind played out of the south. Beside the mailbox in the ditch a yellow barn tom stalked a hidden something in the grass, a mouse, a snake, a cricket. The cat's sand color made me think of Dad. I watched the creature for a time and watched him watch me back. When he shut his eyes against the sun, I glanced behind me to see Call's place, just once. I felt myself no different, no pillar hewn of salt. When I turned around the cat's gaze held me still. In my hand the leather suitcase strap felt as crumbled as Dad's leather Bible. I thought, *Etta's hands have been here.*

A black sedan came from the east, slowing when it hit the washboard patch of road before Call's lane, slowed further, the blown dust overtaking it in a cloud of grit. I shaded my eyes until the air cleared, walked up to the car. In the backseat were two Hannahs, the twins who called each other Sister, driven by a man I'd never seen. On their laps were towel-covered dishes. A warmish meat-and-onion smell came from the window. "Well," said one, "if it isn't little Mackie Spoon."

They took in suitcase, middle, knew the truth that these were telling, a truth they'd known before they knew it, all in that twin look.

"Soon-to-be-big, don't you mean?" one said, snickering. The other said, "Brother, just drive away."

I backed off from the window, but the brother stuck his head out, pushed his straw hat from his forehead. "Hot one today. Is there someplace we can take you, Miss?"

"The wayward home at Carmen is too far away," one sister said wickedly.

Flat-handed, the other spanked the seat. A puff of dust rose, caught a sunbeam. "Emory, that's her. Now, go! You hit the gas."

He turned to eyeball them. "Isn't this where you all wanted to come? To buy yourselves another gander at a scarlet woman with a pork pie ticket? Well, here she is."

"Brother, we did no such . . ."

"Looks to me like she had to have some help to get herself that way. What do you girls reckon?"

"Hisht!" said one. "Brother, shut your mouth." The other shouted, "Drive!"

All this happened fast, and what was said after this last, I didn't hear, for I had moved into the shelter belt to let the ferny leaves of tamarack close around me. Finally, the car began to move, turning into Call's lane. As it passed my hiding place the brother dipped his chin, then raised it, as if to let me know he'd got his sisters good for their mean spirits, wasn't he a sparkplug and a caution?

At this notion something hard and funny seemed to break loose inside me, and before I knew it I was laughing. Maybe at the way the old car jounced along the rutted lane, jolting them like robbers on the lam, or at the way whatever part of me had broken loose could hope that all that jolting spilled their homemade food for Call, their pork pie and their mustard greens, their weepy, tall meringues, had slopped a steaming mess of charity into their flowered laps.

It hit me I was crazy as a bug. I was unsound as Etta, with my feelings yanked around and nothing straight and all there was to do was laugh and laugh and never stop and this made me laugh louder at the sight I must have made, hiding in the tamaracks in my swelling apron, my schoolgirl lace-up brogans with dirty anklets walked down at the heels and pleated into wads that made my arches ache.

When I stopped laughing I was crying and I took the money from the envelope and stuck the bills down my dress front, walked out of the shelter belt, across the road, unlatched the box and threw the empty envelope inside. Missed three times, my hand was shaking so

and me so blind. I set the flag so Call would think he had a letter,
then I set off south.

⌒

I could have just as well stood still, or picked a way and held to it. If
you've ever been bogged down in indecision, where no choice open
to you seems right, you know the way I felt on the long day of my
wandering. I made up my mind to do one thing, and that was to seek
a sign to tell me what to do. I gave myself until the state line to decide whether to turn west and make toward the rescue home at Carmen, which was what girls in trouble did, or keep on south and go on
home to War Drum. I wanted to go neither. I wished a hole would
open in the middle of the road and draw me down.

The road was lined with sapling cedars, smelling of hot resin in
the oven day.

A jay so blue it hurt to look at darted branch to branch.

Far away a dog yipped once, as if somebody'd kicked it.

A few miles away from Call's at the lane head of a pretty farm,
two children had set up a lemonade stand. I was thirsty, and so I
headed toward it.

The children sat on upturned bushel baskets behind their table,
which was made of planks and sweet corn crates and spread with a
cloth printed with a map of Florida. Orange trees and palms and
mermaids all about. On top of this was set a china pitcher, crazed,
some hobnail jelly jars. They had a toy cash register with chipped red
paint, most of the key buttons gone. Both had stuck pencil stubs behind their ears. The boy wore a grown man's necktie, the bottom
tucked into his trouser waist. The girl had on a green isinglass eye-
shade, and she fussed happily with her wares. It seemed to me that
not that long before I'd been her age.

When I stopped in front of them, they grew shy and wouldn't
meet my gaze. I said, "Hello."

The girl pointed to a sign bordered in crayoned bees and daisies. *Lemonade, One Cent,* it read.

In my dress front were the twenty-dollar bills. "I don't have any change."

"That's all right. Here's some." The girl fished in the cash register drawer and drew out a Nehi bottle top. "Use this." She handed me a glass of lemonade. The taste of dirt no obstacle, I drank it down.

Behind them, across a hayfield, some men worked on a bale wagon. A draft horse shook its harness and the jingle traveled all the way across the field. Set in a ring of trees was a farmhouse. A woman appeared at the doorway, then headed toward the swatch of white from towels on a clothesline. I wondered what it might be like to go up to the door, the way Audie once had done, present myself for work. Maybe the children were my sign.

The boy tugged at my skirt. "Who's mad at you?"

"Nobody is."

He toed my suitcase. "Then why you running off?"

"I'm not," I said, "I'm just out for a little walk." I shaded my eyes to look at the sun, seeing the way one lie begot another. "I'd better go. I'm late."

A mile or so beyond them, I bent to take off my shoes, those anklets, now so worked down and dusty that when I peeled them off, they were striped. It was only then that it struck me that I'd left my suitcase at the lemonade stand. I decided not to turn around to fetch it. It would seem like giving in. Worse, I imagined Call stowing my things inside it, and I didn't want to know if he had folded them or thrown them. I was better off without it. I slung the shoes over my shoulder, holding them by the laces, and walked on. For some reason I thought of Etta barefoot, hopeful on the schoolhouse road. I thought, *What have I done?*

I moved into open country. Field on field of seedling beans and melons. Insects hummed, heat rose in waves, mirages shimmered.

Far ahead was a tree line, but oddly low on the horizon, like a stand of sumac. I began to long to reach its cover, as a nameless fear had come upon me, and I felt exposed to someone watching. Someone large and merciless. Each time a shoe nudged at my back, it spooked me, but when I turned around to look, I saw only empty land, that sky.

In those years, dog packs roamed the countryside. Hounds and shepherds, mastiffs, dogs left behind when farmsteads were abandoned, had formed packs, ran wild. They ravaged henhouses and killed stock. They killed goats and cows at calving, yearling colts. Near War Drum a baby girl left napping under an elm tree not six feet from a kitchen window was nearly torn in two. A little boy was maimed, his forehead torn from his skull bone. A woman digging sassafras escaped by climbing a tree, but not before those dogs had bitten both her heels to bone. I wondered whether to put on my shoes, to better run. Decided I should carry them, as they'd be good to throw. There was nothing else of weight, no rock, no stick, but only grass and sand.

A presence had been creeping up behind me. Engine sound, the knock of a thrown rod. Had Call come after me; was that the sign?

I turned to see a sleek gray car, its wirework radiator gleaming, stark. I moved to the roadside, kept walking, waved the driver on. But the car stayed close, slowing to a crawl, so close I felt the engine's heat. My bare heels felt exposed. What I knew of dogs and dog packs mixed with other dangers. Run, the tamest animal will chase you. Stand your ground, and you might have a chance. Best is to pretend you're not afraid and try to keep the smell of fear inside you. I stopped walking, put my hands on my hips, brogans poking outward from my hips like heavy leather wings, and turned to stare down the driver.

Behind the dusted windshield sat a hatted man. He braked the car, its big tires crunched on gravel.

"You go away," I shouted.

He opened the door and got out.

"I don't want a ride. Go on."

He was a wiry, bandy-legged man in city clothes that looked too big for him. From sitting at the wheel, the tops of his pleated trousers stuck out like a shelf below his belt. His pant legs hung like nothing was inside them. He wore a short-sleeved shirt white as a cattle egret. Beneath a straw fedora that was yellow-banded, battered, his face looked wrinkled, as though he'd napped on rabbit wire. Somehow his smallness made him seem more fierce than if he'd been a giant.

I wanted most to run, to put whatever distance between us in whatever time I had before he caught me, for I could fairly feel his stringy grip. In the ditch a redwing blackbird flushed, so close I felt the whir of wings. The strange thought came to me that I needed Etta. With her wicked mouth and look of no-flies-on-me, she would have put him in his place.

He drew nearer. His body cast a shadow that fell between us like a figure in a fun house mirror, squat, zigzagged. The sunlight fell on his hat brim so that specks of light pierced through its weave, and when he moved the spangles raced across the ground toward me, flashing, swift as minnows.

His voice was a surprise. I expected menace, but heard softness, his tone as low and needful as a preacher's in a loving patch of scripture. "Little honey, where you from?"

Something—maybe amazement at his voice, the sweetness of the name he called me, the name Lila had used, and the way in his mouth the word seemed mockery, how alone I was—made me understand that one nice word would be the end of me. "Don't you call me that!" I shouted.

His expression turned to sheepish in an instant, then shaded into mournful slyness. "Alls I did was ask where you was from."

His teeth were yellow as his hatband. His eyes had narrowed into slits as keen as any weasel's. He took a few steps toward me. "How about a ride, wherever?"

I moved back as many steps, careful with my gait so not to give myself away. "I like to walk."

"You'll never get nowhere that way." A husky laugh clicked in his throat. "Honey." His upper lip was thin, the lower fuller, downward-pointing, ugly. "You tell me your name I'll stop calling you that and use your real one. Mine's Dean Dexter."

I doubted this. "It isn't anything."

"You got one, don't you, honey? Missy No-name. Missy Priss."

I started walking toward the tree line, and he took up pace beside me. "Got people waiting for you? Don't know anybody around here has lost a girl like you. Anybody did, I expect he'd be out after her. And ain't it odd that I don't see another soul around?"

Run—the word as urgent as red letters in a Bible came to me, but I walked on.

He kept apace, heat from his body reaching me, closer than a shadow.

I yelled, "Leave me alone!"

And then he fully laughed, as though to say he'd gotten from me what he wanted, but just the taste enough to make him want it more. "Can't do that, honey. Can't just leave you now."

I flung a shoe. It missed and landed in the middle of the road. I flung the other. This one's aim was wilder yet. And then I ran. Barefoot on the soft sand road, I couldn't run fast enough to get beyond him, but he never made to catch me, merely trotted alongside, making catching motions, growling like a beast and saying "Now I gotcha, now I gotcha," and I saw that whatever was upon him—hatefulness or menace, teasing—didn't matter, he was dogging me for sport.

The trees were just ahead, a narrow bridge crossing a wooded gully. My chest felt torn, my breathing ragged. Under my ribs a stitch pierced.

But by and by he fell behind, and when I looked around to check, he stood mopping at his forehead with a handkerchief. I went on, and the next thing I heard was his engine in the lowest gear but gaining speed, a shift, another gear, another, and the car sped past, fishtailing just before the bridge for show. I had to shut my eyes against the dust he spun, but I heard the tires atreadle on the bridge boards. When I opened up my eyes, the car was gone. I was damp between my legs. In all the running, all the fear, I'd wet myself. If Dean Dexter was a sign of anything, it was that I was scared.

I scrambled down the gully and went beneath the bridge, planning to hide in case he was waiting up ahead. The bridge spanned a shallow creek running brownish red between packed clay banks. Near the waterline were tracks of creatures come to drink, possums and raccoons, bird and mice, but over these were laid the footprints of a barefoot child who must have stood a while beside the creek, then moved up the bank. At the water's edge was a raft made out of planks and crooked sticks, tied with wire and clothesline rope, a child's job of work. At the center of the raft was nailed a seat of short board, fashioned like Call's T-bar milking stool. For a time I leaned against a bridge piling to catch my breath, smelled hot creosote and aging wood, the prickling of splinters sharp through my sleeve, felt that dampness between my legs, cold now.

After I calmed down, I stepped out of my drawers and carried them to the water to rinse them, squatting near the edge beside the raft. Jumped when a school of dace darted away. In the rusty-looking water I swirled the drawers, then wrung them, flapped them in the air. I balled them up and put them in my pocket.

A rustle drew my notice to the hollows under the bridge. A boy, a sturdy, wide-eyed child with dishwater-colored hair in a bowl cut like a Dutch boy's, a double cowlick at his forehead so the bangs stuck up like feelers and made him look a little like a locust. Between his knees he held a gunnysack.

His voice sounded clogged, as though he'd been having himself a cry. "I thought you was my pa." The gunnysack appeared to wiggle, and the boy gave it a pat.

"I'm not," I said. "Who are you?"

He sniffed. "Lee Ivey." He was the kind of boy you smiled at just to see, for his look of brotherness. "Who are you?"

I said my name. Thinking of Dean Dexter, I said, "I'm not going to pester you, so don't you worry."

"Wasn't." He said it *wadn't.* He hefted the gunnysack, swinging it a little. "Got six little baby kitty cats in here. I got to drownd them or get skinned."

Dean Dexter still on my mind, I asked, "What color is your pa's car?"

He shook his head. "Skinned raw."

I asked again what color.

He wiped his nose on his shirtsleeve. "It's a truck. It's busted. Blackish tan."

I gathered my skirt and took a seat beside him. The company felt good. The earth beneath the bridge felt moist and cool. I caught a snaky smell. The ground was pocked with holes. From the water came a plop.

"Bullfrog," Lee Ivey said.

"What's that raft? You going to sail away?"

"Won't float." He opened the gunnysack, drawing out kittens until six were lined up on the dirt. "Ever see a bunch so cute and tiny?"

I allowed I hadn't seen their like.

He picked up a calico. One of its eyes was trying to open, a tiny matted seam. He held the little cat so its belly poked out and its hind legs dangled, then he sniffed the belly, ran his lips across the whorled fur. "We got too many." He put down the kitten and arranged it with the others, moving them into a size rank. "This here is Big Boy. Here's Elijah and Buster Brown and Tom. This one is Dan Gray. The runty one is Monk."

"All boys?"

He screwed up his mouth in a little ducklike way to think, then nodded. "Yes'm, ever one."

"Why don't you just move them far away? Make a nest for them somewhere. The mama cat'll find them."

"Done that. She just go gets them back. She hauls them right on back. It's either leave them in the open for the coyotes or else put them in the creek."

He gathered the kittens, putting them gently into the sack, saying their names. "There, Dan Gray, there Buster Brown." As he worked, his cowlicks swayed. When he had finished, he looked me level. His one eye pupil was slotted like a keyhole, black bleeding into blue. "Say they was yours, what do you reckon you would likely do?"

All the while I'd been up on the road with my trouble, he'd been down below with his, and there was no good answer for either of us. I said I didn't know.

"They'll make good mousers once they get grown up." Something about Lee Ivey made me think of Teeny Birdsall, how he was persuasive and a seller, and he seemed to know his mind. Knew right from wrong and could divine what mattered most whether it had to do with pigeon eggs or kittens. I wondered if he was my sign.

He opened the sack and stuck his face inside, drew a long breath. His face looked hopeful, blinded more than by that eye. "You want to smell them?"

I knew the smell, which broke your heart for its familiarness, warm milk and fur, wet bran, and I knew he wanted me to love them, take them with me. No matter what I did with them, he could believe a kinder end for them than the one he had to be the author of.

"I have to get on, now," I told him. Sign or no, I didn't want those cats.

"Maybe I'll walk a ways with you. Is your foot plain crooked, or did you step on a sticker?"

I told him I guessed it was plain crooked, and he nodded. "Ol' Buster Brown is poor-born, too. Got one just like."

"I have to hurry. I'll be late." I turned away and made to leave.

"To where?"

I wanted to say "Home," if only for the comfort of the word, but couldn't, as I didn't have one. And suddenly I couldn't say the other—*rescue home*—not even in my mind. I lied again and said, "The doctor's."

From his look I saw how powerfully he wanted to believe me. "For your foot, I reckon."

I said, "Yes." I said, "I'll see you, then."

He held out the gunnysack. "They don't weigh a feather. Looks like I run up on the just right person at the just right time." He smacked his forehead in a show of revelation. "A doctor'd take and feed them with a dropper!"

"No," I said, but then, so help me—maybe as payment for my lie, or because he put me in mind of Teeny, or maybe just to hold off deciding where to go—I took the kittens. Reached out and snatched the sack from him and started walking.

He followed me up the bank and onto the bridge, where he stood waving as I crossed the wooden planks. "Eyedropper's the ticket," he called out. "And don't forget their names." He said them one by one, Big Boy, Elijah, Buster Brown and Tom, Dan Gray and Monk.

It was late afternoon. The air sang loud with locusts and grasshoppers. Out on the plain, a prairie chicken gave a barrel-thumping drumhead call—a whoomp-a-whoom that made my heart pound. I hadn't gone a few steps past the bridge when I turned off and left the road and went back into the ravine where I felt safer, thinking to follow the creek bank in the shelter of the trees, for I was scared again.

I felt a cross between a woman and a girl, nothing to nobody, not a sister, daughter, woman, wife. Only a lone person who had left behind her shoes, her suitcase, and her pride, who had traded all for the burden of a sack of cats. As I made my way along the creek I had the sense of being watched, but every time I turned around I saw only the shadows of the leaves above me. The steps I thought I heard were just the gurgle of the creek. I walked and walked, intending to find a deep spot near the bank and hold the gunnysack beneath the water. When I was satisfied Lee Ivey hadn't followed me, I stepped down the muddy bank and waded out into the middle where the water came up to my knees.

I thought of all that had happened since the morning, felt I'd lived a year in just a day. I wondered what the others I met on the way were doing at this hour, now nearly dusk. The Hannah sisters, had they gone to town and told the tale of Lucas's hired girl hiding in a hedgerow? The children on the road, were they splashing in a tin tub in their side yard, telling their mother of the walker, showing her the suitcase? The man who chased me, was he sitting down to supper, elbows on the table, hat pushed back, his necktie loosed, that wicked leer turned bland, the image of a simple, hungry man? I tried to feature who was serving him his plate, and did she know the kind of man he was when he was by himself? What would Lee Ivey tell his pa about the girl out on the road? Call, I couldn't fathom. Was he going about his chores washed clean by work? Mending harrow, milking, hammering, or was he a lone man in a darkened kitchen, his head down on the table? Had he gone to a prayer meeting, was he standing in the pew beside the others singing "Throw Out the Lifeline?" Did he think of who was truly sinking? I thought of Etta, Audie, Dad. Of Mam and Lila somewhere in the air. There was no one who loved me or who didn't who could know where I was standing at that hour.

The gunnysack was still, no movement, but when I shook it gently there came a little shift, a mewling sound. I put my hand beneath it. Warm. The kittens wouldn't last without their mother. *Lost without me,* came Mam's voice.

To make their suffering short would be a kindness. There was nothing else to do. And so I lowered the sack into the water, held it down. I waited. I tried to cry for them but couldn't. They were better off. And then I crossed over to the northern bank and stepped out of the water on the side I had just come from, and I started back for Call's, dry-eyed and determined.

This was my reasoning: I'd read the first signs wrong. In the awful minutes while I waited for the burlap to soak up the water, waited for the little cats to cease their struggling, I saw how wrong I was to read the signs that morning as a message I should leave. I understood how shame caused me to read them so. The suitcase on the doorstep might have meant only that I was to move out of the house until a proper time had passed, stay in my little house a while. The money was a gift for the extra care I gave to Lila at the end. He needed time to grieve. He deserved a second chance. He didn't know about the child—I hadn't told him but had kept the knowledge to myself the same way I'd once bottled up my love for Audie.

This reasoning let me push time forward and see us at our supper table, two old people with our grown child going off to make his way. "Remember when you thought . . . " Call would begin, and my long walk would turn into a story he would tell on me when we were old. How we would laugh.

The way back seemed shorter. Along the shoulder of the treeless stretch I found my shoes, just where they'd landed. I didn't find my suitcase; at no lane end was there a sign of any lemonade stand. I walked, thinking of how the seasons of our life were now beginning, how once we were past this one, another one would come, another, then another, until this present one was so far behind us it would be forgotten. Beneath these thoughts I said Lee Ivey's cat names like a prayer, until they finally became one.

The moon was on its way back down by the time I reached Call's lane. My apron was still draped across the mailbox, as though I'd merely shucked it off to take a walk. The empty envelope was still inside the box. I took it out and started down the lane toward the side house. As I passed the back door of the big farmhouse, June bugs sizzed and popped against the screen. Moths flurried at the porch light. Which Call had left on.

I woke up to light cast from the west across the windowsill to see the iron bedstead at my feet, the chest of drawers, the washstand, and the wooden table. It was late afternoon, I'd passed the day in sleeping. My legs cramped when I lowered my feet, as stiff as hooves and swollen, to the rag rug on the floor.

I went to the window, hoping my mind would snag on something to recall the day, the time. As though through sleep, it came to me that it was Thursday. A Thursday in late May of 1938.

Thirst parched my throat, but a pain low in my belly pulsed. I bent over from the pressure, trying to decide which relief to seek. Even this small choice seemed too hard to make.

I stepped outside, passed by the water pump, and hurried to the backhouse. Mare's tail clouds streaked crimson with the sunset gave evidence of wind at sometime during the day, but now the air was still and close as in a weekday sanctuary. *You are at Call's,* I told myself, *you're back at Call's where you belong. You're pulling at the thread spool on the backhouse door.*

Inside, I shut the door, pulled up my dress, and sat. Wondered where my drawers had gone and found them in my pocket. Above, a wasp spun wildly, buzzing in the rafters. Afterward, I went out to the well and primed the pump until it gushed, drank waughts of warmish, nickel-tasting water. I couldn't get enough.

I turned to wipe my mouth with the back of my hand, and there was Call, two brimming milk pails yoked across his shoulders. The milk gave off a green, spring smell of clover. He stood between me and the setting sun.

I wanted to tell him where I'd gone and what had happened, how I turned around and why. But his very shadow seemed rebuke, and when I found my voice, the driest croak despite all the water and sounding so like Etta's that it made my throat lump up in pain before the words would come, "I'm going to have a baby."

I looked down at my feet, streaked and dirty as in the worst days of the storms, but then something made me raise my head and look at him full face.

When he asked me whose it was, the question sank inside me like a stone dropped in a well.

His shoulders quivered as a horse's will to shuck the reins. Turning slowly to keep the pails from sloshing, he set out walking toward the house.

I went inside, lay on the bed, the sheet still damp from earlier. Found the twenty-dollar bills still stuck inside my dress, made sodden by my skin. I slept.

The next morning on the sandstone slab at my door was an enamel basin turned bottom up, and beneath it was a plate holding a heel of bread, a ham rind, and two hard-boiled eggs. I had eaten nothing since the day after the service, and then only a dab. I looked around for Call, but he was nowhere near. With the dishpan between my knees for a table as in my old chicken dinner game, the plate of food on top, I sucked the sweet fat of the ham rind, cracked and peeled the eggs, devoured them.

Beside the water pump, he had propped the scuffle hoe. I picked it up and shouldered it. No one who came up in hard times could fail to understand the bargain. It told me, too, that never mind his awful question, he full and well knew whose. It would take time.

Behind the henhouse lay the garden—a half acre of tomatoes, melons, squash, cucumbers, beans. I went there to weed. I hoed away the morning, looking up from time to time to see if in my diligence he saw me, but I caught no glimpse. The heat that day was terrible. The minute any weed was severed from its root, it wilted up and browned.

The noon hour came. I wondered if he was waiting for me to go into the kitchen and cobble up some dinner, if, as with his leaving of the scuffle hoe, I was to act on signs. With my dress hem I wiped my face and neck. I went to the pump to wash the field dirt off, made ready to go in. If there was bread on hand, I'd make a pudding. There should be raisins soaking in a jar, as I had set them only days before. My mouth went all to water at the memory of their dark taste. At the kitchen door, I propped the hoe so he would see it there and know.

The door was locked.

The next morning on my step I found the same dishpan, beneath it a crude wedge of apple pie, another ham scrap, and some butter cake—funeral food now going stale and dry. I wolfed the ham and cake, but though I craved it with a power that was near murderous, I saved the pie for noon.

I hoed again that morning, working slower to save my strength. When the sun was overhead, I went into the shade of the mulberry tree to eat the pie. In the distance I heard his tractor chug. Set among the elms, the house looked fine and peaceful. With its shutters green as pasture grass, its purple hollyhocks in bloom beside the porch, it looked serene. Then I saw, beside the kitchen door and mounded high, the woven laundry basket.

I fairly ran. The basket held the wash of several days, his shirts and overalls, his good white Sunday shirt. The back door was un-locked.

Inside, I lit the stove. Put on the kettle. Set another pot to boil and into it dropped navy beans, a hock, some bay leaves, salt, and pepper. Chopped an onion, dumped that in as well. Piecing on left-over funeral food, I straightened things and set the kitchen right. All afternoon the cooking smells rose up in clouds of steam, and I cared nothing for how hot it got, for joy rose just the same in me. I did the wash and hung it out, set the table with white plates and forks and knives that matched. In a bowl I set some hollyhocks to float and had the fool's dream of our sweet reunion.

Midafternoon, to make myself presentable, I took a shower bath and washed my hair. I brushed it dry, then tied it with a ribbon. When I opened Lila's jar of Pond's cold cream to smooth onto my sunburned face, I found it gone to grease, only a trace of smell behind. For the first time since she died, her absence seemed to pin me to the spot. I shut the jar lid, quick. I tidied the bathroom, gathering towels for another wash load, but no bustling and no task could take away the cold cream smell, and so I cut the fire under the beans and dashed the hollyhocks and water out the door and ran outside. Even I could see it was too soon.

⌒

Here are the sayings I took comfort in: All things come to those who wait; Providence helps those who help themselves; Patience is a virtue. I allowed myself one pleasure, which was to write imaginary letters to my sister.

Dear Etta, I wrote in my imagination, *by the time this reaches you I'll be a married woman, and so that makes two of us, could you have imagined? I hope you're well and happy. If you get up this way, drop in. Our place is small but pretty. I am turning into quite the cook! My husband Call will likely weigh three hundred pounds before the year is out. In our garden we grow this-that-and-the-other.* On and on and in my mind I built a picket fence around the sorry truth. It didn't strike me then that in these letters in my mind there was no mention of my coming child, or how clearly you could see another's blindness and yet stay blinded to your own.

⌒

Of letters, I had one from Call. A note. I used a certain mug for coffee, and one morning when I went in to start the housework it was on the table, a folded piece of foolscap paper stuck inside. *Town this afternoon. Write down what you need. C. Lucas.*

Well, I thought, snatched up the pencil, wrote down, *You.* Burned this in the pilot light and took another scrap of paper from his desk.

Staples—flour, sugar, salt, black pepper, coffee, yeast. We were fine for meat and vegetables and dairy, as most came from the farm. Toward the end, Lila craved lemons, and I had taken on a taste for them as well. *Some lemons,* I wrote at the bottom of the list, *and I'll make you a pie.*

All morning as I did the housework, the list lay on the table, and every time I passed it I thought of something new to add—cocoa, coconut, bananas—but I held back. These things were rare, expensive. I didn't want to ask too much, too soon. But I knew things had changed, and when the noon hour rolled around and he came in I wouldn't scuttle off. I'd stay inside to greet him. I would hand him the list in person and tell him he could drop me at the market as we had done before. It had been a week since I'd been off the place, and I was eager for the sight of people.

He didn't come at noon. Whether it was that he was busy elsewhere, or that he saw I hadn't left, he stayed away. I ached to dump his pork chops in the garbage, or sling them to the chickens, to eat the food myself, but I left the plate in the warmer box and went out.

That afternoon I set myself the task of scraping the henhouse floor. With the grain shovel I dug at the shaling layers, heaved slabs of mess outside, and raised dust thick with the malty smell of straw and oyster shell and feathers. I set my jaw, gritted my teeth, and shoveled.

He had taken on two boys to odd-job, to help get ready for wheat harvest, Costins from the farm two sections over. Mornings, I would see them coming down the lane. Towheaded twelve-year-olds in overalls and canvas shirts, lean as herons and all knees and elbows, toting lard pail dinner buckets. Evenings they made their way back up the lane, dragging sorely, but not so beaten that they couldn't kite about after a rabbit if their collie harried one, or flushed a pheasant from the shelter belt.

I learned who they were from another note left in my cup: *Costin kids to help out. Stay if it suits you but keep to yourself. C. Lucas.*

I didn't have to be told the reason. Their mother had traveled with the Hannahs until she gave birth to triplet girls. Zada Costin was a busybody—even Lila said so. As much I yearned to go out to the boys with cold sweet tea or pie, I stayed inside.

In truth, I worried most about the Hannahs. Every day as I worked in the house I checked the windows, ready to hide if any car nosed down the lane. But by now a full three weeks had passed since I met the sisters and their brother in the lane, and unless the pastor paid a call on the day of my long walk, no one had dropped by. This was strange, as it was the custom to keep up the flood of food and social calls after a death. I figured Call had told it at the church that he wanted no visitors, and people were honoring his wishes.

Tramps and drummers and wayfarers sometimes passed through. Some asked if we had work, any job of tinkering or mending, weed-cutting or the like. I didn't presume to give them tasks, but I would feed them. Some of the cleaner-looking ones I invited inside. Against the thought that one would bother me—the memory of Dean Dexter was still fresh—I kept beside the drainboard the bone-handled cleaver, weighty as an ingot.

But if a few of these travelers were shifty-eyed, their gazes darting, most of them were shy and grateful. I asked them questions. Where they were headed, where they had been, who their people were. Some would say and some would not. Some changed the subject onto the weather or the changing times, the threat of war. I heard a good many stories, only half of which I took for truth. Often, as I listened, I was reminded of my long day on the road, of those children who had sold me lemonade for nothing but a Nehi bottle top, of Lee Ivey and his cats, and I wondered if I would someday stand for something in those travelers' minds. What would my message be? A young expectant woman in a well-kept house, a plate of beans and side meat, a kind word. If you discounted that the man whose child I carried wouldn't claim me, I made a pretty picture.

Yes, I'd say, *that is my husband out there. Yes, the baby's due in late Octo-ber. Yes, our first.*

Each day I meant to waylay Call and ask what we were going to do, but each day one thing or another stopped me. Truth was, I was afraid that he would send me off. My walk had shown me that I had nowhere to go, and there was not a thing to do but wait.

Anybody reading might well wonder why I went on wanting him. Truth was, I didn't know. By then I'd wanted him so long, I didn't know how not to.

———

Waiting can make time go cockeyed, dragging now and racing then, with hours lost between the times you come awake again to your own waiting, hours crawling while you wish for something, any-thing, to happen, if only just to end the waiting.

July came around. The first year of no dust storms. No bad thun-derstorms as well, although one afternoon chain lightning out of nowhere popped in fiery balls across the dining room. Crops flour-ished. Call stayed out from dawn to dusk. I felt myself slow down, felt boneless, waiting, big. Days went by like barn-bound cattle on a well-worn path. I wanted sleep. Some days I could scarcely keep my eyelids open.

One afternoon I picked some early green tomatoes and sliced a platter of them, then fried up some bacon so as not to heat the kitchen at the hottest hour. I set these things aside for later. There be-ing nothing left to do except some mending I could well put off, I went into the spare room and lay down on Lila's bed.

I had cleared away the sickroom things. The room looked spare and clean. The oak bedstead, a gate-leg table and a chest of drawers, the crooked closet door stopped with the painted brick she'd once asked me to bring down. Limp curtains hung at the north window, no breeze at all to stir them. From outside came the sounds of guinea clack, cicada chirr, the distant barking of the collie dog. In the window a fly buzzed at the screen, making a drowsy droning sound. I closed my eyes, thinking about the day Call and I would lie together on an actual bed.

Commotion at the back door woke me from a doze. People were in the house. I heard voices in the kitchen, the clank of cutlery and water running in the sink. Heavy-limbed and clumsy, I shot up from the bed and lurched toward the closet, nudged away the brick and went inside and shut the door.

Through the crack I saw my shape still on the bed but I didn't dare slip out to smooth the spread. I crouched back into the hanging clothes, winter items stiff and woolen, smelling strong of naphthalene and camphor, rested against a tottery stack of pasteboard cartons.

A sudden slice of light told me the closet door was creeping open. I snatched the knob to draw the door, but a screw fell off and pinged onto the floor. It rolled across the floorboards out of sight and the knob came off in my hand, leaving only the ridged square bar. I put the knob in my apron pocket, pinched at the bar, and drew it inside the well to hold the door closed.

They were in the kitchen, Hannahs come to minister, to check and clean. The house rang with their voices, with the sound of cupboard doors, pot clatter.

"He's really gone to town in here!"

"Look at this mess of bacon!"

I imagined them inspecting the bacon beneath its blotting paper, looking up at one another, wondering. Tomatoes sliced so neat they'd shuffle like a deck of cards. The dishes in the drain rack. A kettle soaking in Bon Ami.

"Who'd have time for woman's work and farmwork, too?"

"Well, he hasn't been to service or to meeting."

"Some men don't need a woman but for . . . You ask me, that's why she got sick. Because she had the leisure to."

"Hush that."

"Look here, he's left the cleaver out."

"That's odd."

There came a clang as someone set a pot on the stove, the smell of phosphorous as a lucifer match was struck against the stove board.

Then they moved along the hallway toward Call's bedroom.

"I declare, I never met a man who'd make his own bed up, and look!"

I'd made it just that morning, changed the sheets. A nickel would have bounced.

"I'll bet he hasn't touched her clothes."

The closet door in the other room creaked. "Look at all these precious little dresses. Remember this yellow one? Back before her color turned?"

"Girls, we oughtn't."

"He told us he would tend to it."

"Yes, but will he?"

"Some hang on. Refuse to change a thing."

"Do you think we should have put her in this gray batiste?"

"No, she was too salled there at the end. The blue was fine, and with that lily pin."

"He gave her that. He was good to her. Little presents and the like."

Somebody whispered something, and somebody laughed. "A big strong man in his full prime with a sick wife? He wouldn't be the first."

"I don't want to hear that, girls. A man can love a woman plain and simple and not stray."

"Well, Lila was an easy one to love. Never asked for anything. Not once."

Their talk went on. My fingers crabbed up on the doorknob bar. I switched hands, shook out the stiffness in my fingers. To ease my back, now knifing across the hips, I straightened.

"At least that Maggie girl is off and gone."

"Mackie," somebody corrected.

Inside the closet I felt hollowed out and sin-sick.

"Sister and I saw her on the road day after. Toting an old suit-case."

"Who did she think she was fooling? Did she think the world and all us on it was born yesterday? Don't you wonder who it was to get her in the family way?"

"Some field hand or some drummer. Sweet-talked her. A shame."

"Where do you reckon she got off to?"

"Masons had a cousin's daughter who went down to Carmen to the rescue home. Maybe off down there."

"I just wonder if Call knew."

"Oh, no! He'd have run her off."

Now they moved out of his room and down the hall to the spare room. My hand cramped, clutching at the bar. They weren't three feet from where I crouched behind the door.

"Well, here's a thing. He's left this bed arumple. Looks like he maybe laid down for a nap."

"On Lila's very bed."

The room was hushed until somebody said, "We ought to shut that window. Rain is on the way, and it'll wick the curtains."

When the window slammed, it startled me. I jumped. Behind me the stack of cartons shifted, then thumped against the wall.

"Listen," one said. "Hush."

I gave up every hope of hiding, knew the door would open to reveal me. What would I say? That I'd come back to clean the closets, fell asleep? There was no answer for my being there that wouldn't damn us both.

Outside, their silence held, but then they moved away, moved out the spare room door and down the hall.

Call had come in.

"This kitchen gets the Good Housekeeping Seal," one of them said brightly.

I didn't hear his answer. I opened the closet door a crack, reached around and pulled out the outside knob and bar, then pulled the brick back into place. Then I made space on the floor and settled down to wait.

The smell of brewing coffee wafted through the house, and the sound of rattling cups and saucers calmed me. I heard the words *Molasses cake*. I knew they wouldn't snoop through things with Call around. All again I had to do was wait.

Late in the afternoon they took their leave, and at last the back door closed and their cars pulled up the lane. In the quiet house Call groaned, a rumbling, wolfish growl.

This scared me, but I quelled the feeling. I was proud of my quick thinking, proud the Hannahs hadn't found us out. I got up from the floor. My bad foot had gone to sleep, and so I stood on it lightly, putting down the weight and waiting while the electric ring of it shot up my spine until the feeling came back right. Then I went into the kitchen.

In a chair he sat, legs splayed and head thrown back, eyes closed.

I cleared my throat. "I've been in the spare room closet all along. They didn't know it."

He didn't move except to work his jaw.

"All this time." Of a sudden I felt sorry for myself. My throat lumped up, but before I could swallow he was out of his chair, knocked it across the floor and was on me, all grasp and wrench. His breath was foul with coffee as he roared, "I told you!" My skull fair racketed with shaking.

Here is one of the hardest parts to tell. I let him. Let him yank me by the forearms yon and hither in that kitchen. Didn't pull away and didn't fight or cry or yell back at him. Made myself go limp and took it. And I didn't take it thinking it my due. I knew how wrong it was.

But in all the ugliness, in all his wrath and my surrender, there was a brutal thrill. He had feeling for me and I knew it and was glad. No matter that his anger scalded me like lye and his grip fair broke my skin, I rejoiced. I met his gaze, looked level at him, matched his fierceness with my own.

Now something other passed between us, fiercer yet and ancient-feeling, and we both of us could feel it and the feeling flared. He yanked my dress and pushed it upward. I helped him, met his mouth as it mashed into mine. He sheared the counter of its plates and orts of that molasses cake and pushed me up and back across it. I set myself against the wood and wrapped my legs around him as he entered hard and dry and searing and then of a sudden flooded, and for the sounds we made a hearer couldn't tell if we were battling unto death or in another state, and I believe we neither one of us knew, either. What I knew, then, was almighty empty-headed need, its ease.

Anyone who's had this kind of union knows the way we felt, those moments after. Anyone who hasn't, ought to. Once, if only just to know.

My apron had slid around and tangled. In the middle of the act, when the doorknob in my pocket barked against the sink, I couldn't think of what it was, for I'd forgotten putting it there. Now I drew it out, crazed porcelain, egg white, the kind you put beneath a hen to coax her into laying. "This came off the closet door. You ought to fix it."

He took it, held out his other hand for me to grasp, helped me move down from the cabinet to my feet. "That didn't hurt you, did it?"

"Which?"

He pinched his nose bridge and looked down. "Either."

This answer and his seeming shame were enough for me to read apology, and so I told him, "No."

He cast about the kitchen as though for something to fix his notice on. The chair he'd flung, a broken plate, cake leavings on the floor. He asked me, "Do you want a cup of coffee?"

I shook my head. "This mess won't clean itself, but it can wait until tomorrow. I'll see you then."

Standing at the stove, eating the laid-out bacon like a starving man, he nodded.

I was halfway to my house before I remembered that we hadn't spoken of the child, what would become of it, of us. *Next time,* I told myself. *Next time.*

⤳

The wheat was ripe. It looked to be a bumper. The soil was just-right-dry. Nights, I fell asleep listening to the wind rustling the whiskered heads.

Call hired a threshing crew of migrant custom cutters, twelve men as work gang and two women to cook. He came to the door of the side house to tell how things would be. He hoped to cut a twenty-bushel acre. The crew would come the Monday hence. I would help with meals, three big ones every day set out on plank-and-sawhorse tables in the yard. The boss's family would board inside the house. The crew would sleep on bedrolls in the barn. For the duration, I could use the bathroom in the house, leaving the back-house to the hands.

With each new bit of news, another question rose—in all of this, what would I be to him? I had grown past the stage when anyone could mistake for simple weight my woman body. As the Bible put it, I was great with child. But he went away before I had the chance.

All the next day I featured ways to frame my question, but I couldn't catch him long enough to ask. That afternoon, when I was down in the root cellar taking stock of canned goods, working while the daylight held, his shadow fell across me. "Girl, you listen here."

This was the first time he had called me by any distinction whatsoever. He had yet to say my name. I set down a jar of string beans and looked up the stairwell.

"You go on and look in her closet and get you some of her old dresses and let them out. That one's popped out at the buttons." He cleared his throat. "The story is that you're her cousin up from Texas, and you come to me in trouble."

Something—maybe what we had done in the kitchen and maybe his lie, maybe just the fact I couldn't see his face—made me bold. "Who do I say the baby's father is?"

"You make up what you want. Nobody's going to ask."

In the time it took me to look down at the jar in my hand and read the words *Ball Dome,* he'd gone.

~

Down the lane at sundown came the threshers in a caravan led by the John Deere Model D pulling the enormous steam-powered reaper, followed by four mule-driven bundle wagons and two trucks loaded with tools and rakes and forks and spools of binder twine. They would cut first thing in the morning, after the dew burned off.

They had arrived past suppertime and didn't expect a meal, but in our excitement Vesta Tannahill and her girl Mavis and I laid out a spread of cold cuts and set up a vat of sweet tea.

The stack and bundle crew was made up of bindle stiffs, young men and boys whose names I barely caught. A rangy man named Coltis but called Speck for his rat-shot-sized freckles ran the separator. Leo Tannahill was boss. It was his job and joy to man the big steam engine. Somebody made a joke about the gangs of awestruck boys along the wayside, saying that if Leo, from his throne high on the huge machine, had given just a single lordly gesture, those kids would have fallen to their knees and worshipped him. "Everybody worships me," Leo said, "except herself, the speaker of the house."

The crew guffawed, and Vesta Tannahill the loudest.

Pear-shaped, heavy-bottomed, Vesta was a blowsy, sun-scorched woman in blue jeans cinched with a tooled belt that showed a line of Longhorns racing around her waist. She wore a chambray shirt with the sleeves cut off, showing her freckled arms. Her hair was dirt red, short, and so curly she had to wet it several times a day to tame the kinks. She had a booming voice, a croupy cough that sounded like water sucked through gravel. "Dust pneumonia," Vesta said, but Leo rolled his eyes. "It's all that talk gets tangled up down there."

They had a way of throwing insults at each other that was better than a radio show. Vesta's quick, wild laugh was most directed at the world of fools and clowns and jokers, men, the lot. "Yahoos," she called them, "aren't they just a piece of work? Can't tell their own hind ends from a row of holes dug in the dirt. Leo, get your backside over here and give your better half a kiss."

The first time I heard her speak so to her husband, I fairly flinched, but Leo grinned and hied his blue-jeaned backside over. Vesta yanked him round and kissed him on the mouth while he pretended to be suffocating.

I'd never seen the like of her for this—it showed a different way of getting on together, men and women, one I liked—and for the tireless way she threw herself at things. She drove the combine like it was a kiddie car, pitched hay bales, sliced that plate-rail bull snake snap-in-two with one chop of the hoe. She could bone a ham in nothing flat, beat a heavy pound cake batter smooth as butter, her beating arm so fast it was a blur of wooden spoon and flapping collops. At night she lit and smoked a briar pipe tamped with cherry tobacco, jigged her foot against the porch boards in a drumbeat, and told tall tales of her girlhood on the Staked Plain, tales so woolly that her daughter Mavis sighed and stalked away.

Mavis also was a law unto herself. She was a moony girl, thin-legged as a spider, dark-complected but with piebald blotches on her cheeks. She balked at work but got it done, moving at a pace so slow a terrapin's was quicker.

"Look out below," Vesta would say, "the girl's a ball of fire. A regular speed demon."

Mavis only rolled her eyes and sulked, slowed further. She was methodical to Vesta's slap-shot haste, but each of us would finish with our tasks the same, and it came to seem that Mavis, for all her pokishness, provided temper for the gatless, flour-spilling, hands-aclatter mess that Vesta's methods were. I had taken her to be twelve or thirteen, but Mavis was long past middling age, exactly mine, nineteen.

One night we were up late in the kitchen when a talking streak struck Mavis and she began to heave like a wind-broken horse. "Look here, now, I'm a full-grown person and look at how I got to cart around on harvest like a yard child. I got ideas and plans, but what about it? No! It's Mavis this and Mavis that! All I ever hear! Mavis, up and at 'em, Mavis, make the gravy. I pure-dee hate the sound of my own name. I wouldn't answer to it if you didn't make me. If there wasn't hell to pay and hot bejeezus and you wouldn't pitch a skunk-fit sideways. Mavis, Mavis, Mavis," she went on, except she didn't stop and went on saying Mavis in a singsong voice that swooped and darted round the kitchen like a swallow trapped inside a chimney. Half of me wanted to take the broom to her, and the other half wanted her to be my friend, wanted her to grab my hand in hers and the two of us run laughing to the barn to swing on pulley ropes.

"She's worked herself into the fantods," Vesta mumbled around the cotton wadded in her mouth. She had a toothache and her head was tied in a dish towel to snug her swollen jaw. The points of her headdress lopped like donkey ears as she worked at boning boiled chickens for the next day's dinner. "She'll do that every now and then. You just ignore her, and it passes over. Like a cloud. The child's a human dust storm."

Mavis gathered her breath and went on, her neck cords straining, color risen, calling forth her grudges from the cradle forward. How once she fell into a dry well and nobody came to look for her in all the hours she spent down in the snaky darkness hollering her heart out. How once a mean boy cousin shoved her so hard she went rolling out the front room door, out into the yard and past the fence, crying and rolling the whole way to the road, and did anybody care? Did anybody bother to pick her up and dust her off and say poor child and see how bad she'd hurt herself in all that rolling and crying and being shoved by that mean cousin in the first place? Not hardly. She could up and die for all they cared.

I had to laugh. Mavis seemed bent on putting on a show, and she reminded me of Etta on her better days. I had been lonely, and it was good to have a same-age girl around, a funny friend. And in just a few days I had come to love Vesta. If you were allowed to pick a second mother in your life, I would have chosen her for mine. In everything I did I tried to please her.

"Don't give her an audience," Vesta said. "That's exactly what she wants."

"I wish you'd named me Deedra," Mavis went on. "Or Jayrene. Just something halfway cute." She had begun to calm down, setting her mind to the task of thinking of any name cuter than Mavis. Under her breath, she went on, her mouth awork as she went back to folding dish towels, carefully matching the corners so they looked like an ironed stack of Sunday handkerchiefs. "Donita," she said. "Becky Jo. Or even just plain Becky." By and by she resumed her former crawl. I took up the job of pinching off dough bits to form dinner rolls for the coming day, and before long her spell had passed.

Mavis sidled up beside me. "There's a boy on the crew by name of Franklin Ritchie, and I set my name on him. Right across his forehead it says Mavis, spelt like M-I-N-E, hear?" She grinned.

Each night when the work was done the crew gathered outside the barn bay door to smoke and I could hear their slow, deep voices winding down toward sleep. I might hear, "Pretty night," then a lag of silence, a nightjar's call, the flick of whittling knife on wood, and another silence before anybody answered, as though each man had to take time to reckon if the statement was by his lights true. Then one might stir himself to say, "Clear," or "Dry." Apart from them sat Franklin Ritchie. He was ox-eyed, slight of stature, with hair the color of wet sand. He played the dulcimer as if it was a human heart with strings. In a different time and place, I would have loved him, but to ease Mavis's fears I pretended ignorance. "Is he the one who plays that instrument?"

Stealthy as a lynx, Vesta had come up behind us. "You mind that's the only instrument he gets near you with. You'll wind up like our Mackie, here. Or me. You're walking proof ongoing, girl. A regular advertisement. You think on that."

Suddenly Vesta gripped her jaw. "*Dad* gum it."

Mavis said, lowering her gaze to my belly, "At least Mackie's got something she can call her own."

Vesta wiped her hands on a dishrag. "If you think a child is something you can call your own, you've got a long contrary lesson coming." To me, she said, "You tell that man to get you up with bigger clothes. You tell him Vesta said so, or he'll have to answer to her." She flinched, again brought her hand to her jaw. "Dad *gum* it!"

I said, "He did. Some dresses in the closet. I haven't had time to let them out."

Vesta shook her head. "This is an old, old story and I've seen them all and acted my fair part in half. You don't have to tell me what the deal is. I've got eyes."

"In back of her head," Mavis muttered. I giggled at her wit, but then was drawn up short when Vesta worked her mouth around her cotton pack to make a speech that stopped me in my tracks.

"You're not anybody's Texas cousin by a long shot, Mackie-girl, and that baby in the oven is Call Lucas's. Don't try to tell me not. And I'll tell you something else. You may be a quiet little thing but you're not feebleminded, not by any measure of the kind. Slow-witted, my big fat foot, I told him. Gave him a goodly quarter of my mind."

Mavis rolled her eyes in Vesta's direction. "Don't *that* explain a few things, now?"

But I couldn't join her in her laugh. I stood stock-still, letting what Call must have told the others wash over me.

Vesta went back to boning, her quick fingers feeling along the joints, picking meat from bone, tossing flesh and yellow skin and fat in steaming splats onto a platter.

Head down, I went on pinching dough.

"I know what you're doing. You're hoping, hoping, hoping. Hoping you can hope a thing so hard you hope it into life."

"I know what I'm doing," I said.

"If that's so, you make him tell you what you are to him. He can't, or what he says goes sundry-wise to how he treats you, you flat run. Run and don't look back. You tell him to do right by you, you hear? That's your fault if you don't. Hear me, yours. Nobody's but your own. Meanwhile, you tell him he'll have me to answer to if . . . dad gum *it*!

"Wait here," she said. She went into the spare room where she and Leo slept and came back carrying a man's shirt. "You put this on for now."

Mavis had drifted off. I missed her already, felt alone, felt big, felt dumb. Slow-witted.

I put the shirt she handed me over my dress and buttoned it. The blue chambray was soft with washing, smelled of Oxydol, a little bit like Leo, fatherly.

"That's better," she said. "Your mama still around?"

I shook my head.

"Gone before you knew you needed her?"

When I looked down, the pan of dough balls blurred.

She took my hands in hers and shook them. Her touch was warm, her grip was firm. I leaned toward her, wanting to be taken in, to cry against her front, be patted on the back and soothed. Be touched again that close.

She held me at arm's length. "I mean you well," she said, "so don't you take this wrong. You're a nice girl and all. Better raised than most, I'd guess. But now you're lost. I've been in your selfsame trouble, and so I know what's up. And I know how you feel. I'll do what I can to help. You only have to ask."

"I would," I said, "I will."

"But see here, I'm a mother too. And I want to spare my own the mistakes I've made. You'll know exactly what I mean someday. So I'm going to ask a favor."

I didn't yet understand what she was driving at, but I told her, "Anything."

She let me go, picked up the roasting pan to gather the leavings for the chicken yard. "My girl's a case, but she's still innocent, and that's the way I want it kept. I'd appreciate it you didn't cozy up to Mavis. Didn't talk to her or tell her . . . you know . . . things. Didn't influence her, no matter if she asks. Steer clear."

The pan of bones and leavings swam in and out of sight, steaming, yellowish and moist.

"I won't." I wanted to cover up my hurt, go on and say I understood exactly what she meant, but I couldn't get myself to look her in the eyes.

She set the pan on the table. With her big arms she gathered me into a hug and squeezed me hard against her cushiony chest, but all I wanted to do by then was run away.

~

You can go along telling yourself a story of how things are and how you're faring in them and keeping all this ordered in your mind, but if somebody comes along and tells it in a way that's crooked to your thinking, you either have to close your ears or change your tune.

The next morning I was washing the breakfast dishes, looking out the window to mull over what had happened the night before. Call and the crew were in the fields, and Vesta and Mavis had gone to town to find the dentist. Vesta, her jaw more swollen than it was the day before, had been near tears. They'd left in one of the cutter trucks, wheat straw flurrying behind, Mavis in a bright yellow dress prouder behind the wheel than Leo at the steam engine.

Why it was Vesta's speech and not something before—the suit-case and the envelope, the sandstone slab, my hunger, the way Call hadn't spoken to me or the story he had told the others about who I was and what I was doing there, that I was feebleminded—that made me stop and ask what I was doing, I didn't know. I knew only that I stood at the sink, my hands in water gone greasy and lukewarm, making excuses for myself.

Mavis could find ample trouble on her own with no help from me, I told the sudsy water. Who was Vesta Tannahill to judge? She'd done the same thing I had done. She admitted it. And hope, I had to think, was good. What would the world come to without it? Why would anybody get up in the morning? Why do anything at all if you lost hope? Hard times were ending, everybody said, and people *hoped* it so. On and on I went, but at the bottom of it all what Vesta said had stung. I hadn't asked for any of it. None of it was my fault. Even Etta had once said so. *It's not your fault. You didn't ask for this.* Scrubbing the dickens out of all the dishes, trying to chase Vesta's smarting words out of my mind, I said this to myself until again I could feel clean and justified, misunderstood.

The windows were open against the kitchen heat, and the usual sounds drifted in. Birdsong, the far-off drone and clatter of the reaper, men's shouts, the braying of the mules. With these sounds came a noise that made me think of a baby's cry. A poor, forsaken wail, piteous as a cat in heat.

Across the yard, beside the door of my little house, a movement caught my eye. Thinking it was one of the crew men coming to fetch some forgotten something or checking to see if the cutter truck Vesta and Mavis took to town was back, I leaned over the sink to look harder.

A woman carrying an infant came into view. My stomach lurched. The woman was Etta, her dark hair ragged in the wind, a flour sack slung over her shoulder, her nursling baby cradled in her arms. She turned by degrees to look out over the place, seeking me, her loose dress stuck to her back, stained and wet with sweat.

I hurried to the screen door, ready to push it open and run out to her, but something stopped me. What would I say? One look at my popping middle would tell the story, no words needed, and I didn't want it that way. I wanted to ease into the tale, set things up so that they didn't look the way they looked. I went back to the window, hid behind the curtain.

She made her way to the sandstone slab outside my side house and knocked at the door. When the baby wailed, she shifted her weight and knocked again. The child cried louder, and so she sat down on the slab and opened her dress and put the child on to nurse, all the while looking around the empty farm. At the elm trees with their leaves ascurf with dust, the open barn bay door with hay bales spilling out, chickens scratching in the dust behind the garden fence, the well's pump handle. I thought of myself on the same door stone, eating the funeral food on the morning after my long walk.

She finished nursing the baby, then wiped her own forehead with the edge of the swaddling blanket. As if she'd seen a sudden movement in the yard, she glanced up toward the house, toward me at the window.

A better person would have run out the minute she had seen the travelers. Would have drawn a cup of water, hurried out to give a drink, or brought them in to rest in a good chair. The better person I had thought I was when I bought a pigeon egg from Teeny and told her to keep the change or dolloped supper onto Audie's plate, washed Lila's wasted skin with lemon water or gave a plate of beans and corn bread to a hungry stranger, that person would have hurried out to help. That person would run out now, even after hesitating, would not let pass another minute, not take one more breath. But rather than let my own kin see how far I'd fallen, I shifted to conceal myself and stepped back from her line of sight.

When I peeked out again, Etta had the child over her shoulder, patting her on the back. My sister's face was pallid, tired, as hollow-eyed as in the worst of days.

She got to her feet and started up the pathway, walking slowly in her old slew-footed walk and nodding as she came.

The kitchen door from the back stoop was open, but if I ran to close it, she would see me. The screen door was latched with a hook, the wire grid all that stood between me and the back porch, but if I ran past the door toward the bedrooms, she would know.

I ducked down, crawled under the table, the only place out of the view from the screen door. I tried to quiet my breathing, to hold still.

She had reached the door. She knocked. The baby made a mewling sound, a small complaint. A locust set to sawing.

She knocked again, then scratched at the screen. "Mackie, are you in there?"

In the shadows under the table in a crack between the floorboards, half-hidden by a dust mouse snagged beneath the table leg, lay a shard of broken china from one of Lila's Blue Willow plates.

Etta rapped again at the wooden door. A loose board slapped and rattled.

"If you're mad at me because of Audie . . . Mackie, I didn't ask for it. I didn't want to marry him. He did it. He and Dad did all of it."

Under the table on my hands and knees, I felt my chest cramp. The weight of my belly seemed to pull me down, and the small of my back seized. *Not all,* I ached to say. *Not all.*

Her voice was small. "Can't you forgive me?"

If I could have made myself come out to face her, I would have told her there was no need for forgiving. Forgiving wasn't it. I knew by then how your own will could snatch you up and shake you hard and drop you in a place you never meant to land. Forgiving wasn't it. It was my pride. For all my trying to be good, for all my setting up myself as picture-perfect, for every time I'd held myself above my sister in my own esteem, I couldn't let her see how low I'd come.

"Let me in for the day, then I'll go. I can't stay around here anyway. They'll probably look here first. Just don't make me go back."

I couldn't move. Spit came into my mouth, and I couldn't swallow for fear of the noise, so I opened my mouth and let it string down to the floor in a little gout of drool.

Her voice came again, this time heavy with weariness. "If you can't do that, send out something to eat. Some food. Put it outside the door. I'll go off and wait. I won't try to talk to you. I'm famished, Mackie."

On the stove the cast iron Dutch oven held chicken and dumplings. A pan of rolls was rising, sending off its yeasty smell. There were boiled brown eggs in a yellow bowl, leftover bacon in the warmer.

She tried to pull open the door, rattling it on its hinges, but the hook held fast.

Even then, I have to think, if she had forced the door I might have had to look beyond myself and make light of my hiding, might have been able to pick up with her as before. Even then. But suddenly her voice took on a harsher tone, the voice of Etta of old, who goaded, blustered, had to have the final word, who lied to justify her lies, and what she said next made a bitter gall rise to my throat and sealed my heart against her. "Mackie, listen. If you're doing this because I told you you weren't Dad's girl, well, I'm sorry. But you had to know. You had to. Nobody should have kept that from you."

From the wheatfield came the blast of the steam reaper, the men shouting jubilation. The wheat was in, the harvest done.

The locust broke off its whining, then resumed. The shouting died away. In the reach of silence then, and later through the years, what Etta said would trouble me. What if what she said was true? Would it have mattered one iota? I tell myself it didn't matter then and doesn't matter now. That truth or no, it didn't make things worse or better, didn't change a thing. It was a storm blown up and suffered through, and once it passed, it passed, was gone. The truth was that at some point in that silence I had chosen what I wanted to believe. I didn't want to know.

And who can say how things might have turned out if I had gotten up from under the table, let her in and fed her like a human being, or packed up that argued-over suitcase and gone away with her, the two of us out on the road, rootless and ill prepared as anybody else. But on the last day I would look upon my sister, wrath against her burned so hot in me I couldn't think, and I'd gone so far pretending I was not inside the house, I wasn't.

"Sister," she said quietly, "I know you're in there. I can hear you breathing."

I lowered myself to my elbows, put my face into my hands, and shut my eyes. The locust drone went on and on and on and on.

<hr>

That night there was to be a bonfire to celebrate the harvest. The year was bad for Russian thistle, and tumbleweeds grown large as hogshead casks had choked the fence rows. In a fallowing field behind the cattle pen, the men gathered them into a brush pile nearly high as the barn, a mountain of dried thistle.

After supper we gathered round the gasoline-soaked pile. The men brought wet grain sacks and shovels. The wind was mild enough, but a wayward gust could start a wildfire.

The mood ran high as we ringed the brush, but I was worn-out and sickened to the marrow by what I'd done.

Vesta came up to straighten the buttons on my borrowed shirt. She tucked a strand of hair behind my ear. On her breath was the deep, dark smell of sour mash. She wet a finger and dabbed a smudge from my cheek. "Did you tell him what I said?"

"There hasn't been a minute."

"Make one."

All afternoon since Etta walked away, I had been thinking about

what to do, and I had more in mind than to make a minute. I was going to make a spectacle.

Dead across from me behind the brush pile stood Call. I knew
this not because I could see him, for the thistle mound was between
us, but because I had been last to take my place and I had chosen it
on purpose. I intended this: When the fire burned down he would
see me in the rising smoke, and the look he gave would be the final
test. If he gave any sign of feeling, I would stay. When Dad came
looking for Etta, which I knew he would, I'd pay the price, saying
we were getting married. I would make Call tell him so. But if he
gave no sign, I'd go.

Speck Coltis struck a match against his jeans. He held it to his face
to watch it burn and draw out the moment long, then tossed it on the
pile. The match flame flickered and went out.

"Dud," called Vesta.

"You blow on it," Leo teased her, "it'll resurrect."

Speck Coltis struck another match, and this one caught. Caught
so fast there wasn't time to see it spread but there before us was a
flaming pillar gone up in a whoosh that sucked air into itself and
burned quicker than excelsior, dry and crackling, then a rain of
sparks and cinders as the mound consumed itself and buckled to a
bed of snapping, spiny, firelit bones.

We stepped back from the heat. The fire was too bright to see beyond. I couldn't get my answer.

I broke from the ring and made my way around and went to stand
by Call, back and off a bit, but there. I studied him, the way his neck
was set, sun-beaten skin with creases like rivulets or gullies, at his
hair unbarbered since the funeral and curled over his collar like a tuft
of wool, hair I would have gladly cut for him if he had only asked. I
thought of how he looked two ways at once, the narrow, upright
stem of neck that held his hard, unyielding head.

In a voice as loud as I owned, I said, "Call Lucas, look at me."

He turned to Leo, clapped him on the back, and took him off to celebrate the yield.

⌐

The threshing crew was gone before first light. I heard the clang and rattle of their leaving, mule wheeze and harness jangle, engine roar, then their progress up the lane. It was half-light of what would be a low, cloud-scudding day, and hot already. I had slept hard and angry, awakened in that grudging state when even the littlest of wrongs will make you mean. I tried to put on my work dress, but it wouldn't button, and so I hiked it up as far as it would go and found Leo's shirt and put it on over the dress. I was either more myself than I had ever been, or not myself at all.

People say they've felt the devil in their lives, in some ill deed or happening. I didn't then and don't know now if it is true that evil hides itself inside the folds of daily doings—accidents or lies, the things you mean to do but don't, the things you do but haven't meant to. I don't know if evil is present all the while or bides its time and waits for summoning, but I believe that any unfed hunger will invite the touch of its unholy hand.

I wanted such a hand to let me go to Call, meat cleaver in my grip, crack open his hard head. Or else I wanted its or anybody's power to seal us. And I didn't know which end I wanted most. At the bottom of it all I wanted what I wanted, and so I made the red and wicked devil in my mind's eye clear as any graven image, invited it into my heart the same way at long-ago revivals I invited Jesus, and just that fast a presence seemed to walk beside me as I made my way across the yard toward the house, my bare feet gliding on the dewy grass.

I went into Call's room. He was awake, lying on his side, the white sheet drawn up to his middle. I stood in the doorway and I said his name.

With a long look and a lazy hand he lifted up the sheet to show his rising self and bid me in.

I won't stop to say what thoughts went through my mind or why I did what I did next. If you know from being there yourself, you know, and if you don't, then no amount of reason matters.

I crawled in with him.

We lay on our backs. The morning light was spreading, gold and pink. I looked up at the ceiling where there was a crack I hadn't seen before, a long and jagged crack, like a river or forked lightning.

The weight of my great belly on my chest made breathing hard. My pulse throbbed in my throat. A square of pale light traveled over us, while outside the mockingbirds set up. A rooster crowed.

Slowly, Call worked up my dress. With an arm under my back, he rolled me gently to my side so that my back was to him.

I'd like to say that of a piece I found my strength the way I'd found that once-upon-a-time-forgotten doorknob in my apron pocket. Or that I changed my ways like Pharaoh with a dream foretold, or Saul of Tarsus. But there was no writing on the wall, no light on the Damascus road, no sudden vision, nothing. I would be poleaxed later in my memory of the moment, but at the time I knew only that sometimes out of nowhere ordinary grace can strike you like a blow, as simple as the heat that makes you drop a skillet.

I got up and walked away.

From Lila's closet I took a wrapper and a nightgown and some underclothes. An alligator purse. Then I went out to my little house to gather my things. I put my money in the pocketbook. The rest of what I needed I put in a bedsheet, tied it like a bindle, and slung it over my shoulder. Then I walked up the lane the same way Etta and Georgette had gone the day before.

This time I knew where I was going, and I wouldn't stop until I got there, wouldn't ask for signs or portents or see messages in people I met along the way, would only walk until I reached the rescue home. I would go there and give birth like anybody else. Leave the child to orphan out, then take up my place where I belonged, wherever that might be.

And this is what I did, except for one last-minute change. I meant to give the baby up but thought again and couldn't. He was mine. But more than that—for good or not-so—I was his.

I've worked in almost every café from Blackwell to Waco Wego at least once, some more. I didn't marry. Late in life, out here a hundred miles from those old times, I loved a man and he loved me, but that's a story even yet I don't know how to tell. Until he came along, I didn't tell a soul what really happened. For too long I let my son believe his father was a boy I loved who moved away before he knew, and only I saw Call's straight chin in my son's son. I never had another chance with Etta, and this I added to the blame I held for Call for how I hid myself from her. But a time would come when I'd have one with him.

You'd think I would have given up, but I kept waiting, waited forty years for him to seek me out and tell me he was sorry. Went about my days like anybody else, but there before that little gilded altar in my heart I waited.

Field by field, acre by acre, town by town, the haggard land came back or didn't, the dust tamped down and sown with grass or left to fallow, those who stayed here edging bit by bit into their lives and those who left it gone for good and never to return. But me, I stopped the world with waiting, not to start again until he walked through the door of whatever place I worked and looked me in the eye, and told me, "Mackie Spoon, I'm sorry," for I believed that day would come.

In the turning of a hundred seasons I saw only Call come begging. Seasons turned and winters moved through springs and summers, and I waited, growing old, but all that while, when sand plums fell, their ripeness gone to bruise, it happened so that he could see the shame in waste. Leaves blew from their branches just to show him that the wrong he'd done me was a grievous one. Frost was to remind him of a harsher cold. Ice, the sharp, cracked color of his heart.

I would forgive him. Easy. All he had to do was ask, and in my dreams he would rise up and call me blessed for the way I had forgiven him. This moment I could see in rain, and we would then be whole again and new, the way we were at first.

Over the years I caught a few short glimpses of his truck, of him. Truth told, I'd sometimes put myself in his potential path to make it likelier that he would see me, but then, heart hammering, I'd hide. Duck down in the driver's seat or slide behind a fence. Whether he saw me or he didn't, I don't know, but only one time did he look at me straight on, one summer night during the year Dad died—the year I met the man I called my husband—when I was on my way back home from War Drum.

Trying to loop around a line of nasty weather, I took the old road rather than the highway; and then I just kept driving into the dark, and pretty soon I found myself over the Kansas line. Along a stretch of unfamiliar road not far from Call's place an abandoned farmstead had caught heat and burned, and people had come out. I stopped the car, got out to have a look. This was a thing that everybody did, a ritual of respect, a tribute to a place's loss, a kind of funeral for all the work that went into the land, but I had the feeling he would be there, and he was.

The barn still smoldered, but the house had gone. People shined flashlights over the ash pile, but there was nothing left to see but charred wood and one lone teapot on a blackened stove. Across the ashes that had been the house, against the smoke that was the barn, stood Call.

I thought I'd gone past fleshly things, but deep inside me something moved at seeing his remembered mouth. Still, I faced him square. He looked at me across the burned-out house, full face, an old, old man. He saw me and I knew it and I knew the day had come.

If we were to end in fire, I understood that at the thistle fire I'd jumped the gun by forty years.

There is a way a summer storm will come up from the west, from mountains I have yet to see but know are there, a sudden way that, when you see the dark cloud tower looming, you can almost think the walls of dust are come again until you feel the wind is sharp and clean, until you finally catch the smell of coming-closer rain. In the storm head rolling high and heavy over us, there was something of my waiting, of a watching of the goings-on on earth, something of wrong that will not be forgotten rising to be stored in thunder, and I waited for the lightning to appear, for the flash of reckoning that would scorch Call for what he'd done.

But on the last night I was to see him, I saw instead the message of the fool I'd been on earth to fit the signs of heaven toward the purpose of my will, and when the lightning flashed across his eyes I saw in them my own, by awful trick of light, the hard and high-and-mighty vision of my own.

I felt my bones grow laden at the sight, with wasted years and with the sudden want of mercy, for the very ground to hold me so I wouldn't fall, and I called out to him, "I'm sorry."

What was in him I can never know, but what was in him made him turn away.

I didn't think. I ran into the rubble and the ashes and I grabbed the teapot. The handle seared my skin but I held on and ran toward him as he walked away. The sound my throat made was a noise like none I'd ever heard—a terrible dark language or another tongue— that wouldn't cease until I threw the teapot at him, hard. It struck him in the back, a clank, a rattle hollow as a far-off clap of thunder. He stopped, stood still, began to turn, then caught himself and kept on walking into rain that came in short quick gusts, then began to fall like rain, like only rain.

Out here past the Dry Line, trees are scarce and people scarcer. This isn't land to leave your mark on. Signs of human habitation stand out stark, and if they last a hundred years, it's something. The place is not called No-Man's-Land without a reason. Gus, who was born here and has never left, hung up a sign penciled *All hope abandon, ye who enter here.* Customers complained, though, so he had to make do with *Help Wanted,* which he sees as his own private joke.

When counter-sitters at the café ask me how I came here, why I stayed, I cock my head, draw back and squint as if to ponder. "Luck all the way," I finally say. "What kind of luck is up for grabs."

"Maxine," they'll tell me, "you're a pistol."

"Yes," I'll answer back, "an antique with a rusty trigger." Truth told, it tickles me, that name, and I'd say almost anything to hear it.

Gus says that as the years go doddering on I've grown cantankerous, and likely he is right. For crotcheting around I sometimes sound so much like Dad did at the end it gives me chills. Most days I feel so pert I half believe I might outlast myself. I have my reputation as an elder to consider, though, and so if anybody asks me how I'm getting on, I shake my head and say, as puny as I'm able, "Oh, failing along."

They laugh, but I believe it comforts them to think the end is nearer me to them, the door ajar between my stringy self and the whatever-after.

Speaking of the afterlife, the old brothers went to blows concerning heaven and the proper end of mortal man, which is what started me to writing this and maybe ought to end it. About religion, I've been back and forth my whole life through, on-again and off-again, coming forward, then falling back, trying to decide exactly how much of the story to put stock in. Gus, who's more right than he knows or I'd admit, calls me a Half Believer. At the bottom of it all, religion's always been another wrestling match where *want-to* fights with *can't* too close to call, and I don't know anything for sure except there's no use for a faith to make me ready for the life to come when what I always stood in need of was a faith to make me better fit for this one.

The other day I said to Gus, who has commenced again to making noises about pulling out and moving on to Denver, "Augustus, I don't care where it is you come to rest. Garden, desert, or your all-fired mile-high city, wander where you want, but at some point you've got to find a place and stick. Whatever's right or wrong with it, you get one plot to tend. What grows there will depend."

He worked his toothpick round his mouth to say, "You think I'm not aware of that, Max Factor?"

"Gus," I said, "if that was meant as wit, you're slipping, bad. Seems to me if you stay put, anybody who's trying to find you will know where to look."

Himself could summon no comeback to this that wouldn't string him upside down, and so he had to satisfy his pique by setting pans to clatter.

I've got more to say to him, and I mean to go downstairs to the café in just a minute and pick up where we left off, but just now I want to wind this up. Two notebooks almost filled, yours truly's written out. In the weeks it's taken me to write them, we've had babies born and people die, people fall in love and others out, people getting sick and getting well, arriving and departing. Son Jesse called for no real reason, just to check on me. Made me gladder than he knows. We lost one of our regulars, the older of the two who went to words. The ghost of Wheeler Alford wields his judge's gavel at the sacred window table while the Old Bulls talk of war and weather, one on the way, the other lingering, this late October still too mild and pretty to believe. Talk, too, of hard times coming once again, dust, no water, weather out of whack, another Dust Bowl on the way, no stopping it. Me, I doubt I'll be around to see it. Hope not, in a way.

I have to say that while I've been up here living in the past, I've half expected Etta to appear, drawn by blood or memory or love, summoned by my longing. The other half of me knows better, knows that some we've wronged or who've wronged us will go away and won't come back, leaving us with no good way to reach them, and so we just go on, certain only that there are some things in this world not given us to fix.

But if wishes were black horses, she'd ride in on one, dust herself off, and plunk down in a booth as if no time at all had passed and I'd slide in beside her, pour us both a good strong cup of coffee, take her hand in mine if she'd allow it, tell her this whole story in two words.

Book Two

How Okies Look to Natives

1

⌒

No Liquor Sold to Indians
Past Dark

In their after-school race through north Wichita on streets crowded with war-boom bungalows, hamburger stands, and storefront markets, Jesse beat his friend Pete Boylan to the alley machine shop for the fifth day running. He slammed a palm against the plank door to prove his win, then slipped inside before heavy, halting Pete could pound around the corner.

Pete's father Cade stood at his bench, mask down against sparks thrown by the torch's rosebud as he worked a butt weld on a three-point plowshare. With his broad back silhouetted against the starry bursts, Cade brought to mind the fire god Vulcan in the book of myths at school—ugly, lame, but kindly and beloved.

"Arc!" the old man yelled, but Jesse didn't need the warning. Even thirty paces off, the blue-white oxyacetylene flame made his eyes ache, the afterburn like sunspots. He knew better than to look at the fire straight on; Cade Boylan's eyes were burned so raw from years at the forge that he had to bind them every night with potato parings.

Jesse studied the display of auto plates and road signs nailed into the wall studs. WHEAT STATE, SOONER STATE, LAND OF ENCHANT-MENT, the walleyed spectacles of I.O.O.F, a buckshot-riddled GREEN RIVER ORDINANCE ENFORCED. Under Cade's prize, a yellowing plac-ard lettered NO LIQUOR SOLD TO INDIANS PAST DARK—DURANT, OKLAHOMA 1929, a pinup cowgirl winked at him from the present, March 1953.

When Pete puffed in, Cade took his finger off the torch's trigger. The hiss and crackle died, the last spark embered out. Cade set down the wand, pushed up his mask. "Crack the door, men."

Jesse loved the shop's dark smell of burned oil, carbide, and pig iron, and he loved hearing Cade call them "men." He hurried to slide open the shop's bay door. Sunlight poured into the gloom. Two days before, the temperature had been at zero, but now, although the hackberry trees were bare and grimed ice laced the snowdrifts, the day was warm. Even so, inside the shop a deeper cold seeped from the packed-dirt floor into the cardboard half soles of his brogans.

Cade took off his asbestos gloves and picked up a handbill from the workbench. He thrust the paper toward his son. Pete was as slow at reading as he was at running, as he was at anything except trying to dodge the jabs his father threw to test his guard and lumbering to his mama's table to wolf her chicken-fried steak and mashed potatoes. To Jesse, who was wiry and a quicker study—even though he got in trouble almost every day, he was the smartest in the school, he knew it, the class knew it, and the teacher knew it too—big, clumsy Pete ran slower than cold 3-in-1.

"Me and Ray Ellis are going," the old man said. He tucked a chaw behind his lower lip. "You gentlemen of a mind to join us?"

"Yeow," Pete said.

In his first days in Wichita, Jesse learned that "Yeow" meant "Yeah," but he had yet to master the way the natives whanged it, couldn't get his mouth to slide around the local diphthong. He had a tin ear, his mother said, and it was just as well. She was a country-woman, but she had notions about grammar, insisting that clear speaking was the measure of a man, and Jesse wanted Cade, no matter that the old man's talk was Ozark as it came, to see that even though his mother was a lunch-counter waitress and he didn't know his father, he was a boy to reckon with. "Yes, sir," he said, not knowing yet what he was signing on for.

Pete let the handbill dangle in his mitts for so long that Jesse wanted to knock his block off, but finally he forked it over. Made up like a Wanted poster, in Old West letters beneath a cartoon drawing of a mustachioed jackrabbit in a bandit's mask, the flyer announced a coursing meet in Reno County.

Another drought was on, as bad as in the worst years of the dust storms when big black-tailed jackrabbits overran the plains, and now the pests were back. Three feet tall, with strong hind legs that sent them leaping in stretches longer than a hayrick, they ate the top crops, then gnawed the roots. In the old days, Co-ops and Last Man Clubs offered bounties, but there were so many jackrabbits that sponsors ran out of funds, and so coursing meets were held. His mother told of seeing a roundup where brush-beaters numbering in the thousands had spread out for miles, starting far apart but closing in and closing in, banging pots and chanting until they drove some thirty thousand rabbits to the center to be clubbed. Although some of her hard luck stories were a stretch, Jesse believed this one, and his heart seemed to beat quicker now than when he'd raced Pete through the streets. He was good at running; he would win the money prize. He'd had his eye on a pair of saddle-leather boots at Harry Shepler's.

"Be here first thing tomorrow," Cade said. "Take us a couple hours to get out there, pick up Cousin Ray Ellis, get signed up. Coursing starts at ten."

Pete winked as if to say wasn't his old man swell, but Jesse was too heated up about the hunt to smart at Pete's smug attitude. He felt a grin come on and knew he must be lit up like a jacklight to be included in the day. "Yes, sir!" he said again.

"Get a note from your mama, hear?" Cade said. "Under sixteen, somebody's got to vouch. And bring a stick, what-have-you, for a club."

Jesse had read the handbill's small print. No firearms—too many beaters jammed together at the end, when all the rabbits were penned. No axes, knives, machetes, no pitchforks and no blades. Blunt objects only.

When he tried to hand the paper back to Cade, the old man brushed it off. "You keep it, bud." Without the welding gloves, Cade's hands were black, his nailbeds dark half-moons. Jesse felt himself warm to slush when Cade cuffed him on the shoulder.

He was halfway home before he remembered his delivery job. He ran for the corner of Eighteenth and Waco, a hole-in-the-wall butcher shop that smelled of sawdust and cut bone where he worked after school and Saturdays. As he pedaled the delivery bicycle along the brick streets of the North End, he considered his good fortune. The promise of a rabbit drive was only part of all the luck that had come his way. At fourteen, he had already lived in a dozen jerkwater towns along the highways where his mother could find work. Sprawling, railhead Wichita was the biggest town he'd lived in, a city. Going on a year now, and he felt as if the place were made with him in mind. He could range and wander and explore. His mother waited counter at the Continental Trailways station, and once a week he was allowed to go in and order what he wanted, free of charge.

He always chose a bowl of chili and a grilled cheese sandwich, washed them down with a Grapette on ice. He tried not to guzzle the pop so he could linger, listening to the stationmaster auction off the town names like livestock at the pens on Twenty-first. He loved to hear the names of the cattle towns the big buses were bound for— Ponca City, Oke City, Dodge City, Strong City, Abilene, Kansas City, Omaha, names so wide-open and powerful they sounded like a spell—and he loved the charged air when the vehicles rolled in, brakes hissing, black fumes rolling, the passengers lurching down the steps, testing their land legs on flat ground. Cowpunchers from the Flint Hills, black-hatted Indians up from reservations, soldiers, sailors, dark-eyed Syrians and Gypsies, rawboned, big-knuckled Swedes from Lindsborg, bearded Mennonites from Halstead, gangsters and zoot-suiters down from Kansas City, with swanky gals in veiled hats, seamed stockings, and high heels. Wichita was the gunslinger capital of Wyatt Earp and Doc Holliday, and in his imagination Jesse Spoon, the smartest gentleman-desperado in the land, was at its hub. He had been named after the runner Jesse Owens, and he liked this well enough, but he told it around school that he was named for Jesse James. Besides, he didn't know his father's name, and so the lie was less a stretch.

When he wasn't at school or on his job, he haunted the alleys in the shadows of the Beacon Building or the Forum, maybe the Eaton Hotel out on Douglas Avenue, where skid row bums lounged in the doorways, a wicked Nineveh where Carry Nation had once axed the painting behind the saloon's bar. *Cleopatra at the Bath,* the painting was, and Jesse'd heard that you could still make out the hatchet marks. At S. S. Kress's, when the salesclerk's back was turned, he'd kyped a dented kaleidoscope from the clearance bin. He never tired of gazing into it. The jagged paper shapes inside the tube never lined up the same way twice. The town reminded him of that.

He pedaled down Ninth Street, through the part of town his mother called the colored section. Her genteel name seemed to drain life from the place, rendering the people bland as Presbyterians on their way to Calvary Church. To his way of thinking, black people knew better than white ones how to live, closer to their insides. He could tell this from the laughter he heard as he passed the alley nip joints, from the sassy, singsong jump-rope girls and mumbledy-pegging boys at the curb who mocked and jostled, the arguing old men smoking home-rolled on tipped-back chairs, the porch grannies cussing out the kids one minute, the next minute squeezing out their stuffings. He loved to hear their voices—as if they understood the world was messed up but also funny—and once, alone out on the mudbanks of the Little River, he'd tried to mimic the swooping vowels and slurring consonants, but he gave up when his own voice came out strangled, fake.

The tougher Negro kids at school called the neighborhood Niggertown, saying the word defiantly, but Jesse wouldn't call it that either. *Nigger* was a bad word even if it was in *Huckleberry Finn*. He never said it and he tried never to think it, even though sometimes it came into his mind, but secretly he liked the way it sounded when the tough kids said it. And kids weren't the only ones he'd heard. "You need to find me, I stay up in Niggertown," a rickety old grandpa said. He'd come into the machine shop to ask for work. "Holler down and anybody tell you where I'm at." Cade said the man was a shiftless coot who never did a lick of work, but he said it in a hearty way that made Jesse think he admired the old man, and so he paid no mind to his mother when she fretted that if he hung around the shop, he might pick up Cade's biases. Something about the Boylans rubbed her wrong, but she worried too much anyway, and she didn't know Cade from Adam's off ox. She'd met him only once or twice.

Besides, it seemed to him the black kids were the ones who set themselves apart. At school they sat in the back of the classroom, bunched together on the playground. At the Orpheum they cut up in the balcony, dropping chewed Walnettos onto people's heads. When he wondered aloud why they didn't sit below, Pete said it was the law. They—Pete used the bad word—weren't allowed on the theater's main floor, weren't allowed to try on clothes at Geo. Innes. Jesse knew better. It was 1953. Kansas wasn't Mississippi. It was a free country, and Kansas especially was a Free State, framed by abolitionists and known for Border Wars and Bleeding Kansas, Osawatomie John Brown raising high his rifle on the statehouse wall. He'd seen the mural on a field trip, and the righteousness of John Brown's cause had sent him.

Where Ninth Street gave onto Minneapolis Avenue, a bunch of kids had blocked the alley with bedsprings and broken chairs to set up an obstacle course of rusted oil drums, and there was Sanders Moody sprinting toward him. Sanders held Horace Mann's low hurdles record. Jesse stopped to watch him take the oil drums in his stride. Sanders was in his English class—the only other smart kid, Jesse thought, except that Sanders always read the homework while Jesse winged it.

Jesse stood down from the delivery bicycle, straddled it. "Hey," he said, when Sanders came to a stop. He had tried before to get in with some of the corner kids, making a point of smiling to show that in his mind all people were the same, twisting his grin a little more off plumb to say that maybe for all the trouble they'd gone through they were even better, wiser, or more noble, something *more* he couldn't put his finger on, but they always chased him off, and he could find no way to let them know that in his book they were tops. "Hey," he said again, but Sanders, bent over to catch his breath, didn't answer.

"Good run," Jesse said. He wanted Sanders to notice the delivery bike, a red Schwinn rigged with a metal icebox with bright fittings. He pressed the spring bell's lever.

Sanders wiped his brow. Jesse thought of trying to talk about school, but he couldn't think of anything to say except that their teacher was a goofus and Horace Mann was for the birds, and so instead he asked if Sanders knew about the jackrabbit drive.

When Sanders said Yeow he'd heard, Jesse found himself bragging that he would win.

"Money prize?" Sanders was paying attention now, looking at him straight on.

"Fifty fat ones." He was boasting, but it felt all right, felt good. Normal, not that he was white and Sanders black, just friendly, usual.

Sanders grinned. "Says you. Where's this supposed to be again?"

Handbills had been posted on telephone poles along his route, but Jesse dug the flyer from his pocket and stood by while Sanders read.

"This white-only?"

"What?" He wasn't sure he'd heard right; nobody spoke that kind of thing aloud. "Come one, come all, it says." His own voice sounded false and hopeful as an eager beaver teacher's. To ease the awkwardness, he repeated a phrase he'd read on a donkey basketball game flyer. He'd thought it was clever and it seemed to carry the right tone. "Bring your in-laws, bring your outlaws."

Sanders handed back the flyer. "You sure it doesn't cost?"

"Free," said Jesse, more grandly than he meant to, making it sound like he was in charge, was inviting Sanders. "Says so right here." He raised the handbill as proof.

"Maybe I'll beat you to that prize." Sanders winked, then clicked his tongue against his teeth the way you'd giddy-up a horse. Jesse wondered if he was putting him on, and after Sanders went back down the alley he practiced the noise to see if he could detect Sanders's intention. Hurdle champ or no, if he showed, Jesse would beat him, then Sanders would see what he was made of. Maybe they'd pal around sometime. They could hang out in Riverside Park, maybe jump off the boathouse balcony into the slow, brown water. If he discounted age and other things, they'd be like Huck and Jim.

His last delivery took him near the stockyards, where he always stopped to study the stuffed two-headed Brahma calf in the display window of the auction barn, trying to imagine how the world would look if one set of his eyes faced one way and the other set of eyes another. Then it was a quick dogleg down Waco past the armory, where he pulled the bike into the back room just as Ab Murdock was closing up.

"Couple of big orders in College Hill tomorrow. Be here on time for once." Ab shot the bolt before Jesse, his mind still on the calf, could think to say he wouldn't be at work.

All the way home he concocted excuses for his no-show, deciding that on Monday he would tell Ab he'd been sick, a polio scare, maybe. Nobody'd question that. He might get a talking-to, but Ab was a soft touch. As Jesse walked along he practiced croaking in a fever-thickened voice until he could almost believe that he was coming down with some bug or another.

It was past dark when he got home to Water Street. He took the stairs up the side of the rented duplex, passing the kitchen window of the lower rooms where Letty Burdin lived with her little girl. His mother sat at Letty's kitchen table, looking more worn-out than usual. Letty held his mother's hand, petting it as if to comfort her. Jesse stood outside the window to watch them, feeling sneaky, sly, an outsider looking in.

His mother had met Letty on the bus from Blackwell. Seated behind the driver, Jesse endured their chatter all the way, the two of them hoping to hire on at Boeing and build B-52s, worrying loudly, embarrassingly, that they were Johnny-come-latelies, Okies come a day late and a dollar short. Their cornball expressions and their shrill high spirits made him squirm, and he turtled his head into the collar of his pea jacket, stared out the window at the prairie towns they passed, pretending he didn't know them. The women tried the big plants, Boeing, Cessna, Beech, but it was no soap, and things were looking bad until his mother found the Trailways job and Letty found a place at Hollabaugh's.

Every night they visited downstairs at Letty's, drinking cup after cup of tea, waiting on each other, pretending to be snooty customers. Mrs. Lady Astor, lah-di-dah, how-do-you-do? What they talked about, he didn't care to know, but they laughed and laughed, his mother saying at least once a night, "You have to or you'd go stark raving."

"There oughta be a law," Letty would say, mopping her teary eyes. They called each other Mrs. Spoon and Mrs. Burdin, like the tearoom ladies he saw coming out of Innes Tearoom and he couldn't stand it. Neither had a husband. He didn't think that either ever had. Both were nice-looking enough—once, he had believed his mother was the prettiest around—but his mother was too small and snippity to get a man, and Letty was too big and loud. They were a pair. If they would straighten up and stop taking on like hayseeds, like Alice-the-Goon, he'd bet a busload full of husbands would turn up.

Letty was laughing now, cawing at what he supposed was another of her Little Moron jokes. Why'd the Little Moron throw the clock out the window? Why'd the Little Moron put his hat in the refrigerator? When Letty got up to go to the stove, his mother sipped her tea. Resting her chin on her hand, she stared at the darkened window, looking out as if right through him. He had been thinking of bursting in to tell his news about the jackrabbit drive, but something in his mother's haunted look made him think better of it. She would hear him above and know that he was home, so he was off the hook. She was a worrywart, always warning of lockjaw and polio and sleeping sickness, bad men at the bus station.

From the clouded water in the enamel pan on the hot plate, he took two shriveled wienies, dosed them with mustard, and rolled them in slices of Sunbeam bread. He stuffed them in, chewing thoughtfully while he considered his reflection in the darkened window, mulling again the constant, satisfying question of who he was, who he wanted to be. Wyatt Earp or Jesse James? A hero-gentleman or a hero-desperado? Was there a way he could be both? He felt on the verge of either, but it was too confusing to sort out, and he was tired, and so he crawled onto his pallet in the closet that served as his bedroom and went to sleep.

He woke up in the dark—he never needed a clock, he could set *way early* in his head. The linoleum floor was cold. His head ached, and his ears felt plugged, his throat was scratchy. He rooted for a sheet of tablet paper, but he'd left his book strap in the delivery bike's basket, and so he dug out the handbill. On the back he wrote a vouching note he thought would pass.

Jesse Spoon has my consent, he wrote in a hand as close to his mother's even loops as he could manage, *to participate in any sporting contest under the auspices of Mr. Cade Boylan.* He was proud of the phrase *sporting contest,* the word *auspices.* His teacher often praised his vocabulary. Jesse imagined Cade's face when he read the note. He signed her name. It was wrong, and he knew it, but he told himself he didn't want to wake her.

He found his best plaid flannel shirt. A sniff under the sleeve told him it could serve another day. He dug in his pile of clothes for his trapper cap. His shoes were cracked and flimsy, the cardboard half soles shredding, but there was nothing he could do about them. A slurp of water from the bathroom tap made his throat feel better. If he slugged back some milk, it might improve further. He went into the kitchenette.

He hadn't counted on his mother being awake, and he stopped just outside the door where she sat at the table, wrapped in her Woolworth's kimono. The robe was cheap, too big, too loud, like Letty'd picked it out. Even though his mother cinched the garment around her waist, it seemed to swallow her. The arms drooped, which made her look smaller than she was and half-loony to boot. She had a lift shoe for her lame foot; the shoe was already on against the cold. To make things worse, she had a way of rolling down her anklets to make them look what Letty called "snazzy," and the habit as well as her use of Letty's silly word made him want to punch the wall.

His mother was a case. Often he would catch her looking off into space in a spooky way that made him want to come up behind her and say "Boo!" He used to think her mooning had to do with his missing father, and sometimes he would ask. But she wouldn't speak of the man except to say he'd gone away before he knew that Jesse was on the way. Things were different then, she said. It was the times. People scattered everywhere, no telephones to speak of, the Great Depression she harked back to twenty times a day if she harked once, as if it was an excuse. Sometimes he tried to pry a name from her, but she wouldn't give one up. When he examined the mystery of his own face in the mirror, trying to see more deeply into it, to memorize its planes, the cast of his jaw, the way the skin lay over his eye sockets, it was as though he couldn't know the boy in front of him and yet he could, could sometimes catch a glimmer of what the father of a boy like him—blue-eyed, a thatch of sandy hair that stuck up in a cowlick, hands and feet too big for the rest of him—might look like.

Seeing him in the doorway, his mother brightened her look. It miffed him that she pretended to be cheerful when she was downhearted, that she tried to cover up her troubles. If she was sad, why didn't she just come out and say so? Why didn't she ever level with him?

"What's the matter?" His own voice sounded foggy, cracked, impatient. A sick hot taste had risen in his throat.

"Nothing." She dabbed at her eyes with her kimono sleeve, then surprised him by bursting out, "Letty's getting married. Moving back to Oklahoma."

The isinglass stove ticked loudly but gave only feeble warmth. He felt like the stuffed calf at the stockyards, seeing two ways at once. He was sorry for her. She seemed happier in Wichita than anywhere else they'd lived. But he also thought Letty's departure served her right. For all his mother's trucking him from town to town, uprooting him and living like a nomad, somebody else was leaving first. He didn't know what to say, and so he went to the icebox and opened it, staring blindly, his throat aching. The motor kicked on with a racket that shook the floor. There was no milk.

"Close the door. Make sure the latch is caught." She watched a penny like it was a gold piece.

"Ma, I'm going on a hunt."

When she stood up he saw again how small she was. He was taller by a head. Her eyes were rimmed in red and for a minute he considered letting her in on Cade's potato-peeling cure. "What kind of hunt? You don't have a gun, and I won't . . ."

The want of a shotgun—even in the city most boys his age had them—struck him as one more unfairness. "A coursing meet. No guns. It's a jackrabbit drive."

"Son, those things are cruel. Barbaric. When I was growing up they . . ."

"Cade wouldn't go on it if they were. Everybody's going." He thought of telling her that Sanders Moody would be there. That could earn some points. One of her everlasting saws was how all colors ought to get along.

"*Mister* Boylan," she corrected. "And you don't know yet what cruelty is."

The haggard look she gave him seemed to weigh him down with his own cruelties to her. His shame at their straits, his haste to get away when she told her yarns of starving livestock, of lack and dust and hunger. Lately he'd come to think two ways, that not only did she relish her hard luck, it was due to some flaw in her, and she had somehow brought it on herself.

Before she could get going on the tired subject of hard times, he said, "I know all that. It's just a hunt." He told her he was going to win the fifty dollars, buy himself some boots, she ought to be glad. It struck him that for such a sum he could buy boots *and* a shotgun, maybe a .22.

"It's a massacre, and I won't have it. You don't have my permission."

He never backtalked, but there was a saying at school and it came to him in the bitter voice of a boy whose father was in Korea. He wasn't sure what it meant, but it sounded good, and so he said it. "Who's going to stop me, you and Coxey's army?" He shouldered his pea jacket and made for the door.

When she darted between him and the doorway, bracing her hands against the jamb, he tried to angle past her, but she set her weight. In a movement he didn't think was rough, only determined, he lifted her up and set her to the side. His last sight of her was of her shocked gaze, and he felt hollow and apart, but in a strange way good. He was a boy at large, a man almost. He would go where he wanted.

He and Pete rode in the back of the flatbed Ford among hay bales and canvas tarpaulins. Cade drove out Highway 54 toward the town of Ninnescah, a trip of forty miles across the shortgrass plains of the Arkansas River Valley. The late-winter wind bit hard, backdrafting around the cab to buffet them as they rode through the darkness. His nose ran in the cold; his ear hurt worse. He wedged his head between two bales and tried to sleep.

They stopped at a filling station at the halfway point, a round stucco structure with a gaslight beacon, its beam dimming against advancing daylight. CAIRO LIGHTHOUSE, read the sign in the lot. Joking, Jesse said to Pete, "Hey, where are we, Egypt?" but Pete only stared dully and later Jesse learned that natives pronounced Cairo *Kay-row,* like the syrup.

Cars and trucks were nosed in toward the door, and the dirt lot looked like a carnival, filled with people headed for the drive. Pete went inside the café with Cade, but Jesse had no money to spend on breakfast and so he stayed in the truck bed. While the others were inside, a gray DeSoto spluttered past, its dragging tailpipe throwing sparks. In the back window Jesse thought he saw Sanders Moody. In the half-light he couldn't tell for certain, but he waved regardless, just in case. He wished he hadn't shot his mouth off; he'd forgotten that outside the city limits things were pretty white. All white. Whoever was driving the DeSoto ought to have known that. Still, he wished he hadn't bragged.

Cade and Pete came out with a skinny, freckled, red-haired man who wore a Sam Browne belt over GI fatigues. Even at a distance Jesse smelled whiskey and Wildroot Cream Oil.

Pete climbed back in the truck bed. "Old Ray Ellis," he said, his voice sounding worshipful, "he's got a big Colt semiautomatic. Eleven to a clip. He showed us. Now we're gonna have some fun, you watch."

"They'll take it off him," Jesse said. "No guns allowed."

Pete snorted. "Tell that to Ray Ellis." His hard look made Jesse drop the subject. Besides, what use was it to argue when the rules were firm?

Pete shared his sack of sorghum molasses doughnuts. Jesse ate three. Breakfast made his head feel better, so he sat up the rest of the way, considering that he might have shaken the bug. He considered too that he might have brought his illness on himself, as punishment for lying to Ab. But he hadn't yet told the lie, so as of this minute he was still in the clear at work except that now his lie was halfway true.

Several miles past Ninnescah they pulled into a pasture where cars and trucks were parked in rows. Women at camp stoves fried bacon and venison sausage, made flapjacks, boiled coffee over Sterno cans. Kids darted through the clusters of men lolling at tailgates. Some of the men had smeared their faces with soot and bear grease; some had garbed themselves like warriors from forgotten tribes. Most wore Big Smith overalls and barn coats, but among the farmers and ranchers Jesse saw army-issue flak jackets and bandoliers from which dangled hammers, nunchucks, homemade saps.

He shouldered the hoe handle he had brought and carried his

counterfeit vouching note to Cade. The older man read it, then gave him a lopsided look he couldn't read. Cade spat tobacco juice, then tucked the note in his shirt pocket.

Around him, beaters compared weapons. Broomsticks and two-by-fours, stovepipes, mallets and pipe wrenches, marble pouches, leather saps loaded with buckshot, birdshot, bearings. Billy clubs, belaying pins, a tennis racket in a wooden press, gun stocks and lamp poles, cast-iron skillets. Pete had a monkey wrench and Cade a square-blade shovel. Jesse waited for somebody to take it off him. The shovel seemed to ride the line. But nobody came around to check. Ray Ellis, making like it was a joke, swung a caveman cudgel like Alley Oop had in the Sunday funnies, saying the club wasn't old Sam Colt but it would do. When he winked at Cade, who laughed, Jesse wondered whether the gun was safely in the truck or if Ray Ellis had concealed it.

On the crowd's fringe stood the man who'd driven the DeSoto. Sanders and a smaller kid Jesse thought might be his cousin—Feeney, his name was—hung close by. There were no other black people in the crowd. Ray Ellis eyed them, slung his club over his shoulder. "Get me some jungle bunnies, maybe."

The Boylans laughed at his wisecrack, but Jesse felt sick again. As the truck rolled into Ninnescah he'd seen the usual signs. VFW, ANCIENT AND ACCEPTED SCOTTISH RITE, KIWANIS, LOYAL ORDER OF MOOSE. Behind them was a smaller sign painted on plywood, NIGGER DON'T LET THE SUN GO DOWN ON YOU HERE. He'd seen such signs before, but never when there'd been any black people around. Looking at it had made him feel bad, feel strange, almost as if he'd written the words himself.

The organizers came around with maps of the acreage. In the center of the four-mile section a stake fence the size of a ball diamond's infield had been erected, a stack of hay bales in the center. The idea was to flush the rabbits from the brush and drive them into the stockade. The coursers were numbered off and directed to as-

semble at check stations at the corners of the coursing area, then
spread out ten paces from the next man in line. Grouped with the
eastern line, Jesse took a place between Cade and Pete. Down the
line next to Cade, Sanders stood with Feeney. The two looked small
and citified, out of place, alone. Sanders wore his track shoes. The
man who brought them made ready to head for his line assignment.
Ray Ellis had drawn a number for another line, as well. Jesse was
glad; with him gone the day might turn out all right.

But Ray Ellis didn't leave. Jesse looked around for an official who
would come and send him away, but nobody seemed to care. "We get
the chance," Ray Ellis said, "we'll give them little Rastus-juniors
what for!"

Pete guffawed, but Jesse looked at the ground until Ray Ellis
walked back to his place, then he stepped forward from the line,
hoping to catch Sanders's eye and let him know he had no part.
When Sanders glanced his way, Jesse raised his hand. The other boy
ignored him, bending down to say something to Feeney that made
him snicker, putting on for his cousin, Jesse knew, and acting tough,
above it all, like Jesse was beneath his notice.

Cade had been watching. He crossed to Pete, snaked out a fist to
sucker punch him in the belly. "Oof," Pete said, sounding like a cartoon bad guy with the air knocked out of him. When his turn came,
Jesse dodged the feint. Cade roughed his hair. "Go get 'em, boy.
Show everybody them fine auspices you got!"

He'd said it *aws-pisses,* growling something else under his breath,
but all Jesse caught was the tag end, something about Jesse trying to
rise above his raising.

The day was now more messed up than before. His lies, his acting
big for Sanders, the way he'd barged past his mother, Ray Ellis's
meanness, and Cade's mockery, all these clotted up with his sore
throat and seemed to bore through him like a molten rod; but before
he could sort out the way he felt, the starter fired a shot and the drive
was on.

The line surged forward, a rear guard of girls and women banging pans, gobbling like turkeys. Men and boys whooped Rebel yells and war cries as they coursed through the thigh-high brush, and Jesse forgot about the others when the first leaper flushed, a big buck jackrabbit with a frowsy patch of mange where skull met shoulder blades bounding ahead of him, the creature's black-rimmed ears laid back, haunches vaulting the tawny body forward.

One of the rules of the drive was to keep an even pace, but still he stepped up speed. The back of his neck crawled, his ear throbbed as he stumbled over a hidden lay in the tall grass where leverets curled like a nest of mice, exposed without the doe that sprang up harum-scarum. She zigzagged to decoy him, her shrieks so human that the urge to yell tore in his own chest, and it was all he could do not to burst into a run. Another sprang up—a buck or doe he couldn't tell—then more and more, too many to keep track of, and the prairie was alive with them, thick as the beggar's-lice that clung to his jeans, jumping at random, haphazard as hot popcorn in a hopper. Ringnecks and bobwhites sometimes startled up, a whir of wings and displaced air, his own heart thumping, catching at the fear and glory of it.

For a mile or so they harried the field, the line of beaters tightening, now only a few feet from each other and close enough for Jesse to hear Pete goading Sanders with a schoolyard joke so ignorant and ugly that he couldn't believe that in the clean wide-open country he'd be hearing it. "What's pink and purple on the outside, black on the inside, has four wheels, no brakes, and hollers?"

Pete had circled around so that the Boylans flanked Sanders and Feeney, who came on, their faces grim, holding their ground but closer to each other than they'd been before. "Hey, Moody, you! Big track star! I said, 'What's pink and purple on the outside, black on the inside, has four wheels, no brakes, and hollers?'"

Jesse knew the punch line. Everybody knew it. The joke was going around; you heard it at the Orpheum and in the street, in the halls and on the playground no matter how the teachers tried to stop it. The answer was: a Caddy full of niggers driving off a cliff.

Sanders and his cousin slowed their pace, hanging back as Pete renewed his baiting. "What's pink and purple on the outside, black on the inside, has four wheels . . ."

". . . no brakes, and hollers for their mamas!" Ray Ellis bellowed, taking up the shout.

Cade called forward, "Hey, aws-pisses, I bet you know the answer!"

Pete yelled, "Get back here, Spoon, you little runt!"

Jesse wanted to do right. If he could only always do right, there'd never be a reason for him to think that he was less than anybody else. But no matter how he wanted to do right, he always did wrong anyway, and all his fine intentions came to squat. If he went back, what could he do? Say stop? He knew what Pete would call him. They would have to fight. He couldn't blurt the punch line just to get it over with. It was ugly, wrong, but also there was this: Even though he hadn't meant to, the first time he heard the joke he'd laughed. Alone behind his locker door, until his belly ached, he'd laughed, and he wasn't laughing because everybody in the hallway was or because it was contagious, he was laughing because the picture struck him funny, because an awful cartoon reel rolled in his mind, unstoppable as a bad dream, the lurid car cram-packed with dark-faced riders yelling bloody murder as the Cadillac went airborne off a cliff. The cartoon was horrible, but it struck him so hilarious it hurt, it cracked him up, even though he knew how wrong it was and tried to stop. What if the awful urge took over and he cracked up again? What if Sanders knew he'd laughed, had seen him? Even if he hadn't, what if his guilt was written on him now, was rising off him thick as fumes?

With the rabbits swarming ahead of him across the plains, the Boylans bawling out the joke behind him, he couldn't think fast enough to see how right and wrong shook down, and when another jack flushed close and he felt the rush of air and heard the scrabble of hind legs on turf, that seemed to set him free to run. He ran and nothing mattered but the way his feet pounded the earth and blood thrummed in his aching head. He was no fire-eyed John Brown with beard-tails streaming in the wind, no hero, no defender, he was an eighth-grade country boy with shirt cardboard in his shoes, who couldn't help his running any more than he could have helped his laughing. It was not on him. He hadn't started it.

Ahead of the others, he passed through a sheltered draw, a dry creek bed where scrub elderberry grew head high. Out on the other side and headed for the center pen now visible in the distance, he heard behind him in the thicket a commotion. Shouting, a scuffle, then a thunk, the wind-knocked-from-you sound like Pete gave out when Cade socked him a good one. He slowed, then turned to jog in place. He couldn't see but he could guess at what was happening. The Boylans were bushwhacking Sanders and the littler kid, cracking their knees or heads with club or wrench or shovel, maybe with all three. He thought of running back, but he couldn't get himself to do it and soon enough Pete came out, then Cade and Ray Ellis, breathing hard and walking fast. Pete whooped, cuffing Ray Ellis on the shoulder, and Cade yelled "Teach you!" back into the thicket.

Jesse tried to make it look like he'd been heading forward all along, fast-walking, but there was a crawling feeling between his shoulder blades, as if he bore a mark, a target, and whether or not Ray Ellis had a gun—he couldn't think—it felt like any second he would hear a shot and feel a bullet in his back.

With a surge of copper in his throat, a swelling in his chest, a second wind rose in him, and he was running again, leaving them behind as he plowed through the dry waist-high grass into the clutter of jackrabbits in a boiling sea of pelts that streamed toward the stockade. Heart hammering, he sprinted the last hundred yards to the pen where a big man in a suit coat and a string tie hoisted an arm around his neck and hefted him so that his feet came off the ground. Another man grasped his hand and raised it like a boxer's at the Forum, and then he was in a press of men who ringed him, saying, "Attaboy, fine job."

Jackrabbits in a ragged river ahead of them, the four lines of beaters converged, flapping coats and hats and driving toward the pen. Jesse saw the Boylans shouldered up, yee-hawing like it was a rodeo. Sanders, his nose streaming blood, straggled in, limping on Feeney's shoulder. The man who vouched went to them and stood by, looked sick, looked blank, looked something. Jesse couldn't read the look except to know it was a mix of shame and anger and the bitter knowledge there was nothing he could do. Jesse fixed his gaze on Sanders, willing him to look his way, trying to make his face say it was not his fault, but things were happening too fast, and Sanders never looked his way, not once.

A man with a bullhorn shouted to the crowd for quiet and the human din diminished, overtaken by the rabbits' shrieks, the sound of thumping from the pen, low and thundering, the frantic drumming of hind feet. The bullhorn man yelled, "Folks, if we all tried to go in we'd only mangle our own selves, so here's ten of our early birds to do the honors. Two sawbucks out of my own pocket—plus the fifty—for the young man who clobbers down the most."

Hands shoved Jesse inside the pen. He waded in among the screeching rabbits to a place near the stacked bales. Dirt flew thick as some of the jackrabbits dug, trying to scuttle under the fence or squeeze through the gaps between the stakes. Some climbed each other's backs, some leapt against the fence like beetles at a screen. One of the men had thrust a ball bat on Jesse and he raised it, brought it down against the swarm, struck dirt.

He tried again but all the rabbits had blurred into one sorry-looking mass. Outside the pen the crowd yelled, laying odds and making bets, but in his mind he heard the team captains in the schoolyard at Horace Mann as they chose sides for a kickball game,

one captain saying *hell, can't anybody tell you guys apart,* and everybody
standing there uneasy, laughing because for some dumb reason it was
funny—the captain said it funny—and even the Ninth Street kids
waiting to be picked were laughing, laughing with an edge to it like
they didn't want to but they couldn't either stop. They too were
helpless not to laugh, they had to be good sports and go along if they
didn't want to be the odd man out, and Jesse hated it that nobody—
not him, not them, not anybody—could slam on the brakes, say
stop. The stupid joke was funny in the first place because a pink-and-
purple Caddy was a tricked-out heap nobody but a bunch—he
brought down the bat, again struck dirt; he *wouldn't* think the
word—of *morons* would be caught dead in. If it wasn't halfway true,
nobody'd have to laugh, and so whose fault was that? Letty said that
only morons planted moss rose in their ratty dirt front yards because
of being layabouts too shiftless to mow grass and so the moss rose
grew up in a riot, and Jesse thought the tender little flowers should
have looked innocent and pretty to anybody who passed them on the
sidewalk, but morons like big, clumsy Letty had to laugh behind
their backs because they knew better, they were above such things
and had to laugh to prove they were. Why couldn't everybody know
the same damn things, see things the same damn way? Why couldn't
they see that the pink-and-purple Cadillac set them apart? That moss
rose in a front yard might as well have been a kick-me sign? If everybody understood these things, none of this would have to happen,
and the Caddy wouldn't have to screech over the guardrail and nobody, especially a boy who didn't want to, would have to laugh. Even
if nobody ever changed, he wouldn't laugh again, he promised, but
he thought it might be hopeless anyway, awful and ridiculous and
doomed, so wrong a thousand John Browns couldn't stop it, it bored
into you so deep, stealing in as silently as polio or sleeping sickness
until it worked its way back out, and who was he to think it could be
shaken off by any good intentions? Everybody put himself above

somebody else. It was no secret. It was a big unspoken rule. The world was ringed like Saturn, and on every ring somebody bigger, smarter, faster, somebody *more* something stood lording down, and it was wrong. He didn't want to be lorded over, and he didn't want to be above. He wanted to be with, among, the same, getting along and usual, but still sometimes those thoughts, even that word he'd never say, would come into his mind and rise up like a sign, *Don't Let the Sun Go Down on You.* No matter that he wanted to be pals or good or noble, those thoughts, his *over-ness* sprang up unwanted even as he looked straight in somebody other's—Sanders's, anybody black's— eyes, and something sick—infected—deep inside him made him think them. He brought down the bat on the packed dirt so hard his arms burned in their sockets, raised it, brought it down again.

Swinging wildly at the rabbits, he missed, and missed again. It made him want to throw the bat. It made him want to cry. He couldn't hit a single one although the screaming rabbits milled so thick around him that they scrabbled at his feet, one snagging its hind leg in his jeans cuff, wriggling out. Their heat and shit stench choked him. The other boys inside the cage were bashing them like sixty and the blood and fur were flying and the swarm became a picture of the messed-up world laid out and asking for it. The world was not just messed up, it was broken, as shot to hell and blasted as the garish Caddy's brakes. It was a joke you had to laugh at or you'd go stark- raving and there ought to be a law but even if there was people would break it. Hell, *he* would break it.

He brought the ball bat down and down again until at last he struck a rabbit, a dazed, weak animal that darted toward him, stun- ning it so raw he had to beat it dead to end its suffering. Its eyes rolled crazy as outside the cage shouts urged him on, and he could swear the rabbit held him in its golden gaze as life leaked out, its eyes glazed over, and it learned for good the lesson that it had to learn. The lesson was *Give up,* but Jesse couldn't, and he brought the ball bat down so many times the turf grew slick, and he was spewing snot and tears. And then the ground itself began to pitch and heave, and he went down.

They'd hauled him from the pen, he guessed when he came to in the truck bed halfway back to Wichita. He'd been covered with a tarp. Feverish, he had passed in and out of awareness, his jaw rattling so bad he bit his tongue, bringing him awake to his own stench. He reeked of mud and vomit, his own body odor fouler than the stockyards on days they cut the bullocks. His jeans and shirt were stiff with blood. One of his shoes was gone.

The Boylans rode in the cab, and when they stopped along a hedgerow to make water he gathered dimly from their talk that Ray Ellis had gone off to raise Cain somewhere else. When Cade passed the truck bed and saw Jesse sitting up, he said amiably, "Guess you shoulda stood in bed. You're one sick little bast . . . boy, ain't you? And us the fools to put good money on you."

Jesse tried to move his mouth but couldn't. He had heard the other word behind the one Cade had come out with. He didn't know if Cade had meant to cuss him or to brag him up, to say that Jesse had been one tough kid. He didn't care. The word stung, and the holding back stung worse, but he felt numb, as if he'd waited all his life to hear the word, and when it came it wasn't any big surprise.

Pete had wrapped an oil rag around his knuckles and he cradled his hand, rubbing it as if he wanted Jesse to notice his injury. "Had to lug you two hard miles acrost a field. You went down like a sack of rocks before you whopped a single bunny," but Jesse knew that wasn't true. Pete was either trying to get his goat or cover him for bawling, but it didn't matter which.

Later in the machine shop the Boylans would crow about the day, saying wasn't Ray Ellis just a pure-dee hotspur, wasn't Pete a chip off the old block, but Jesse wouldn't be there. He would not go to the welding shop again. Sanders and his family would rage or grieve over his banged-up nose, over the broken way of things, but Jesse wouldn't go to Ninth Street either. He'd be a solitary ring, a ring of one, so far off in the outer dark no other ring could touch him. He knew why from the start the corner kids had spurned him and why Sanders looked away, why Cade had mocked him for his airs. Part of it was maybe that they knew him better than he knew himself, but the biggest part had to be that they too were ashamed of how they measured up and how they squared excuses for themselves the same way Jesse had squared his, all of them, Pete, Cade, Ray Ellis, and himself, Sanders, Feeney, and the man who vouched, trying to close the distance between the *not-enough* they feared they were, the *over-ness* they needed to believe in. The man was brave or lucky who could step across the line, and for his own failure his punishment was perfect: He could not again look straight in anybody else's eyes without the knowledge of that distance showing in his own.

The Boylans dropped him at the duplex. Upstairs, his mother stood at the hot plate, putting on the kettle. From her day at work, she wore her uniform with its brown-checkered collar, her frilled cap bobby-pinned to her thin hair like a limp crown. Just before he sank into a kitchen chair, he marveled at how she held herself upright, how anybody did. Her lift shoe was off, the angles of her hipbones out of kilter as she pivoted, turning her back to him as she waited for the coil to redden. "Mr. Murdock telephoned the Trailways. I had to tell him where you went. He said he hated to do it, but he'd have to let you go."

He knew she would say no more. About small things she could go on and on, but about the big ones he could count on her to hold her peace. The ruin of the day was his alone, and she would let him bear it. It came to him that he knew her in a way he'd not known her before, that he understood her silences, knew that her acquaintance with regret ensured that she would understand its hold on him.

She took a chair across from him, sat gazing at the darkened window but with her stare turned inward, as if to listen for an old lost certain voice to tell her what to do. "Son," she said, shaking her head, and that was all.

His throat caught when he heard the homely, simple word for what he was to her. He swallowed, wanting to tell her he was sorry but he didn't know for what exactly and he understood she knew this and there was no need for words. Soon enough, he guessed, they would move on, leaving the city for another place along the road, and soon enough the time would come when he would leave to make his way alone. Someday his mother might forgive herself enough to speak about his father; he hoped he would be strong enough to take it like a man. For a long moment he considered that he'd been born lonely, but when he put his head down on the table and felt her cool hand smooth his cowlick, a touch that if he had felt well he wouldn't have held still for, he knew this wasn't true.

"Would you like me to fix you a cup of tea?"

"No," he told her, his head still resting on the table, "but thank you, Mama. I appreciate it." He didn't sound quite like himself. His own voice sounded distant, as if he'd left already, had come back a stranger.

"Well, then," she said. Although the words meant nothing and she said them all the time when she was at a loss or when she wanted to move past things, a shy pride in him seemed to weight her tone. "Well, then," she said again.

Up the window glass frost flowers bloomed, precise and intricate and beautiful, the streetlamp outside the pane refracting them like shards; but just now it hurt to look at anything, and it felt best to sink into himself and close his eyes.

2

~

Garden of the Gods

Yes, she knew them. They were her grown sons Sam and William and she loved them dearly but she wished they wouldn't loom over the bed to ask her did she. Wished they wouldn't block the patch of sunlight that stole across the floor. If they stood aside, and if the fog would lift, the view would show the gray Pacific, and she wanted to see it, see the far edge of the continent, the place she'd come to rest, having gone as far as she could go. She tried to nod so they could see her answer, the part she hoped they would remember.

A breeze soughed through the open window. It was late afternoon. The sheets were snowy, freshly changed. The nurse had spread a clean sheepskin beneath her. In the bedside chair sat her husband of thirty years, stricken by her fast decline but trying not to show it. Del worked the Sunday crossword, stuck on a word he'd given clues for at least twice. Soon enough, as if she'd spoken it aloud, he would supply the word himself, talking either to keep her in his world or keep himself in hers.

The chart clipped to the footboard of the bed her body lay in gave her name as Marlene Delaney, but her history was invisible, and she had long ago determined she would keep it so. No deathbed confession; she had heard one once—her mother's—and the keeping of it from her sister was a part of what had driven her from home. For her sons, there would be none of that. Even if she had the breath or strength to speak, she would keep her silence to the end; it was the price for bartering her old life for the new.

Long before she felt the mass under her ribs, she'd known its source, its name, how long it had been hidden in her. She'd married young, her first as near a shotgun wedding as her pride allowed. There she was like yesterday before the magistrate, wearing the horrid dress, a limp sack of a flowered thing she'd given up trying to belt over her swollen middle, standing between her father in his black Sunday coat too big for him and her lank boy-husband Audie with the smear of dried soapsuds behind his ear. He was a hapless hired boy she'd lain with only once. Simple figuring told her he was the baby's father and not the man who had come after, a man she wished she didn't want but couldn't make herself stop wanting.

That one had left without so much as a good-bye. She'd walked over to his home place to seek him out and found the clapboard house abandoned, dusty curtains waving out the open window. When she set a match to them, the tattered cotton went up like a torch she'd borne for him. Later, even as she stood on the puncheon floorboards of the courthouse, the magistrate's sour breath making her gorge rise as he said the words *love, honor, and obey,* binding Mary Etta Spoon to Audubon Jay Kipp, she vowed she would go after Becker Birdsall, force him to believe the child was his and make good on his promise.

The child, Georgette, was five months old when she made her getaway. She packed a few things in a flour sack—her sister had made off with their straw suitcase—and waited until the men had gone out to a far field, then she left on foot. Even as she walked, she puzzled at the bundled presence in her arms. Why had she not left the child behind? The answer came quickly enough: The men would be away for hours; she didn't want Georgette to cry. No love for the infant had yet crept into her heart—only a weary sense of duty—but she feared something she left behind would draw her back.

Keeping to back roads, she made it to the Kansas farmhouse where her sister worked. She remembered hunger, heat, the drone of locusts, the open screen door, and the smell of bacon wafting out. Mackie wouldn't let her in, and that, she knew, was just. An eye for an eye; her sister loved the boy who was her legal husband, and she, Etta the Bad, had known it from the start. Worse, maybe, she'd told her sister a truth she didn't want to hear.

In those times most travelers were good to help one another, supplying blankets, BC powders, sympathy, advice, a sack of nickel hamburgers from a roadside stand. Once, when the baby bit her breast so hard she cried, an Arkie granny woman from the cotton fields predicted that her milk was drying up, and it was so. But before long she had a feeding bottle with a big black rubber nipple and cow's milk almost anywhere she asked.

Walking, she practiced reasons to be on the road. A sailor husband out in San Diego. A cousin in San Bernardino. A lost pocketbook. Good lies, but no one pried. She gave her name as Marlene Smith, the first name pronounced like the actress's. Smith, she always joked, was said the usual way.

She could have guessed Audie would try to follow her, but the first time she saw her father's Model A as it juddered past with Audie behind the wheel, she nearly knocked over the bench where she was sitting with a family who shared their lunch. She had been reaching under the picnic table for an orange that had rolled there, and when she swung back up she saw the car. Audie hadn't seen her, but she knew he'd either read her mind or found Becker's address in Manitou jotted on a scrap and knew where she was bound. At the next crossroads she headed north.

Her outstretched thumb earned her a ride as far as Las Animas, Colorado. Begging milk from a filling station market, one thing leading to another, she had taken up with Vaughn and Nita Richard. Pulling a new silver trailer behind a sleek green Hudson, they were on their way to the Garden of the Gods, near Manitou. College teachers from Baton Rouge, long-married, carefree, with no trace of the wind-bitten doggedness of the others who fled the plains, Vaughn and Nita laughed a lot—so many things were *just outrageous*—and every evening they drank Scotch whiskey from crystal tumblers with initials etched into the glass. They wore rolled dungarees and flannel shirts and saddle oxfords. A pair of glasses perched on Nita's nose. Vaughn smoked a pipe.

They said educated things in foreign languages, calling their trip *der Wunderjahr*. They traveled with boxes full of books. Vaughn was writing one himself, he said, and every day he'd lug out a big black Royal and set it on a card table. The keys clacked steadily, the table shook, and pages piled up beside the typewriter, weighted with a rock. At night they cleared the table and played cards.

To Vaughn and Nita it was a given that she was running from a man. Past that, she hadn't had to say much. She made up a tale about a bull-riding uncle she was meeting out in Winnemucca. The Nevada town's name rolled off her tongue; she wasn't sure exactly where it was. "Uncle Pug is after me to join the rodeo," she'd said.

"How fascinating that would be," said Nita, but Etta wasn't sure she really meant it. Sometimes the Richards looked at her as if the things she said were strange. Their quickness often made her shy, so she took care to be helpful, quiet, good, to laugh when they said something was outrageous, to mind her p's and q's. Now, she knew they must have seen her as a crazy, lying, Okie girl trying to make herself bigger than she was, and the memory of the airs she put on could make her wince. But mostly the couple had been kind.

They delighted in Georgette, singing lullabies she hadn't thought to sing, familiar songs she'd been too numb to recollect as she tended the baby in a fog of duty, and the baby yearned toward them, resting her head against their shoulders. Nita held the child for hours on end, crooning and making silly noises, and Vaughn was a baby-loving man, extravagant in his affection. Darling bitty, he would call the child. One afternoon when Etta was sitting on a blanket in the sun, the baby in her lap, Vaughn picked a dandelion and in a courtly gesture he bowed low to present it to Georgette. The baby grasped it by the stem and slowly brought the flower to her nose. Vaughn was charmed. He snapped their picture with his Leica. "You moved," he said to Etta, "but I think I caught the bitty."

In the Garden of the Gods they camped in a pine forest. The air was thin and dry, the park immense and beautiful, spreading out over the countryside of red ochre sandstone rising in spires and pillars, craggy boulders balanced on thin stems, stern marvels of a palisaded wonderland that made her think of the red walls of Jericho, a thought she pushed away for the way it reminded her of her father's Old Testament religion. Sunlight struck the juts and angles of the rocks so they appeared to change each time she looked at them, their otherworldly shadows shifting on the valley floor. Pikes Peak hulked in the distance. From the doorway of the tent her new friends set up for her beside the trailer, she could see its summit.

Vaughn and Nita planned to stay until the first snow fell, and Etta was so enchanted by them that she almost forgot her plan to seek out Becker. She was off him anyway, enough time had passed for her to understand she'd been a fool. Instead, she began to spin daydreams of going back to Baton Rouge with them. They could be a happy family, a society of three, talking of books and politics and playing cards to all hours of the night, drinking highballs from etched crystal. They would all write books.

When the Model A passed by again, she had been walking down the path from the pit toilet at the trailhead. Although she wasn't in the line of sight, she ducked into a stand of spruce. Audie was bent over the wheel and peering straight ahead, turtle-eyed and sleepy. She wondered if it was chance that led him to her or if someone had seen her—maybe as she'd begged the milk, the scene she'd made before the Richards came to her rescue.

"You look as if you'd seen a ghost," Nita said, when Etta returned to camp. She was dealing a hand of cards at the fold-down table under the awning. "Gin, anyone?" Nita laughed her hearty laugh, and ice cubes chinked so loudly that Etta feared the noise would wake Georgette, sleeping in her apple crate in the tent beside the trailer.

"I'm sick," she said, the lie springing to her tongue. What if he'd stopped around the bend, was waiting for nightfall to make his ambush?

She jerked her head toward the privy trail she'd just come down. "Watch the baby, will you?"

Vaughn's gaze sought Nita's, and she wondered if they doubted her story about feeling ill. She'd lied enough to know when people suspected untruth—that eye catch was a certain sign—but just now she couldn't care.

Out of their sight, she threaded her way through the trees, up a sandstone outcrop that overlooked a bend in the road near Balance Rock, and there was the car, parked in a turnout. Audie slouched in the seat, his beat-up Stetson covering his face. She didn't know if he was catnapping or if he meant to sleep for the night, but she couldn't trust him either way, and so she set up watch, wedging herself among the rocks and pulling her skirt over her knees.

Woodsmoke drifted past, and with it the smells of cooking from other campsites. The sun slipped behind the ridge, and darkness fell. The wind was cold. In the distance, the baby cried, then quieted. A sudden fear rose in her that the Richards would worry, would come to check on her, and so she hurried to the campsite to show herself.

"Are you all right?" Vaughn asked when she appeared.

"No," she told them, needlessly whispering. She made a show of gripping at her belly.

"Marlene, we're worried about you," he began. "We think you ought to tell us what you're—"

"Don't," she said. Her answer sounded harsh and so she softened her voice. "Don't worry. It's just something I ate." She told them she'd feel better if she spent the night close to the privy.

Nita shook her head, then pressed a woolen army blanket on her. "Take this, then."

She was glad for the blanket. It was cold in the woods, dark among the trees behind the privy. She was afraid of bears and rattlesnakes and mountain lions, and her heart raced at the slightest rustle in the underbrush, but by the gleam of moonlight on the Ford's fender she was able to keep Audie and the car in view. In the morning, when the coast was clear, she would go down. She would be much improved although still weak. They would take up as before. She would stop her needless lying, level with her friends.

The sound of a car engine grumbling to life woke her early, as the sun was glinting off the ridge, and she peered out from her hiding place to see the Ford making a turn to head back down the mountain. Scrambling through the forest, she made it to the campsite's clearing in time to see Audie knocking at the trailer door. He'd taken off his hat, and she noticed how long his hair had grown, longer now than the rawhide tie he gathered it into.

Vaughn stepped out under the awning. In the doorway behind him, Nita cradled the baby. Audie talked to Vaughn awhile, then pointed down the road, seeming to ask a question. Vaughn shook his head. Nita shook hers, too, hefting the baby to her shoulder so the child faced the inside of the trailer. When Audie brought out a piece of paper, she knew it was one of the pencil drawings he had made of her during the suffocating months they spent as man and wife, when his longing for her seemed more stifling than the heat. Both looked at the drawing and shook their heads, and with relief and gratitude she understood her friends were lying for her. Nita jiggled the baby in a protective way, drawing up the swaddling blanket as if the child were cold. She vanished into the trailer's interior. Again Vaughn shook his head.

It would have been so easy, after the car had trundled down the mountain road, for her to step into the clearing. But she couldn't move. The lies she'd told seemed to close in on her, jumbled up and teetering like rocks about to fall, too many to sort out, too many questions to remember or to count, too many to make sense of, and she was lost inside them, and so she turned away, working her way through the trees toward the road.

She walked all day. It had to be a sin to feel so light, so free, released, but the sin of it was not that she felt free, but that to turn away had been so easy. She knew that what she'd done meant something she could not take back. She knew that there was no forgiveness for it. But there she was in the middle of doing it. Wrong as it was, she determined she would do it, and the solitary power of her resolve seemed to burst in her brain like sparks, recalled to her the girl she'd been before she had been trapped. The daredevil who walked around a silo rim, wind in her hair, who raced a coal black horse to town alone and made it back before they missed her and they never the wiser, the girl whose will could not be bent, whose spirit wouldn't break. No one could make her do a thing she didn't want to do. Not her father and not Audie, not Vaughn or Nita or the baby. Nothing could change her mind, not guilt or sense, not even love.

The road wound down the mountainside toward Manitou. By dusk she'd nearly reached the outskirts. A steady stream of cars went by, park visitors, sightseers, but she kept well back from the road unless a hairpin turn took up the roadcut, then she waited in the brush until she saw her chance. On the steep downhill slopes, she had the sense of hurtling toward the future stretching out before her, shining like the lights of town below.

She reassured herself of her clean break. She'd given a false name; they couldn't track her. She'd made no mention of her home, of her father or her sister, had left no token of herself that they could use to find her. When she recalled the Leica and the picture Vaughn had snapped, it was this small thing that slowed her steps. Not because it was a clue, a sign, or evidence, but because she'd seen the picture in her mind as he had taken it, and now she couldn't seem to get it out. There was the baby on her lap, the dandelion wilting in her hand. What charmed them then was what had stopped her now—the way Georgette had taken the flower, received it gravely, with the surest hand, seeming to understand it was a tribute, accepting it with solemn grace. That meant something. What? Power, will, a soul? She didn't know, but something.

She began to walk again, but her steps had become heavy, and she found she was resisting the momentum that pulled her downhill. She didn't want the baby, but yet she did. What kind of selfishness was that? Not to want a child but yet to balk at her loving someone else? Was it jealousy she felt, the stir of mother love? She didn't know that either.

The road had leveled off, and she walked out onto the shoulder and stood out in the open for a while. To rest, she told herself, but then longing settled like an ache deep in her bones, a simple longing for the child's flesh, for the way, setting her feet against Etta's belly and grasping her fingers, Georgette would pull up to a stand, all will and all determination stiffening her body as she squealed the thrill of her achievement. Even now, forty years later, she could feel the baby's grip around her thumbs.

Step after step she took away and down the mountain told her she would soon turn back, would begin to make her way back up, but still she couldn't make herself stop walking. Any minute, any minute she would turn, go back and finish what she'd started, make her excuses and start fresh, begin her life, one different from the one she had imagined, but livable.

It was ridiculous, the kind of thing her superstitious sister might have done, but she sought a sign, a trigger. A falling leaf, a scuttling mouse, a rustle from the pines, something to mark the moment, urge her back, something to release her from the great spell of herself. When the sweep of headlights from a car coming around the bend toward her lit the road, habit made her crouch behind a boulder while her heart beat wildly but with joy at knowing what she wanted and for knowing, for the first time, that her choice was right, and more, that it was good.

It was only after the car sped past her hiding place that she saw it was the Hudson, packed to the roof, the silver trailer coming on behind.

On the chance they would come looking for her where she told them she was headed, she went to Winnemucca and took work as a hotel maid. A year went by, then another. No one came. Often she thought of writing them in Baton Rouge, but the telephone book had no listing for a Vaughn and Nita Richard. And even if it had, what would she say? That she'd changed her mind, she didn't mean it, it was all a big misunderstanding? By the time she met Del, another exile, a South Dakota boy fleeing the plains, in one word, *Gone,* she had erased her past.

"Marlene," he was saying now, his voice hesitant, uncertain, on the cusp of his desire, as if he didn't know whether to try to speak her name to bring her back or to release her. His crossword puzzle was finished; the folded newspaper lay on the tray beside her water pitcher. It was coming on dusk. He alone was in the room with her, Sam and William having left while she was drifting. At her unspoken question about the boys, he said, "They went out for a bite to eat. They won't be long."

How could she have foreseen, as she walked on down the mountain road telling herself the child was better off without a mother who could walk away, that the willfulness that wrecked her girlhood would depart, and she would live a placid life, unable to summon even the ghost of the reckless yearning that once drove her? That she would be happy, that she would wear rolled dungarees and flannel shirts and glasses, would settle near an ocean where water in absurd abundance rolled against the shore, causing her to wonder if she'd just imagined dust and drought, the dirty years she'd lived through. That she would own books, tall shelves of them she came to love like friends, and that once she would even try to write one, giving up when shadows seemed always to fall across the sunny stories she set out to tell. That she would have two sons, the leisure to spend days at the beach with them, smiling while they threw their bodies into the breakers, the boys exuberant when she joined them in the vast, mind-numbing roar, all of them emerging sunburned and salt-crusted, clean.

Times when her desire to find her daughter haunted her, she willed the want away. *Vanity of vanities,* she heard her father's voice. It would be selfish vanity to barge into her life, to upset things, to prod old scars, should there be any. Was it wrong to hope they'd lied to her, had in a backward way returned the favor, telling Georgette that she was only theirs? What if they'd changed her name? And what if her lost child was happy, was at peace the way her sister was in her illusion, steadfast in her adoration of the man she believed to be her father? She would make no attempts, would do no further harm. If she had had to play with fate, let her have done it once and then no more.

She must have twisted in the bed, for Del was straightening the sheets. Soon her sons would come into the room, smelling of salt air and the sea, to hover, to ask her did she really want the window open, wasn't she too chilly? At Del's gesture—he understood she couldn't bear a stillness in the air—they would agree to leave it open for the breeze. Soon, in their need for comfort, in their belief a word from her could ease their grief, the boys would hover over her to ask again if she knew them. Behind this question, she understood, was the ache to hear again the answer to a deeper question: *Do you love me?* If she could pit her will against her strength a final time, she'd try to nod. She'd tell them *Yes* as often as they needed. And if somewhere another voice was asking, she would send the answer out again, again, and hope the air would hold her message, pray, beyond deserving, it was heard.

3

Great Men and
Famous Deeds

After she forgave me and our long week of questions ended with the resolve to put my mistake behind us, my wife asked one last, rhetorical, unanswerable. "Thomas James O'Hanlon," she said sternly, as if using my full name for the first time in our half a century of marriage, "what *could* you have been thinking?" Whether the cause had been her manner of dismayed affront or my relief at being off the hot seat, her question struck me funny, and I laughed, idiot laughter, helpless, an outburst sudden as a sneeze that left me wheezing like the old man I'd become, and for a second time in need of accounting for myself.

We were in the kitchen of the house we bought when we retired from our law practices and moved to Virginia's Eastern Shore. Outside, beyond the marsh, across the Chesapeake, the sun was going down. I hadn't been acquitted altogether of my crime, but I'd been easing back into Eleanor's bristly graces. Then, on her way to the pantry to see what we might prepare for dinner, she tilted her head as if to consult her better sense and asked her question: What *could* I have been thinking?

Two weeks before, we'd had a visit from a former colleague, a lovely young woman named Anne whose specialty was medical malpractice. Apparently I'd made a pass at her. I say "apparently" not because I dispute Anne's word or mean to diminish her charge, but because I have no memory of the event and am able to recall only in a blurred way the events of what she later, in her letter, called "the incident."

On the second morning of her stay, Anne and I had taken our coffee to the dock. The morning was beautiful, the mist burning off, the light rosy and diffuse. "Lambent," I'd said, glad that in all the lost and errant thoughts that had begun to trouble me, in all the dead-end sentences and fugitive words, I'd found the word I wanted. Maybe because of the word's recall, maybe because a feeling had been dogging me—an amalgam of dread and desire and the sense that time was moving too fast when I wanted most for it to stand still—when she pointed out the periwinkle snails that clung to the spartina just above the tideline, I moved toward her. It wasn't until she was shoving me away, saying, "Tom!" that I understood that something had gone wrong. She'd left that afternoon, cutting short her visit.

A few days later a letter arrived addressed confidentially to Eleanor and thanking her for our hospitality but expressing worry about my health. The letter avoided diagnoses, but Anne's meaning was plain. She valued our friendship, I was a wonderful man, she enjoyed my company, et cetera, et cetera, but . . .

"You goat," said Eleanor, flinging the letter to the hall table. "How could you?"

"*Non compos mentis,* my big foot," she said, after I tried to convince her I didn't remember what so obviously I must have done. "You *had* to know, and now you plead diminished capacity?"

Her charge of dissembling troubled me almost as much as the fear of a memory lapse, one of those white reaches of time that my father, who suffered from them in his later years, called "spells." This much was clear: I'd touched Anne's breast, had left my hand there too long for accident.

The following week, as I've said, was difficult, with me trying to recollect the events of that morning and to defend myself, Elly hurt and miserable. "Admit it," she'd say, "just admit it and get it over with." She held so firm in her conviction that I'd knowingly groped our friend that I began to wonder what fears of her own about my worsening forgetfulness she'd been holding off, and so at last, although it wasn't true, I confessed. "Eleanor, you're right," I said. "I'm sorry."

My owning-up, however false, seemed to draw me back into my wife's affections and us into our usual peace, but then my outburst— once laughing, I broke up again and again—shattered this. I wanted to make things right between us, and so I pulled out a chair for Eleanor at the table, took one myself, and began to lay out an explanation, a memory, a story that in all our years I'd never told her, that rose to mind as perfectly, it seemed, as that found word on the morning at the dock. I write it now as a stay against its loss, and as an answer to the other question she had the kindness—or the fear—to leave unspoken: "How bad is it?"

Some miles past the outskirts of my flatland hometown lived a hermit known as Audie Kipp, who was rumored to have a fortune in silver ingots buried on his property. As misers went, he was unlikely. He lived in a squat trailer parked in a locust grove at a bend where Highway 81 curved around an oxbow of the Ninnescah. Aside from the bounty on coyotes he shot and the return deposits from bottles he scavenged from culverts, he had no apparent source of income. Every now and then he hauled a load of bottles into town in a buckboard drawn by a fat old jennet, a creature so gassy that it was one of the town marvels anyone could tolerate a ride behind her, the malady renowned enough to prompt one of the few ribaldries my father—before he left town, the Methodist minister—allowed himself. "A farting mule never kicks," he'd say, leaving me and my younger brothers to guess at his meaning, vaguely understanding that it had to do with the economies of pleasure.

Tormenting Audie Kipp had become a tradition in a place that took its few thrills from the rattlesnake hunt across the Oklahoma line and the fleabag carnival that set up each summer in the pasture behind the Meadowlark Drive-In, and so when word circled that the old man had been seen trolling ditches for pop bottles and was away from his place, carloads of high school boys mustered. Speculating all the way as to how by means of explosives and contraptions he might be delivered of his loot, some deputations went so far as to spang rocks against his rust-blighted trailer, and it was maintained that some seniors on a graduation dare were blasted with a volley from his sawed-off, but most war parties confined their derring-do to whooping through the wide loop of his lane. Because he never called the sheriff, the tale grew up that the old man's fortune was ill-gotten.

I've called him an old man though in that year of 1956 he must have been only in his middle thirties. The facts of his life, insofar as anybody knew them, represented that a family of Kipps had lived out at the Ninnescah Bottoms, but most had died in the Spanish Flu epidemic, orphaning Audie, who had been found wandering beside an icebound stock pond. Owing to his mother's tribal status and a fine point in the Dawes Act, he was sent to the boarding school at Chilocco. He wasn't heard from again until the late forties, when he turned up on the spit of land on the ten-year floodplain.

He was lank-framed, had huge hands and feet, a beetled brow that made him look sometimes Lincolnesque and sometimes apelike. He wore U.S. Navy dungarees and bull-hide boots, a flannel shirt, a flaps-up hunting hat. His single vanity was barbering, his straight gray hair clipped neatly across his nape. Years of rough living had crabbed his stance, and vandal raids had made him more suspicious than he might have been by nature. An offhand greeting—"Hey, Mr. Kipp"—would yield a pop-eyed startle before he could collect himself, tip finger to brow in an uneasy salute. He was thought to be simpleminded, but somehow he'd come by enough learning to allow him in a letter to the *Waco Wego Register* to liken his tormentors to Ostrogoths. The epithet had become the name of a loose brotherhood of mischief to which most town boys laid claim.

One afternoon in March it occurred to my mother that she hadn't seen the old man for several weeks. We'd had a late-winter blizzard, a cattle-killing prairie storm with ice-blade winds and four-foot drifts, then overnight a turn-wind had set off a thaw, blowing in a watery day of false spring. She determined that someone should go out to check on him.

She caught me as I was passing through the kitchen on my way to the garage. I planned to spend the hour before supper tinkering with the Chevy I'd saved up for, a '51 the color of lye soap. The car handled with a lurch and yaw that hinted at an agency more demoniacal than simple bad alignment, but I loved its stolid lines. I washed it every other day, polished its pitted chrome, had named it, for its grayness and its girth, Leviathan.

"Just to see if he's all right," she said. She pulled a threaded needle through the frayed cuff of a shirt that belonged to the town's druggist. When the new school year started and after the scandal of my father's betrayal died down, she would go back to teaching fifth grade, but until then, to supplement the checks he sent, she took in ironing and mending.

"He's fine," I said. "Ain't nothing going to kill old Odd Wad off."

Her stern look told me that as well as taking a dark view of the nickname we had for Audie, she had caught all my offenses against English usage. But in our town good grammar set you apart, and I was already a misfit—captain of the debate team, sophomore spelling champ, a shock-headed, girlfriendless, fallen preacher's boy who put himself forward as a wit—and so to fit in at school I flavored my speech with ain'ts and might-coulds.

She took a last stitch, knotted the thread, then snipped it. "You haven't been out there, have you?"

Although around town I'd roughed up my talk, in debate class I'd seen the way rhetoric might be cross-examined and convicted, and so at home I entertained myself by parsing my mother's most innocent utterances. Raising an eyebrow, puffed-up as a bantam barrister, I asked, "Madame, 'out' where?"

Her eyes brimmed, her chin pitted. Whether or not she intended her effect, in the six months since my father left she had taken on the dread power of the wronged. The story of his betrayal was as threadbare as the clerical collars he left in a drawer: He fell in love with a woman he was helping through a divorce. From time to time letters postmarked Little Rock arrived for me, but until my mother put them in an El Ropo box they lay unopened on the hall table. "No, ma'am," I said.

Sssk went the hot iron against a dampened shirt. "You drive on out there, son. What earthly good is that great whale if you won't put it toward some higher use?"

I stopped myself from asking what, precisely, she meant by "good" and how did "earthly" differ?—what constituted "use" and by what scale was "higher" measured? I sulked.

She brought down the iron in a final-sounding sear against the broadcloth. "Tom," she said, the line of shirts behind her hanging from the lintel like a row of ghosts, "I am not asking."

"It's wall-to-wall mud," I said lamely, thinking of Leviathan. Highway 81 was macadam, but after that the county road would be a mud-slick, the lowland timber route that led to Audie Kipp's place even worse.

She handed me a foil-wrapped package. "Meat loaf. You make sure he gets it."

The package was warm and dense as flesh, domestic, comforting, but I held it as if it had dropped from Pluto.

She shook out a shirt so starched it crackled. "Don't put on like that. I'm asking you to be a man." She slid the shirt onto a hanger. "To do what's right."

I fished my key ring from my pocket and headed for the back door, passing through the sunroom, where my brothers lolled on the floor watching Soupy Sales. They shot dire looks as I hovered over them, flinched when I pretended to stumble onto their bellies. Together, they piped, "Jerk."

"Take the boys along," my mother called, but she'd inflected her order in a way that let me take it as a question. "That's all right," I called back, "I'll hunt up Ranse." I took my jacket from the hook and went out.

Even in those days Waco Wego was a settlement gone past its purpose, a failing prairie railhead; by now it's all but vanished. Once you left the section where our white stucco foursquare—we were staying in the parsonage until my mother could find another place—and a few others like it ranged along the town's one elm-lined street, once you passed the downtown storefronts of the Ark Valley State Bank, the Rexall, Blaine's Hardware, and the Western Auto where I worked summers, any charm the place possessed was undone by the broken-windowed armory, the thistle-choked siding platform, and the tumbledown Santa Fe depot that housed Kickapoo and Kiowa Baptist. Beyond them, the defunct grain elevator cast a shadow over Bender's Fourth, a tract of war-boom cracker boxes shingled in cobweb gray asbestos. The place was home to aircraft workers who staffed the assembly lines of Boeing, Beech, and Cessna, and to my friend and hero, the outcast Ransom Kuschnerheit.

Three years older than I, at nineteen he was still in high school, his jaw peppered with stubble even early in the day. In all seasons he wore Levi's and a T-shirt, a faded jeans jacket, army-issue steel toes. He drove a Studebaker truck, a primer gray '49 rattletrap we called the Cyclops for the way one headlight dangled and the other slewed outward like a wandering eye. He'd installed a radio he kept tuned to Voice of Oklahoma, which broadcast from his old hometown below the line; but you could barely hear the music over the rumble of the straight-six and the clatter of tools and junk beneath the sprung excelsior seats. He was past tough, answered to no one, was, I believed, his own man. He called me Tombo, or Kemosabe, which I liked. "His race has not a thing to do with it," my mother said when, accusing her of prejudice, I pressed to know the grounds of her objection to him, "but upbringing does. It's just that his situation is a little rough." I suspected, given her feelings about the flashy woman my father left town with, that it wasn't Ranse, or that he was what was called in Waco Wego in those days a half-breed, who was the source of her worry, but his mother, Toby, whom she must have known I had a calf-eyed crush on.

"Mrs. Kuschnerheit sounds like somebody sneezed," Ranse's mother would say in a purr that made my belly quake. "Call me Toby." Summers, she wore cut-off jeans that showed her pretty legs, legs slightly knock-kneed so that at the backs of her knees the pads of flesh protruded sweetly. She smoked Parliaments, and the sight of her pink lipstick on the crushed butts in the jar-lid ashtray could stab me through the heart. Her straight hair was glossy as a blackbird's wing; she wore it loose and down her back at a time when most women cut theirs short. Once, she'd offered to cut my hair—she fashioned Ranse's ducktail with precision—but her breath on my neck, her fingers on my scalp, set off a spasm that made me blunder from the kitchen chair. Rumor held that she carried on with lowlifes from the juke joints of South Wichita and otherwise kept bad company; but in heroic daydreams I defended her, lifting from the Beatitudes and the

Bill of Rights in a speech I featured as more eloquent than the Son of Man before the bar. In her presence I went stumble-tongued and oafish. On my father's bookshelf was a volume titled *Great Men and Famous Deeds*. The book recounted the lives of saints and martyrs, statesmen and war heroes. I'd read it to shreds, and yearned to prove myself to Toby Kuschnerheit on some grand sacrificial scale, the perils I placed her in ranging from flat tires and dead solenoids to Russian spies and Titan missiles, from mad dogs to rogue tornados.

She worked swing shift at Boeing and so her old humpbacked maroon Dodge wasn't parked at the curb, but Ranse's truck was rump-up in the gravel driveway, aimed as if to make a getaway. I tapped the Chevy's horn, cut the engine, and got out and crossed the yard to knock at the punch-bellied screen door.

A giggle from inside the house told me that his girlfriend, Linda Weir, who waitressed at the bowling alley, was with him. Out of Ostrogoth honor I made to leave, but then the door opened and Ranse appeared, pulling on his T-shirt. He wedged a steel toe between the sill and door, then shot out a ropy arm to hold it open. Linda must have seen her chance to slip outside. "Hey, Tom-kins," she greeted me. Her chin was chafed with whisker burn. "I'm late for work."

She jumped over a privet at the edge of the slab porch and headed across the barren yards. Ranse crossed his arms over his chest, a signal that I should explain myself.

Leaving out my mother and the meat loaf, I did. "All we have to do is ride out and check on him." With my sneaker toe I kicked at a curl of dried mud on the slab's edge. "Might be he's dead out there."

A jerk of his head indicating that I should follow, Ranse ducked into the house where the torn paper shades were drawn, casting the shabby front room in murky light. From a coffee table strewn with bologna strings and a block of Velveeta shrinking from its wrapper, he took his jacket and pulled it on. While he shot the cuffs I stole a look at the mural behind the couch. The painting, done by his mother, showed a naked woman, her long hair streaming out to form a black lake on which she appeared to float feetfirst into a full white moon, her breasts impossibly high and buoyant. The work was crude, but at the time I found the mural beautiful, haunting for the way it suggested all the mysteries of women at once, love and art and carnal knowledge, prurience and worship. I studied it every chance I got, often wondering aloud how Ranse could see it every day and not go crazed with lust. He'd shrug; the questions that consumed me were beneath his notice.

Eleanor cleared her throat, fiddled with the sugar bowl; I was woolgathering. But as I got deeper into the story, I became aware of how it built on itself, each detail leading to the next in a way I couldn't have predicted, threatening to derail the tale like freight cars on a siding, but I went on. The charge of woolgathering aside, I was proud of all I'd remembered and meant to get from the beginning of the trip to Audie Kipp's to what I'd done there, then to its end, an intention I would make good on, forgetting only that stories tend to go on ending long after their telling.

Ranse picked up his keys and shook them; we would take the Studebaker. Outside, I fetched the meat loaf from the Chevy and hoisted myself into the truck's cab.

He gave the package the stink eye.

"We're supposed to give it to him."

He shook his head. "Tombo, son, you got a lot to learn."

This was why I'd sought him out: With Ranse along, even the mildest errand took on possibility and menace; the day had turned.

Beyond the salvage yard the landscape gave way to open fields. Melting snow had left dirt-crusted drifts and exposed the new winter wheat, furrows fanning so that it seemed the moving Cyclops was at the still point of the turning world. Ranse steered by means of a Bakelite steering knob—illegal even then—his palm resting easily on the cylinder. He flipped on the radio, but the six o'clock stock report crackled between blasts of static and so he snapped it off. From his jacket pocket he pulled a pack of Pall Malls and his Zippo. He shook the pack toward me.

The one time I'd lit a grapevine twist I'd horked myself into the dry heaves, but I helped myself. "For later," I said, tucking the cigarette behind my ear like the renegade I hoped to be.

One-handed, he flicked the lighter and lighted up, releasing the aphrodisiac aroma of naphtha and tobacco.

I trained my gaze on the swag of power lines along the road and tried to figure how to bring up the subject of what he and Linda Weir had been doing under the mural. At last the expression came to me, perfect in its strategy and its use of our high school's current vulgarity. "You and old Weir," I said, "bet you didn't get any on you, did you?"

He curled his upper lip. I socked his arm. My gesture proved just right; his smirk was my reward, inducting me into the company of men as well as holding off for a time the sorry certainty that I would at no time soon get any on me.

Low in the west a cloud bank glowered, the sun setting beneath it casting long light against the treetops, but by the time we reached the river bend and turned west onto Audie's road, the light began to wane, dusk setting in. At our approach to the first of his two lanes, some turkey buzzards flapped away from a carcass in the ditch. Ranse braked beside a cedar stump where an ax-head crate served as his mailbox, hand-lettered Aud. J. Kipp.

I said, "His royal crest."

Ranse hadn't laughed the first time I'd made the joke; he didn't now.

I tried again. "What do you suppose the J stands for? Jerk-off?"

Beside the mailbox a coyote pelt was stretched between the

strands of a barbed-wire fence. Ranse gave a low whistle. "That fresh?"

The tattered pelt riffled in the wind. "Looks to me like."

At this sign the old man was alive we could have turned back to town, lobbed the meat loaf into a wheatfield, and called it good, gone off to eat fried chicken at the Buckaroo.

Ranse appeared to consider. "We head down his lane, he's liable to shoot at us." His Oklahoma accent rendered "liable" as "lobble," making the word sound posselike and Western, dangerous. He smirked. "And us just doing the neighborly thing, just checking up on him."

"Our Christian duty," I put in, giving myself a bad case of the snickers.

I dummied up when he squinted down the road. He said, "Might ought to go on foot."

It was decided that we'd park the Studebaker on the oil lease behind the property, make our way through the timber, and come up on the trailer from behind. As we jolted down the lease road toward the edge of the woods, I hefted the meat loaf. "We can sneak up and plunk this on his doorstep. Odd Wad'll never know. He'll think the meat loaf bunny left it."

In the time it took to ease the truck around the pump jack, make a three-point turn and park nose out among the weeds, Ranse had been quiet. Now he said, "God's dangling objects, Tombo, screw the meat loaf." I left the package on the Studebaker's seat.

We entered the woods, picking our way through the underbrush. Above us, withered catalpa pods clattered in the wind. Ranse picked up a rifle-sized shank of deadfall cottonwood, slung the limb across his shoulders, and draped his arms over it GI style. I found a limb and did the same, but after a while it hurt my neck, so I dropped the shank.

When a jackrabbit bounded across our path into a sumac thicket, I jumped. Ranse punched my arm. "Spook you, did it?"

A taste of copper in my throat, I told him, "No."

After a few hundred yards we came up on the old man's compound, a stand of outbuildings we hadn't seen on prior raids. Nearly hidden in a tangle of woodbine stood a crumpled Butler building, its round steel roof stove in. Inside, a mound of empty pop bottles, furred with dust, glinted in the falling light. Wind swirled around the open bottlenecks in an unearthly fluting.

Just past the bottle shed we came upon the buckboard, iron wheels sunk into the loam, and a ramshackle paddock, its slat fence smooth as driftwood and laced with borer trails. We bellied up to the corral fence. Ranse rested a boot on the bottom rail as if surveying his domain. Inside the paddock was an array of abandoned farm equipment. In a corner near the mule shed the jennet stood, dirty ice beading her winter-shagged hide. She gave us a sidelong glance, then shifted on the frost heave to face away from us.

The scene seemed fashioned out of junk and chance and loss made somehow more pitiable by the clarity of detail: chafed rails, a rickety manger, a bull-tongued plow blade jutting from the boggy ground, the mule. Emblems of defeat, of bygone lives, cobbled out of nowhere, then suddenly too present, there. It occurred to me that I didn't know what we were on the brink of—rout or robbery or worse—but to show that I was up for any wrack my idol had in mind, I propped a foot on the rail as well, and we stood so, side by side, until he motioned us on.

We crept forward until the trailer appeared through the trees, light shining from its single window. Just as we were ready to break out of cover—our plan was to stay low, weaving from stump to woodpile to butane tank—we heard a laugh, low, full-throated, female. We put out arms to halt each other. Needlessly I said, "Hear that?"

Out on the open plain someone was burning trash; a smell of char collected in the spectral woods. Just as I began to think the woman's voice had been the eerie whistling from the bottle shed, the old man wheedled, "Hey, go easy, hon."

Again we heard her laugh. "Hold still," she said. She lowered her tone in an intimate, familiar way, "you big galoot."

Though at the time he gave no sign, Ranse must have recognized his mother's voice. Later it would occur to me that if we'd taken our usual route, we would have seen her Dodge parked in front of the trailer, but at the moment I had yet to fit a figure to the voice's sweet, low lilt, its teasing edge. What I knew was that we had the chance to make the exploit of all exploits, to get the kind of eyeful no painted mural could deliver—the talk inside the trailer augured a sure thing—and we would have a tale to tell in town, a tale—one of my father's phrases came to me—the likes of which for badness would be never seen in all of Egypt.

"I'm holding still," we heard Audie's slow, good-natured whine, "it's you the wiggleworm."

In a slewed look I meant as comic, I let my mouth go slack and doltish, leering at Ranse with an expression he must have seen as canny, simple-headed cruelty. "Come on, man," I whispered. "He's got a girl in there. We might see"—no one word came to mind that held the promise of what we might witness and so I finished—"tits."

He brought a fist so near my jaw I felt its heat, smelled its Pall Mall reek, a whiff of bologna and Velveeta. I flinched, but he merely plucked the cigarette I'd forgotten from behind my ear and jabbed it in his mouth. He turned away and walked into the woods.

Any other time I might have followed, but I was ticked at him for bailing, for the fake-out punch that showed me up for what I was. From the timber's cover I made a run to the butane tank, a steel cylinder set on cinder blocks. From here it was a short shot to the trailer. My idea was to steal up to the window, take a peek, then swagger back to the truck, full of myself and what I'd seen, what Ranse, quailing at the final hour, no man at all, would never own the rights to tell in town. Suddenly the moment seemed to call for spectacle, for violence, and so without a thought beyond the outlaw power it made me feel to act and let the consequences catch up later,

I gave a curdled yowl and sprang into a run. Flinging myself at the trailer's window, I mashed my face against the pane, leering like a pirate, a berserker, then dropped to the ground, flattening myself against the dank earth.

My heart, hammering before, now seemed to thrum as the scene I'd glimpsed inside the trailer caught up to me: in the glow of a kerosene lamp, bare-chested, ham-backed, his old dugs lopped over his chest, Audie seated on a stool, head bowed, and behind him, her belly pressed into his back, Ranse's mother shaving his nape with a straight razor.

I barreled over, vaulted up and lunged into the thicket. Crashing through the brush, I tripped over a grapevine, sprawled, but scrabbled up and kept on running. I'd almost reached the oil lease when the old man's shotgun blasted in the distance.

Gray in the twilight, the Studebaker hulked, its engine running. I yanked open the passenger door and jumped inside, yelled, "Gun it!"

Ranse slouched at the wheel, spun the steering knob.

"Go!" I shouted, voice ragged in my throat.

He looked out across the field, then back at me. The Bakelite knob ticked like a ratchet, like a clock. At last, his voice so low I barely heard, he muttered, "Guess you got yourself a look?"

Jaw rattling from cold, adrenaline, and shock, my molars knocking, I blurted the lie that even crashing through the woods I'd known I had to tell, a lie that hurt to see how much he wanted to believe. "Too dark. I couldn't see a thing!" I stomped a phantom pedal. "Go!"

For a long minute he searched my face, as if to gauge the truth. My nose ran, but I held his gaze. Then he seemed to settle something in his mind, and he smacked the steering wheel. "Goddamn it, Kemosabe," he crowed, "you flat out slammed that trailer! Good thing I had old Cyclops running . . ."

He slugged my arm in a way that felt too hard, too false, and in a hollow, heartsick way I understood that we were fixing on the story we would tell at school. He put the truck in gear. Threshing through the tall weeds, we pulled across the field and headed back toward town.

"Is that it?" Eleanor asked when I placed my palms on the table, a gesture she called my peroration stance. The last of the daylight had gone from the kitchen, and though it was hard to see her face, I understood that she was baffled by the story. I'd made it through the tale, but there was something missing, a stray wire, a lost connection.

"Did it not make sense?"

"It did," she said slowly, "but what does it have to do with anything? He wanted to save face. Who wouldn't?"

"You're missing the point." I said this more irritably than I meant to, but just then I couldn't think of what the point had been.

She harrumphed, a dear, gruff, skeptical sound that made my eyes fill unaccountably, then she rose to flick on the light. She sat down again and folded her hands, waiting. "Then tell me."

I told her that after that night Ranse and I saw little of each other, that in April he quit school to take a job as a burr bench operator and moved to another prairie town on the verge of the Flint Hills, that he enlisted shortly after that, was killed years later at Da Nang.

I told her that the one time I saw Toby Kuschnerheit when she came into the Western Auto the summer before I left for Georgetown, and she stood helplessly—in the cut-off jeans that had once driven my dreams—in front of a battery display, I'd ducked into the stockroom to hide behind a stack of Bardol cases.

I remembered all these details, but I couldn't recall why I'd thought the story would provide an answer to what I'd been thinking on the dock with Anne, why I'd thought it would supply the reason for my laugh. "How does any story fit together?" I shouted. "How does anybody?"

She got up and went to the pantry and pulled out an onion, re-

garding it as if it might tell the future. The moment drew out long—
Eleanor looking at the onion, holding it by its shoot. When she spoke
again, it was gently, as if to bring the subject to an end, to move us
past my outburst. "What became of the old man?"

Screwing up an eye, I lowered my voice, and said mysteriously,
"Nobody knows."

I'd hoped to draw a laugh, but she looked away. "He's the one I'm
sorry for, Tom. Silver ingots, the idea! The poor old guy." She busied
herself with the cutting board, with choosing a knife from the
drawer. Her back was to me, but from the way she canted her head
it was clear that she was struggling with some mix of feeling—love,
fear, pity, resignation?—and that if she'd turned to face me, I would
have seen the unasked, the unbearable question in her eyes.

I crossed the kitchen to stand beside her at the sink. This close, I
wanted to lay my palm against her cheek, to tell her things would be
all right, that it wasn't time to worry yet, that I would let her know,
but I was afraid that any touch would remind her of the morning on
the dock. Instead, I asked what she was making.

"Eggs," she said briskly, as if she'd settled on the tack to take. She
handed me the onion and the knife. "You chop."

Although she called me twice to come to bed, that night I sat up
late, worrying the problem of what had made me start the story,
musing in a general way about what the mind held on to, what it lost,
how the past could shoot through the present, then as quickly as a
shifting wind reverse itself, how sense could vanish into the space between what you meant to do and what you did, for the way all memories nested in each other, one inside the next, the next, the next,
until they amounted to a life that couldn't be lived again, a dream no
other could recall, lost even to the dreamer, the illusions that it took
to live and how the heart could bear their loss.

The sky had gone black but for a lowering moon that cast a path
across the slick-calm water of the bay. Through the open jalousies

came the sounds of the rowboat creaking in its moorings, a heron's prehistoric shriek. It felt as if the world itself were in a lull, waiting for something that it couldn't name.

If the memory had not arrived—from a place past summons, then suddenly stark and present as the desolated scene in Audie's paddock—what I am saying here would be so different that I wonder if I would try to say it at all. But through mercy, chemistry, or luck, it did, and it felt like such a proof that I started from my chair to wake Eleanor. But as I reached the bedroom door I understood how she—peeved to be disturbed—might see only more evidence of addlement, her husband a rumple-headed stranger looming above the bed, the old lunatic who laughed.

And what could I have told her that would make a difference? That I laughed out of a logic that I couldn't reconstruct. For the way a person could be taken by a reckless urge and still be mystified by what had led him to it. For loving her, for failing, for wanting a second chance, a second life.

I eased into bed beside her and put my hand on her hip the way I had most nights for almost fifty years. For now, it was enough that I remembered that on our ride back to town, the Studebaker's closed cab sealing in the smells of motor oil and sweat and meat loaf grease, Ranse and I were quiet, the silence growing thick as the purling smoke from his Pall Mall, and that for all the urgency I felt to break the stillness, I had known there was no word, no feat that would restore us to our former selves.

I don't know if he felt the same, but for reasons of his own when we reached the raised Santa Fe track bed outside town he punched the gas and floored the truck. We took the grade full throttle, jolting off the seats and battering our heads against the cab roof. A mindless, rakehell thing we'd done before, the lurch seemed to sever us from something dire and human, and we laughed.

Ranse threw back his head and gave out a bray, a yowl as wild as mine when I ran at the trailer. Not because I wanted to be like him, but because I couldn't not, I echoed him, and this seemed to be the signal we should turn around and take the hump again. Fishtailing, bald tires spitting sand like vengeance, plowing zigzag cuts like scars along the empty road, speeding toward a vandal hall of fame where we paid tribute to the secret lives of men, to knowledge that we hadn't asked for, didn't want, again and again we steeled ourselves and clenched our jaws and hit the grade.

Lofted to a place where past us there was nothing but the blue-black night, where we held sway over a world we had the power to wreck, a world as full of us as we were full of it, we laughed until our bellies ached, our throats were raw, until the stars we saw were artifacts of feeling not of light, until tears streamed. With yelps and slugs and slaps against the dashboard we made it known between us each time the truck went airborne that some kind of victory had been won, some ruinous event outrun.

I cranked down the window, hurled the meat loaf at the shot-pocked RR sign. It hit; we howled. Ranse snapped on the radio and Voice of Oklahoma came in clear, the music swirling out into the plains, into the darkness gathered at the edges of the moonlit road, and we bellowed out a song whose words are gone from mind but which must have been the anthem of the age until a rush of static whited out the signal and he turned it off and quiet fell around us as we hurtled toward the town lights up ahead.

4

How Okies Look to Natives

The summer before he left for college, Gib Harrell had been haunted by a fear too deep for reason. It was 1969, he was eighteen, and he felt stalked by something terrible and mortal, afraid he was going to die before he'd lived. Nothing he tried, not beer or weed or backseat groping, could take his mind from his dark thoughts, and so when his uncle offered a job clearing some land out on the high plains of New Mexico, Gib took it.

While his friends sweated the draft lottery back home in Memphis, he was camped alone in a stone sheepherder's hut out on the Llano Estacado. Under a sky so wide he could track the passage of the sun from horizon to horizon, he hauled rocks the size of nail kegs and piled them into cairns. Nights he sat at the hut's door, alert for rattlesnakes, many thicker than his arm. His shouts and wild stomp dances failed to rout them, and he slept uneasily until he laid a rope around the hut to ward them off. He wasn't sure the trick was anything but television cowboy lore, but it seemed to work, and he began to enjoy the night. Star clouds glimmered pale as glass, the Perseids shot sparks, and he liked to imagine he was the lone recipient of light from ages past. At the end of August he went off to Vanderbilt to begin the life that had proceeded without obstacle until the present.

Now he was fifty, the millennium had newly turned. He had a sturdy marriage to a woman he loved, a son at Tulane and twin daughters in their last year of boarding school in Vicksburg, a radiology practice with congenial colleagues in his hometown, an orderly, contented life into which the black dog had come again.

He saw death everywhere, in the starry efflorescences on X-ray films, shadowy tumors, a near miss on the freeway, even when he mowed the lawn. His parents were in robust health, his children flourished, but these mercies somehow made it worse, made loss more imminent. His luck, he feared, was running out, his number coming up. He decided that at summer's end he'd take time off and drive west on the back roads to the stretch of badland between Milnesand and Lingo to see if what had cured him before would cure him now.

In the last days of August he drove the twins to St. Margaret's, mustered them on the dormitory steps to deliver what they called his "danger talk," cautions about hair dryers near bathtubs, reminders about sunscreen and vitamins. They'd heard it all before. Listing toward their classmates gathering in a grove, they pledged to be careful. "Nothing bad will happen, Dad." He stood by while they murmured endearments to Hal, the deaf red setter who had come along for the ride, hugged them, then remanded them to the delta heat and the other beautiful immortals waiting under the tupelos. He held open the car door so Hal could ricket his long body inside, then got in himself, belted up, and drove out of town and onto the bridge.

The Mississippi was down. Sandbars stretched nearly to the middle where barges plied the coffee-colored water. As the bluffs of the battleground—so many dead, a mountain—receded in his rearview, it struck him that he'd taken a wrong turn. The hitch rattled him, but there was no way to check the map until he reached the Louisiana side and pulled into the parking lot of a barbecue stand.

A homemade sign proclaimed Lucky's open for business. On the sign in front of Lucky's name a vandal, or maybe Lucky himself, had spray-painted the letters UN. In a clump of knotgrass a billboard teetered. Across its collapsing scaffold plywood farm animals, a paint-scabbed cow, a pig in a top hat, a rooster wearing a jauntylooking bib, jigged on hind legs. Smoke roiled from the chimney pipe of a meat smoker parked hazardously close to a propane tank. Briefly he wondered if he'd warned the twins about what to do in case of fire.

When he cracked the window, the hickory-and-vinegar smell of pulled pork drifted in, alerting Hal, who nosed the air. Gib rubbed the dog's ears, then unfolded his map. He had just smoothed it across the steering wheel when Lucky's screen door slapped open and out stormed a girl in purple shorts and a T-shirt the color of a Creamsicle. She hurried to a banged-up white Chevy Caprice, yanked open the squawking door, got in, and started the engine, which roared like the big V-8 it was. For a moment she rested her forehead on the steering wheel, then she swung out to pull the door shut and slammed into reverse just as a young man appeared in the doorway. He wore a paper hat and a butcher's apron smeared with what looked like blood or barbecue sauce. In a clotted voice he bawled obscenities at the girl. She braked, then shifted into drive. As she pulled across the lot the young man ran alongside her, then heaved himself sideways in a martial arts kick so violent it dented the passenger door and left a waffle-grid boot print. She sped away, spattering chat as the sedan lugged onto the highway.

Beyond wondering whether the scene had been a fragment of an ongoing argument or a final, overwrought parting, he gave little thought to the encounter except to marvel that if he hadn't been just where he was just when he was, he never would have seen it. By the time he and Hal stopped for the night at a motel outside Little Rock, he'd almost forgotten it.

The next day he was passing a buffalo preserve in Oklahoma when he became aware that a car was bearing down behind him. He took it for a state trooper—the car was white, it rode low, its wide grille appeared to leer. But then the driver leaned on the horn and passed him. In the white blur he saw the dented door, the boot smudge still intact.

Across the ribbed and gullied ranch land he marveled at the coincidence, and when in the early afternoon he saw the car a third time, crossing his westbound route and speeding north on a county road a hundred miles past where he'd last seen it, he veered off to follow. His act was rash, foolhardy. Anyone who knew him would be shocked by what he'd done. *He* was. But he was oddly exhilarated. In a harebrained way, he felt as if he were destined to take the chance, to follow her on whim, a breakaway. He told himself his trip to Milnesand had been put off so long, a few more hours wouldn't make a difference. He stayed back a quarter of a mile, but in such empty country it wasn't hard to keep her in his sight.

Late in the afternoon as they sped north on a sandy road to cross the Kansas line, his exhilaration had left him. His cell phone signal was a flat line, his fuel gauge needle below *E*. To save gas—he wasn't sure if it mattered, but to be on the safe side—he cut the air-conditioning and rolled down the windows, letting the hot wind buffet him. He'd exhausted his imagination as to her circumstances. His fantasies of offering aid had dimmed. It struck him that the bare bones of his act were at best suspicious, at worst criminal, and he'd put himself in peril of running out of gas on the road to nowhere, a road so treeless that even the buzzards gathered around an armadillo carcass had no perch to flap away to and merely moseyed to the shoulder to let him pass. His warnings to his daughters oozed an irony that was ludicrous, and his tea-leaf-reading for symbols and portents—Lucky's, a Caprice?—was more crackpot than phrenology.

In the distance a grain elevator promised a town he hoped he had enough gas to make. He wished the girl would turn off onto yet another side road so he could go on alone, leaving her to whatever fate she was bent on, but she made straight for the elevator. At the outskirts of a prairie town she pulled in beside the single pump of a rundown filling station, and he had no choice but to turn in. In order not to alarm her, he parked some distance away, out near the culvert by a heap of asphalt slag.

He left the engine running, rolled up the windows, and turned on the air conditioner for Hal, still dozing in the back, his chest falling and rising in heavy, old-dog sleep. He was so relieved to reach safety that when he got out of the car and hit the locks and shut the door, he didn't notice that he'd left the keys in the ignition.

He nodded to the attendant, a rangy youngster tipped back on one of the chrome-and-vinyl kitchen chairs on the concrete apron outside the door. The attendant touched his cap brim and went back to chalking a pool cue. Gib fed quarters into the pop machine, then punched the button for root beer. When he'd walked past the Caprice, the girl had been in the driver's seat, but suddenly she stood behind him. "What are you, some kind of stalker?"

His root beer can clunked into the bin. He retrieved it and straightened to face her. Her outfit and her size, so small and bony she seemed held together with wire and string, had made him think she was a girl. This close, he was shocked to see she was a woman, sixty if she was a day. She looked so hot and frazzled and sorely used that if she hadn't sneaked up on him, he might have felt compassion for her and asked her what was wrong.

She took a long pull from a blue bottle of antacid, recapped it, and dropped it into the pocket of her baggy shorts. She put her hands on her narrow hips. The Creamsicle-colored T-shirt, billowing behind her in the hot wind, was plastered to her front. Beneath the shirt was a lump that made him think it was a colostomy bag. Training made him look for a MedicAlert bracelet, but she wore none.

"Nothing better to do than follow me across the country?"

When he opened the root beer, the fizz sloshed over the can's rim to drizzle down his hand. He held the can away so it wouldn't spatter his khakis. "I thought you might be lost." This was a lie, but how could he tell her why he'd followed her when he wasn't sure himself?

"It occur to you maybe I intend to be?" There was a burned texture to the dark, dyed hair she'd gathered into a stringy ponytail, and her skin seemed stretched over her cheekbones, giving her a skeletal look. At her scalp line ran a scattering of ulcerated sores. She stalked back to the pump to wrestle with the hose, shooting him a hateful glance.

He raised a hand to show he meant no harm.

"Just so you don't go getting any big ideas, I've got this." From beneath her T-shirt where the lump had been she produced a pistol, a tiny thing, pearl-handled, a Ladysmith, he guessed. "Don't think it isn't loaded." He almost laughed; her squint-eyed sneer made her look like a pint-sized Dirty Harry.

Disgusted with himself and impatient to get on his way, he stood in front of the station window waiting for her to fill her tank, pretending interest in a display of Tom's Peanut Logs. Heat waves rose from the hardpan lot.

"Your engine's about to quit," offered the attendant, jerking a thumb toward the idling Cherokee. Embroidered on the attendant's blue shirt were the initials R. D.

"I know that," Gib said shortly.

R. D. sighted along the cue, balancing the fulcrum on his thumb, then flipped the cue, rolled it deftly across his hand and snapping into shot position. "Just saying, is all."

Gib thought of walking over to turn off the car, but he didn't want to pass the pump and give her another opportunity to snarl. He went around the corner of the station to the men's room. He would give her a head start, then take the opposite direction and work his way back to his mapped route.

When he returned to his car, she was inside the station, jotting something on a notepad. His tag numbers, he guessed, so she could report him. On what charge, he wondered. Superstition? Folly?

R. D. craned around the cash register as if to size him up. At the precise moment Gib tried his car door and spotted the keys still dangling from the ignition, the engine died.

He went around to all the doors, including the hatch window behind which his camping gear lay neatly stowed, but the car was sealed. On the backseat, Hal lay as before, so deeply sacked that not even the ceasing of the engine vibrations roused him.

R. D. had taken up his duty post on the kitchen chair and was working something out of his thumbnail with a jackknife blade. The woman's car was still at the pump, but she was nowhere to be seen. Gib waved to get R. D.'s attention. "Locked myself out," he said, "do you have one of those . . ." He couldn't think of the word for the tool he needed. R. D.'s look told him that he knew it but he had the live-long day to wait for him to get the phrase out, which he finally did, ". . . a Slim Jim?"

Canting his chair so he could reach a clump of foxtail that sprouted from a crack, R. D. pulled up a stalk and clamped it between his front teeth, for no purpose Gib could detect other than so he could mumble around it. "No can do. Illegal."

"A wire hanger?" Gib reached into his pocket and brought out his wallet to see if he'd tucked an extra key inside. He hadn't. "The dog's locked in," he said, hearing the rise in his voice. "He's old and deaf," he added, as if this made it worse. Sweat trickled into his eyes, making them sting from the sunscreen he'd put on that morning.

R. D. got up and ambled to the car. He peered inside, considered Hal, now standing at the window, and went into the station bay to root in a disordered tool bin. Gib, unable to meet the setter's baleful gaze, followed.

Discarding one object after another, R. D. at last brought up a narrow-gauge file and a tangle of solder wire. He tripled the wire and twisted it, wound it around the file, then fashioned a noose at the end.

"Looks like it'll work," Gib said, trying to keep the urgency from his voice.

"Pretty tricky deal." R. D. tested the noose with an oil-blacked forefinger, then went to the car, set his stance, and began paying the wire into the space between the glass and gasket.

Hal now stood on the backseat, tongue lolling. When he caught sight of Gib he gave a hopeful tail swipe.

R. D. fiddled with the loop, wiped his brow with his sleeve. "Catch on these is pretty tricky."

Hal had sagged back down. Gib had brought the dog along because the girls had begged—he was often mystified by the fragments of their childhood they hung on to, what they left behind—but also because he liked the company. Hal was a riding dog; say *car* or even mouth the word when he was looking, and the setter was at the door, chest out, nose up, alert. Now Gib didn't know whether to look at Hal or not to. Both seemed like betrayal. "Let me try," he said, reaching for the file.

R. D. shouldered him off, resank the wire. "Just needs a little English."

The woman had come over to watch. In her gritty little voice, she said, "I read that three minutes in a hot car can broil your brains."

Gib ignored her and R. D. went on working with the loop, each time coming up empty. She drifted off.

In desperation, Gib ran to the slag pile and picked up a good-sized chunk of asphalt, intending to break a window, but by the time he returned, the woman stood over the driver's side windshield, gripping a maul.

ed that as soon as he got himself spruced up, he was
re. "Play me some pool. I could pick you up a windshield
it back tomorrow. Put it in right here." He gave Gib the
, taking in the expensive watch his wife Barbara had given
d cost you."

n Gib didn't respond, R. D. said cagily, " 'Course you could
rive it. Get you some duck tape and some visqueen. Maybe
our head out the side window. We don't have none of that
though. Duck tape or visqueen, either one." His eyes darted
ly to the station bay, then back to hold Gib's gaze.

ib took out his wallet. "How much?"

R. D. consulted his thumbnail. "Four, five hunnerd."

When Gib said he didn't have that much with him but that he had
redit card, R. D. looked at his boots, his expression blank as sand.
ot to be cash. No credit. Bad experience."

"Is there a bank?"

"Sure, but it's closed. Saturday afternoon."

"But there's an ATM?"

"In Dodge there is."

Georgette put in, "I could drive you, but you'll have to wait until
tomorrow. I want to see that hand-dug well."

As if sensing his chance slipping away, R. D. delivered a smart
slap to his own forehead. "I got it. You could just send me into Dodge
with that credit card. I can get the cash out of the ATM. Done it before for customers. Plenty of times."

Gib said he'd call Triple A.

"Shop phone's on the blink," R. D. reported.

"I'll check into a motel and use the phone there."

R. D. cast an eye at Hal, who had returned from a foray into the
sunflower field across from the station. "Days Inn don't take dogs."

At last he wrangled from R. D. the name of the nearest dog-
taking motel, which turned out to be a short mile away and to cater
to pheasant hunters. He arranged with R. D. to leave the car

"Hit the side one!" R. D. y⟨
down the maul, the windshield⟨
down his rock on the hole she'd ⟨
reach inside and pop the lock.

The woman opened the back do⟨
chest, and hauled him out. She set hir⟨
he sank to his haunches. "Water," she ye⟨

R. D. said, "Gotcha," and loped away.

Stupid with relief, Gib knelt before the o⟨
drooped more than usual. Still, Gib didn't ⟨
damage. "Thanks," he said to the woman.

"Georgette Boudreaux."

He looked at her, not comprehending; he tho⟨
speaking in a foreign language.

"As in 'Thanks, Georgette Boudreaux.'"

Although her smug prompt annoyed him, he wa⟨
about Hal's rescue to take issue. He stood up and ⟨
thanks, this time using her name.

R. D. returned, sloshing water over the rim of a dinged
Moon hubcap. He set the hubcap on the pavement. While Ha⟨
noisily, he inspected the shattered windshield, giving out ⟨
whistle. To Gib he said dolefully, "I told her to hit the vent."

Georgette shrugged, taking another pull from her antacid bott⟨
A chalky imprint ringed her upper lip.

"It's all right," Gib said. "It can be fixed." He asked R. D. where
the nearest glass shop was.

R. D. pulled at his earlobe. "Closest anything's in Dodge."

"Dodge City? Where are we?"

"Zenobia, the Pheasant Capital of the Sunflower State."

Georgette looked around. "I thought we were near Greensburg.
Home of the World's Largest Hand-Dug Well."

"How far?" Gib asked.

"From Dodge? Thirty, forty mile." Gazing down the empty road,

R. D. allow⟨
headed the ⟨
and bring⟨
once-ove⟨
him. "It'⟨
Wh⟨
try to ⟨
hang ⟨
here, ⟨
swift⟨

overnight in the station bay so he wouldn't have to unpack his camping gear, gathered a few things, and prepared to leave, thanking them again for the help.

"Sorry I yelled at you," Georgette said. "And about your windshield."

"No, I'm glad." He hazarded a laugh. "The windshield part, I mean."

Hal had come to lean against her leg. She patted his head. "Just about lost you, didn't we," she said tenderly. "You were almost a goner. A doggie goner." She smiled at her feeble joke, and the lowering sun glared on her features, on her thin, yellowish skin, the wrinkles around her eyes as she looked up at Gib. "I'm going to camp down at that little creek we passed. You two can join me if you want. It's the least I can do, since I'm the one who bashed your window."

The little laugh she gave was surprisingly pleasant, but more than anything, Gib wanted to be done with her. "I should be here when the tow truck comes, but thanks." He added, "Georgette Boudreaux."

"At least let me drive you to the motel." When she opened the Caprice's dented door, Hal lumbered in and sat at ride position on the center of the bench seat.

"Thanks, again," Gib said. He got in beside the dog.

"Sure you don't want to camp?" she asked when they pulled up to the motel office and got a look at the tumbledown building.

He thought of her gun, her earlier attitude. One heedless act was enough. "This is fine." He thanked her a final time and watched as she drove away.

The Crescent Motor Lodge was a long, low cinder-block affair, the doors stenciled with crescent moons so that the effect was of a row of outhouses. Beside the building ran the tall chain-link fence of a defunct kennel, and the place, he thought as he checked in, looked more UN than Lucky's. His room, equipped with a swamp cooler that dripped into a Maxwell House can and a matted shag carpet that smelled of hound, boded a miserable night. But the telephone worked and he called Triple A. They promised to send a tow truck in the morning.

In the middle of the night he was startled awake by a noise that seemed to come from the bathroom, a drawn-out scrape that sounded like a metal ladder being dragged across a rock bed. Hal's knobby backbone was pressed into his side, and the dog hadn't stirred. The scraping grew louder, rhythmic now, and so he got up and went into the bathroom. He pushed open the frosted glass of the window and stood on the tub rim to look outside.

Moonlight washed over the white façade of an abandoned ell that abutted the motel. Midway down it was a storm door, the top screen bellied inward and the lower one shredded, leading from a mound of broken boards and carpet scraps into the darkness of the ell. Above the rubble, protruding from the door's lower opening, were the hindquarters of a large brindle dog, its back paws scrabbling against the pitted aluminum, head and forelegs having made the hurdle. The sight was so surreal that Gib couldn't help thinking about all the events that had led up to his seeing it. Just as it occurred to him to stop making the sight a private omen and go outside to help, the dog heaved its weight inside the ell, the door rattled and shook, and all was still.

He was awakened early the next morning by the sound of a horn. He got up and opened the door, expecting to see the tow truck driver, but there stood Georgette. Hal thumped his tail against the chenille spread, then lolloped off the bed to greet her.

Clutching a faded Power Rangers beach towel and a box of baking soda, she looked worse than she had the day before. The skin on her face was inflamed, her arms and legs striated with long red wheals, some already suppurating. "Picked out a dandy campsite," she said, "but a bunch of chiggers beat me to it." She tried to laugh, but her lower lip drew up and her chin pitted the way his daughters' did when they were hurt but trying to be brave. Then she cleared her throat and jutted her jaw, her truculence regained. "Since you owe me one, you could let me use your bathtub."

Despite her mean little bulldog face, she looked so miserable he couldn't refuse. He gathered his things, leashed Hal, and went outside to wait.

The tow truck arrived while she was still in the bathtub. He tapped on the bathroom door to tell her he was leaving, then went out and climbed in beside the driver, relieved once again to be done with the personage known as Georgette Boudreaux.

When he got to the station, he found his Cherokee still in the bay, but the station was closed, the doors locked tight. R. D. was nowhere to be found. The tow truck driver called the Zenobia sheriff, who roared up in a dust-caked Suburban studded with antennas, but there was nothing he could do. R. D. was famous for his Dodge City benders. It would take an act of God to see him back in town before late Sunday night. Monday was more likely.

Gib suggested a locksmith, but the sheriff shook his head. "Legal issues. Court orders, all like that. Be Monday, Tuesday at the outside. Best you can do is wait him out. Old R. D. will come on back." He took off his hat and spanked it against his Levi's to shake the dust off, then put it back on. He sighed. "Kid never hasn't."

There was nothing to do but go back to the Crescent. The Caprice was still parked outside his door, which Georgette was just closing behind her.

"Hello, puppy. Hello, hello, hello." She bent to pet Hal, who leaned against her legs as if for shelter. Though her skin was still inflamed, she seemed a bit improved. Her hair was wet, which made her look older and smaller than before. As she slung her things into the Caprice, Gib told her what had happened at the station.

"Look here," she said, "I was going to see the world's largest hand-dug well, but I overshot it. Now I owe you one. For the bathtub. I was thinking fair is fair, and I might as well drive you up to

Dodge. We can hunt down R. D. and get the station key from him. How many pool joints can there be? We could be back here by noon. It might be fun. A big adventure. What do you say?"

The idea that they would "hunt down" R. D. sounded ominous. He hadn't forgotten her pistol. And there was the violence with the boy—he *was* a boy, Gib was certain of it—back at the barbecue stand. "I'll wait."

"Seriously. What else have you got to do?" She eyed him quizzically. "What are you doing out here anyway?"

He explained about Milnesand, his time there, that he wanted to see it again.

She crossed her arms over her meager chest. Today she wore the same baggy purple shorts and orange T-shirt, but she had added a black sweatshirt emblazoned with red flames licking at the words *Bad to the Bone*. "Just to look at it?"

"Maybe camp a night or two. Take some pictures." It struck him only then that his Nikon was locked inside the station bay.

"Hey, I'm not as mean as I let on," she said. "Why don't we just go out there? You can have your look, then we'll turn around and come back. By then your car'll be fixed."

The idea was oddly appealing. Barbara didn't expect him for days, and she didn't expect him to call; the trip was open-ended. Still, he wanted to know more about Georgette, a diagnostic interview from which he could determine whether she was a full-bore sociopath or just a rough little character. "What are you doing way out here?" he asked. "Aren't you from around Vicksburg?"

At her startled look, he explained that he'd seen her at the barbecue stand, the coincidences that led him to follow her.

She nodded as if his act had fallen in the realm of normal, and to his surprise—he'd judged her as a simpler person, probably unread—she said, "Kismet?"

"Sort of."

"My son lives in Vicksburg, but I'm from Jackson."

It embarrassed him to repeat his question, but he wanted to know. "And why are you all the way out here?"

"Long story." She knelt to pet Hal, giving his ears a roughing up and addressing her explanation to the dog. "I'm on a pilgrimage. Oh, yes, I am." She held her pose, stroking Hal but looking up at Gib. "Going around to see weird roadside things. World's largest ball of twine. Quigley's Castle—thing is built out of rocks and bottles. The stuff people make, the pitiful wonders of the world."

"You took off work to do this?"

"I'm"—she gave a comic cough—"retired. Can you believe I once taught high school science?"

"Why not?"

"And then I decided to become an outlaw?"

He wasn't sure how to take her, but he laughed.

"What about you? What do you do for a living?"

When he told her, she nodded, as if the fact of his profession fit somehow into her scheme of things. She straightened up and looked at him levelly. "Is the inquisition over? Do I pass?"

He hadn't asked about the boy who kicked the car door—her son, he guessed—but suddenly this didn't seem to matter. "Do I?"

She cocked her head and squinted. "No funny stuff?"

He took her meaning. Though the idea would have been last on his mind—with her or anyone—the fact that this scrawny little bug-bitten person worried that he might have such designs pulled his heart toward her. "No funny stuff."

"I already know your name and where you're from." She gestured toward the motel office, where from a crack in the Venetian blinds the clerk was observing them. "When I came to find you this morning I couldn't figure out which room you were in, so I told him I was undercover FBI, and you were a fugitive traveling under an alias. I had a good look at the registration. Pretty tricky deal, eh?" She pulled a cagey, sly-eyed face that looked so much like R. D.'s that he had to laugh. He shook his head in astonishment. "You're unstoppable."

"I wouldn't go that far," she said drily, but he could tell that she was pleased.

By noon they'd driven through the Texas panhandle, taking a side trip so Georgette could see an immense white cross that dwarfed the trees at its base. She traveled without a map. "Dead reckoning," she said, narrowing her eyes against the road glare, against his incredulity.

The day was hot and windy. Russian thistle blew across the road, piled up along the fence lines. She was a lead-foot driver, and more than once he jammed his foot flush with the floorboard. Outside Clovis on a county road she tailgated a mufflerless pickup, green as arsenic where it wasn't laced with rust, its bed piled high with microwave oven boxes. Three surly-looking men riding on the boxes glowered, but when Gib suggested she slow down, she shrugged. "Pistol's in the glove box."

The more time he spent with her the more he noticed her age. When they stopped to rest she had to walk around a while so she could unkink herself. She moved as arthritically as Hal. She traveled with a case of Maalox. Stowed in her backseat where Hal rode were blankets, pillows, a tent, a camp stove, a box fan, and brown paper grocery bags full of various supplies. One bag appeared to hold dozens of empty orange prescription vials, but he didn't think she was an addict. He hadn't seen her put anything in her mouth except the eggs she ate for breakfast, a ham sandwich for lunch, innumerable sips of antacid. There was something not quite right about her, but she appeared to be glad for his company, and she had set herself into a fine, determined mood, and so he gave up speculating. The Caprice rode smoothly, lulling him into a pleasant out-of-body-ness, an anesthesia of hot wind and tire rhythm, the everlasting sameness of the rolling plains.

She handed him a bag of pork rinds. "Open that for me, will you?"

Holding back his opinion of her dietary habits, he opened the bag and handed it to her.

She took a rind and crunched meditatively. "Remember when you were a kid and you'd go on family trips, those guessing games? I see something green? Let's play one, all right? I'll give you three guesses to figure out what I have."

"In your hand? A pork rind."

"No, what disease. What diagnosis?"

She was ill. He should have known; she had all the signs. The look about her eyes, her skin. Once, when she smiled, the word *rictus* had come to him. He'd been so busy judging her on other counts—clothes, pistol, temperament—he'd missed the obvious. "Why don't you just tell me?"

"Here's a head start. It's a connective tissue disorder."

His curiosity kicked in. "Rheumatoid arthritis?"

"Good guess, but no. Too easy." She bit down on a pork rind and then mumbled around it, spewing crumbs. "And it isn't scleroderma. At first they thought it was. They wished it was."

In his mind he went down the list, and in a flush of dread it came to him. "Not polymyositis?"

She toasted him with another pork rind, then popped it into her mouth.

There were scores of questions he could ask, numberless details, but the disease was incurable, heralding a painful death. "What are you taking for it?"

"Nothing. I flushed the lot, and I don't want to hear a word about it."

They were far out in the country, the road leading through folds and rises, across unexpected arroyos. In the distance herds of bounding antelope flashed white as wheeling gulls. When they passed a bloated, flyblown Hereford by the side of the road, its stiffened roan red legs straight up, he looked away, trying to pretend he hadn't seen it.

She reached over to tap the glove box. "I'm out of here before it comes to that."

Suddenly he understood the violence at Lucky's. "Your son . . ."

"Robbie doesn't like it any, but he'll understand when . . . the kid is twenty-two. He thinks he knows it all."

"But he cares . . ."

With a fierceness that closed the subject, she said, "So do I." She shrugged, then made a show of peering through the windshield. "Shouldn't we be coming up on that rock of yours?"

They were closing in on the area where a limestone pillar slashed with three diagonal cuts would mark the turnoff to the land he'd cleared, but nothing looked right. In his vision of the trip, he came over a crest to see the stark brown hills stretching to the edge of earth, the sky blue and high, but even the view seemed off.

He was unnerved by her casual announcement that she planned to take her life. He'd never settled the question in his mind, and now its equivocations reared in all their confusion. On the occasions he'd been called to deal with it as the resident on call, when there wasn't a DNR, *Do Not Resuscitate,* on a patient's chart, he'd gone by the book.

The light changed, the hills cast in shadow as a cloud passed overhead. He said, "I think we missed it. We should turn around."

She pulled to the side of the road, staring ahead, her face impassive. "Get out, Gib. This is the end of the line."

At first, thinking she was joking, he laughed at her bad movie dialogue and its clench-jawed Dirty Harry delivery, but when she deepened her glare he understood that she was serious.

He didn't know what he'd done or failed to do. He'd barely reckoned with the news. Again, the consequences of his rash action swirled around him, seeming to settle like the dust now drifting through the open window. It was late afternoon. They were at least ten miles from the last town in land trackless but for the road. He would have to carry Hal, who couldn't walk more than a quarter of a mile before he gave out. "Water," he said, thinking of the plastic jugs they'd filled outside Clovis. "Will you let us take one?"

The dog stood up, nose over the seat back. Georgette gave Gib a sidelong look. "Hal can stay. But you get out."

"Oh, God," he said. Hal's hot breath wafted over his shoulder. Something made of cellophane crackled under the dog's feet.

He could overpower her. She was so small and sick she'd have no strength. In front of him was the glove box, the pistol wrapped in a red oil rag.

As if she'd read his mind, she said, "Don't even think about it."

"Listen," he began, but he didn't know what to say.

A smile played at the corners of her lips. "If you can't bring yourself to get out of the car, then at least just look around."

Fear, chagrin, disgust with himself had stupefied him.

"Let's play another guessing game," she said, now patiently, the high school teacher she claimed to be. She gestured out the window. "I see something made of limestone with three slashes clearly marking . . ."

He saw it then, the pillar in the weeds beside the road, smaller than he'd remembered, and he went limp with relief.

"Did you really think I'd kick you out?" She cut her eyes at him. "Don't trust me for a minute, do you?"

Before he could lie and say he did, she shifted into reverse, backed up, then aimed the car toward some high ground that provided a passage across the ditch, and set off bumpily across the grassland. "Don't feel bad," she said. "I wouldn't either."

She yanked the wheel to dodge a boulder. "How far in?"

"A mile or two."

She looked at him out of the corner of her eye. "Thanks, by the way."

"For what?"

"Not putting up an argument. You really would have gotten out, wouldn't you?" With a fist she pounded on the steering wheel, crowing, "Boy, I must be tough!"

What he'd had in mind was to walk the acres, spend the night camped near the hut, courting the feeling he'd had before, but now, as they threshed through prickly pear and Mormon tea, across loose rock and shaling outcrops, the place felt wrong. In its boundlessness he felt dislocated and unreal, unable to connect the man he was now to the boy he'd been at eighteen.

A mile or so in they found the sheepherder's hut a pile of rubble, its tin roof gone. They walked down the grass around it, pitched her tent, fed and watered Hal and made a bed for him, then spread another blanket outside so they could sit to watch the night come on. In such wide space, the sun seemed to take its time going down. Darkness crept in from the east and in the last light the rolling ground looked molten. Overhead a goshawk dived, then soared again. Bats swooped. It was too dry and windy to make a fire, and so in the moonlight they ate the sandwiches they'd bought in Clovis. The sky was spangled, and the Milky Way stretched like a broad white road. Falling stars crisscrossed each other. She pointed out the Seven Sisters, glittering.

He couldn't shake his mind from what she planned to do. "What about the rest of your family?"

"Long gone. I'm a stray." She stretched out on the blanket, put her hands behind her head. "Orphaned, divorced, a foster person."

"Did you ever try to . . . ?"

"Find them? Sure. I'm trying now. Well, not trying actively, but I always think when I'm out driving that I'll run into somebody or some thing, catch the tag end of a conversation or see something that rings a bell and that will put it all together. But I don't even know my real last name. It's like this lost word out there that if I hear it everything will come back."

He nodded. Milnesand had been named for a windmill in a dry

gulch that settlers called "the mill in the sand," slurring the phrase to form an oddly pronounced word. The mill was gone, and the name was all that remained of the place. He considered offering this information, but in the face of the unknowables she lived with, the observation would be heartless.

"My mother came from Oklahoma, but I don't know where. It was the Dust Bowl, so I didn't come with papers. No birth certificate, no nothing. Well, a picture of us when I was a baby, but that's all. Her face was blurred, so it's just me in her lap, holding this dandelion. Nita—that's my foster—wrote a caption on it. *How Okies Look to Natives.* I'd ask her what it meant, but she couldn't say exactly. The separateness in people, the strangers they can be, something like that.

"She was just a girl, my mother, when she left me. She meant to come back, my fosters said, but something must have happened. She followed rodeo, so maybe . . . did you know that Pretty Prairie, Kansas, is home of the world's largest night rodeo?"

He shook his head. Hal yawned widely, stretched. The last full moon of summer shone a silvery path across the darkened bench land.

"But then Nita was a talker. She made up a lot of things. Probably to spare my feelings."

"But you believed her?"

"Sometimes. She said I was part Indian, too, but that's the kind of thing drunks brag about in bars. Used to be nobody would admit it, but now everybody wants to be one. More romantic. Mystic. But I'll tell you, if as many people were as claimed they were and even halfway cared to, red people could take back the country. At least the western half. That's my idea of revolution. Wouldn't that be something?"

From the arroyo coyotes yipped and howled. Hal lay drowsing, too deaf to hear them, too old, Gib realized with a pang, to howl back.

"Now I figure I'll know everything when I'm a ghost." She sat up and began to pick through Hal's coat for burrs, collecting them in a neat pile. "What about you?"

As he told it, his life sounded privileged and charmed. Because it shamed him that he'd had things so easy, he tried to put a wry tone to his account to show he was aware how mild and safe his life had been. She didn't speak for a time after he had finished, and he thought she might have dozed off, but then she said, "Don't feel like you've got something over me because you know who you're related to. Sometimes it's best if you don't. Besides, I figure everybody's got to be somebody's second-cousin-once-removed."

He could make no sense of her theory of lineage, and so he gave up trying. "Maybe so," he said.

"You sound like that radio guy on the prairie show," she said. "You sigh when you talk, and you make these little whistling noises when you breathe."

"Sorry."

"No, it's a good sound. Like somebody's voice you sort of think you know." She gave Hal a pat and pushed up from the blanket, getting to her feet. "Except I have to tell you, Gib, it puts me and my pal Hal to sleep."

He planned to bunk on the bench seat of the car while she took the tent, but she wouldn't hear of it. She'd rest better sitting up in the front seat, she said, it eased the pain of reflux. "Besides"—she gave him the half eye—"a fugitive such as yourself, how do I know you won't hot-wire the car and leave me stuck out here in bee-eff Egypt?"

Getting into the spirit of her banter, he said, "You don't. Maybe I'm an outlaw, too."

She cackled, pleased.

He walked off a ways from the campsite to urinate, to give a last look toward the stars. He tried to let his mind expand to take in the vastness, but he was too weary for long thoughts. Maybe when he

was in his own car driving home something profound would come to him.

When he crawled inside the tent, Georgette was already there. "Hal insisted," she informed him.

"It's fine," he said. "The car's just fine for me. No problem."

She patted the pallet. "No, you too. Our mutual friend insists. There's room enough."

Hal, tongue lolling, gathered himself beside her, thumped his tail against the blankets as if to ratify her invitation. On his hands and knees, Gib hesitated until she said exasperatedly, as she might to a house cat havering at a door, "Gibson, in or out. We're only going to sleep."

Later, when he was back in Memphis and he came to the part in the story of his absurd trip that he would tell himself but no one else, he would remember how fragile the bones of her spine felt when she nestled hers against his. Hal lay backed into her; her arm was slung over the dog's chest. For a long time they lay that way, Gib conscious of her breathing, of her smallness, of the unlikely tableau they made, dog, woman, man a thousand miles from home in a dark tent on an empty plain under a moon close enough for light but too far away for warmth.

He turned over so that the three of them faced the same direction, and when he put his arm around Georgette, she gave a tired sigh. "Cousin, that feels better than you know." Her breath, acrid, ketotic, seemed to gather in the air above them. They slept.

The next morning in the gray light of false dawn Hal stood over him on stalky legs, tethered with his leash to a tent stake. A look outside told him the car was parked where they had left it, but Georgette was gone.

He called her name, his voice insignificant in the endless space, but no answer came, and so he put on his shoes, went out to check the car, thinking she'd given up on the tent and bunked up on the car's bench seat.

The red oil rag lay on the seat, the glove box hung open, empty. He swore.

At a run, trying to recall whether or not a shot awakened him, he set off for the rise from which he had framed his imaginary photographs, trying to steel himself. He saw himself finding her body in the arroyo, driving her car to the nearest town and trying to explain. Hal followed as if they were on a romp, tail waving, in high spirits.

Just before they reached the arroyo Hal sniffed at the air and turned off in a rachitic lope toward a low-lying thicket of sapling cottonwoods. The wind licked at the leaves to flick them white side up, and the quaking cottonwoods shimmered like a mirage, from which Georgette emerged.

Fury dizzied him, then a feeling of relief so callow and self-serving that he gasped.

She walked toward him, slinging the pistol as if it were an extension of her hand, and suddenly he was yelling at her.

She tucked the pistol into her shorts. "How could I do *what*? Go out to whiz?" Hal swagged his tail across the tall weeds, licked her hand.

Struck dumb, Gib gestured toward the lump the pistol made.

"Rattlesnakes, why else?"

"Then why did you tie up the dog?"

"Same reason, Sherlock. I'm supposed to be everywhere at once? Aren't you going to ask me how I feel?"

He could only stare.

"Never mind, I'll tell you. Like a million bucks, all green and wrinkled. Worse for wear. You're not the quietest bedmate. You snored worse than a troll. And you drive, okay?"

After they broke camp and packed the car, she said, "Look, Dr. Kildare, I wouldn't put another person in that spot. Not even a stranger. I'd leave a thank-you note, for pity's sake."

All the way back to Zenobia, they rode in a silence that if he didn't feel so foolish and unsettled, he would have called companionable. She swigged Maalox, served as a morbid little tour guide pointing out turkey buzzards circling on updrafts, a road-killed bobcat, a rest stop on the high plains where a sign painted in Park Service yellow warned WATCH OUT FOR SNAKES.

As they sat at the counter in a motel coffee shop in the heat-blasted state-line town of Texhoma, he asked, "Where will you go after you drop me off?"

"Up to see that well, then maybe over to have a look at the Garden of Eden. Some old jasper forged all the scenes from the Old Testament in scrap iron. Or concrete or whatever. Quite the deal, I hear." She took a sip of coffee, grimaced, then shook off a shudder. "Hey, last night I think I figured out the reason people build the things they do. World's biggest this, world's only that."

He waited, wondering if it would offend her if he invited her to come back with him to Memphis. Care could be arranged, a place found, he could visit and watch over things. Barbara would come around. She'd probably be glad he heeded an impulse, even one that put her out. One of the few contentions in their marriage was that she found him too straitlaced.

"They make the little ones because they're poleaxed by the big ones. What do you think of that?"

He didn't know if what made him speak was guilt or compassion or some combination of the two. "I was thinking that maybe you'd come up to Memphis. You'd be closer to your son. There's hospice care, and I know a couple of good . . ."

"Forget about it, Gibson. I know what I'm doing. I figure I started on the road, and that's where I'll wind up. End to end. A balance. Poetic whatever."

He wanted to do something, but she seemed to have shut all the doors. "Is there anything?"

She rolled her eyes, then smirked, jabbing him with her elbow.

"Look me up when you're a ghost. We'll have ourselves another campout."

He made a noise low in his throat he hoped passed for a chuckle.

"Look, Gib, if it will make you feel any better, I'll go back and talk to Robbie. I don't like things the way I left them, but I had to clear my head."

He nodded, but he wasn't sure if he believed her.

That afternoon when they pulled into the station at Zenobia, his Cherokee was parked out front, a new windshield installed. R. D. was scraping at the sticker. "Howdy, howdy," he hailed them, his welcome both hangdog and hearty. "You're good to go. I even gassed her up, no charge."

R. D. explained that the sheriff tracked him down in Dodge and blessed him out. "So I done it on good faith. You can just mail me the check."

When Gib asked him how much, R. D. said grandly, "Cost." He pantomimed a twist on an imaginary cue. "Won me a little something."

Gib went inside to settle the amount and copy the station's address, and when he came back outside, meaning to say a farewell stark enough for Georgette to countenance, even if it was just to say thanks for the ride and he was glad he met her, no solicitude, no vows to keep in touch that she could growl at, she was already steering the Caprice across the culvert. Beside her on the seat, Hal sat at attention, a paw on the dashboard to steady himself, his long nose lifted toward the road ahead.

Gib called out, but she didn't stop.

"Wait!" he shouted, but she rolled on.

R. D. hurried to the door, and he shouted, too. "Pull over!"

Despite the loss it meant, despite the explanation he would have to make when he got home, Gib called out to tell her Hal was hers, that she could take him, but he wasn't certain she heard, was less certain she cared.

She stuck her arm out the Chevy's open window and raised two fingers in a salute that to her generation had meant victory but that to his meant peace, then she hit the gas and sped away.

R. D. stood beside him. "That's your *dog* she's running off with, dude."

Gib said, yes, it was.

"That's wrong," R. D. said. "You get her tag number? Mississippi plates . . ."

"It's all right."

"You want me to call up J. D.?"

"J. D.?"

"My dad. The sheriff. He could head her off."

When Gib told him there was no need, R. D. seemed at a loss as to how to be of aid. He gestured toward the chair next to his in front of the station. Absurd as the offer was, Gib was grateful for it, and he took a seat, tilting back to rest his head against the wall. In the field across the road sunflowers bowed and waved in the prevailing breeze. A meadowlark swooped from a power line to disappear among the blooms. From an unseen place the bird sang out, its bright trill sounding for all the world like language, like the answer to a riddle or a question he had yet to form. Watching the field, he waited for the meadowlark to rise, for the song to come again, but all was quiet. It was as though the bird had never been. For a long time before he stood up to be on his way, he sat quietly beside his host, dazed by chance and sorrow, time and, for a wonder, love.

5

~

All of the House That Stood

We met out at Meg Garrett's farmhouse on a bitter February night. The meeting had been called to order, the last month's minutes were approved, and we were ready to take up our study of the poems of Robert Frost when a charter member cleared her throat. "Madame Chairman, if it please the court."

"Honey, you don't have to talk like that," Meg told Rebecca Alford. "This is not a trial, it's us."

By *us* she meant our book club, a dozen readers gleaned from the panhandle towns of Eva, Guymon, Slapout, Goodwell, Hatcher, and Texhoma. We met round-robin style, men welcome to attend but none in evidence, although depending on the place and season the sons and/or nephews who drove some of the elder members might barbecue an elk haunch or tinker with machinery in somebody's shed or barn.

About the legal talk, Rebecca's husband Wheeler had been a county judge, and she'd picked up his speaking habits. It was party-of-the-first-part this and party-of-the-second-part that, to wit and heretofore, but if it made her miss him any less, nobody minded, and it sometimes gave a needed weight to our proceedings. We were given to artistic dustups, as will be seen in this account, respectfully submitted this night of March 18, 2007, in place of the usual minutes and with apologies for liberties that cause offense.

"We've done Robert Frost before," Rebecca went on. "Eisenhower was president. We thought we were so smart because right after that Frost read the poem for that other inauguration."

"JFK's," said Puffy Branch, who ran the Z-Bar-T and styled herself a maverick.

Rebecca said, "I was a young mother then. Wheeler had just opened his law practice down on Front Street . . ."

"Maybe it's déjà vu," somebody suggested, cushioning the likelihood that at eighty-nine Rebecca had a memory that was shot.

Rebecca shook her head. "I'm certain of it. By all signs and presents, Robert Frost's a repeat."

We had a firm bylaw against repeats. Jane Bellamy, at ninety-two the only other member with a history long enough to confirm the charge, dozed in a chair beside the fire. We couldn't check the record because the logbook had been left at Puffy's, ten miles across the Texas line. A norther had blown up, a blizzard on the way, and we were in a quandary.

In our book club there were factions. For reading tastes we split between readers who leaned toward fated romance leading down the aisle to happy endings and those who favored loss and suffering and ironies, the deadly virtues. So far—with one slip-up for a bodice-ripper about which ruffled feelings still remained—the pull of gravity held sway, but times were changing, and as members died off and new ones joined, our list was tending away from tragic classics toward more popular works, some of these so feathery, some maintained, that if you blew on them, they'd float away.

At January's meeting we had a wrangle about the next selection. One faction pressed for romance. February was the month of valentines, if not love then, then when? The other faction lobbied for *The Brothers Karamazov.* There were strong words. Insult was given, umbrage taken, and poetry was the compromise, agreed to when somebody said, "If you can't depend on poets to write about love, who can you trust?"

A vote was taken, Robert Frost anointed, and the waters stilled until somebody else observed, "And death. Poets are huge on death." And so you can see why, when the repeat issue reared its head, the uplift faction moved in for the kill.

Delilah England named a bestselling title from years back that some of us called *the book whose name should not be uttered.* "We can finally talk about it. We've waited ages. Most of us have read it or else seen the movie. The library has almost all our names on the card. I checked."

"Not mine," said Puffy, and a murmur went up as others protested they had only checked it out for nieces, maiden aunts, shut-ins.

Puffy went on, "That book's not fit for pig feed." She kept up with *The New York Times Book Review,* and she had saved us more than once from clinkers. If she was often coarsely frank in her opinions, they at least held some weight.

Nancy Jameson took up Delilah's cause. "Puffy, do you never tire of going against the grain?"

"I don't get tired of thinking, no."

Delilah said, "Well, I do. Sometimes I just want to go to a strange place and get lost in a story and let it take me away."

Puffy said that if Delilah wanted strange places and more lift, why didn't she drive down to Amarillo and shop for new brassieres. Delilah pointed out that some people ought to climb down off their high horse, and things were getting out of hand until Meg tapped a spoon against her coffee cup. "Let's hear Rebecca out."

Every schoolchild knew about the yellow wood and the road less traveled by, and so at first Rebecca hadn't worried about the familiar feeling she was getting, but when she found herself in tears she remembered weeping over Frost's crow in the hemlock tree a long time back. She remembered exactly where she'd been, in her kitchen chopping chestnuts for Thanksgiving stuffing, looking out the window at a cardinal in the snow and thinking of the hemlock poem and how it pierced her in the way its plain words put a picture in her mind of what it felt like when a gloom began to lift.

In the absence of the logbook, we had to trust Rebecca, and so it was either break the bylaw and go on with Frost or talk about *the book whose name should not be uttered.* "Let's leave it to our hostess," Delilah said, and everybody looked to Meg, who had been known to tilt uphill.

It was then an odd thing happened. Old Jane Bellamy started from sleep, blinked as though possessed, and began reciting one of Frost's poems as if speaking from the great beyond. "The house had gone to bring again to the midnight sky a sunset glow. Now the chimney was all of the house that stood, like a pistil after the petals go."

When no one interrupted, Jane fluffed her hair, which had flattened on one side from being mashed against the chair's wing, and went on to recite the rest of the poem. Her voice was low, melodious; it seemed to hold us in a loving hand. She ended with, "One had to be versed in country things, not to believe the phoebes wept." She petted the bow of her pink blouse. "I can't remember if the club's done Frost before, but I memorized that poem as a girl. Some things you don't forget."

"Recite another," Delilah urged.

"We should get back to business," Meg said. "We need to make a choice. If it's up to me, I say we ought to . . ."

Whether it was that Jane was loath to give up the spotlight or that she meant to stave off the inevitable, our eldest member went on to say, "If it's love we're fighting over, I could tell a story. This one didn't happen in any exotic place, though"—she glanced toward Delilah—"it happened right out here. The people in it are all dead or gone, and so it isn't gossip."

When someone sets to storytelling we usually ride herd, alert for misremembering and embellishment. Members will put in with missed details and side perspectives, how it really happened, until the version we arrive at bears, if not the whole truth, then at least a satisfactory allegiance to it. But on this night we yielded the floor. Not only was our attention a token of respect for Jane's surpassing age, we would say a short week later when she was laid to rest, it was that it felt good to sit back on a cold night in a warm place and listen to a story.

"In Hatcher there were two men with the same name, John Wright Freeman," Jane began.

"Both of them were big men. They were the same age, and neither had a nickname and neither went by his initials. Both ran diners, one between the bank and the Otasco store and the other out on the county road beside the tracks. To keep them straight we could have called them Town John and Country John, but they were known as Married John and John the Bachelor.

"Married John was black-eyed handsome with a strong-jawed face that looked like it hadn't been slapped enough. He had a curl of black springy hair over dark eyes the high school girls who stopped by to look at movie magazines called hypnotic. He was a Casanova and a Fancy Dan, but his looks and ways felled women by the score. Young and old and smart and not-so, even some who ought to have known better." Jane cleared her throat, petted her pink bow, and went on.

"Married John wasn't married at the time the story takes place, but he had been through four wives, and every one of them had left him. He never made excuses for himself. He said he just loved women, found something beautiful in each one, from the plainest to the proudest. He couldn't help himself, he said, it was his hot Greek blood. He came from Philadelphia but had lived in Hatcher for so long he thought he had a franchise on the town's affection, at least the female half's.

"John the Bachelor had appetites as well, but he had a loner's nature. He arrived in the late fifties from somewhere else back East, saying he wanted to live in a place as far away from war and water as he could reach by rail. He bought the abandoned feed store that sat out by the Noah place, built some rooms above to live in, and opened a café.

"He was portly as the tenors whose arias he played on his phonograph, with a broad face and sad eyes, a brushy mustache. He'd been in World War Two, was taken prisoner behind German lines, but to hear him talk no one would ever know it. The Wharton kid he hired to wash dishes—even as a boy Gus was a snoop, but he meant well—found the medals in the bottom of the drawer where John kept pay stubs. A Purple Heart, some others. He told it around town. Curiosity led some to try the place, others followed, and pretty soon the café was doing a land-office business.

"For cooking, John the Bachelor had a gift. No one around had ever seen the like. He sponsored game dinners for the hunters, cooked their quail and dove and pheasant fixed up to perfection with berries, nuts, and mushrooms, not just slapped into a skillet with a stick of oleo. His roast goose bore no trace of grease, his chicken was sublime. Pork, it was his calling, beef a holy thing. What he could do with new spring lamb could break a heart; under his hand even old mutton was delicious. He had such success with local food that he branched out and cooked dishes from foreign lands. Borscht and latkes, blintzes and pierogies, gumbo, jambalaya, cassoulet, frittata, things no one had heard of. Whatever it was he put in any dish, it made people wish they could be natives of whatever place they ate that way.

"Married John's nose was out of joint, but there wasn't much he could do except oil his springy curl and go on flipping hamburgers. Hoping to win back the teetotalers at least, he spread it around town that the other John's secret ingredient was bootleg whiskey, but this tactic didn't work, and by the end of the 1970s, John the Bachelor's place had siphoned customers until the only ones at Married John's besides the bank kaffeeklatsch were those star-eyed high school girls.

"About this time a woman came to town. Some of you may have known her. Maxine Spoon, her name was. She drove one of those half-truck, half-car affairs, and she pulled it into one of the empty parking spots in front of Married John's. She got out and looked around. It was a gritty day in spring and wind blew down the street and tore the bun out of her hair, which made it fly about wrecked as the *Hesperus,* but she had a quick-eyed face, and she had kept her figure. It was this last that drew John's roving eye. Watching from the window, he fixed his curl and geared up to work his charm. But he couldn't get his hot Greek blood to rise, and so when she came in to ask about a job, he decided to use her to get his rival's goat.

"She was too tiny to lift a tray of coffee cups much less a heavy bus tub, and she was the wrong age to flirt with—like him she was nearing sixty—and so he thought it would be worth a good haw-haw to play a trick on John the Bachelor. He leaned across his counter on his black-haired arms and told her to go out and try the place beside the tracks. 'Tell him the governor of Kansas got wind of his fancy food. Joan Finney in the flesh is headed down to Hatcher with a party of eighteen. Tell him it looks like he could use your help.' He chuckled like the skeezicks that he was and saw her on her way.

"John the Bachelor didn't believe the business about Joan Finney, but he hired Maxine on the spot. He told customers he'd been getting by with only Gus as backup and he'd been thinking about hiring more help, but the truth was that he'd fallen hard and fast in love.

"No one could figure the attraction. Yes, they were the same age, and Maxine was nice enough, but the kink in her getalong made people worry for her as she hoisted heavy trays. Except for pies and chicken fry and gravy, she was a washout in the kitchen, all thumbs and too much salt, forgotten pepper, baking powder lumps to make you pucker up. But the big stove was John's bailiwick, and at serving meals and cleaning up she worked like killing snakes. Love, however, wasn't on her menu.

"She had a soft spot for young mothers with small children, and she kept a jar of penny candy for them. She was tidy and efficient. But the regulars were used to John the Bachelor's easy ways. They didn't cotton to Maxine. She was pecky as a biddy, and she had notions about blue language, about men doffing their hats indoors. The men maintained they took their headgear off in church and never swore too loud on Sunday, and that seemed to be enough for God, who hadn't filed complaint. A hat-and-cussword war began, business began to fall off, and it looked like Married John might win back his customers.

"What turned the tide was the way Maxine could singe somebody's puffed-up feathers. It happened one day that a bunch of cattlemen were lolling around a table, holding forth on politics, religion, and what have you. Maxine had waited on them all morning, with one well-known windbag filibustering on, when a stranger whose car had broken down out on the road came in and asked if anybody in the place knew how to fix a flat. Maxine drew up and fixed the windbag with a look. 'Well, Cap,' she said, her quick little monkey face squinched up so sly that anyone could guess at what was coming, 'why don't you hurry out and blow it up?' This brought down the house, which loosened up Maxine and made her feel at home enough to call a cease-fire about the hats. About the language she held fast, but the men called it a draw and curbed their tongues.

"By now John was more in love, and from all signs Maxine was coming around. She was blooming on his cooking, and she began to cushion up a little. Since she'd come to town she'd been living in an alley walk-up, and John the Bachelor wanted her closer by. He decided he would move out of his rooms above the café and take up living in the long bunkhouse beside the café that the Noahs had once used for migrant workers in the beet fields. Maxine could settle in.

" 'Only if I pay rent,' she told him. 'How much would you charge?'

" 'Cash on the barrelhead?' He narrowed his eyes into a study of greed, for he loved to tease Maxine about her seriousness. 'Two bucks.'

" 'A day? Why, that's outrageous.' She meant his price was low, of course.

" 'All right, two bucks a month,' he countered, raising an eyebrow.

" 'Forget it, Buster Brown.' She had caught on to him by now.

"He crossed his arms. 'Okay, two bucks a year, but that's my final offer.'

"Finally, he agreed to take the going rate, and it was a good arrangement as it put Maxine closer to the café. As a bonus, every night when they tallied the receipts they could sit out on the bunkhouse porch to watch the sun go down. John's cooking got even more inspired. The whole town put on weight, and everybody knew it wouldn't be long before John popped the question.

"The first thing he did was drive to Amarillo for a ring. He bought a pearl and stashed it in the walk-in cooler behind the gallon jars of pickles. Next, he checked the *Old Farmer's Almanac* for the moon phase and settled on the night. He planned to drive out to Black Mesa, and as the harvest moon rose over the hills, at a table set with a starched white cloth and candles in hurricane globes, he would propose.

"Then he planned the meal. For three long days he cooked, and the good smells drifting from the café's windows stopped traffic on the road. When the evening came he was beside himself with nerves, but he was ready.

"It went around town that the dinner went well. The moon hung low and red, the wind for once was down, and so the torches flared just right. Maxine sat there smiling, tasting this and tasting that and smiling, but she turned him down. She liked things the way they were.

"Back at the café, he worked on her. 'Maxine, we're not getting any younger.'

" 'I am,' she said in her crooked little voice and went on counting setups.

" 'We could wake up together, go to sleep together.'

"At this she rolled her eyes, as anyone could track their progress from the porch to Maxine's upper room, and on certain mornings Gus could hear the creak of John's weight on the floor above the café's kitchen.

"John tried to understand. She had been hurt before. Who hadn't? She didn't want to depend on anybody else. For what, he asked, shaking his head, for love? But she held firm.

"Every night they sat on the bunkhouse porch, rocking and talking. Not even Gus knew what they talked about so many nights together, but they made a peaceful scene to pass when you drove down the road at dusk and saw them there, their heads together.

"About this time her son blew in, down on his luck. He was trouble, the kind of son who's grown but not grown, wanting everything he didn't have and ready to stand in the way of anyone who had it. He nursed a grudge against his father, whose name Maxine had kept from him too long, she confessed to Gus, blaming herself for letting the secret fester so that when she finally told him, Jesse's anger had long since turned to pity for himself. There wasn't room enough for Jesse to stay upstairs at Maxine's, so John suggested he take the migrant house. He'd move in upstairs with Maxine.

" 'Not in this talky town,' she told him.

" 'We could move you in beside me,' John suggested. 'There's a wall between the sections.'

" 'Even thick walls,' she said, cutting her eyes at Gus, 'have ears.'

"There was no arguing with Maxine when she made up her mind, so John gave up. They found Jesse a bed and some things he needed, and he moved in next to John. Nights when they'd have their porch-talk, there sat Jesse with them, a forty-year-old child strumming his guitar and asking if they liked his singing, which sounded to Gus like sick cats wauling in a cardboard box.

"John was philosophical. He worked it around in his mind that if he wasn't her boss, Maxine would marry him free and clear, and so he hired Jesse, saying he'd been thinking of retiring. Gus tried to warn him that no good would come of this arrangement, but of course John went ahead.

"For a while things went all right. John taught him to cook, and to everyone's surprise the younger man, as flighty as he was, took to it. One night a week he prepared the dinner special, and if his offerings weren't a match for John's, they were still a big success, and Maxine was giddy with the changes in her son.

"But soon the café started losing money, and they couldn't figure how. Every day they had the same number of customers but every night the till count came up short. Of course, Jesse was pilfering. One day Maxine caught him red-handed, snaking a twenty out of the register drawer. 'Put that back, or I'll call the police.'

" 'I thought it might be counterfeit.'

" 'Son, you know I have to tell John.'

"John thought he could father Jesse into going straight, and Jesse took the second chance. He promised to do right. But he didn't, or he couldn't, and after a few more weeks went by he stole again. This time he staged it like a break-in. Smashed out the back window, crept to the floor safe everybody knew was broken, and made off with the money bag.

" 'Let it go,' John told Maxine, who said, 'That isn't fair to Gus.' Even though he was a meddler and a one-man party line, he was honest as the day was long.

"It was the hardest thing she'd ever done, she told Gus later, but she put the law on Jesse, and he served six months. The first week of his sentence Jesse wrote an apology and promised to pay John back. But he didn't, at least not then. As for John, he didn't care. With Jesse gone, he was working up to pledge his troth again when Maxine walked up as he and Gus sat at the window table going over invoices.

"In front of him she dropped a ten-dollar bill clipped to a piece of notebook paper on which he read that Maxine Jane Spoon owed John Wright Freeman three thousand, some-odd hundred dollars and change.

" 'Honey, there's no need for this. Why should you pay for what he did?'

" 'Maxine's the name, and why should you?' Brandishing a ballpoint pen, she wheeled on Gus. 'You be our witness.'

"By then Gus was a man in his full prime with children of his own. He stayed at the café in part because his wife was happy with her sisters and their families around, in part because he liked his work, and he was good at it. The café'd go broke without him, so he liked to say, as John and Maxine would likely run it to the ground the way they both gave food away. But still it troubled him that he hadn't proved himself by going out in the world, and so when John shot him a look that could have seared a brisket, Gus said he would be moving on to Denver any day so not to look at him. He wasn't going to witness anything, nosirree-Bob. Wasn't going to get involved. Was keeping his trap shut. Hands off. No dice. None of his never mind. And on and on the endless way Gus could protest.

"Maxine rolled her eyes and heaved a Gus-ward sigh and tacked the paper to the corkboard by the telephone in the back room. Then she stomped off, shaking her head at both men.

"Over the next two years the paper grew smudged with ink and grease but the debt went steadily down. For John, it was uneasy consolation that as long as the I.O.U. was up, it meant Maxine wasn't going anywhere. But while it was up, it meant she wouldn't marry him. In the meantime, although he knew it would make her mad enough to spit, he put the money in the bank with her name on the account, letting it build for a rainy day.

"Their wedding day, he decided. He was getting on toward seventy, and Maxine wasn't far behind. He figured that if they were lucky they would have at least fifteen or twenty more years, and he wanted to live them married to Maxine. When it came to him that to hasten the payoff he could give her a raise, he wanted to kick himself for not thinking of it earlier.

"To his surprise she accepted. 'High time,' she said. 'Inflation. Cost of living. Good help isn't cheap.'

"At last the day came when she crossed off the final balance on the tally sheet, but by then John was failing. Gus had worked beside the man for twenty years, and he'd begun to notice a slowness to John's movements, a falling-off of strength, a liverish look around the eyes. John had lost weight. If he'd fallen fast in love, in sickness he fell faster.

"Maxine was devastated. She moved him into her bed upstairs and hardly left his side. The man was dying, it was plain to see, but still she wouldn't marry him. She dug in her heels, refused, until half the town was up in arms against her.

"One night when he stopped by to bring a bowl of banana pudding, Gus heard them arguing. 'It isn't that,' Maxine was saying. 'It's that you might think I did it for the wrong reasons. People might.'

" 'There were always only right ones, Max. And to hell with people.'

" 'I haven't set foot in a church for sixty years.'

" 'Who said a word about a church?'

"On and on they went until Gus, standing outside on the landing, had heard enough. Gus had ripened to the kind of person who did anything he did—even his meddling—for reasons of love. He knew his heart contained his doom, which was to stay with those he cared about. He had a family to support and he should have left town long before but here he was still in the same place and it looked like he was stuck, as now he loved Maxine as well. Hidden in his heart, which Gus searched for a way to break the stalemate between the two behind the door, he found the other half of what had always stopped him from moving on, and this other half was fear. For all her acting tough and independent, Maxine was afraid.

"Gus knew what he had to do. He barged into the room without a knock, set down the pan of pudding, and began to yell. He yelled at Maxine that she ought to be ashamed for waiting so long and that if she were his to spank, he'd spank her blue. He told John it was a low-down trick to get himself so sick that Gus had to take over as the unpaid boss, but if that was the way it was, he would be laying down the law. Common law, he said, to be exact. He told them both that if theirs was not a union, there was no such thing. 'You fools can get yourselves a stack of Bibles, put your hands on top, that's fine with me. But by the vested powers in anybody in the round world has to watch this mess, you're married. End of subject.'

"What the two said to each other after he stormed out, nobody knew, but the next day when Gus came to open the café for breakfast Maxine had the pearl ring on her finger and even after John passed on he never saw her without it . . ."

Jane coughed delicately. She asked for water, and Meg brought it. With a quaking hand she lifted the glass and sipped. She coughed again and took another sip. "The end. That's all I know."

Meg went for a bottle of Jack Daniel's and a tray of communion cups she'd brought home from church to wash. She filled the cups and passed the tray around.

We drank. Outside the wind was howling, and sleet peppered the windows, while inside by the fire we silently considered love and death. We drank again.

Rebecca said, "I remember Maxine. She came to Wheeler's service. She thought the world of him, she told me. She didn't last long after that, as I recall."

None of the rest of us had known Maxine, but we wanted to know what had become of Gus. Jane had lost touch with him when he left town, she said; the café by the tracks had been boarded up for several years.

Someone asked, "What about the bad John?"

Jane's voice was raw from talking. "Well, bad is relative, of course. But, yes, he struck again. Went on to marry the woman he brought with him to John's funeral."

Rebecca, whose memory, if on some counts vaguer, was almost as long as Jane's, gave her a pointed look.

Jane knocked back the last of her whiskey. "Who then had to go to the trouble of unmarrying him."

Our Jane had been the picture of a lady, and many of us were surprised to learn this bit of her story lost in the past. We considered her, with her palsied hands and her stiff white hair, her peony pink blouse with the bow at her creped neck, out of whose whiskery mouth the story had come, and at least one of us was moved to wonder how she herself would appear at great age, what account, near the end of her days, would she give of the choices she'd made?

"Sometimes you just have to do wrong," Jane said defiantly, to no one.

Delilah said we'd had such a good discussion we should stick with poetry.

"Here's an idea," said Puffy. "How about for March we talk about the actual poems the actual Robert Frost wrote?"

On the principle that some bylaws needed breaking, we concurred, and Frost it was again for March. After that we turned to setting April's book. In the spirit of the evening it was moved and seconded that a little lightness wouldn't do us in and that *the book whose name should not be uttered* had waited long enough. When Rebecca asked, "What say we, yea or nay?" *yeas* rose from most quarters.

"And I know just the book for May," said Puffy. "It's a classic, but it's got romance enough to choke a horse." On Puffy's trusted word we added *Madame Bovary.*

By then it was past ten o'clock. In the yard the men were starting cars and scraping windshields, stamping boots on porch boards. Snow swirled in a driving wind to veil the headlight beams, turned on against the darkness. The lane would soon be drifting over, and it was time to make our separate ways onto the night, onto the gleaming roads toward home. All other business tended to, or tabled for another time, our meeting was adjourned.

Epilogue

Worldly Goods

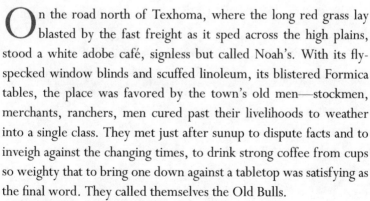

On the road north of Texhoma, where the long red grass lay blasted by the fast freight as it sped across the high plains, stood a white adobe café, signless but called Noah's. With its fly-specked window blinds and scuffed linoleum, its blistered Formica tables, the place was favored by the town's old men—stockmen, merchants, ranchers, men cured past their livelihoods to weather into a single class. They met just after sunup to dispute facts and to inveigh against the changing times, to drink strong coffee from cups so weighty that to bring one down against a tabletop was satisfying as the final word. They called themselves the Old Bulls.

Thursday mornings Wheeler Alford and Cap Russell joined them in deploring a world it pleased Wheeler, at eighty-one, to announce he would be leaving. "None too soon," he liked to say. "For parts unknown." This was his great joke, and that he made it every Thursday did nothing to dim the glee he took in its effect on his half brother Cap, who found the outlook sour and fatal and a slap at heaven's face.

For years the two had fallen out with each other, then in again. The town saw this as ritual sparring between men as different from each other as their fathers, and so their final fight was at first viewed as only the most recent in a never-ending chain. Not until after Wheeler's heart gave out a few days later did speculation start as to how the blows the brothers came to figured in his end.

The argument took place on a Thursday morning in September, a morning so serene in Oklahoma that it seemed at odds with the terrible events that had happened across the country in the days before. Whether or not the faraway disaster played a part in the brothers' trouble, the two witnesses to their quarrel agreed it had a hand as surely as if it had slouched into Noah's, a stranger to the place, to take up one of the wobbly stools at the counter. On this morning, the men were to meet as they had for almost half a century of Thursdays but—owing to a meeting Cap had at his church, hinting at high doings of a confidential nature—two hours past their usual time.

Wheeler, the elder, arrived first. Broad-faced, jug-eared, of middling height but wiry enough in his youth to box welterweight, he had settled into stoutness. His robust health belied his forecasts; among his few nods to age were a gouty foot, a dewlap from chin to collarbone that jowled his face, and nearsightedness that required glasses. He had their mother's brown eyes, but where hers had been mild and deep-watered as a hound's, Wheeler's were sharper, the irises more light-filled and acute, giving his face a wolfish, sly expression. He had worn a suit and tie all his working life—he had kept a Front Street law practice and after that he served as county judge—but after stepping from the bench he'd taken to wearing work shirts and bib overalls, imagining himself the mechanic he sometimes wished he'd become. He put himself forth as a man unshocked by the downward turn in human sense, but his cynicism was a pose that had fooled no one but himself.

Many years before, he'd lost his teenaged son in a motorcycle accident in the sand hills west of town, an accident from which Wheeler walked away unhurt. He hid his grief with skepticism, avoiding bitterness though an affability that could make you wince, some who remembered the accident said, to witness. But enough time had passed to allow most people to see him as he wished to be seen: genial, salt of the earth, dry-witted.

The night before this particular Thursday, he and his wife Rebecca had buried their aged pet, a terrier mix called Packer for his pack rat habit of hoarding bones, lengths of frayed rope, bits of fur, and carpet scraps in a messy lair under the back porch. Wheeler had loved the little fice and—selfishly, he had to admit—he had hoped to go before the dog went. He didn't think that he could bear another grief, and he knew the loss of Packer would undo him. He had determined that today at Noah's he would gut it out and keep his sorrow to himself, but he was counting on his visit with Cap to take his thoughts from the heartbroken moan that in his mind's ear he still heard himself give out when Packer's spirit left him.

He stepped from his car just as the other Old Bulls were trailing out. They greeted him gravely, with none of the usual back and forth. He could count on Gene Hembree to call him *Hizzoner,* on Chess Fugate to say, "Here comes the judge," on Dolph Gunderson to look him over with his doctor's eye and pronounce him hale as ever. But today, given the shock of the days before, his friends touched their hat brims, and said only, "Wheeler," as they passed.

On the one hand, he was put out at missing the morning talk, but on the other he was glad. He'd watched the network news the first two days, until Packer had begun to fail; he wouldn't watch again. He was resolved to meet any talk of the catastrophe—the magnitude of sudden loss gave lie to numbering, to comparison—with silence, which seemed the only way to honor it.

Inside the café, he hung his Open Road on the hatrack and took the window booth the others had vacated. The elderly proprietress hunched over the counter, peering at the screen of an old TV set that sprouted a tangle of hanger wire and tinfoil. The set—thrifty Maxine would not replace it—had radio calipers soldered onto the knobless terminals, and the picture was so bleared that she had to lean close to make out the images.

Behind the pass-through window, Gus the fry cook scraped at his griddle. Always aggrieved—in middle age he hadn't made his threatened break to Denver—Gus appeared more put-upon than usual as he bulldozed the spatula across the smoking slab. Against Gus's threat of leaving, a waterfoxed HELP WANTED sign languished in the window. A wag had penciled on the back *All hope abandon, ye who enter here,* but the marks had been there for so long Wheeler had almost stopped seeing the message.

Neither Gus nor Maxine seemed to notice Wheeler's arrival, and so he called, "Hello, the house!"

Gus raised his spatula but didn't look up. Maxine glanced over, regarding him bleakly.

"If you can tear yourself away," Wheeler said. Often he and Maxine passed some pleasant moments in teasing each other about their common age, their nearness to being booted off the rim of earth. He relished her cranky humor, but today she fixed him with a stunned look.

As she poured his coffee, he filled her in on the reason the Old Bulls' routine was out of whack—Cap's mystery meeting with the pastor. He hoped to take his mind off Packer by sparking some banter about his brother's churchly airs, but Maxine had drifted off to take up her post in front of the TV set.

The day was off to a bad start, and it took Wheeler no time at all to lay the cause on his brother's lateness. He took off his glasses, his habit when he wanted to think deeply, and settled into his secret indulgence, which was to ruminate on Cap's flaws.

They had almost nothing in common. Cap at seventy-five was tall and bony, bald but for a monk's fringe of white hair that ringed his high-domed head. He had a blade nose and dark, deep-set eyes that gave him a look of hawklike intensity out of keeping with his nature, which was gullible, hale-fellow, loud. Cap was a believer to Wheeler's skeptic, garrulous to his reserve. He had a high, wild, yelping laugh and the glib tongue of the Irish father who had left him the packinghouse Cap ran until he retired. Since his retirement, Cap had led Young Life trips to Acoma Pueblo, Mesa Verde, and once as far away as Israel.

These trips galled Wheeler. Cap Russell was the last man on the planet who ought to be allowed to guide the innocent through ancient sites. If Cap didn't know a fact, he'd make one up, embellish it, then defend his crackpot ideas: the earth was six thousand years old, Indians were the migrant remnants of the Lost Tribes, dinosaurs died out during the Flood. Cap's heaven was a place with harps and gates and golden streets from which the dead looked down upon the living. "Through the portholes of heaven," Cap would say, as if the firmament were an enormous cruise ship. He filled his charges' minds with mangled notions, spackling the fissures in his logic with scripture, but the worst was that when Cap returned from one of his trips—Cap who'd sat out his last year of high school as well as the war, while Wheeler, after earning an engineering degree and before going to law school, had been at Iwo Jima—he would lecture Wheeler on foreign travel and history, on politics and religion.

Wheeler had given up trying to change his brother's opinions. He sat quietly when Cap blored on about Hillary's offenses and the proper place of women in the home, salvation and the end of days, the need for laws more in line with the way the Lord intended man to live. Still, Wheeler loved his younger brother with the kind of love bred in the blood, however thin, and just now he missed him. On this morning of all mornings, with the world in ruin and Packer in the ground, he needed the consolation of the one kinship he knew inside and out. He put on his glasses, glad to be taken from the brink of ill feeling by the rumble of the nine-fifteen freight, which set his cup and saucer quaking and knocked out, for a time and for a mercy, the TV's reception.

For a good half hour after he stormed out of his meeting, Cap had raged up and down the county roads, slewing his red Dodge Ram between the sand shoulders, once scattering a pack of coyotes from an armadillo carcass, trying to shake off the blow he had been dealt. Now, alone on the road that led across the tracks to Noah's, for a dark red minute after the bells clanged and before the crossing gates started down, he was struck by the simplicity of the two courses of action in front of him.

The first was to brake and let the Santa Fe go by. The second was to clamp the cherry top he kept from his Fire Squad days onto the roof, yank out the siren stop, and floor the gas. Smack the train and go out in a flare. Life or death, that simple. Of course he didn't mean this, but so help him he was mad enough to cuss. The train came on, its air horn blaring, and Cap finally hit the brakes.

When the new pastor called the private meeting, Cap was nearly driven to his knees with gratitude at the sudden notion that the purpose of the sit-down was to let him in on the announcement that the church would bestow on him a lifetime stewardship award. He loved to usher, loved to volunteer. He was civic-minded, and he loved a gathering—wedding, funeral, lodge meeting, sausage supper, fire. He'd done forty years on the Fire Squad—he still raced to any disaster that came across his bandwidth—and for that same number of years he had stood in the vestibule every Sunday, a Buddy Poppy or a fresh carnation pinned to his lapel, a sheaf of programs in his hand. Even minus pew-card-one, he could sort out the children's children's children who showed up at Christmas. He could spot a newcomer in a batch of every-now-and-thens and hardly-evers. When the hymns were sung, he opened his heart to heaven, wishing his lone voice could belt out melody, harmony, bass, and descant, every organ stop and trill.

Pastor Gary Bledsoe had laid waste to his hopes. "Mr. Russell, with all respect, you've done your part, but it's time to think of stepping down."

A light-headed feeling made Cap wonder if he'd strung his bolo tie too tight.

The board felt that others might want the chance to usher.

"What is it? I'm too old?"

The pastor sat back in his chair. "We're hearing that you take it on yourself to speak for . . ."

"The Almighty?" Lately the sermons had been no more fiery than ingredients mumbled off a Grape Nuts box. What Cap wanted to say was, "Somebody has to," but he stilled his tongue. Sure, he'd sometimes tell a prodigal the Lord rejoiced at his return. He might give a new widow—along with an arm to guide her down the aisle—the Heavenly Father's report on her late husband. But he meant only to give a helping hand to grace, to bring back the forgotten glories of Sunday mornings. "I can stop."

The pastor fidgeted with his desk toy, a row of ball bearings suspended from an armature. He set the first bead into motion, holding his silence as the click worked down the line.

Though he felt hypnotized while the gizmo was going, Cap recalled that a newcomer named Margaret Means had weaseled her way onto the Board of Deacons. Every time he turned around there she was, trying to change things. His wife Dorrie said he was imagining things, but Cap knew otherwise. The woman was tall and mannish, and she talked in bursts as sharp as rock salt shot against a barn side. He knew her overbearing kind. Now he leaned forward, deciding to talk man-to-man. "Is this some kind of female problem?"

The pastor made a temple of his hands, folding down his fingers two by two. "We have to make way for change. I'm in the middle here, Cap. Help me out."

The pastor stood, extending his hand, and Cap stood too, stung to see that the younger man wore rumpled shorts and a T-shirt when for the occasion Cap had put on his best blue suit and his chrysolite bolo. Before he knew what he was doing, he'd shaken the pastor's hand. That tore it.

He was never big on rough language, but suddenly a string of ugly words sprang to his tongue. "You pissant. You dungball-rolling stinkbug. I'll see your sorry hind end in a court of law."

Now, as he watched the freight cars trundle past and the caboose—unmanned—come into view, he wiped his hand on his pant leg. Once he got to the café, he would lay his trouble on his brother. Wheeler would take up his cause.

By the time Cap's truck swerved into the parking lot, a cloud of dust backdrafting against the window, Wheeler had finished a second cup of coffee. The first had burned his palate so that the ridge behind his teeth felt puckered and sore. He needed to eat, but out of manners he had waited. As well, he didn't want to cross Gus, who was done with his griddle and was now hacking at a heap of onions as if he bore a grudge against it. Gus chopped in time to a fiddle tune that sawed from his radio. Maxine had cranked up the TV's volume so that a reporter's commentary dueled with the fiddles. At the counter, a newcomer—a thin, road-worn, older woman in an orange T-shirt—dandled a spoon over a cup of coffee, a steaming plate of scrambled eggs before her.

When Cap burst in and sank into the seat, the vinyl bench sighed, and stale air gusted across to Wheeler. "Well," said Wheeler pleasantly, "what do you know?"

The phrase "What do you know?" wasn't so much a question as it was a ritual greeting. The Old Bulls' Thursday morning talk followed an order: first pass-the-times, then projects—those delegated by wives followed by projects the Bulls actually intended to do—then goings-on in town or in the larger world that got somebody's dander up, and then the floor was open. His brother's answer should have been "Not much."

"Plenty," Cap said. "Plenty," he said again, but that was all. He had remembered that between himself and his brother lay the bone of faith. Wheeler was a scoffer. Say anything about religion, Wheeler snorted, and if the subject went to words, he quoted verse for verse, twisting scripture and if not mocking Cap outright, then at least holding holy writ in light too dim to see by. He'd have to work up to his topic.

Cap wasn't one for strong spirits, but the thought of whiskey crossed his mind. Whiskey in the morning. A kick of the white mule his father had once given him to show the way the world could go blood simple. But when Maxine came by with the coffeepot, he said only, "Sanka."

Wheeler handed Maxine the menu he knew by heart. "The usual," he ordered. Two over easy, bacon, one big flaky biscuit, butter-soaked. His blood sugar was so low that floaters blurred his vision.

Usually Maxine went off straightaway, but today she lingered, fussing with the sugar caddy. Tilting her head toward the TV set, she said in a quavering voice, "They're saying it's like Pearl Harbor."

The comparison irked Wheeler. He'd said as much to Rebecca as she stood in their den, watching with a stricken face each time the towers crumbled. Not two hours in, and the words had been all over the news, as if no one could bear to let the horror stand for itself, its own calamity, analogy a fool's reach.

He set his jaw, an artery athrob in his neck, and waited for his brother to liken the disaster to Armageddon. But Cap was glaring out the window where a flock of blackbirds swirled around the grain elevator, their shadows fleeting across his face.

For Maxine's benefit, Wheeler nodded. "It's terrible." But she had swung around, her gaze drawn by the snowy images on the set.

Now that his order was in, Wheeler hoped to set the morning back on track. Again he said, "So, what do you know?"

Cap shrugged.

"Your meeting went all right?"

"It went."

Wheeler gave up. His brother couldn't keep a secret any more than he could stop his every thought from showing on his face. Soon enough, his trouble would come out.

Around Cap's head swirled all the moments of his morning—the pastor's words, his shock, his suspicion about Margaret Means, the lone caboose that seemed to bear a message—but before he could pluck one from the array, a disturbance broke out in the kitchen.

A stack of pans clattered to the floor, and Maxine shouted, "Don't put me in the middle of this, Augustus Wharton! *You* tell him!"

There came another clatter, then Gus's mutter. "Griddle's off. No breakfast."

Maxine, flustered, was back at the table, her white hair springing from its combs. "He gets this way near lunch. The blue plate's beef tips. He gets rattled."

A sign on the door read BREAKFAST SIX TO TEN. By Wheeler's watch it was only nine-forty. He had clearly seen the newcomer buttering a biscuit. "Any doughnuts left?"

"One jelly."

Wheeler ordered it, and Maxine went to fetch it. She served him, then went back to the counter, where she cranked up the TV's volume. Gus did the same with his radio and so there was a cluttered sense of cross-purpose in the air.

Cap, steam from his coffee seeming to well up behind his eyes, said, "Look here," and with no warm-up at all, he spilled it, every nickel, dime, and quarter of it. He had a reputation for blowing up his talk to fit his feeling, and so he took pains to relate the meeting word for word. "Wheel," he finished up, "I want to sue. I need your help."

Wheeler bit into his doughnut: stale. He hated confrontation. It soured his stomach. He'd been glad to leave his practice, leave the bench. Too many clients said they wanted justice when what they aimed for was revenge. The truly wronged, the numb who sat past utterance, their pain too deep for speech, he ached to comfort, if only to agree there was no fixing wrong that was unfixable; but most grievances, he'd come to think, were two-way streets.

His brother waited, jaw ajut. "Well?"

In the long view, Cap's complaint was mild and, if Wheeler knew anything, Cap had made a pest of himself, theologically and other-wise. But in his brother's stubborn look there seemed to be genuine injury, and Wheeler wanted to do right by it.

He fished in his pocket and brought up his mechanical pencil, then drew a napkin from the dispenser. He posed the standard question: What damages was Cap asking?

"Damages?" Wheeler's question had come too soon. It was too businesslike, bone-cold. Cap wanted his brother to share his out-rage, for the two of them to chew on it until the offenders were ground down to cud.

Wheeler put down the pencil. "You want my advice? Let it go. It's wrong," he said, trying to show a matter-of-fact sympathy, "but there it is. What isn't?"

Cap had taken his wife to dinner the night before, the two of them nearly alone in the Stuckey's on the highway, the cooks and waitresses gathered around a television set. Dorrie had toasted his news of the possible award with her iced tea glass. Now he slammed the flat of his hand on the table. "It's the principle!"

Just then Maxine appeared at the booth, carrying a tray. She un-loaded a creamer, a spoon, and a bowl of oatmeal, and set them in front of Wheeler. "Peace offering from himself. He got to feeling bad."

At the pass-through window, Gus touched the brim of his Broncos cap. "Not a griddle item," he said. "All I had to do was boil the water."

Maxine beamed. "Isn't that just Gus all over?"

"What do you think?" Cap prompted his brother. "Do we have a case?"

Above them, Maxine drew a determined-sounding breath. "Wheeler, I want a word. A legal matter."

"Look here," Cap said, rudely, he knew, but Maxine was out of order. Dimly, he recalled another slight she had delivered years before, making him the butt of a joke, a laughingstock. "We're in the middle of some business."

Maxine worked her mouth, then spat out, "So am I!"

While Cap nursed his temper with a sip of Sanka, Wheeler studied her. Maxine had shown up from time to time in his office for minor matters, a quitclaim on a scrap of land three counties over, a disclaimer for debts public and private. She lived above the café. She had never been married, as far as Wheeler knew, but she had a grown son who once stood before him on a burglary charge. Wheeler hadn't pried, but from his own familiarity with sons and regret, he understood she blamed herself for something.

They were of an age, but suddenly she looked impermanent, a wisp, and Wheeler saw that she was truly old. He felt a rise of pity—not because her look told him she wouldn't last much longer, but because even after all this time he hardly knew her, a person he had seen once a week for years but who had slipped into the cracks of daily life.

He got up, leaving Cap to stew, and led her by the elbow to the counter, settled her on the end stool. "What is it, darling?"

She swiveled on the stool, twisted the calipers to turn down the TV's volume, and then swiveled back. "Now then," she said, twisting the pearl ring on her finger, "I don't suppose I'm going to live forever."

Behind her on the screen a harried-looking reporter was speaking into a microphone. "Sure you are," said Wheeler, trying to resurrect their usual banter, but his timing was off.

"I mean it. And I want Gus to have this place. My son can take what's in my bank account, but this place"—she swept her arm in an arc above the counter—"should go to Gus."

From the kitchen came the sound of a stainless-steel bowl toddling across a surface, then a *clang* as it hit the floor. Gus appeared, his frizzed gray hair awry from his having yanked off his Broncos cap, which he spanked on the pass-through shelf. "I don't want it! I never wanted it!" He turned on his heel, went deeper into the kitchen, and undertook to bang and rummage.

"I could die tomorrow," Maxine shouted, "and then where would you be?"

The walk-in cooler door clunched shut. Gus was heard to grumble, "Denver."

Maxine drew her order pad and pen from her apron pocket and put them in front of Wheeler. "Write it. Say that I bequeath my worldly goods . . . write whatever you usually write."

Wheeler looked across the café. Cap had taken up the pencil and was scribbling notes on a napkin, paying them no mind. "Come by the house later, Maxine," Wheeler said. "We'll talk."

Maxine crossed her arms. Her uniform rucked emptily, a phantom bosom. "It has to be right now."

Wheeler lowered his voice. "Cap's got a problem. This isn't a good time."

She set her jaw. "It never is."

Gus yelled that he would burn the café to the ground.

She rolled her eyes and pushed the order pad toward Wheeler. "Write."

Thinking that by morning she would calm down and he could better advise her, that he could determine if she indeed owned the café, Wheeler wrote a few lines attesting to her wishes. She inspected them, then took the pen, and signed her name.

"I want a witness," she said, throwing a hot look toward the kitchen, "so it's legal."

Wheeler looked down the counter for the newcomer, hoping to enlist her in the charade, but at some point she had left the café. Over at the booth, Cap had stopped writing and was now jerking his head to summon Wheeler.

Wheeler knew better than to trouble his brother when he was in his firebrand mood, and so although it was against his better judgment and against a code of ethics he could not just then recall, he took the pen and signed his own name.

Maxine tore off the page, folded it, and stuck it down her dress front. "Ha," she said. She reached over the counter to turn up the TV's sound.

Gus appeared in the pass-through. "If I'm the boss, I'm ordering you to turn that off."

Spry as a sparrow, Maxine hopped off the stool and went to the fountain and drew herself a coffee cup of ginger ale and drank it down. "I'm not dead yet," she said, but she went to the counter and turned down the volume. As Wheeler made his way back to the booth, Gus turned down his radio, and the café fell back to its usual hum.

A nagging feeling that he was in the wrong, that he was out of sorts for reasons greater than the treachery at church, had come over Cap, but he didn't wait for it to overtake him fully, blasting by the notion in the same way he'd scattered the coyotes. When Wheeler came back to the table, he took up where they left off. "I figure we can nail them on breach of promise."

Cap's wife Dorrie had often told him that if he spent as much time thinking about others as he thought about himself, he'd be a better man, and so, to undo the jinx that might be brought on by his single-mindedness, he gestured toward the counter. "What was the matter with old Max?"

"Feeling it," said Wheeler. "Tending to what's left to tend to."

Wheeler felt something loosening within. He felt ready to speak his mind, to cut through jokes and gutting out and unsaid things to talk openly about how endings figured in all human doings, how loss lay over everything they did. What held humanity together wasn't contracts, torts or laws or physics, wasn't place or time or blood or love but—maybe—death, their own to come, those near and far away, the thousands in the days before, the knowledge of the common end of all.

"You know the way," he went on in words more earnest than he'd ever used with Cap, "those thoughts will sometimes come to you?"

Cap shook off what he suspicioned was his brother's ploy to lead into his sorry joke about heading for parts unknown. "I'm talking about the here and now," he said. "The case." Starting with the importance of faith and acts, working in legal phrases when they came to him, he laid out his argument. "Implied contract," he'd often heard Wheeler say, and he seized the concept.

As Cap went on, Wheeler felt himself lapsing into the catalogue of his brother's failings, but then instead of the well-worked grudges, the deeper and more ancient one he tried to hide appeared: his brother had lived a life touched only by expected grief, by sorrow in its proper time—the passing on of parents—and at remove—church members, someone else's uncle, sister, child. Cap's grown children, two sons and a daughter, were living. Thriving, to hear Cap tell.

Rebecca kept their son's memory the way at first she'd kept his room, but Wheeler couldn't speak his name. He worked. At law. At projects, taking down to parts a '36 Caterpillar earthmover and rebuilding it, fashioning a single-axled tractor with a cantilevered front end and a revolving differential. At the back of his property he put up a barn for his tools and his equipment, his saws and compressors, welding torches, lathes and forges, hulks and engines. A heap of scrap iron spilled into the yard, but it was while he worked among the orderly laws of physics, the elegant equations of mechanical design, that he came closest to forgetting.

But even then, as he worked late into the night under the shop light, thinking of nothing more than the task at hand, the ring of a fallen wrench on concrete or the immaculate burring of a cylinder would recall to him his last summer with his son while they tinkered with the 650 BSA, the clean smell of the boy's breath—a smell like Beechnut gum and new-cut hay—as in a light moment Charlie, pretending to be a surgeon, had used the needle-nose pliers to hand Wheeler a sprocket.

Across from him, Cap was in full throat. Stewardship, reward, the good and faithful servant. Heaven.

Wheeler hadn't believed in heaven since boyhood, and even if he could have summoned his old faith—he had tried, bringing himself to the brink only to fall away—it would have been dishonest, a calculation made to ease an anguish that could not be eased.

He didn't know if it was the off-ness of the morning or Maxine's will, Cap's picayune concerns against the horror of the days before, the memory of his own loss, losses—he knew a dog's death could not compare, but there it was, each new sadness, he ached to realize, an echo of the first—but he wanted to shock his brother into seeing the difference between what mattered and what didn't, to stand up for one small thing in all the silences he'd chosen. He wanted, he understood in the moment he raised his coffee cup so he could bring it down against the tabletop, to hurt his brother for his innocent, his lucky life.

"Cap," he said, "we're old. We're going to die, and death is death. The end."

Although they'd argued scripture all their lives, he'd never really contradicted Cap about the afterlife, but now he did. "Heaven's just a fine idea to make it go down smoother. Heaven is a story for the living."

Every name Cap called his brother in his private thoughts—Joe College, Clarence Darrow—threatened to burst from his throat, but he was too furious to open his mouth. All his life he'd suffered Wheeler's acting like the devil's counsel paid-in-full, snarling his ideas until Cap lost his train of thought. That business about parts unknown, when everybody knew that heaven was the best and final hope of God-made man, and Wheeler Alford, Esquire, of all people, stood in need of it the most.

Cap crossed his arms. "What is there, then?"

Thinking it might be possible—even this late in their lives—to find a different way of talking to each other, one closer to what he believed, Wheeler took off his glasses, intending to clean them as he worked out his answer, but instead he laid them on the table. A shaft of sunlight fell across the lenses, which were motty with dust, but he quelled the urge to hide behind activity, and instead, although it was so painful it made him want to look away, he met Cap's glare. "What's here at hand. What everything goes back to. Rock. Carbon. Iron. Dust."

He was about to say that just because these things were simple, it didn't mean they bore no meaning, but something seemed to catch in his throat and he heard his own voice saying, weakly, "Cappy, little Packer's . . ." The word would not come out. He finished with, "He's . . . gone."

This last news didn't register with Cap. It passed him by. He'd never asked for anything. Not help, not money, not advice. He saw to his own house and didn't trouble anyone. The one time he did, this was what he got. Dust and iron. His faith pared down to filings.

Again he went hot behind the eyes, then hot his whole brain over. Heat raced down his backbone to his arms and legs, his hands and feet, and he bolted from the booth, stepped back to set himself, brought up his fists. "You and your books and big ideas," he said. "Put up your dukes. Just put 'em up."

Cap's ridiculous threat allowed Wheeler to master his emotion.

"Brother, simmer down." Once, he'd tried to teach Cap to box, the two of them behind the henhouse, Wheeler home on furlough and Cap crossed sideways by his uniform and yet in awe and spoiling to take him down. Wheeler went over the Queensberry rules, showed him a few moves, but Cap—too trusting to keep up his guard, so gullible he followed every feint—was so on fire to fight that Wheeler felled him with one punch. "I'm saying what I think. That's all."

Cap jabbed the air. He felt foolish, out of bounds, but also good. Strong and righteous, wronged. What he wanted was for Wheeler to admit that he, Wheeler, was wrong about the present case and wrong before, wrong backed up to the beginning. Cap couldn't drive a nail without his brother instructing him on how to swing the hammer, couldn't shift a gear without a lecture about flywheels, cogs, and rpms, Wheeler acting muck-almighty and high-cockalorum. "Show me what you got," Cap said. Then, knowing it was cruel, he added, "Left."

Gus came out of the kitchen, wiping his hands on the sullied patches of his apron. "You old boys, there's flat no call for this."

Maxine clutched her collar to her throat.

Another surge of grief for Packer warned Wheeler that his earlier pitiable display would repeat itself if he didn't get out of Noah's, and so he forced a wink. "Folks, hold your bets."

He stood up from the booth. His glasses still lay on the table, but when he reached out to pick them up, Cap, in the moment just before the news of Packer pierced his consciousness, sideswiped the glasses and, with his fist, caught Wheeler with a cross.

The blow broke over Wheeler as though in slow motion. Stars, floaters, scotomata; funny, Wheeler thought as he went down, that he should know only three words for the myriad lights that swarmed his vision before spangling into darkness.

When Wheeler came back to his senses, Gus and Cap pulled him to his feet and helped him back into the booth.

Gus studied Wheeler's eye. "Looks like a shiner."

Maxine, after a time during which—later when she and Cap apologized to each other—she would say that she hadn't known what to think or do or say, in a gesture that had less to do with Cap and Wheeler and more to do with whatever sideways, tangled thing was working in her, untied her apron and flung it to the floor. She stormed across the café, out the side door, and up the wooden staircase to her rooms. A prolonged thumping was heard, as if Maxine were ransacking a closet.

Cap had pulled up a chair, and now he leaned in toward his brother. He was about to say he was sorry, but then he realized he wasn't. His own loss at church was small, but still it hurt. What could it have cost his brother to pay it heed?

"I didn't know about old Pack," Cap said, "but you have to know you had that coming."

Gus went to the kitchen and came back with a frozen beefsteak, a bowl of water, a clean dish towel. He placed these on the table and left the brothers to themselves.

Above them, the café's old plumbing grudged on—a clank, a shudder, a gurgle through the pipes.

To hold the steak to his eye made Wheeler recall a winter night of his boyhood when he'd fallen asleep in the woodshed after being punished for some misdeed and an ice-encrusted leaf had frozen to his cheek. He hadn't felt wronged then—he had deserved the switching—and he didn't feel wronged now. There was a cockeyed harmony to Cap's punch, and it came to Wheeler that by taking the blow he had repaid a debt.

Cap studied his brother. Wheeler's face looked different, but it wasn't just the swelling eye. There were the jug ears and the wattled neck, the wolfish eyes, the left one coming on blue as a plum. But there was something other, a look he saw on elders brought back to church for one last service, a naked look, prophetic and farseeing, all hardness and all falseness gone, as if the mask that faced the present world had fallen, nothing in the space between that new gaze and the world to come.

Wheeler had that bare look now, and in its openness Cap understood his brother only half believed his own bitter opinions, had kept them up so long that Cap had almost forgotten finding Wheeler in the sand hills after the accident, Wheeler blind with grief and praying in a voice so torn that Cap's own heart felt ripped in two, the way no touch, no word, no prayer, nothing Cap could do or say could help his older brother. The burden of the recollection swamped him. However cussed and high-handed Wheeler was, Cap ached to have him back the way he'd been.

From overhead came the wrenching off of the water tap, then the sound of Maxine's footsteps. Hoping to outride his welling loss, to weld himself and Wheeler back together as the skunks who shared the blame for the old woman's wrath, Cap said, "Looks like we got her riled."

Wheeler knew what Cap had seen—the knowledge of his coming loss was written on his brother's stricken face—and so he grinned to show that he was as strong as ever, but he worried that his swollen eye had turned his wink to a grimace.

For every one thought Wheeler kept to himself, Cap sent out a dozen into the world. He knew that on the other side of the gift of his lucky tongue lay his greatest flaw, which was that he put it to use too soon. In a corner of his mind there was a strongbox so packed with heedless, haywire things he'd blurted that a dark hour of the morning visit to it left him sleepless. Now, as he came back to his senses to admit to himself that he never meant to sue a soul and all he wanted was to blurt the tale, then go off to lick his wounds, he saw that he had brought the day down on himself by reason of his own hot head.

But even as he understood this, he knew that he was going to say another haywire thing. He would mean the words as help, as comfort, as a span across the gulf he now felt widening between them, and even as the words came to his mind to say, he knew Wheeler would take them wrong and that they weren't enough. Still, they were all he had, and so he said them. "Brother"—he held out a hand—"why won't you make peace with the Lord?"

Slow as swelling, starting in his belly and moving up through his chest and throat, Wheeler's laugh came on. His eye hurt, and his face hurt, but he couldn't stop. He wasn't laughing at the invitation. Cap had made it before, most often as a roundhouse in an argument. And he wasn't laughing at the way Cap phrased the words or that he now held out the same hand that had decked him. He laughed because he loved—admired—his old hair-triggered, bullet-headed brother, who even at the uttermost would not stop being who he was.

Wheeler felt as if the sand had gone right out of him, but better than he'd felt for days. With the dish towel he wiped at his good eye. "Cap, I didn't mean to laugh. I don't know anything. I never did."

"Sure you do," Cap said, aiming for heartiness but missing, "why, sure you do." He had heard the admission he had suddenly gone too far past wanting, but there was a prickled feeling behind his eyes, deep in the sockets where he'd felt so hot before, and he knew that if he didn't leave the café that instant, the feeling would spill out and scald him.

Cap stood. When Wheeler held out his hand, he shook it, feeling the shift of skin on living bone, his brother's knuckles knobby and misshapen, then made for the door.

Outside, the Dodge Ram roared to a start. From the window Wheeler watched Cap pull across the parking lot. He expected to see the brake lights flash as his brother made his trademark tap before he barreled past the stop sign, but the truck came to a full halt and idled for a time, as if Cap couldn't figure out which way to go.

How hard would it have been, Wheeler considered, to thank his brother for his trouble, for his maddening, his overbearing love, for the prayers he knew Cap prayed for him throughout his life, Cap on his knees beside his bed, he'd bet, his bald pate shining in the lamp-light and his beetled brow knit toward Wheeler's redemption? What bitter thing had wrapped itself around his, Wheeler's, heart? He didn't have an answer, but he knew one thing: If he but said the word and meant it, Cap's heaven would open to receive him. He would be welcomed back into the host to march among them, and there would be his brother, glad-handing at the gates and proud to usher him to glory. What was it in him that could not surrender? What was it that he couldn't bear? The smug certainty, the blind faith required to patch the story's holes, or that the hope of heaven cheated sorrow of its power? He didn't know. He was too old to ask these questions.

A smell of stewed beef wafted through the café. In the kitchen, Gus worked the potato masher at a steady clip against a rubber bus-tub. Maxine had come back down. She took the seat across from Wheeler. Her face looked younger, pinker, new, as if she'd had her-self a cry. They sat quietly until she said, "That eye smarts, I'm bet-ting."

"It does," Wheeler admitted, and again they sat in silence, until Maxine asked, "What are you going to tell folks happened to you?"

He grinned. "That a flyweight by the name of Maxine down at Noah's tried to sock me in the nose and missed."

She pursed her lips and looked at him as if from far off in the sky. "I wouldn't," she said, "miss."

"Did you ever," Wheeler asked, surprising himself, "think you'd last so long?"

She gathered some torn sugar packets, made a halfhearted swipe at the table with her apron, then answered a question he didn't think he'd asked. "There are things I would do over."

Wheeler worked his glasses over his ears.

Maxine tilted her head toward the silent TV screen. "Sorry to be such a pill before. It must be everything that's going on."

Wheeler motioned toward her bodice where the paper testament peeked like a tucked sachet. "Come by the house with that, why don't you. We'll fix it up the way you want."

She pushed up from the table, cocked an eye toward the kitchen. "Hail Caesar's almost finished with his special, I believe. I'll bring you some. On the house. To make up for . . ." She lifted a hand as if to implicate a single cause that had set off the morning but, as though finding any gesture fruitless, let her hand fall to her side.

Wheeler gave the tabletop a knuckle rap. "I'll hold you to it next time."

He rose, took his Open Road from the rack and squared it, then made his way outside.

The wind was up. A dust devil whirled across the parking lot to vanish against the white wall of the café. In an old white Chevy with Mississippi plates, the newcomer sat, her head resting on the steering wheel. She appeared to be deep in thought, or else in tears. If she was crying, Wheeler reckoned, the malady was going around. He thought to tap on the window, ask her trouble, offer a word, but he didn't want to intrude, and just then a car pulled in to park near a barrel Maxine had planted with red petunias, now gone leggy with the dying season, and two young women got out. Bank tellers or secretaries from the next town over, Wheeler guessed. The wind whipped at their dresses, causing their skirts to flutter and bell. The women laughed.

The sight charmed Wheeler and he smiled, but when the women saw him they ceased their laughter, as if mindless joy at such a time, in front of such a battered-looking man, were wrong. They made their faces solemn and looked down.

Don't, he thought to say to them, *don't stop.* He meant, he thought: Just live. Recover and be changed, but live. But it was too soon for them, he knew, and so he only tipped his hat as they went past him into Noah's.

He looked across the dry red grass at a county mower cutting a swath along a rise, at the straightness of the railroad tracks as they

paid out to the horizon, then toward the sun at zenith in a sky impossibly high and clear. *Wild blue yonder,* Wheeler thought, his chest
seeming to widen with a sudden ache to rise and enter it. One of
Cap's pet questions came to him—What is man that thou art mindful
of him?—and he tried it out, but there came no revelation and no answer, only the vastness of the weather-beaten land that seemed to
throw the question back at him.

Standing alone in the bright parking lot, unsteady on his feet but
feeling good, the sunstruck caliche radiant with warmth, Wheeler
marveled at the rolling earth, at himself standing upon it, held up by
legs that didn't seem his own. He could almost believe he felt beneath
his feet the ancient aquifer, the hidden sea of rain no stay against the
drought, against the long slow murders of the dusty years, a well
lasting through sorrows and leave-takings without number, through
stories he could never know and lives lived out of reach of all but his
imagination.

It was no vision or apparition Wheeler saw then. He was in his
right mind, and he knew it. It was no sign, no portent of the future,
only the sense made present that the air was full of spirits, the dead,
the living, those yet to be born, in no majestic cavalcade proceeding
each by each in like and kind but stumbling, ragged and aslant, veer-
ing off and merging with each other in no pattern he could track,
only an inconstant, dazzling, matchless disarray, but his presence in
it seemed so simple and inarguable and glorious that he ceased his
struggle to fix order to the way things worked. Before he could shore
the illusion in his mind, it went away, but he believed that for the
time left to him he would not forget, and he hoped it was enough to
bear him toward the time to come.